U0141094

高等学校英语应用能力考试（B级）
全真试题透视

主编： 崔艳萍　　冯新艳

编者： 鲍春燕　　陈　蓓　　胡百慧
　　　　梁　熹　　刘春丽　　彭　丹
　　　　王　敏　　王琴芳　　汪雅琴

外语教学与研究出版社
FOREIGN LANGUAGE TEACHING AND RESEARCH PRESS
北京　BEIJING

图书在版编目(CIP)数据

高等学校英语应用能力考试（B级）全真试题透视／崔艳萍，冯新艳主编；鲍春燕等编 . — 北京：外语教学与研究出版社，2010.1
ISBN 978 - 7 - 5600 - 9307 - 9

Ⅰ.①高… Ⅱ.①崔… ②冯… ③鲍… Ⅲ.①英语—高等学校—水平考试—试题
Ⅳ.①H319.6

中国版本图书馆 CIP 数据核字 (2010) 第 023201 号

出 版 人：于春迟
责任编辑：付分钗
封面设计：张苏梅
出版发行：外语教学与研究出版社
社　　址：北京市西三环北路 19 号 (100089)
网　　址：http://www.fltrp.com
印　　刷：北京京科印刷有限公司
开　　本：787×1092　1/16
印　　张：17
版　　次：2010 年 2 月第 1 版　2010 年 2 月第 1 次印刷
书　　号：ISBN 978 - 7 - 5600 - 9307 - 9
定　　价：26.90 元 (含 MP3 光盘一张)
＊　　＊　　＊
如有印刷、装订质量问题，请与出版社联系
联系电话: (010)61207896　　电子邮箱: zhijian@fltrp.com
制售盗版必究 举报查实奖励
版权保护办公室举报电话: (010)88817519
物料号: 193070001

前　言

本书依据教育部《高等学校英语应用能力考试大纲》和《高职高专教育英语课程教学基本要求（试行）》编写，旨在帮助高职高专学生顺利通过高等学校英语应用能力（B 级）考试。书中收录了自 2005 年 6 月至 2009 年 12 月的高等学校英语应用能力考试 B 级真题共 10 套。全书主要分为四大部分。第一部分为高等学校英语应用能力考试（B 级）题型透视；第二部分为高等学校英语应用能力考试（B 级）真题；第三部分为高等学校英语应用能力考试（B 级）参考答案与应考指南；第四部分为高等学校英语应用能力考试（B 级）听力录音文本。

在第一部分，编者对高等学校英语应用能力考试（B 级）的每一种题型都进行了详尽的剖析，并进一步提出了各种实用的解题思路和技巧，帮助考生在较短的时间内正确、高效地把握全真试题的命题原则与规律，题型特征和应试策略，真正做到有的放矢。

第二部分包括 10 套近年来高等学校英语应用能力考试的 B 级真题。

第三部分包括第二部分 10 套真题的参考答案以及与考点相关的应考指南。在本部分，编者不仅对 A 级考试中出现的各种考点进行了分析和归纳，以便帮助学生抓住要点，而且还根据不同题型的侧重点开设了其他栏目，如语法结构题中的"用法拓展"、"参考例句"，阅读理解题中依据大纲和试题而设的"核心词汇"和"难句分析"等，使学生能从点到面、举一反三，整体提升对 B 级考试深度和广度的认知和掌握，从而切实提高自己的应试能力和语言能力。

第四部分是听力录音文本，包括第二部分 10 套真题听力部分的录音文本。

在附录部分，编者通过分析和总结归纳近几年 B 级考试真题的考点，在结合考试大纲的基础上对常考和必考语法点进行了分类梳理，提供了系统精辟的讲解，并配有相应的练习题。语法基础较强的学生可以利用此部分检测自己的语法水平，而语法基础相对薄弱的学生则可以利用此部分系统地自学语法，巩固所学语言点。

本书配有 MP3 光盘，便于学生对听力部分进行强化训练。

本书由崔艳萍、冯新艳主编。参加编写的有：鲍春燕、陈蓓、胡百慧、梁熹、刘春丽、彭丹、王敏、王琴芳、汪雅琴。全书由崔艳萍、冯新艳统稿和审稿。在编写过程中，我们参考了近年来出版的一些相关书籍，在此特向这些书籍的作者和出版者表示感谢。

由于编者水平有限，书中难免出现纰漏，敬请读者和专家不吝指正。

祝同学们学习进步，考试成功！

编　者
2009 年 12 月

目　录

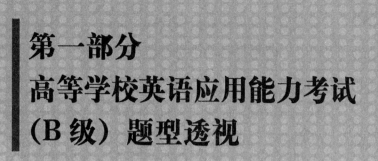

第一部分
高等学校英语应用能力考试
（B 级）题型透视

听力理解

一、题型概况

听力理解是高等学校英语应用能力考试测试的第一部分，主要测试考生通过听来获取英文信息的能力。根据大纲的要求，听力材料的语速为每分钟 100 词，以日常交际和简单的业务交际内容为主；词汇限于《高职高专教育英语课程教学基本要求（试行）》的"词汇表"中 B 级 2,500 词的范围，交际内容涉及其中的"交际范围表"所列的 B 级全部听说范围。

本部分的得分占总分的 15%，测试时间为 15 分钟，测试的题型包括以下三种：

1. Proper responses
2. Short dialogues
3. Short passage

二、题型透视与应对技巧

上述三种题型的特征各有不同，所以做题时的策略也不一样。

1. Proper Responses
● 题型透视

这一部分主要是测试考生理解所听问题并作出恰当回答的能力，本部分共 5 个问题。问题的内容一般以简单的日常交际内容为主，包括问候、介绍、感谢、道歉、道别、指路、购物、游玩、学习、饮食、健康等日常生活的各方面。句子结构和内容都不太复杂，一般以特殊疑问句或一般疑问句的形式出现，有时也可能是表歉意、祝贺、致谢等的陈述句。该题型具有以下几个主要特点：

1）特殊疑问句的提问方式以五个 W（who, what, where, when, why）和 how 等形式为主，其提问的内容主要涉及数字（时间、距离、价格）、地点、感受、天气、原因等。

2）一般疑问句的提问内容主要涉及请求、建议、习惯、状态、日常问候、日常会话等。常见的回答方式以 Yes/No 作答，或者 Certainly./With pleasure. 等。

3）陈述句的内容主要涉及问候、祝福、道歉、祝贺等。

4）全部问题均朗读两遍，每个问题之间有 10 秒钟的停顿时间便于考生答题。

● 应对技巧

针对以上特点，考生可以采取以下对策：

1）在听之前，仔细快速阅读各选项，判断出各选项之间的差别，划出不同点。读完之后要通过选项中的已知信息对题目进行猜测，便于在听的时候抓住重点。例如：

A. Oh, yes.　　　　B. With pleasure.　　　　C. Thank you.　　　　D. Here you are.

从这些已知的信息中，考生可以发现这四个选项的内容侧重点都有所不同，但基本可以推测此题的询问方式是一般疑问句。

2）在听的过程中，要快速弄清交际场景，抓住关键词。一般来说，特殊疑问句中的疑问词往往是表达句子主要意思的关键词，如果是一般疑问句，则情态动词、系动词、助动词是关键词。例如：

A. Far from here.　　　　　　　　　　B. From 9 a.m. to 6 p.m.

C. Five people.　　　　　　　　　　　D. One hundred dollars.

根据以上四个选项的已知信息，考生不难猜出此题的提问与数字有关。考生在听的时候应该密切注意录音材料中的疑问词。例如，在听到 Mr. Johnson, when is the library open? 时，考生能立刻判断出该句的疑问词是 when——询问时间，因此就能预测该题的答案是 B 项。

3）在听的过程中要注意中英文回答方式的不同，排除干扰项。

4）在听完问题后，要果断选出答案，然后阅读下一题的四个选项；切忌仍然左思右想而影响后面题目的听力。即使在不确定答案的时候也要果断做出决定或者暂时放弃，为后面一题做好准备，千万不要在没有准备的情况下去听。

2. Short Dialogues

● 题型透视

这一部分主要是测试考生理解所听对话的能力，本部分共 5 组对话，通常是一男一女各读一句，然后第三人就对话内容提出一个问题。对话内容一般以日常生活和日常交际内容为主，命题主要围绕日常生活、工作、学习等展开。该题型具有以下几个主要特点：

1）问题均以特殊疑问句的形式出现，以五个 W（who, what, where, when, why）和 how 等形式为主，其提问方式主要涉及以下几个方面：

① 就谈话内容直接提问。这类题型主要针对对话中的某个细节提问，答案往往是对话中出现的关键词或关键词的近义词、同义词等。例如：

W: I'm here to see Miss Brown.

M: Miss Brown? Er..., she is in her office.

Q: Where is Miss Brown?

A. In her office.　　　B. In the meeting room.　　　C. At home.　　　D. At the bank.

② 就对话内容的语用意义提问。这类题型难度比较高，需要对对话者的态度、观点、情感等做出推理，分析其言外之意。例如：

W: I'm afraid we will be late for the party.

M: Don't worry. There is still twenty minutes to go.

Q: What does the man mean?

A. They won't go to the party.　　　　　B. They won't be late.

C. They will be late.　　　　　　　　　D. They will stay at home.

③ 就对话内容的场景提问。这类题型主要就对话发生的地点、对话的人物关系或人物身份等提问。考生需根据对话内容作出合理推理。例如：

M: I want to mail these books to New York.

W: By ship or by air, sir?

Q: Where is the man?

A. In a post office.　　B. On board a ship.　　C. In a booking office.　　D. On an airplane.

④ 对数量、价格、具体时间提问，此类问题可能是直接提问也可能需要进行简单的计算。例如：

M: These cups look nice. How much are they?

W: They are $10 each.

Q: How much will the man pay if he buys only one cup?

A. $5.　　　　　B. $10.　　　　　C. $15.　　　　　D. $20.

2）很大一部分问题是针对第二个人所说的话进行提问，另一部分是针对整个对话进行提问，少数部分是针对第一个人所说的话进行提问。例如，在 2008 年 12 月高等学校英语应用能力考试（B级）的听力部分中，该题型全部是针对第二个说话人所说的话而提出问题。

3）全部对话及问题均朗读两遍，每个问题之间有 10 秒钟的停顿时间便于考生答题。

● 应对技巧

针对以上特点，考生可以采取以下对策：

1）听之前认真快速阅读四个选项，对题目所提问题进行正确的预测并判断出题目所提问题的关键信息。例如：

A. From his friend.　　B. From his brother.　　C. From his boss.　　D. From his teacher.

从这些已知信息中，考生可以发现这四个选项的内容均和"来自某人"相关，因此基本上可以推测出此题问的是 Who...?

2）听的过程中应快速弄清会话主题（通常由第一个说话人提出），在听到与某个选项一样或相近的内容时，在该选项上划上记号，预测该题的答案，同时不断修正自己的预测直至与原听力内容保持一致为止。例如：

A. Cold.　　　　　B. Warm.　　　　　C. Wet.　　　　　D. Hot.

根据以上四个选项的已知信息，考生不难猜出这是一道关于"天气"的题目。考生在听的时候应该密切注意录音材料中哪些词或短语与这些选项联系最为紧密，从而选出正确答案。例如，在听到第一句话 It's very cold this morning. 时，考生可以预测该题的答案是 A 项，然后在听的过程中进一步确认自己的答案是否正确，做到心中有数。

3）本部分会话内容问题均朗读两遍。在听第一遍录音时，不要忙着答题，应在听的过程中把握该会话的大概内容和与选项有关的信息，重点是要听清楚会话后的问题，在选项旁写出问题的关键词。在听第二遍录音时，可以结合听第一遍时掌握的会话大概内容和问题选出正确选项。

4）对于细节判断题，由于其细节信息直接在对话中出现，考生可在听的时候结合选项的已知信息对答案作出预测，一般来说直接听到的就是答案。此外，考生平时应养成记录的好习惯，学会边听边记，记录有关事实细节的关键词，这样就会很容易解答问题了。

3. Short Passage

● 题型透视

本部分要求考生听一篇约为 100 词的短文，其中设有 5 个空格，每个空格要求填入一个单词或词组，主要考察考生的听力理解能力、听写能力和速记能力。该题型具有以下几个主要特点：

1）短文的第一句话通常不设空格，考生可借此更好地把握短文的主旨。

2）每道题只要求考生填入单词或者不多于 3 个单词的短语。

3）全文朗读三遍，三遍皆以正常的语速朗读，第二遍朗读中在需要填空的句子后有10 秒钟的停顿时间，以便于考生填写答案。

● 应对技巧

针对以上特点，考生可以采取以下对策：

1）在听之前，认真仔细阅读短文，尤其是短文第一句话，把握文章主旨，理清文章层次。此外，考生可以根据短文的已知内容，通过自己所掌握的语法知识和上下文语境预测出空格部分所缺的词语。

2）在听的过程中注意运用正确的做题方法。在听第一遍时以听为主，以便明确地了解短文大意和主旨，并验证所预测的单词是否与录音内容相符。在听第二遍时要以记为主，尽可能写出听到的空格处应填的单词。如果个别词没听清楚要果断放弃，以免影响后面的听力内容。在听第三遍时，考生要仔细核对自己的答案是否与听力录音中的单词一致并对答案进行调整和补充。

3）在答完题后，考生需要再次运用自己掌握的语法基础知识检查所填写的单词或短语的拼写、时态、语态和词性等是否与上下文相符。

除了掌握听力考试题型的基本特征及解题对策，更重要的是坚持多听，踏踏实实地提高自己的英语水平，这样才能以不变应万变，成功地突破听力考试。

词汇与语法结构

一、题型概况

语法结构是高等学校英语应用能力考试（B 级）的第二部分，旨在测试考生运用语法知识的能力。词汇测试范围包括《基本要求》中"词汇表"所规定的 B 级 2,500 个单词。

语法测试范围包括高职高专大纲要求掌握的所有语法，主要有七类词（名词、动词、形容词、副词、代词、冠词、数词）、主谓一致、时态、语态、语序、独立主格结构、定语从句、虚拟语气、强调句型、倒装句等。测试内容包括词汇用法、句法结构、词形变化等。

本部分共 20 道题，占总分的 15%，测试时间为 15 分钟。该部分包括 Section A 和 Section B。其中 Section A 是 10 道选择题，Section B 是 10 道填空题。

二、题型透视与应对技巧

上述两种题型的特征各有不同，做题时的策略也相异。

1. Section A: Multiple choice（多项选择）

● 题型透视

本部分给出 10 个不完整的句子，要求考生从所给的四个选项中选出最合适的一项使句子完整且正确。每题 0.5 分，共 5 分。

● 应对技巧

做此类题目时，考生首先应当**读懂题干，理解句意**。然后依据题干中的语法特征、相关的标志词或信息词来**判断此题的考点**：是虚拟语气还是非谓语动词、抑或是固定结构等等。再根据自己的句法、语法知识**进行选择**。选择完毕后一定要将所选的答案放到句中，**再读一遍进行检查**，看一看是否符合语法结构，是否符合句意，句子是否通顺，是否符合英语中的语言习惯等。

2. Section B: Filling the blanks（填空）

● 题型透视

本部分同样有 10 个不完整的句子，要求考生用括号里所给单词的正确形式填空。每题 1 分，共 10 分。此类型的题目不仅考查考生的语法知识（如时态、语态、虚拟语气等），同时也考查考生的词汇量及正确使用词汇的能力（如应将所给单词转化成形容词、副词、动词还是名词、加上何种前缀后缀等）。

● 应对技巧

考生首先还是要认真细心地**读懂题干**，简要划分句子成分，判断句子的结构及空格处应添加什么句子成分，确定本题考的是**词形转换**还是**语法结构**。如果是考查词形转换，要明确括号里所给单词的词性、确定应填词的成分和词性以及该如何对所给单词进行形式变化：如果要填**名词**（前面通常有冠词、形容词或介词等，在句中充当主语、宾语、表语等）时，应考虑到该名词是可数名词还是不可数名词，如果是可数名词此处应填单数还是复数。如果要填**动词**（在句中通常作谓语），应使用什么时态、什么语态。如果是**形容词**（修饰名词，在句中作表语、定语等）或**副词**（在句中通常修饰动词、形容词、副词或全句，在句中主要作状语），应该用原形还是比较级、最高级，等等。如果考查的是语法结构，则要认清考查的是什么语法点，是虚拟语气、独立主格结构还是主谓一致，等等。

答完题后，考生应将答案放入题中再检查一遍，看看最后成形的句子是否完整而准确。由于没有可供选择的选项，考生必须自己写出单词，因此单词拼写、句首字母大写等细节也很重要。

Section B 部分涉及到大量的词形转换，因此平时我们在背单词时，不能仅仅记住它们的汉语意思，还应注意这些单词的词性和相关的词形转换。很多考生觉得 Section B 部分很难，它也的确是在 Section A 的基础上又提高了一个层次，但只要平时多加积累，考试时细心做题，难题也可以迎刃而解。

关于英语应用能力考试中语法结构部分常见的考点，请参见书后的附录 1。

阅读理解

一、题型概况

本类题型旨在测试考生通过书面文字材料获取信息的能力。按照高职高专英语课程教学的基本要求，要达到 B 级考试阅读的要求必须做到以下几点：一是能够阅读中等难度的一般题材的简短的英文资料，并能正确理解；二是在阅读生词不超过总词数 3% 的英文资料时，阅读速度不低于每分钟 50 个单词；三是能读懂通用的简短实用的文字材料，如信函、产品说明等，并且能基本正确地理解内容。

测试题的主要题型包括以下四种：主旨题、推断题、词汇释义题和细节题。

二、题型透视与应对技巧

为实现有效的阅读，需要掌握阅读的一般过程，具体如下：

1. 浏览全文，掌握文章主题	4. 确定主题句和支持主体的部分
2. 根据段首句抓住文章中心思想	5. 根据衔接用语识别段落之间的关系
3. 再次细读原文，找出与题目对应的关键词句	6. 得出文章结论

特别注意：阅读题要求根据问题选择正确答案，考生做题时不必要求自己读懂每个词，遇到生词可根据上下文猜词义，如与题目无关则跳过。

下面将针对测试题的四个主要题型分别进行解题技巧的讲解：

1. 主旨题

● 题型透视

这一部分测试考生对短文主题的把握能力，要求考生能从选项中选出表述全文主题的句子。有的短文有题目，从题目就可一目了然知道全文讲述的内容，有的短文没有题目，这就对考生提出综合归纳的要求。主旨题的常见提问形式有：

Which of the following sentences best expresses the main idea of the passage?

What is the passage mainly about?

The passage mainly discusses about _____.

The main idea/point of the passage is _____.

A suitable title for the passage would be _____.

● 应对技巧

针对该题型的特征，考生可以采取以下对策做题：

1）明确主旨题一般会出现下列词语：main idea, main point, theme, title 等；

2）粗略读全文，确定文章中心思想；

3）确定主题句在文中的位置；

4）识别主旨题干扰项。干扰项的特点如下：a. 用某段的信息代替主旨，或是某段中某句未展开论述的话，或是某一段中某几句的主要内容；b. 概括内容过于宽泛，这种干扰项中所包括的内容多于文章阐述的内容，过于笼统；c. 与文章无关的信息，即莫名生出的信息，在文章中根本找不到细节根据。例如 2009 年 6 月真题的第 40 题：

Subways are underground trains, which usually operate 24 hours a day. They are found in larger cities and usually run between the suburbs and the downtown area. Maps and schedules are available from the ticket office. If you take the subway often, you can save money by purchasing a monthly pass（月票）.

City-operated buses run on various routes（线路）and are designed to be at certain places at certain times. Maps and schedules may be posted at certain stops, or they may be available at local banks, libraries, the student union, or from the bus drivers. Buses run mainly during the day. Fare is paid by exact change in coins, or by monthly passes.

Taxis are generally more expensive in the United States than in other countries. If you use a taxi, be sure you ask the amount of the fare before you agree to ride. The driver usually expects a tip（小费）of 15 percent of the fare.

40. The passage mainly tells us about _____.

  A. the bus and train fares in the US B. the ways of paying a taxi in the US

  C. the public transportation in the US D. the advantage of subways in the US

本题询问全篇大意，选项 A，B 和 D 都只涉及到一个方面，选项 C 最为全面，能概括大意，故选项 C 为正确答案。

2. 推断题

● 题型透视

阅读中推断题有一定难度，往往不能从原文中直接找到答案，而要根据对上下文的理解和全篇主旨的把握来推断，即通过对事物全方位的理解来推出作者的言外之意。一般情况下，推断题的干扰项具有以下特点：直接选取文章中的细节信息；做出无关紧要或片面的结论；给出与文章内容完全相反的结论；或是提出不合常理或不合逻辑的结论等。因此做这类题应注意：首先要全方位分析相关信息，切忌片面思考，得出片面结论；其次要忠实于原文，切忌脱离原文，主观臆断；再者不可选择表层信息答案，应该透过现象看到本质。这类题目要求可包括推断作者观点、推断写作目的、推断细节等。

推断题的常见提问形式如下：

It can be inferred from the text that _____.

The author's purpose of writing the passage is that _____.

When the author talks about..., what the author really means is _____.

The story/author implies/suggests that _____.

We can conclude from the passage that _____.

● 应对技巧

应试者可针对不同的题目要求采取不同的对策：

1）推断作者观点：要正确推断作者观点需要抓住文章中的暗示词以及作者在文中的措辞，尤其是表达感情色彩的形容词、副词、动词及所举的例子，以推断作者的观点。

2）推断写作目的：不同类型的文章写作目的也不相同，但写作目的通常有以下几种：娱乐读者、让人发笑，说服读者接受某种观点，或者告知读者某些信息。第一类常见于故事类的文章；第二类常见于议论文或广告类的文章；第三类多见于科普、新闻报道、文化或社会类的文章。

3）推断细节：文章为了说明一个观点，作者往往会给出一系列的论述或解释，采取的方法包括摆事实、举例、论证、提问或给出原因，因此对细节进行推理时应从原文字里行间中找到推理的依据，然后进行推断。

例如 2009 年 6 月真题第 41 题：

> Dear Ann:
>
>   I'm going to give a dinner party next month. I want my guests to enjoy themselves and to feel comfortable. What's the secret of giving a successful party?
>
>   Mary

41. From the letter we learn that Mary _____.

    A. is asking for advice on giving a dinner party

    B. knows the secret of giving a pleasant party

    C. is going to attend a dinner party

    D. has successfully held a party

根据第一封信的最后一句话 What's the secret of giving a successful party? 得知，玛丽向安询问成功举办晚宴的秘诀，与该句意思相符的只有选项 A，而选项 B，C，D 都与原文意思背离。

3. 词汇释义题

● 题型透视

词汇释义题是英语阅读理解必考题型之一，既包括对大纲词汇和短语的辨义，也包含对超纲词汇的推断。这类题型主要用于测试考生根据上下文语言环境理解关键词汇确切含义的能力。词汇释义题常见的提问形式如下：

Which of the following is the closest in meaning to the word...?

The word...could best be replaced by _____.

In the...paragraph, the word...means/refers to _____.

● 应对技巧

应试者可利用定义、同义关系、反义关系、常识或句法结构（如定语从句和同位语）等推断词义。解题时通常要综合应用多种方法，但是，这些方法的应用都离不开对特定语境的正确理解。以下将分别举例介绍：

1）根据定义猜测词义：

定义常用的符号标志为破折号、冒号和分号等，正确理解符号后句子的内容就能推断词义。定义常用的谓语动词多为：be, mean, be considered, to be, be called, define, represent, refer to, signify 等。有时定义也通过定语从句或同位语来体现。例如：

In fact, only about 80 <u>ocelots</u>, an endangered wild cat, exist in the US today.

由同位语 an endangered wild cat 我们很快就能猜出生词 ocelots 的义域：一种濒临灭绝的野猫。

2）根据同义关系或者反义关系猜测词义：

常见的表示同义关系的信号词有：similar, like, as...as, the same as 等。常见的表示反义关系的信号词包括：but, yet, however, while, whereas, otherwise, in spite of, despite, although, unlike, instead (of), rather than, nevertheless, on the other hand, by contrast, on the contrary 等。例如：Green loves to talk, and his brothers are similarly <u>loquacious</u>.

该句中副词 similarly（相似地）暗示 loves to talk 和 loquacious 意义相近。由此我们可推断出 loquacious 的意思是"健谈的"。

3）根据常识猜测词义：

Husband: It's really cold out tonight.

Wife: Sure it is. My hands are practically <u>numb</u>. How about lighting the furnace?

根据生活经验，天气寒冷时，手肯定是"冻僵的，冻得麻木的"。

4）根据句法结构猜测词义：

He was a <u>prestidigitator</u> who entertained the children by pulling rabbits out of hats, swallowing fire, and other similar tricks.

此句中，who 引导的定语从句对生词 prestidigitator 的词义给出了非常清楚的定义，指能从帽子里拉出兔子、吞火和玩其他类似把戏的人，这不就是变戏法的人吗？因此，prestidigitator 的词义应该是"变戏法者"。

4. 细节题

细节题在阅读理解中占了相当大的比例，主要测试考生对文章中某一细节（常与 who, what, where, when, why 等相关）或者某一句话的理解。解此类题的关键是灵活地运用"定位"原则与"同义改写"原则。例如 2009 年 6 月第 42 题：

Dear Mary:

　　Cook something that would let you spend time with your guest. If a guest offers to help you in the kitchen, accept the offer. It often makes people feel more comfortable when they can help.

　　Before serving dinner, while your guests make small talks in the living room, offer them drinks. Some guests may like wine, but make sure to provide soft drinks for people who don't.

　　At the dinner table, let your guests serve themselves. Offer them a second serving after they finish, but don't ask more than once. Most guests will take more if they want.

　　Perhaps the most important rule of all is to be natural. Treat your guests as you want them to treat you when you're in their home — that is, act naturally toward them, and don't try too hard to be polite. Have a good time in a pleasant atmosphere.

Ann

---

42. Ann's first piece of advice is that Mary should _____.

　　A. get the food ready before the guests arrive

　　B. keep the guests away from the kitchen

　　C. spend some time with the guests

　　D. accept the guests' offer to help

根据题干关键词 first piece of advice 可将答案定位在第一段，由该段第二句话 If a guest offers to help you in the kitchen, <u>accept the offer</u>. 得知，选项 D 为正确答案。

翻　译

一、题型概况

根据大纲，该部分的分值占总分的 20%，要求学生在 25 分钟内完成四个句子和一个段落的翻译。其中，句子翻译为选择题，选项给出四个答案——最佳的答案，较好的答案，较差的答案和最差的答案，分值依次为 2 分、1 分、0.5 分、0 分。段落翻译一般由四个英语句子组成，共 12 分。该题型旨在测试考生正确理解英语书面语并综合运用基本翻译技巧将其准确译为汉语的能力。

二、应对技巧

在做句子翻译时，考生应首先阅读原句，仔细比较四个选项的不同之处，再找出原句中相应的翻译重点，利用排除法选出最佳答案。做段落翻译时，应首先阅读全文，正确理解原文内容，然后综合运用各种基本的翻译技巧，尽量准确地译为汉语。下面我们将从词汇和句子两个层面来讲解一些常用的翻译技巧。

1. 词的翻译

1）词义的选择

英语词汇一词多义的现象远比汉语突出，且一词多义的词汇现象又和一词多词类的语法现象结合在一起。这就使得英语词义的选择更加依赖词的语境，简单地说也就是上下文。例如：

What our company <u>values most</u> in employing people is their basic quality and practical skills. （2005 年 6 月）

A. 我们公司的最大价值在于它所雇用的员工具备了基本素质和实用技能。

B. 在培训员工时，我们公司大多会重视人的基本素质和实际技能。

C. 在招聘员工时，我们公司最看重的是人的基本素质和实际技能。

D. 我们公司最值得称道的是它培训员工的基本素质和实用技能。

比较四个选项可发现翻译的重点是单词 value 和 most，这两个词一词多义且多词类。value 作为名词表示"价值"，作为动词表示"重视，看重"。在原句中，它位于 what 引导的主语从句中，从句的主语是 our company，value 应是动词，表示"重视，看重"。most 作为指示代词表示"（数量上）最多，最大；大多数，几乎所有"，作为副词表示"最"。句中，它位于动词 value 之后，显然是副词，表示"最"。两者结合可知选项 C 最佳。

2）词义的引申

词典中的基本词义并非是固定不变的。在实际运用中，我们往往可以根据词汇的内在含义和具体的语境，将其意义延伸，以使表达更准确、通顺。例如：

The manager tried to <u>create</u> a <u>situation</u> in which all people present would feel comfortable. （2007 年 6 月）

A. 经理在设法创造条件，让所有的人都得到令人满意的礼物。

B. 经理试图营造一种氛围，让所有在场的人都感到轻松自在。

C. 经理在设法创造一种条件，让所有人都能够显得心情舒畅。

D. 经理想努力营造一种气氛，让所有的人到场时都觉得畅快。

在词典中，situation 的词义是"情况，状况，形势，局面；地理位置，环境特点"。如果我们照搬这些词义进行翻译，句子就会显得特别别扭。因此，可以根据语境将 situation 的意义延伸为"气氛，氛围"，这样更符合汉语的表达习惯。同时，将 create "创造"引申为"营造"，能更好地和"氛围"搭配。选项 B 最佳。

3）词类的转译

虽然英语和汉语的词类大多相似，可以直接进行转换。但是在英语句子中可以充当某个成分的词类是有限的，例如充当主语的只有名词、代词、动名词和不定式，动词不能做主语。因此在翻译时要灵活处理，不要死板地将名词译为名词，动词译为动词，一种词类可能被灵活地转译成另一种词类。例如：

The <u>successful</u> <u>completion</u> of the book is the result of the cooperation and confidence of many people.（2001 年 6 月）

A. 本书的写作很成功，是因为许多人互相合作、具有信心。

B. 成功地完成本书的写作是许多人互相合作、坚信不疑的结果。

C. 这本书成功了，结果使许多人更加合作，更加信任。

D. 许多人的合作和信任导致了本书的成功。

句子的主语是名词短语 the successful completion of the book，如果直接翻译为"这本书的成功完成"，会显得非常生硬，不符合汉语的表达习惯。所以我们不妨将其中的名词 completion 进行词类转译，译为动词，将形容词 successful 转译为副词，则整个主语译为"成功地完成本书的写作"，这样就非常顺畅了。选项 B 最佳。

4）词义的增减

由于英汉两种语言在表达形式上的区别，在翻译时我们经常要酌情增补或删减一些词语，以使译文忠实地再现原文的内容并合乎汉语的表达习惯。增补的词语往往是原文暗含的词语、注释性的词语、句中省略的词语等等。删减的词语一般是代词（尤其是物主代词）、介词、连词等。例如：

Great changes in a country's social structure have always caused <u>stresses</u>.（2004 年 6 月）

A. 一个国家社会阶层的重大变化总会带来压力。

B. 一个国家社会结构的压力总会引起巨大的变化。

C. 一个国家社会结构的巨变总会导致紧张状态。

D. 一个国家社会阶层的重大变化总是很突然的。

句中，stress 是抽象名词，意思是"压力，紧张，重要性"。汉语词汇在形式上显示不出抽象名词的特征，它和名词、形容词是完全同形的。在汉译时需要增词，使其所指更加具体，这并不是无中生有。因此，stress 一词结合语境选择词义"紧张"，并增译为"紧张状态"，选项 C 符合。再如：

· It gives <u>us</u> much pleasure to send you the goods asked for in your letter of September 10.（2002 年 6 月）

A. 很高兴发去贵方 9 月 10 日来函索购的货物。

B. 我们很高兴寄去你们 9 月 10 日来信询问的商品。

C. 我们十分高兴贵方 9 月 10 日来函询问我们的商品。

D. 我们很高兴贵方来信要求我们 9 月 10 日寄出优质产品。

该句话是商务用语，从叙述者的角度出发，翻译时必须做到精练简洁。因此，us 不用译出，选项 A 最佳。但一定要注意，减译是减去不必要译出或者译出会使译文显得啰唆、繁复的部分，而不是随意地删减。

2. 句子的翻译

B 级对句子层面的翻译考得较为简单，只要能理解句子的意思，把握句子的基本结构，熟悉一些特殊的句式，并参照汉语的语序和表达习惯来翻译即可。

1）语序的调整

语序的调整在翻译中是非常普遍的，这主要是由英汉两种语言在句子结构上的差异造成的。在翻译时，考生不可生搬硬套，而应该在正确理解原文内容的基础上，根据汉语的表达习惯灵活地进行调整。例如：

...We encourage card-holders to use the card as often as possible, and they will be awarded with prizes when their marks（积分）reach a certain amount...（2005 年 6 月）

英语句子的扩展方向是以主句为中心倾向于向后扩展，而汉语句子的扩展方向倾向于向前。因此在翻译时，我们可能需要调整句子某部分的位置。例句中的 when their marks reach a certain amount 在英语句子的后边，但为了符合汉语的表达习惯，翻译时应向前移动，故后一分句应译作"卡上积分达到一定数额将有礼品相送"。

2）特殊句式的翻译

● 被动句的翻译

英汉两种语言在语态上有明显的区别。英语中，被动语态使用得非常广泛，这主要出于以下四个原因：不知道或不必说出动作的执行者；不愿说出动作的执行者；强调动作的承受者；衔接上下文。但汉语中普遍使用的是主动语态。因此，在英译汉时，考生应尊重汉语的表达习惯，适当地进行调整。一般来说，可以将英语的被动句译为汉语的被动句、主动句或无主语句。例如：

The lecture was supposed to start at eight, but it was delayed an hour.（2000 年 12 月）

A. 讲座以为在八点钟开始，但一个小时以后就开场了。

B. 讲话被认为在八点钟开始，但延误了近一个小时。

C. 讲演本该在八点钟开始，但迟了一个多小时。

D. 讲座应该在八点钟开始，但被耽搁了一个小时。

该句子包含两个分句，前一分句的主语是 the lecture，后一分句的主语 it 指代 the lecture。在不知道动作执行者的情况下，我们最好将其翻译为汉语的被动句，以保持上下文的连贯性，故选项 D 最佳。汉语中表示被动的常用词有"被"、"受"、"给"、"为"等。

All of our four objectives of this trip have been fulfilled, which is more than I had expected.（2005 年 12 月）

A. 我们此行四个目标的完成情况比我预期的要好。

B. 我们此行的目标一共有四个，比我预期的还多。

C. 我们此行总共完成了四个目标，比我预期的要多。

D. 我们此行的四个目标均已达到，比我预期的要好。

句中出现了被动态的完成时结构 have been fulfilled，动作的执行者显然是"我们"，因此可以根据汉语的表达习惯，明示主语将其翻译为主动句"我们此行的四个目标均已达到"。选项 D 符合。

Candidates should be given the company brochure to read while they are waiting for their interviews. （2007 年 6 月）

A. 求职者应帮助公司散发有关的阅读手册，同时等候面试。

B. 在阅读了公司所发给的手册之后，求职者才能等待面试。

C. 在求职者等待面试时，应该发给他们一本公司手册阅读。

D. 求职者在等待面试时，可要求得到一本公司手册来阅读。

该句中没有必要说出 give 这一动作具体的执行者，强调动作的承受者 candidates，如果将 should be given 翻译为"应该被给"不符合汉语的表达习惯，因此只能将原句译为无主语句，即"应该发给他们一本公司手册阅读"。选项 C 最佳。

● 定语从句的翻译

英语中，定语从句对先行词起着修饰限制的作用，可分为限制性与非限制性两种。它的翻译方法主要有四种：前置法、后置法、融合法和译为状语从句。使用哪种翻译方法和它的分类是密切相关的。一般来说，限制性定语从句采用前置法，非限制性定语从句采用后置法。融合法是将主句中的先行词和定语从句顺译成一个句子，限制性和非限制性定语从句都可以使用这种译法。当定语从句含有状语意义，例如表示原因、条件、时间等，可以直接译为状语从句。例如：

...Our idea is to offer you a place where you can enjoy shopping without interruption by others... （2003 年 12 月）

在该句中，关系副词 where 引导的限制性定语从句修饰先行词 place，可以采用前置法将定语从句译为作定语的汉语偏正结构，即"我们的理念是为您提供一个不受他人打扰的享受购物乐趣的场所"。

Congratulations on purchasing from our company the C800 Coffee Maker, which is suitable for home use. （2008 年 6 月）

A. 我公司隆重推出 C800 型家用咖啡壶，欢迎各界人士惠顾。

B. 您从我公司购买了最新款的 C800 型家用咖啡壶，值得祝贺。

C. 恭喜您购买本公司 C800 型咖啡壶，此款咖啡壶适合居家使用。

D. 您购买的咖啡壶是我公司最新产品——C800 家用型，特此致谢。

翻译时，可采用后置法来译定语从句 which is suitable for home use，即先译主句，然后将定语从句译为并列分句。这时需要重复先行词或使用代词来指代先行词。因此将定语从句译为与主句并列的结构"此款咖啡壶适合居家使用"，用"此款咖啡壶"指代先行词 the C800 Coffee Maker。选项 C 符合。

Mr. Smith has cancelled his trip because an urgent matter has come up which requires his immediate attention. （2007 年 12 月）

A. 史密斯先生推迟了旅行，因为发生了一件大家都十分关注的突发事件。

B. 史密斯先生取消了旅行，因为发生了一件紧急的事件需要他立即处理。

C. 史密斯先生取消了旅行，因为有一件棘手的事情需要他予以密切关注。

D. 史密斯先生推迟了旅行，因为要处理一桩已引起公众关注的突发事件。

该句可采用融合法，忽略关系词 which，直接将主句的先行词 an urgent matter 和定语从句除关系词以外的部分 requires his immediate attention 顺译为一个句子，即"发生了一件紧急的事件需要他立即处理"。故选项 B 最佳。

Candidates who are not contacted within four weeks after the interview may consider their application unsuccessful.（2005 年 6 月）

A. 面试后四周内仍未接到通知的求职者可以考虑再申请。

B. 未在面试后四周内来联系的求职者则可考虑申请是否已失败。

C. 求职者在面试后四周内不来签订合同则被认为是放弃申请。

D. 求职者如果在面试四周内尚未得到通知，则可以认为未被录用。

读完整个句子可以发现，由关系词 who 引导的定语从句实质上是一个表示假设的状语从句，因此可以直接将其译为状语从句"如果在面试四周内尚未得到通知"。选项 D 符合。

总之，考生应本着"忠实"（忠实于英语原文）和"通顺"（汉语表达通顺）的基本原则，在翻译的过程中灵活运用各种词汇和句子层面的翻译技巧，真正做到正确地理解、准确地表达。例如：

...We encourage card-holders to use the card as often as possible, and they will be awarded with prizes when their marks reach a certain amount...（2005 年 6 月）

在翻译时，该句子运用了词汇层面的翻译技巧——词义的引申和增减，award"授予，奖励"被引申为"送"，they 和 their 的词义被删减了，还运用了句子层面的翻译技巧——调整语序，将 when their marks reach a certain amount 向前移动，故译作"我们鼓励持卡人尽可能地使用此卡，卡上积分达到一定数额将有礼品相送"。此外，考生应注意多学习和积累英语中的固定短语和搭配，这也是翻译部分考查的要点，并多加强翻译练习，以做到熟能生巧。

写 作

在英语应用能力考试中，写作占总分的 15%，测试时间为 25 分钟。该部分着重考查学生套写应用性短文、信函、填写英文表格或翻译简短的实用性文字的能力。

纵观历年 B 级考试真题，可以发现写作部分主要考查便条、通知、书信类（包括感谢信、求职信、祝贺信、电子邮件）等文体的写作；而且几乎每次在中文信息之后均提供了文章的基本框架，考生只需在题目要求中找到对应信息翻译后填入即可。但是信函的写法以及正确的信件格式是许多其他文体应用文写作的基础，故仍然是考生备考的重点。

一、写作应注意的问题

写作部分按综合方式评分，从格式、内容和语言三方面衡量，只给一个总体印象分。据此，考生欲在写作部分得高分，必须注意以下几个方面：

1.内容完整

应用文必须为读者提供所有必需的信息，或者答复读者所提出的一切问题和要求，务必使所有的事情都得以阐明和论述，所有的问题得到答复和解释。故仔细审题，按照中文提示完整地表述内容是取得高分的必要因素。

2.表述具体

应用文给读者提供的信息应该具体、明确，尤其是合同、通知、启事、海报中关于时间、地点、事件等信息必须言明。

3.言简意赅

应用文写作应避免文字冗长、重复，且应注意不要产生歧义。

4.格式问题

考生在写作时一定要严格遵循各种应用文的格式，不能遗漏或错误地书写某个部分，否则会被酌情扣分。譬如，有同学将书信里的日期按照中文的习惯写在文章的右下角，像这样的错误会直接影响考生的作文得分层次，所以应尽量避免。

5.时态问题

时态问题也是容易被考生忽略的问题之一。写作之前，不妨仔细考虑该文章的基本时态是什么。一般来说，应用文最常见的时态是一般现在时；若文中出现陈述过去或将来的情况，则应根据具体情况调整该句的时态。

6.句式调整

句式单一，毫无生气也是影响作文得分的一个原因，因此鼓励考生在确保句子正确的前提下，尽量使用不同句式表达意思，使文章富有节奏感，从而有利于取得高分。但考生也要注意避免走极端，不可一味追求复杂、冗长的复合句或并列句以求高分。

总之，只要考生能加强基础英语知识的学习，熟练掌握大纲要求的词汇与句型，同时多阅读应用文，熟悉应用文的基本结构和常用句型，并依据以上要点反复进行应用文的练习，必定能在写作部分取得理想的成绩。

二、写作步骤

掌握正确的写作步骤往往可以使考生在考试过程中更加从容不迫，提高写作效率。

1.审题

首先不要急于动笔，应该先花一些时间看清题目要求。一般来说，题目会明确要求所写文章的体裁、情节、人物、日期，甚至字数等等；而这些都有可能在写作中用到。

2. 构思

读懂题目之后则应根据具体的要求安排文章的格式和内容。题中汉语提示部分给了相当多的信息，考生应尽量把涉及的信息融入到写作之中。若时间允许不妨列一提纲，既可增加条理性又易于从整体上把握文章；列提纲时应注意既不要遗漏也不要画蛇添足。

3. 写作

第三步则是参照提纲及内容进行写作，写作过程中考生应注意筛选句型及词组，力求准确生动，且要尽量避免语法或常识性错误！

三、英文信函格式

英文信函主要由以下六部分组成：信头（heading）、信内地址（inside address）、称呼（salutation）、正文（body）、结束语（complimentary close）、签名（signature）。

1. 信头

信头一般位于右上方，包括写信人的地址和写信日期。一些正式信函的信头还包括发信人或单位的电话号码、传真和邮政编码等。写信头时，地点的名称按由小到大的顺序排列，然后是其他项目和发信日期。信头的具体次序是：第一行写门牌号和街名；第二行写区名、市（县）名、省（州、邦）名，往国外寄的信，还要写上国家的名称；第三行写邮政编码；最后一行写日期。例如：

16 Fuxing Street

Haidian District, Beijing, People's Republic of China

100035

August 20th, 2009

此外，写发信日期时应注意以下几点：

1）年份应完全写出，不能简写；

2）月份要用英文名称，不可用数字代替；

3）月份名称可用公认的缩写式，但 May, June, July 因为较短，不可缩写；

4）写日期时，可用基数词 1，2，3……等，也可用序数词 1st, 2nd, 3rd……等；但最好使用基数词，简单明了。日期可有下列几种写法：① Oct. 20, 2009；② 10 May, 2009；③ 3rd June, 2009；④ Sept. 16th, 2009；其中第①种写法最为通用。

2. 信内地址

信内地址是收信人的姓名和地址，一般与信头之间空一两行，从信纸的左边顶格开始写。其书写次序依次是收信人姓名、头衔、单位名称（占一二行）及地址（可占二至四行）。例如：

Prof. Edward Smith

Department of Humanities

University of Nottingham

Nottingham, England

3. 称呼

称呼是指写信人对收信人的称谓，写在低于信内地址一二行的地方，从信纸的左边顶格开始写，每个词的开头字母都要大写。称呼之后，英国人用逗号，但美国和加拿大英语则多用冒号。称呼用语可视写信人与收信人的关系而定。

常用收信人称呼如下：先生（男人）Mr.；夫人（已婚）Mrs.；小姐（未婚）Miss；夫妇二人 Mr. and Mrs.。

常见的头衔（汉英对照）如下：

教授 Professor	博士 Doctor（Dr., Ph.D.）
总统或校长 President	副总统或副校长 Vice President
主席或董事长 Chairman	副主席或副董事长 Vice Chairman
首相 Prime Minister	总理 Premier
省长或州长 Governor	市长 Mayor
大使 Ambassador	秘书长 Secretary General
系主任 Dean, Head, Chair	院长 Director, Dean

4. 正文

正文与称呼之间一般空一至两行。根据结束语和签名的位置不同可将其分为齐头式和折中式。齐头式常在商贸官方以及一些正式的信件中使用，以显示信件内容的严肃性、真实性和可靠性。用齐头式写作，每段的句首无需空格，且段与段之间需空一至两行，最后的结束语和签名均须置于左下方。而折中式则显的比较随便，主要用于家人、朋友、私人之间来往的信件；如果两人之间不是第一次通信，相互比较了解，可以省略信内的双方地址。用折中式写信，每段的第一行应往右缩进四五个字母，段落间无需空行，且结束语和签名都写在信件的右下方。本部分的最后将提供省去了信头与信内地址的齐头式正文例文和折中式正文例文各一篇。

5. 结束语

结束语是写信人本人的一种谦称，只占一行，低于正文一二行，从信纸的中间或偏右的地方开始写。第一个词的开头字母要大写，末尾用逗号。一般用：Yours (very) truly, Yours (very) faithfully, Yours (very) sincerely 等等；写给上级和长者的信一般可用：Yours (very) respectfully, Yours (very) obediently, Yours gratefully, Yours appreciatively 等等。在欧洲一些国家，多把 Yours 放在 sincerely 等词的前面；在美国和加拿大等国，则多把 yours 放在 Sincerely 等词之后，且 Yours 一词有时也可省略。

6. 签名

签名位置在结束语之下，一般要用手写。

以下为一篇省去了信头与信内地址的**齐头式**正文例文：

Dear Professor Sullivan,

　　This is a request for admittance to your university as a visiting scholar. I hope it will be possible for me to take some courses and also do some research work in your department. Our government will provide me with all traveling and living expenses. Enclosed please find my application and three letters of recommendation, which I hope you will find satisfactory. Thank you for your kind consideration. I'm looking forward to your earliest reply.

Sincerely yours,
Liu Ping

以下为一篇省去了信头与信内地址的**折中式**正文例文：

Dear Mr. Smith,

　　We acknowledge the receipt of your letter and its enclosure of February 10 about the supply of washing machines.

　　We regret that it is difficult for us to consider the purchase as our company does not need the item for the time being. We have recorded your quotation of our further use.

　　Thank you for your kind attention to this reply.

Yours faithfully,
Li Xiang

第二部分
高等学校英语应用能力考试
（B级）真题

2009 年 12 月高等学校英语应用能力考试（B级）真题

Part I Listening Comprehension (15 minutes)

Directions: *This part is to test your listening ability. It consists of 3 sections.*

Section A

Directions: *This section is to test your ability to give proper responses. There are 5 recorded questions in it. After each question, there is a pause. The questions will be spoken two times. When you hear a question, you should decide on the correct answer from the 4 choices marked A, B, C and D given in your test paper. Then you should mark the corresponding letter on the Answer Sheet with a single line through the center.*

Example: *You will hear: Mr. Smith is not in. Would you like to leave him a message?*

You will read: A. I'm not sure.　　　B. You're right.

*　　　　　　　C. Yes, certainly.　　D. That's interesting.*

From the question we learn that the speaker is asking the listener to leave a message. Therefore, "C. Yes, certainly." is the correct answer. You should mark C on the Answer Sheet. Now the test will begin.

1. A. Never mind.　　　B. Yes, I am.　　　　C. No problem.　　　D. Here it is.
2. A. I like it very much. B. That's a good idea.　C. Thank you.　　　　D. You're welcome.
3. A. Let's go.　　　　　B. Don't mention it.　　C. It's delicious.　　　D. Here you are.
4. A. He's busy.　　　　B. He's fine.　　　　　C. He's fifty.　　　　D. He's a doctor.
5. A. That's difficult.　　B. It's sunny today.　　C. Yes, please.　　　　D. This way, please.

Section B

Directions: *This section is to test your ability to understand short dialogues. There are 5 recorded dialogues in it. After each dialogue, there is a recorded question. Both the dialogues and questions will be spoken two times. When you hear a question, you should decide on the correct answer from the 4 choices marked A., B, C and D. given in your test paper. Then you should mark the corresponding letter on the Answer Sheet with a single line through the center.*

6. A. A telephone.　　　　　　　　B. A watch.
　 C. A T-shirt.　　　　　　　　　　D. An mp4 player.

7. A. Travel to Australia.　　　　　　B. Start a business.
　 C. Work part-time.　　　　　　　　D. Write a report.

8. A. Prepare a speech.　　　　　　　B. Send an e-mail.
　 C. Type a letter.　　　　　　　　　D. Make a phone call.

9. A. The first floor.　　　　　　　　B. The second floor.
　 C. The third floor.　　　　　　　　D. The fourth floor.

10. A. In a bank.　　　　　　　　　　B. In a bookstore.
　　 C. At the airport.　　　　　　　　D. At a hotel.

Section C

Directions: *In this section you will hear a recorded short passage. The passage is printed in the test paper, but with some words and phrases missing. The passage will be read three times. During the second reading, you are required to put the missing words or phrases on the Answer Sheet in order of the numbered blanks according to what you hear. The third reading is for you to check your writing. Now the passage will begin.*

Ladies and gentlemen,

　　Welcome to you all. We are pleased to have you here to visit our company.

　　Today, we will first ___11___ you around our company, and then you will go and see our ___12___ and research center. The research center was ___13___ just a year ago. You may ask any questions you have during the visit. We will ___14___ to make your visit comfortable and worthwhile.

　　Again, I would like to extend a warmest welcome to all of you on behalf of our company, and I hope that you will enjoy your stay here and ___15___.

Part II　Vocabulary & Structure (15 minutes)

Directions: *This part is to test your ability to use words and phrases correctly to construct meaningful and grammatically correct sentences. It consists of 2 sections.*

Section A

Directions: *There are 10 incomplete statements here. You are required to complete each statement by choosing the appropriate answer from the 4 choices marked A, B, C and D. You should mark the corresponding letter on the Answer Sheet with a single line through the center.*

16. How much does it _____ to take the online training course?
    A. cost　　　　　　B. give　　　　　　C. pay　　　　　　D. spend

17. If you need more information, please contact us _____ telephone or email.
    A. in　　　　　　　B. by　　　　　　　C. on　　　　　　D. for

18. Mr. Smith used to smoke _____ but he has given it up recently.
    A. immediately　　B. roughly　　　　C. heavily　　　　D. completely

19. He was speaking so fast _____ we could hardly follow him.
    A. what　　　　　　B. as　　　　　　　C. but　　　　　　D. that

20. Please call me back _____ you see this message.
    A. as well as　　　B. as early as　　　C. as far as　　　D. as soon as

21. We haven't enough rooms for everyone, so some of you will have to _____ a room.
    A. share　　　　　B. stay　　　　　　C. spare　　　　　D. live

22. Before _____ for the job, you will be required to take a language test.
    A. apply　　　　　B. applying　　　　C. applied　　　　D. to apply

23. If you want to join the club, you'll have to _____ this form first.
    A. put up　　　　B. try out　　　　　C. fill in　　　　　D. set up

24. _____ the rain stops before 12 o'clock, we will have to cancel the game.
    A. As　　　　　　B. Since　　　　　　C. While　　　　　D. Unless

25. As the price of oil keeps _____, people have to pay more for driving a car.
    A. to go up　　　B. going up　　　　C. gone up　　　　D. go up

Section B

Directions: *There are 10 incomplete statements here. You should fill in each blank with the proper form of the word given in brackets. Write the word or words in the corresponding space on the Answer Sheet.*

26. What a (wonder) _____ party it was! I enjoyed every minute of it.

27. The film turned out to be (successful) _____ than we had expected.

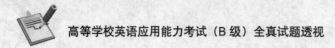

28. Readers are not allowed (bring) _____ food and drinks into the Library at any time.

29. The manager has promised that she will deal with the matter (immediate) _____.

30. We are looking forward to (work) _____ with you in the future.

31. Today email has become an important means of (communicate) _____ in daily life.

32. The visitors were (disappoint) _____ to find the museum closed when they rushed there.

33. Because of the (improve) _____ in the road conditions, there have been fewer accidents recently.

34. When you arrive tomorrow, my secretary (meet) _____ you at the airport.

35. John has worked as a sales manager since he (join) _____ this company in 2002.

Part III Reading Comprehension (40 minutes)

Directions: *This part is to test your reading ability. There are 5 tasks for you to fulfill. You should read the reading materials carefully and do the tasks as you are instructed.*

Task 1

Directions: *After reading the following passage, you will find 5 questions or unfinished statements, numbered 36 to 40. For each question or statement there are 4 choices marked A, B, C and D. You should make the correct choice and mark the corresponding letter on the Answer Sheet with a single line through the center.*

Thank you for your interest in Calibre Cassette (盒式录音带) library. This letter tells you about our service. With it we are sending you an application form, so that you can join if you would like to try it.

Calibre library aims to provide the pleasure of reading to anyone who cannot read ordinary print books because of sight problems. We currently have over 7,000 books available for reading for pleasure, including 1,000 specially for children. All our books are recorded cover-to-cover on ordinary cassettes and can be played on any cassette player. They are sent and returned by post, free of charge.

When we receive your application, we will send you a book and an information tape. They will explain how to use the service. The easy way to use Calibre library is to tell us what sorts of books you like, and we will keep you supplied with books we think you will enjoy. Or you can send us a list of books you would like to read, and we will then send you books from this list whenever possible. In that case you will need to use our website, or buy one or more of our catalogues (目录).

36. According to the first paragraph, the library sends the application form to the readers so that they can _____.

    A. read ordinary books   B. order cassette players

    C. buy Calibre cassettes   D. use the library service

37. Calibre library provides service mainly for people who suffer from _____.

    A. hearing difficulties   B. mental illnesses

    C. sight problems   D. heart troubles

38. The service of sending and returning books by post is _____.

    A. not available to children   B. paid by the users

    C. free of charge   D. not provided

39. The easy way to use the library service is to _____.

    A. inform the library of your name and address

    B. tell the library the sorts of books you like

    C. buy the catalogues of the library

    D. ask the library to buy the books

40. The main purpose of this letter is to _____.

    A. introduce the library's service to readers   B. recommend new books to the readers

    C. send a few catalogues to readers   D. express thanks to the readers

Task 2

Directions: *This task is the same as Task 1. The 5 questions or unfinished statements are numbered 41 to 45.*

    People in some countries cannot use their native language for Web addresses. Neither can Chinese speakers, who have to rely on pinyin. But last Friday, ICANN, the Web's governing body, approved the use of up to 16 languages for the new system. More will follow in the coming years.

    The Internet is about to start using the 16 languages of the world. People will soon be able to use addresses in characters (字符) other than those of the Roman alphabet (字母表). The change will also allow the suffix (后缀) to be expressed in 16 other alphabets, including traditional and simplified Chinese characters.

    But there are still some problems to work out. Experts have discussed what to do with characters that have several different meanings. This is particularly true of Chinese.

    Most experts doubt the change will have a major effect on how the Internet is used. "There will be some competition between companies to obtain popular words for addresses."

41. For Web addresses, Chinese speakers now have to use _____.

    A. pinyin   B. signs   C. numbers   D. characters

42. The approval of the use of 16 languages by ICANN will allow web users to _____.

    A. change their email address
    B. email their messages in characters

    C. have the chance to learn other languages
    D. use addresses in their own language

43. The new system will allow the suffix of a Web address to be expressed by _____.

    A. any native language
    B. figures and numbers

    C. Chinese characters
    D. symbols and signs

44. Which of the following is one of the problems in using the new system?

    A. Certain characters have several different meanings.

    B. Chinese is a truly difficult language to learn.

    C. People find it difficult to type their address in characters.

    D. Some experts think it is impossible to use Chinese characters.

45. Many experts do not believe that _____.

    A. there are still some problems to work out

    B. there will be competition to get popular addresses

    C. companies are willing to change their web addresses

    D. the change will affect the use of the Internet greatly

Task 3

Directions: *The following is an advertisement. After reading it, you should complete the information by filling in the blanks marked 46 through 50 **in not more than 3 words** in the table below.*

Hard Work, Good Money

We need:

    Staff (员工) to work in a busy operations center.

    You to be working in Hangzhou.

We are:

    A rapidly expanding international IT company.

    Based in the UK and USA, with 500 employees worldwide.

We want to:

    Recruit (招聘) staff for our office in Hangzhou.

    Recruit 30 staff members in the first year.

You should be:

    Chinese;

    A college graduate, majoring in Computer Science;

    Flexible, efficient, active;

    Willing to work in Hangzhou;

    Able to work unusual hours, e.g. 7 p.m. to 3 a.m.

You should have:

Good basic English language skills, holding Level-A Certificate of Practical English Test for Colleges (PRETCO)

Keyboard skills.

Way to contact us:

0571-88044066

For more details about the job, please visit our website: www.aaaltd.cn.

A Job Advertisement
Recruitment: staff to work in an operations center
Work place: ____46____
Qualifications (资格):
Education: college graduate majoring in ____47____
Foreign language: English, with Level-A Certificate of PRETCO
Personal qualities: flexible, ____48____, active
Working hours: ____49____, e.g. 7 p.m. to 3 a.m.
Ways to get details about the job: visit the website: ____50____

Task 4

Directions: *The following is a list of terms related to employment. After reading it, you are required to find the items equivalent to (与……等同) those given in Chinese in the table below. Then you should put the corresponding letters in the brackets on the Answer Sheet, numbered 51 through 55.*

A — annual bonus   B — basic salary
C — benefit   D — commission
E — head hunter   F — health insurance
G — housing fund   H — job center
I — job fair   J — job offer
K — labor market   L — labor contract
M — minimum wage   N — retirement insurance
O — trial period   P — unemployment insurance
Q — welfare

Examples: （A）年终奖   （O）试用期

51. （　）招聘会	（　）最低工资
52. （　）劳动合同	（　）福利
53. （　）养老保险	（　）住房基金
54. （　）猎头	（　）基本工资
55. （　）劳务市场	（　）失业保险

Task 5

Directions: *Here are two letters. After reading them, you are required to complete the statements that follow the questions (No. 56 to No. 60). You should write your answers **in not more than 3 words** on the Answer Sheet correspondingly.*

Letter 1

December 1, 2009

Dear Mr. John Campbell,

We have received your letter of November 20, 2009 about your latest model of mountain bikes, in which we are very much interested. We believe that they will sell well here in the USA Please send us further details of your prices and terms of sales. Your favorable quotation (报价) will be appreciated. We look forward to hearing from you soon.

Yours sincerely,

Robert Loftus

Marketing Manager

Letter 2

December 4, 2009

Dear Mr. Robert Loftus,

Thank you for your letter of December 1st inquiring about our latest model of mountain bikes. We are pleased to send you the catalogue (产品目录) and price list you asked for. You will find our quotation reasonable with attractive terms of sales. We are looking forward to receiving your order at the earliest time.

Very truly yours,

John Campbell

Sales Manager

56. What product is inquired about in the first letter?

The latest model of _____.

57. What information of the product does Mr. Robert Loftus ask for?

Further details of the prices and _____.

58. What is enclosed with the second letter?

The catalogue and _____.

59. Who writes the second letter?

John Campbell, _____ manager.

60. What does Mr. John Campbell say about the quotation of the product?

He says it is _____ with attractive terms of sales.

Part IV Translation — English into Chinese (25 minutes)

Directions: *This part, numbered 61 through 65, is to test your ability to translate English into Chinese. Each of the four sentences (No. 61 to No. 64) is followed by four choices of suggested translation marked A, B, C and D. Make the best choice and write the corresponding letter on the Answer Sheet. Write your translation of the paragraph (No. 65) in the corresponding space on the Translation/Composition Sheet.*

61. Not until this week were they aware of the problems with the air-conditioning units in the hotel rooms.

    A. 这个星期旅馆里的空调间出问题了，他们没有意识到。

    B. 直到这个星期他们才意识到该修理旅馆房间里的空调了。

    C. 直到这个星期他们才知道旅馆房间里的空调设备有问题。

    D. 他们查不出旅馆房间内空调的故障，这个星期会请人来检查。

62. We sent an email to your Sales Department a week ago asking about the goods we had ordered.

    A. 一周前你方销售部发来电子邮件，询问我方是否需要购买该产品。

    B. 一周前我们给你方销售部发了电子邮件，查询我们所订购的货物。

    C. 一周前我们给你们销售部发了电子邮件，想核查我们要买的货物。

    D. 一周前你方的销售部派人来核实我们的订购货物的有关电子邮件。

63. Candidates applying for this job are expected to be skilled at using a computer and good at spoken English.

    A. 申请该岗位的应聘者应熟练使用计算机并有良好的英语口语能力。

    B. 本项工作的申请人希望能提高使用计算机的能力和善于说英语。

    C. 本工作的受聘人员在应聘前应受过使用计算机的训练并懂得英语。

    D. 申请人在应聘本岗位时有可能被要求使用计算机和说良好的英语。

64. It is widely accepted that the cultural industry has been one of the key industries in developed countries.

    A. 发达国家广泛接受，文化是支撑国家工业发展的关键事业。

    B. 发达国家已普遍接受，文化产业应看成是一种关键性的事业。

    C. 大家普遍接受，发达国家应把文化事业看成一种关键产业。

    D. 人们普遍认为，文化产业已成为发达国家的一个支柱产业。

65. Journalist Wanted（招聘记者）

    Student Newspaper is looking for a journalist. Applicants (申请人) should be studying at the university now, and should have at least one year's experience in writing news reports. The successful applicant will be expected to report on the happenings in the city and on campus. If you are interested, please send your application to the *Student Newspaper* office before the end of June. For more information, please visit our website.

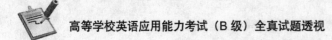

Part V Writing (25 minutes)

Directions: *This part is to test your ability to do practical writing. You are required to write an Invitation Letter based on the following information given in Chinese. Remember to do your writing on the Translation/Composition Sheet.*

写信日期：2009 年 12 月 20 日
邀请人：UST 电子公司总经理 Mike Kennedy
被邀请人：张威
内容：

　　UST 电子公司为庆祝公司创立三十周年，定于 2009 年 12 月 29 日（星期二）晚上 7 点在假日酒店举行庆祝晚宴。

　　为了感谢张威先生多年来的支持和合作。UST 电子公司总经理邀请他出席庆祝晚宴。

Words for reference:

电子公司：Electronics Corporation　　　　　三十周年：30th anniversary
庆祝晚宴：dinner party　　　　　　　　　　假日酒店：Holiday Inn

2009 年 6 月高等学校英语应用能力考试（B 级）真题

Part I Listening Comprehension (15 minutes)

Directions: *This part is to test your listening ability. It consists of 3 sections.*

Section A

Directions: *This section is to test your ability to give proper responses. There are 5 recorded questions in it. After each question, there is a pause. The questions will be spoken two times. When you hear a question, you should decide on the correct answer from the 4 choices marked A, B, C and D given in your test paper. Then you should mark the corresponding letter on the Answer Sheet with a single line through the center.*

Example: *You will hear: Mr. Smith is not in. Would you like to leave him a message?*

You will read: A. I'm not sure.　　　　B. You're right.

*　　　　　　　　C. Yes, certainly.　　　D. That's interesting.*

From the question we learn that the speaker is asking the listener to leave a message. Therefore, " C. Yes, certainly." is the correct answer. You should mark C on the Answer Sheet. Now the test will begin.

1. A. Never mind.　　　　B. Thanks a lot.　　　　C. Yes, of course.　　　D. With pleasure.

2. A. Hold on, please.　　B. It's interesting.　　　C. That's nothing.　　　D. He's all right.

3. A. Next month.　　　　B. So long.　　　　　　C. Very funny.　　　　D. Two weeks.

4. A. It's too late.　　　　B. Yes, it is.　　　　　C. Take it easy.　　　　D. It doesn't matter.

5. A. Of course.　　　　　B. You are welcome.　　C. It was excellent.　　D. Yes, I do.

Section B

Directions: *This section is to test your ability to understand short dialogues. There are 5 recorded dialogues in it. After each dialogue, there is a recorded question. Both the dialogues and questions will be spoken two times. When you hear a question, you should decide on the correct answer from the 4 choices marked A, B, C and D given in your test paper. Then you should mark the corresponding letter on the Answer Sheet with a single line through the center.*

6. A. 11：00.　　　　　B. 11：50.　　　　　　C. 12：00.　　　　　D. 12：10.

7. A. To see the woman.　　　　　　　　　B. To send the email.

　C. To go to the bank.　　　　　　　　　D. To write a letter.

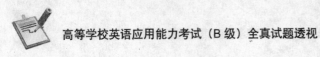

8. A. The woman will drive tonight.　　　　B. The woman doesn't like fruit.

   C. The woman has given up smoking.　　D. The woman is leaving now.

9. A. In a bank.　　　　B. In a restaurant.　　　　C. In a hospital.　　　　D. In a bookstore.

10. A. Tell her the price.　　　　　　　　　B. Wait for a while.

   C. Examine her computer.　　　　　　　D. Go shopping with her.

Section C

Directions: *In this section you will hear a recorded short passage. The passage is printed in the test paper, but with some words and phrases missing. The passage will be read three times. During the second reading, you are required to put the missing words or phrases on the Answer Sheet in order of the numbered blanks according to what you hear. The third reading is for you to check your writing. Now the passage will begin.*

Hello, everyone. This is the captain (机长) speaking. ____11____ to Flight JK900 leaving for Chicago.

Our flight time today is 2 hours and 35 minutes, and we will be flying at an average altitude (高度) of 31,000 feet. The ____12____ in Chicago is a quarter past twelve, and the current weather is cloudy, but there is a chance of ____13____ later in the day. We will ____14____ at Gate 7 at the Chicago Airport.

On behalf of our Airlines, I wish you an enjoyable ____16____ in Chicago. Sit back and enjoy the flight.

Part II Vocabulary & Structure (15 minutes)

Directions: *This part is to test your ability to use words and phrases correctly to construct meaningful and grammatically correct sentences. It consists of 2 sections.*

Section A

Directions: *There are 10 incomplete statements here. You are required to complete each statement by choosing the appropriate answer from the 4 choices marked A, B, C and D. You should mark the corresponding letter on the Answer Sheet with a single line through the center.*

16. What are the essential differences _____ selling and marketing?

   A. between　　　　B. from　　　　　　C. among　　　　　D. for

17. Jack called the airline to _____ his flight to Beijing this morning.

   A. improve　　　　B. believe　　　　　C. confirm　　　　　D. insure

18. It was in the year of 2002 _____ they set up a branch company in China.

   A. as　　　　　　B. that　　　　　　C. what　　　　　　D. which

19. You'd better _____ advice before making a project plan.

    A. put down   B. take in   C. turn out   D. ask for

20. Young people now live a lifestyle _____ their parents could hardly dream of.

    A. which   B. why   C. when   D. where

21. While traveling in France, he _____ some everyday French.

    A. gave up   B. picked up   C. drew up   D. got up

22. Hardly _____ at the office when the telephone rang.

    A. I arrived   B. I had arrived   C. did I arrive   D. had I arrived

23. To work _____ with the machine, you must read the instructions carefully.

    A. firstly   B. naturally   C. efficiently   D. generally

24. We'll have to continue the discussion tomorrow _____ we can make a final decision today.

    A. unless   B. because   C. when   D. since

25. If you have three years' work experience, you will be the right _____ for this job.

    A. person   B. passenger   C. tourist   D. customer

Section B

Directions: *There are 10 incomplete statements here. You should fill in each blank with the proper form of the word given in brackets. Write the word or words in the corresponding space on the Answer Sheet.*

26. It is reported that the sports meet was (successful) _____ organized.

27. Some people think (much) _____ about their rights than about their duties.

28. It is reported that foreign car sales in the country (rise) _____ by 8% last year.

29. The adviser recommended that Mary (start) _____ the training program as soon as possible.

30. The job pays well and you get a 20-day holiday a year — it's certainly an (attract) _____ offer.

31. It (announce) _____ yesterday that the game was to start in a week.

32. Because many people will come to the meeting, we need some (addition) _____ chairs.

33. No reader is allowed (take) _____ any reference book out of the reading room.

34. The course is designed to provide a general introduction to computers and (practice) _____ skills training.

35. We've only got one day in Paris, so we'd better (make) _____ the best use of the time.

Part III Reading Comprehension (40 minutes)

Directions: *This part is to test your reading ability. There are 5 tasks for you to fulfill. You should read the reading materials carefully and do the tasks as you are instructed.*

Task 1

Directions: *After reading the following passage, you will find 5 questions or unfinished statements, numbered 36 to 40. For each question or statement there are 4 choices marked A, B, C and D. You should make the correct choice and mark the corresponding letter on the Answer Sheet with a single line through the center.*

Subways are underground trains, which usually operate 24 hours a day. They are found in larger cities and usually run between the suburbs and the downtown area. Maps and schedules are available from the ticket office. If you take the subway often, you can save money by purchasing a monthly pass (月票).

City-operated buses run on various routes (线路) and are designed to be at certain places at certain times. Maps and schedules may be posted at certain stops, or they may be available at local banks, libraries, the student union, or from the bus drivers. Buses run mainly during the day. Fare is paid by exact change in coins, or by monthly passes.

Taxis are generally more expensive in the United States than in other countries. If you use a taxi, be sure you ask the amount of the fare before you agree to ride. The driver usually expects a tip (小费) of 15 percent of the fare.

36. According to the passage, subways are underground trains, which usually run _____.
    A. within downtown areas   B. away from city centers
    C. in or outside big modern cities   D. between suburbs and city centers

37. You can get the maps and schedules of the subways _____.
    A. at bus stations   B. at local banks
    C. in any bookstores   D. from the ticket offices

38. From the passage we learn that _____.
    A. buses are always available in 24 hours
    B. bus riders have to buy monthly passes
    C. bus fare is paid by exact change in coins
    D. buses are the best means of transportation

39. When you take a taxi, you'd better _____.
    A. buy a monthly pass   B. ask about the fare first
    C. agree on the amount of the tip   D. pay by the exact change in coins

40. The passage mainly tells us about _____.

    A. the bus and train fares in the US

    B. the ways of paying a taxi in the US

    C. the public transportation in the US

    D. the advantage of subways in the US

Task 2

Directions: *This task is the same as Task 1. The 5 questions or unfinished statements are numbered 41 to 45.*

Letter 1

Dear Ann:

    I'm going to give a dinner party next month. I want my guests to enjoy themselves and to feel comfortable. What's the secret of giving a successful party?

Mary

Letter 2

Dear Mary:

    Cook something that would let you spend time with your guests. If a guest offers to help you in the kitchen, accept the offer. It often makes people feel more comfortable when they can help.

    Before serving dinner, while your guests make small talks in the living room, offer them drinks. Some guests may like wine, but make sure to provide soft drinks for people who don't.

    At the dinner table, let your guests serve themselves. Offer them a second serving after they finish, but don't ask more than once. Most guests will take more if they want.

    Perhaps the most important rule of all is to be natural. Treat your guests as you want them to treat you when you're in their home—that is, act naturally toward them, and don't try too hard to be polite. Have a good time in a pleasant atmosphere.

Ann

41. From the first letter we learn that Mary _____.

    A. is asking for advice on giving a dinner party

    B. knows the secret of giving a pleasant party

    C. is going to attend a dinner party

    D. has successfully held a party

42. Ann's first piece of advice is that Mary should _____.

    A. get the food ready before the guests arrive

    B. keep the guests away from the kitchen

    C. spend some time with the guests

    D. accept the guests' offer to help

43. Ann suggests that Mary offer drinks _____.

    A. while the guests are having small talks

    B. when all the guests have arrived

    C. after the guests finish small talks

    D. after the dinner comes to an end

44. When having dinner, the guests are expected to _____.

    A. eat their food slowly   B. help the host serve food

    C. serve each other at the table   D. help themselves to more food

45. The most important rule for Mary to follow in treating her guests is to _____.

    A. be as polite as she can   B. let them feel at home

    C. prepare delicious food   D. create a formal atmosphere

Task 3

Directions: *The following is a notice. After reading it, you should complete the information by filling in the blanks marked 46 through 50 **in not more than 3 words** in the table below.*

Email or Call Tip Line (举报热线)

    Have you seen a crime being committed (犯罪) on a bus, train, or near a bus stop, or train station? If you do, email us or call Tip Line.

Tip Line

    If you would rather give your information by telephone, call the Police Tip Line at 612-349-7222. You can leave information anonymously (匿名地) or leave your name and phone number and an officer will call you back.

Call an Officer

    You can speak directly to any Police Department staff member who receives the call weekdays, 8：00 to 16：00. Call 612-349-7200.

Contact the Chief

    If you haven't received any reply to your Tip Line information for half a day, directly call 612-349-7100 or email: chief@metrotransit.org.

Report on a Crime

Use Tip Line

1) Tip Line number: 612-349-7222

2) Ways of reporting:

   1) Give ____46____ anonymously;

    2) Leave your name and telephone number, and wait for an officer to ____47____ .

Call the Police Directly

1) Service time: weekdays, ____48____

2) Telephone number: ____49____

Contact the Chief

1) Reason: receiving no reply to your Tip Line information for ____50____ ;

2) Telephone number: 612-349-7100;

3) Email: chief@metrotransit.org.

Task 4

Directions: *The following is a list of terms used in weather forecasting. After reading it, you are required to find the items equivalent to（与……等同）those given in Chinese in the table below. Then you should put the corresponding letters in the brackets on the Answer Sheet, numbered 51 through 55.*

A — breeze   B — calm sea

C — clear up   D — dry

E — fog   F — heavy snow

G — high seas   H — light rain

I — partly cloudy   J — shower

K — southeast wind   L — storm

M — the highs   N — the lows

O — typhoon   P — wet

Q — windy

Examples: （A）微风   （O）台风

51. （　）天气放晴	（　）大雪
52. （　）最高温度	（　）局部多云
53. （　）东南风	（　）小雨
54. （　）有雾	（　）海面大浪
55. （　）天气干燥	（　）暴风雨

Task 5

Directions: *Read the following two ads carefully. After reading them, you are required to complete the statements that follow the questions (No. 56 to No. 60). You should write your answers **in not more than 3 words** on the Answer Sheet correspondingly.*

Ad 1

Personal Assistant to Sales Manager

We are a small but growing computer software company. We are looking for someone to assist the manager of the sales department in dealing with foreign customers and orders from abroad. If you know English well and have previous experience in this job, and between 21 and 30, please write us a short letter giving details of your previous jobs, current employment, etc. Some knowledge of Spanish and Italian would be an advantage.

Write to:

Soft Logic

23 Alfred Street

Winchester

Hants

Ad 2

Part-time Drivers

King County Metro Is Hiring Part-Time Bus Drivers

Great Pay! Great Benefits!

Start at $14.50 an hour,

Plus paid vacation and sick leave, paid training

Must be 21 years or older, have a Washington State driver's license

and acceptable driving record.

Call (202) 684-1024

Or log on (登录) to www.metrokc.gov/ohrm

56. In the first ad, which department in the company is seeking an assistant to its manager?

   _____.

57. What is the major responsibility of the assistant manager?

   Dealing with foreign customers and orders _____.

58. What is mentioned as an advantage for the application in *Ad 1*?

   Some knowledge of _____.

59. What is the age limit for the position of the part-time bus drivers in *Ad 2*?

   _____ years or older.

60. What kind of driver's license should the candidates have in order to get the position?

They should have a _____ driver's license.

Part IV Translation — English into Chinese (25 minutes)

Directions: *This part, numbered 61 through 65, is to test your ability to translate English into Chinese. Each of the four sentences (No. 61 to No. 64) is followed by four choices of suggested translation marked A, B, C and D. Make the best choice and write the corresponding letter on the Answer Sheet. Write your translation of the paragraph (No. 65) in the corresponding space on the Translation/Composition Sheet.*

61. This matter is so important that it should not be left in the hands of an inexperienced lawyer.

A. 如此重要的事情，没有经验的律师不敢接手。

B. 这件事事关重大，不能交给缺乏经验的律师来处理。

C. 这件事也很重要，不应让有经验的律师处理。

D. 这件重要的事情，没有经验的律师是不敢接手处理的。

62. No matter how hard I tried to explain how to operate the machine, they were still at a loss.

A. 尽管我努力把机器开动了，他们还是觉得非常失望。

B. 无论我怎么努力地说明机器的用法，他们都不理解我。

C. 即使我努力地对机器做了解释，他们还是不相信我的话。

D. 不论我怎么努力地解释如何操作这台机器，他们依然不懂。

63. We accept returns or exchanges within 30 days from the date of the purchase of these cell phones.

A. 手机从购买之日起 30 天内我们接受退换。

B. 手机在试用 30 天之后我们可允许退货。

C. 我们同意 30 天之内可以购买手机，退货或更换。

D. 我们保证 30 天之内购买的手机，包退包换。

64. Good managers can create an environment in which different opinions are valued and everyone works together for a common goal.

A. 大家一定要齐心协力地工作，创造一个良好的环境，发表各种不同看法，要做好经理。

B. 为了共同的目标，好经理应该尊重各种不同意见，与大家一起工作，创造良好的氛围。

C. 好经理能够创造一种氛围，让不同意见受到重视并且每个人都为共同目标合作奋斗。

D. 为了共同的目标，好经理应该能够提出各种宝贵的意见，为大家创造良好的工作氛围。

65. If you want to get a driver's license, you will have to apply at a driver's license office. There you will be required to take a written test for driving in that area. You will also need to pass an eye test. If you need glasses, make sure you wear them. In addition, you must pass an actual driving test. If you fail the written or driving tests, you can take them again on another date.

Part V Writing (25 minutes)

Directions: *This part is to test your ability to do practical writing. You are required to write an email based on the following information given in Chinese. Remember to do your writing on the Translation/Composition Sheet.*

说明：假定你是 Hongxia Trading Company 的雇员王东，给客户 Mr. Baker 发一封电子邮件。内容如下：

1）欢迎他来福州；

2）告诉他已在东方宾馆为他预定了房间；

3）告诉他从国际机场到达东方宾馆大约 20 公里左右，可以乘坐出租车或机场大巴；

4）建议他第二天来你的办公室洽谈业务；

5）如需帮助，请电话联系。

Words for reference:

机场大巴：shuttle bus

An Email

Dear Mr. Baker,

_____

_____

_____

_____

2008 年 12 月高等学校英语应用能力考试（B 级）真题

Part I Listening Comprehension (15 minutes)

Directions: *This part is to test your listening ability. It consists of 3 sections.*

Section A

Directions: *This section is to test your ability to give proper responses. There are 5 recorded questions in it. After each question, there is a pause. The questions will be spoken two times. When you hear a question, you should decide on the correct answer from the 4 choices marked A, B, C and D given in your test paper. Then you should mark the corresponding letter on the Answer Sheet with a single line through the center.*

Example: *You will hear: Mr. Smith is not in. Would you like to leave him a message?*

You will read: A. I'm not sure.   B. You're right.

*   C. Yes, certainly.   D. That's interesting.*

From the question we learn that the speaker is asking the listener to leave a message. Therefore, "C. Yes, certainly." is the correct answer. You should mark C on the Answer Sheet. Now the test will begin.

1. A. Oh, yes.   B. With pleasure.   C. Thank you.   D. Here you are.

2. A. Far from here.   B. From 9 a.m. to 6 p.m.
   C. Five people.   D. One hundred dollars.

3. A. Please sit down.   B. Take it easy.   C. Yes, of course.   D. I'm OK.

4. A. I work very hard.   B. He's a nice person.   C. You're welcome.   D. Certainly not.

5. A. It's far away.   B. I'm afraid I can't.   C. I hope not.   D. It's rather warm.

Section B

Directions: *This section is to test your ability to understand short dialogues. There are 5 recorded dialogues in it. After each dialogue, there is a recorded question. Both the dialogues and questions will be spoken two times. When you hear a question, you should decide on the correct answer from the 4 choices marked A, B, C and D given in your test paper. Then you should mark the corresponding letter on the Answer Sheet with a single line through the center.*

6. A. From his friend.   B. From his brother.
   C. From his boss.   D. From his teacher.

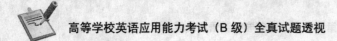

7. A. Attend a meeting.   B. Hold a party.
   C. Take an interview.   D. Meet a friend.
8. A. In her office.   B. In the meeting room.
   C. At home.   D. At the bank.
9. A. It's very boring.   B. That's too busy.
   C. She's going to give it up.   D. She likes it very much.
10. A. A salesman.   B. A doctor.   C. An engineer.   D. A secretary.

Section C

Directions: *In this section you will hear a recorded short passage. The passage is printed in the test paper, but with some words and phrases missing. The passage will be read three times. During the second reading, you are required to put the missing words or phrases on the Answer Sheet in order of the numbered blanks according to what you hear. The third reading is for you to check your writing. Now the passage will begin.*

   People visit other countries for many reasons. Some travel _____11_____; others travel to visit interesting places. Whenever you go, for whatever reason, it is important to be _____12_____. A tourist can draw a lot of attention from local people. Although most of the people you meet are friendly and welcoming, sometimes there are dangers. _____13_____, your money or passport might be stolen. Just as in your home country, do not expect everyone you meet to be friendly and _____14_____. It is important to prepare your trip in advance, and _____15_____ be careful while you are traveling.

Part II Vocabulary & Structure (15 minutes)

Directions: *This part is to test your ability to use words and phrases correctly to construct meaningful and grammatically correct sentences. It consists of 2 sections.*

Section A

Directions: *There are 10 incomplete statements here. You are required to complete each statement by choosing the appropriate answer from the 4 choices marked A, B, C and D. You should mark the corresponding letter on the Answer Sheet with a single line through the center.*

16. Information about the new system is easy to _____ on the Internet.
    A. like   B. go   C. find   D. open
17. We talked for more than three hours without _____ a cup of tea.
    A. to have   B. having   C. have   D. had

18. The big IT company will _____ a new research center in the city.

   A. set up   B. break up   C. get up   D. turn up

19. We had a(n) _____ with him about this problem last night.

   A. explanation   B. impression   C. exhibition   D. discussion

20. She told us briefly about how they succeeded in _____ the new product.

   A. develop   B. to develop   C. developed   D. developing

21. _____ she joined the company only a year ago, she's already been promoted twice.

   A. Although   B. Because   C. If   D. When

22. They had to give up the plan because they had _____ money.

   A. come up to   B. got along with   C. run out of   D. taken charge of

23. I _____ at 130 kilometers per hour when the policeman stopped me.

   A. had driven   B. have driven   C. drive   D. was driving

24. The newspaper _____ two people were killed in the accident.

   A. says   B. talks   C. calls   D. asks

25. I'd like to introduce you _____ James Stewart, the new manager of our department.

   A. with   B. to   C. of   D. on

Section B

Directions: *There are 10 incomplete statements here. You should fill in each blank with the proper form of the word given in brackets. Write the word or words in the corresponding space on the Answer Sheet.*

26. The new (nation) _____ museum will be open to the public next week.

27. This question is (difficult) _____ than the one I have answered.

28. The secretary has been working for the same (manage) _____ for over 5 years.

29. The hotel, (build) _____ 100 years ago, still looks new.

30. We are pleased to learn that that problem (solve) _____ at yesterday's meeting.

31. I want (point out) _____ that a decision about the matter must be made at once.

32. Although she is young for the job, she is vey (experience) _____.

33. The new rules for environmental protection have been (wide) _____ accepted by the public.

34. We demand that the tour guide (tell) _____ us immediately about any change in the schedule.

35. Thank you for your letter of November 15, (invite) _____ us to the trade fair on December 10.

Part III Reading Comprehension (40 minutes)

Directions: *This part is to test your reading ability. There are 5 tasks for you to fulfill. You should read the reading materials carefully and do the tasks as you are instructed.*

Task 1

Directions: *After reading the following passage, you will find 5 questions or unfinished statements, numbered 36 to 40. For each question or statement there are 4 choices marked A, B, C and D. You should make the correct choice and mark the corresponding letter on the Answer Sheet with a single line through the center.*

What is the better way of staying away from the cold winter days? Come out to our Hall Markets in the beautiful countryside, full of color, fun, music and delicious food! With over 350 stalls (摊位) selling wonderful home-made and home-grown goods, this will surely be a great day out.

The Hall Markets are held on the first Sunday of each month from 10 a.m. to 3 p.m. at Hall Village. They are operated by Hartley Lifecare Co. Ltd. All the income will go to help and support service for people with disabilities (残疾).

Volunteers (志愿者) play an important part in the success and pleasant atmosphere at the Hall Markets. Hartley Lifecare is always grateful to have you serve as volunteers with the Hall Markets.

If you are interested in being one of our volunteers and spending a few hours with us each month, please contact us during business hours on 62605555.

36. According to the passage, the Hall Markets are held _____.

    A. in the countryside   B. to attract volunteers

    C. to promote winter sales   D. by people with disabilities

37. There are over 350 stalls in the Hall Markets that _____.

    A. are operated by the disabled   B. offer free food to volunteers

    C. sell home-made goods   D. are open day and night

38. The income made by the Hall Markets goes to _____.

    A. expand Hartley Lifecare Co. Ltd.   B. support service for the disabled

    C. create more fun for customers   D. develop local economy

39. When are the Hall Markets open?

    A. The first Sunday of each month.   B. Every day from 10 a.m. to 3 p.m.

    C. The first day of each month.   D. Every weekend in winter.

40. This passage is written for the purpose of inviting _____.

    A. tourists   B. villagers   C. businessmen   D. volunteers

Task 2

Directions: *This task is the same as Task 1. The 5 questions or unfinished statements are numbered 41 to 45.*

Each time we produce a new English dictionary, our aim is always the same: what can we do to make the dictionary more helpful for students of English? As a result of our research with students and discussions with teachers, we decided to focus on providing more examples for this English dictionary.

Examples help students to remember the word they have looked up in the dictionary because it is easier both to remember and to understand a word within a context (上下文). The examples also show that words are often used in many different contexts. Fore these reasons, we have included 40 percent more examples in this new book.

We edit all the examples to remove difficult words and to make sure they are easier to understand.

We very much hope this new book will be of use not only to the students of English but also to the teachers.

41. The aim of the author in producing this new dictionary is to _____.

    A. correct mistakes in the old dictionary

    B. make it more helpful for students

    C. increase the number of words

    D. add pictures and photos

42. A word is easier to remember and understand if it is _____.

    A. included in a word list   B. pronounced correctly

    C. explained in English   D. used in a context

43. What is special about this new dictionary?

    A. It is small and cheap.

    B. It has a larger vocabulary.

    C. It has 40% more examples.

    D. It is designed for students and teachers.

44. The purpose of removing difficult words in the examples is to _____.

    A. make them easier to understand

    B. provide more useful words

    C. introduce more contexts

    D. include more examples

45. The passage is most probably taken from _____.

    A. a letter to the editor   B. a comment on a novel

    C. an introduction to a dictionary   D. a news-report in the newspaper

Task 3

Directions: *The following is a letter. After reading it, you should complete the information by filling in the blanks marked 46 through 50 **in not more than 3 words** in the table below.*

Dear Dr. Yamata,

　　The Association of Asian Economic Studies is pleased to invite you to be this year's guest speaker at its annual international symposium (研讨会). The symposium will be held for 3 days from December 22nd to 24th, 2008. This year's topic will be Economic Development in Asia. About 100 people from various countries will be attending the symposium. They would be pleased to meet you and share their views with you.

　　The Association will cover all the expenses of your trip to this symposium.

　　As the program is to be announced on December 1st, 2008, will you kindly let us know before that time whether your busy schedule will allow you to attend our symposium? We are looking forward to your favorable reply.

Yours sincerely,

John Smith

Secretary of Association of Asian Economic Studies

Letter of Invitation
Writer of the letter: ___46___
Organizer of the symposium: Association of ___47___
Guest speaker to be invited: Dr. Yamata
Starting date of the symposium: ___48___
Number of guests invited: about ___49___
Topic of the symposium: ___50___ in Asia

Task 4

Directions: *The following is part of an index (索引). After reading it, you are required to find the items equivalent to (与……等同) those given in Chinese in the table below. Then you should put the corresponding letters in the brackets on the Answer Sheet, numbered 51 through 55.*

A — after-sale service　　　　B — business license

C — business risk　　　　　　D — dead stock

E — department store　　　　 F — import license

G — limited company　　　　 H — net weight

I — packing charge　　　　　 J — price tag

K — purchasing power L — seller's market
M — shipping date N — shopping rush
O — show window P — supermarket
Q — trade agreement

Examples: （D）滞销品 （I）包装费

51. （ ）净重		（ ）百货商店
52. （ ）购买力		（ ）商业风险
53. （ ）超级市场		（ ）卖方市场
54. （ ）有限公司		（ ）售后服务
55. （ ）装船日期		（ ）进口许可证

Task 5

Directions: *The following is an advertisement. After reading it, you are required to complete the answers that follow the questions (No. 56 to No. 60). You should write your answers* ***in not more than 3 words*** *on the Answer Sheet correspondingly.*

Yanton Playingfield Committee
Grounds-person (场地管理员) Wanted

The Yanton Playingfield Committee has for many years been fortunate to have Eddie Christiansen as grounds-person at its sports ground in Littelemarsh. However, after 10 years of service, Eddie has decided it's time to retire in July. The committee wishes him the best for his retired life.

However this leaves us needing a new grounds-person. This role is part-time, averaging around 5 hours per week. The duties involve the mowing (除草), rolling, and trimming (修剪) of the field edges. Applicants (求职人) need to drive and use the equipment needed for the above-mentioned duties.

Applicants can either contact Hugh Morris, 42 Spencer Avenue tel. 765-4943780, to discuss or register an interest in the position, or any member of the Playingfield Committee.

56. Which organization is in need of a grounds-person?

The _____.

57. Why is a new grounds-person needed?

Because the former grounds-person, Eddie Christiansen, has decided it's time to _____.

58. What are the duties of a grounds-person?

His duties involve the moving, _____ of the field edges.

59. What should applicants be able to do?

They should be able to _____ the equipment needed for the duties.

60. Who is the contact person?

_____ or any committee member.

Part IV Translation — English into Chinese (25 minutes)

Directions: *This part, numbered 61 through 65, is to test your ability to translate English into Chinese. Each of the four sentences (No. 61 to No. 64) is followed by four choices of suggested translation marked A, B, C and D. Make the best choice and write the corresponding letter on the Answer Sheet. Write your translation of the paragraph (No. 65) in the corresponding space on the Translation/ Composition Sheet.*

61. This new type of air-conditioner is so energy-efficient that it can save the company forty thousand dollars a year.

A. 这种新型空调功率很高，公司电费一年高达四万美元。

B. 这种新型空调高效节能，一年能为公司节省四万美元。

C. 这种新型空调效率很高，公司一年节省了电费四万美元。

D. 这种新型空调效率很高，公司一年仅需支付电费四万美元。

62. All flights have been cancelled because of the snowstorm, so many passengers could do nothing except take the train.

A. 暴风雪使所有航班被取消，许多乘客只能改乘火车。

B. 所有的航班因暴风雪而取消，许多乘客也无法改乘火车。

C. 受暴风雪影响，许多乘客坚持改乘火车，因此所有航班被迫取消。

D. 由于暴风雪的影响，许多乘客不得不放弃乘坐飞机，而改乘火车。

63. The function of e-commerce is more than just buying and selling goods and services on the Internet.

A. 电子商务的功能很多，如提供网上货物交易的服务。

B. 电子商务更多的功能在于做买卖并提供网络服务。

C. 电子商务的功能不只是在互联网上买卖货物和服务。

D. 电子商务的功能更多的是从互联网上买卖货物和服务。

64. Seldom can people find international news on the front page of this popular local newspaper.

A. 人们不会在这份地方报纸前几页上寻找重要的国际新闻。

B. 人们很难在当地这份深受欢迎的报纸头版看到国际新闻。

C. 人们从这份当地发行的报纸第一页上几乎找不到国际新闻。

D. 人们阅读当地发行的报刊时从不查看头版刊登的国际新闻。

65. The ABC Railway Company has greatly improved its public hotline service. Simply dial 3929-3499 to get information about all the services of the company. The telephone information system is working to serve you 24 hours all year round. The customer service staff (员工) are also ready to provide you with the information you need. Their service hours are from Monday to Sunday, 7：00 a.m. to 9：00 p.m.

Part V Writing (25 minutes)

Directions: *This part is to test your ability to do practical writing. You are required to write a letter of thanks based on the following information given in Chinese. Remember to do your writing on the Translation/Composition Sheet.*

说明：假定你是 JKM 公司的 Thomas Black，刚从巴黎出差回来，请给在巴黎的 Jane Costa 小姐写一封感谢信。

写信日期：2008 年 12 月 21 日

内容：

  1）感谢她在巴黎期间的热情招待；

  2）告诉她巴黎给你留下了美好的印象，你非常喜欢法国的……，参观工厂和学校后学到了很多……；

  3）期待再次与她见面。

注意：必须包括对收信人的称谓、写信日期、发信人的签名等基本格式。

2008 年 6 月高等学校英语应用能力考试（B 级）真题

Part I Listening Comprehension (15 minutes)

Directions: *This part is to test your listening ability. It consists of 3 sections.*

Section A

Directions: *This section is to test your ability to give proper responses. There are 5 recorded questions in it. After each question, there is a pause. The questions will be spoken two times. When you hear a question, you should decide on the correct answer from the 4 choices marked A, B, C and D given in your test paper. Then you should mark the corresponding letter on the Answer Sheet with a single line through the center.*

Example: *You will hear:* Mr. Smith is not in. Would you like to leave him a message?
You will read: A. I'm not sure.   B. You're right.
                              C. Yes, certainly.   D. That's interesting.
From the question we learn that the speaker is asking the listener to leave a message. Therefore, "C. Yes, certainly." is the correct answer. You should mark C on the Answer Sheet. Now the test will begin.

1. A. A good idea.   B. No problem.   C. My pleasure.   D. Of course not.
2. A. It's too hot in June.   B. In East Europe.
   C. In the countryside.   D. After December 24.
3. A. It was impossible.   B. It was wonderful.
   C. So do I.   D. I see.
4. A. You are welcome.   B. Sure. Where?
   C. How are you?   D. Long time no see.
5. A. Glad to meet you.   B. I'm not sure.
   C. Go ahead.   D. No thanks.

Section B

Directions: *This section is to test your ability to understand short dialogues. There are 5 recorded dialogues in it. After each dialogue, there is a recorded question. Both the dialogues and questions will be spoken two times. When you hear a question, you should decide on the correct answer from the 4 choices marked A, B, C and D given in your test paper. Then you should mark the corresponding letter on the Answer Sheet with a single line through the center.*

6. A. Tea.   B. Coffee.   C. Water.   D. Beer.

7. A. He can't call a taxi for her.   B. There is no taxi.

   C. The traffic is heavy.   D. The line is busy.

8. A. Husband and wife.   B. Patient and doctor.

   C. Teacher and student.   D. Manager and secretary.

9. A. On foot.   B. By bus.   C. By car.   D. By bike.

10. A. Buy a new computer.   B. Try a new computer again.

    C. Use her computer.   D. Have the computer repaired.

Section C

Directions: *In this section you will hear a recorded short passage. The passage is printed in the test paper, but with some words and phrases missing. The passage will be read three times. During the second reading, you are required to put the missing words or phrases on the Answer Sheet in order of the numbered blanks according to what you hear. The third reading is for you to check your writing. Now the passage will begin.*

Today more and more people begin to understand that study does not come to an end with school graduation. Education is not just a college ____11____; it is life itself. Many people are not interested in studying at college, and they are interested in ____12____ of learning. They may go to a ____13____ in their own field; they may improve their ____14____ skills by following television courses. They certainly know that if they know more or learn more, they can get ____15____ jobs or earn more money.

Part II Vocabulary & Structure(15 minutes)

Directions: *This part is to test your ability to use words and phrases correctly to construct meaningful and grammatically correct sentences. It consists of 2 sections.*

Section A

Directions: *There are 10 incomplete statements here. You are required to complete each statement by choosing the appropriate answer from the 4 choices marked A, B, C and D. You should mark the corresponding letter on the Answer Sheet with a single line through the center.*

16. Please keep a detailed _____ of the work that you have done.

    A. paper   B. idea   C. exercise   D. record

17. _____ our great surprise, the new secretary can speak four foreign languages.

    A. Of   B. In   C. To   D. For

18. The department manager _____ a new plan to promote sales at the meeting.

    A. took away   B. put forward   C. looked after   D. got on

19. What he told me to do was _____ I should get fully prepared before the interview.

    A. what   B. if   C. which   D. that

20. When dealing with a _____ task, Alice always asks for help from people around her.

    A. difficult   B. wonderful   C. funny   D. simple

21. Location is the first thing customers consider when _____ to buy a house.

    A. planning   B. planned   C. to plan   D. having planned

22. Soft drink sales in this city have _____ by 8% compared with last year.

    A. picked   B. moved   C. increased   D. pushed

23. If I hadn't attended an important meeting yesterday, I _____ to see you.

    A. will have come   B. would have come   C. have come   D. had come

24. To obtain a visa to enter that country for the first time, you need to apply _____.

    A. in part   B. in person   C. in turn   D. in place

25. The new model of the car was put into production in 2007, _____ helped to provide another 1,400 jobs.

    A. that   B. when   C. what   D. which

Section B

Directions: *There are 10 incomplete statements here. You should fill in each blank with the proper form of the word given in brackets. Write the word or words in the corresponding space on the Answer Sheet.*

26. My impression is that the sales of this company have (great) _____ increased this year.

27. This picture (take) _____ by a young reporter in Beijing last month.

28. Tom has made the (decide) _____ to apply for a job in the company.

29. No reader is allowed (take) _____ any reference book out of the reading room.

30. Although you may not (success) _____ in the beginning, you should keep on trying.

31. Because light travels (fast) _____ than sound, lightning is seen before thunder (雷) is heard.

32. The doctor recommended that Mary (start) _____ the health program as soon as possible.

33. It took me several weeks to get used to (drive) _____ on the left side of the road in London.

34. This medicine is highly (effect) _____ in treating skin cancer if it is applied early enough.

35. Now the number of people who are working at home on the Internet (be) _____ still very small.

Part III Reading Comprehension (40 minutes)

Directions: *This part is to test your reading ability. There are 5 tasks for you to fulfill. You should read the reading materials carefully and do the tasks as you are instructed.*

Task 1

Directions: *After reading the following passage, you will find 5 questions or unfinished statements, numbered 36 to 40. For each question or statement there are 4 choices marked A, B, C and D. You should make the correct choice and mark the corresponding letter on the Answer Sheet with a single line through the center.*

Falls are the number one cause of death to old people at home. Most old people can live safely at home if they make a few changes. Falls are common as people are getting older. Up to half of home accidents could be prevented by making some very simple changes. Here are a few suggestions.

Mark trouble spots with bright tapes. The first and last steps on stairs are usually high-risk accident areas. Applying bright tapes and using bright light in these areas would make these spots easier to see.

Put grab bars (扶手) in the bathroom. A large number of falls occur in the bathroom. This is unfortunate (不幸的) because it's easy to make the area safe from accidents. Putting grab bars in the bathroom gives something to hang on to.

Invest in a personal alarm. A personal alarm can be started if a person falls or otherwise gets in trouble. With the push of a button, the alarm automatically sends a signal, which gets someone to call and see if person needs help.

36. By making some very simple changes at home, old people _____.
   A. are free from home accidents
   B. can improve their health
   C. are likely to live longer
   D. can live more safely

37. Last steps on stairs may become a high-risk accident area if they are _____.
   A. not painted in a different color
   B. not marked with bright tapes
   C. fixed with grab bars
   D. very brightly lit

38. Falls in the bathroom are considered to be unfortunate because _____.
   A. they can easily be avoided
   B. old people seldom fall in bathrooms
   C. grab bars do not help to prevent falls
   D. bathrooms accidents are difficult to prevent

39. A personal alarm is designed for old people to _____.

    A. detect safely conditions at home

    B. avoid falls in the bathroom

    C. send out signals for help

    D. make phone calls easily

40. The purpose of this passage is to tell people that _____.

    A. most old people die from accidents at home

    B. up to half of home accidents could be prevented

    C. falls at home can be avoided by taking some simple measures

    D. protection of old people should be the first concern for the public

Task 2

Directions: *This task is the same as Task 1. The 5 questions or unfinished statements are numbered 41 to 45.*

    We have created a special rate that will let you travel actually thousands of miles on your vacation at no extra cost.

    In most of our US and Canadian offices, we'll rent you cars of high quality for seven days for $99.

    You can drive as far as you like without paying us a penny over the $99 as long as you return the car to the city from which you rented it. Insurance (保险) is included, gas is not.

    If you rent the car in Florida or in California, the rate is the same, but you can return the car to any city in the state.

    If you'd like some suggestions on what to do with the car once you've got it, we have driving and touring guides for almost every part of the country. No matter which rate you choose, the company comes at no extra cost. You don't just rent a car. You rent a company!

41. According to the advertisement, $99 is the rate offered for _____.

    A. traveling a limited distance   B. renting a car for seven days

    C. hiring a driving guide   D. driving within a state

42. Which of the following is included in the car-renting rate?

    A. Gas used.   B. Car repairs.

    C. The hotel charge.   D. Insurance fee.

43. The car rate remains $99 if you _____.

    A. return the car to where you rent it   B. drive within the same city

    C. buy the insurance   D. pay for the gas

44. The last sentence of the passage "You rent a company" means that _____.

   A. you have to be responsible for the company

   B. you should obey the rules set by the company

   C. you can enjoy all-round services of this company

   D. you may choose the best car from the company

45. The purpose of the passage is to advertise _____.

   A. car-renting services in the US   B. a special rate of car-renting

   C. the advantages of car-renting   D. a US car-renting company

Task 3

Directions: *The following is a job application letter. After reading it, you should complete the information by filling in the blanks marked 46 through 50* **in not more than 3 words** *in the table below.*

Dear Ms. Rennick,

    Professor Saul Wilder, an adviser to your firm, has informed me that your company is looking for someone with excellent communication skills, organizational experience, and leadership background for a management position. I believe that my enclosed resume will show that I have the qualifications (资历) and experience you seek. In addition, I'd like to mention how my work experience as a sales manager last summer makes me a particularly strong candidate for the position.

    I would be grateful if you can offer me an opportunity for an interview with you. If you are interested, please contact me at (317) 555-0118 any time before 11:00 a.m., or feel free to leave a message. I look forward to meeting with you to discuss the ways my skills may best serve your company.

Sincerely yours,

Richard Smith

An Application Letter

Applicant: Richard Smith

Position applied for: a ____46____ position

Qualifications required for the position:

    1) excellent ____47____

    2) organizational experience

    3) ____48____ background

Work experience (last summer): as ____49____

Contact number: ____50____

Enclosure: resume

Task 4

Directions: *The following is a list of terms used in the waybill (运货单) of the Express Mail Service. After reading it, you are required to find the items equivalent to (与……等同) those given in Chinese in the table below. Then you should put the corresponding letters in the brackets on the Answer Sheet, numbered 51 through 55.*

A — original office

B — accepted date

C — posting stamp

D — delivery stamp

E — company name

F — sender's address

G — customer code

H — document

I — parcel

J — name of contents

K — insurance amount

L — sender's signature

M — postal code

N — insurance fee

O — total charge

P — receiver's signature

Q — remark

Examples: （D） 投递日戳　　　　　　（L） 交寄人签名

51. （　） 费用总计		（　） 收寄日期	
52. （　） 文件资料		（　） 邮政编码	
53. （　） 用户代码		（　） 收件人签名	
54. （　） 内件品名		（　） 发件人地址	
55. （　） 收寄日戳		（　） 单位名称	

Task 5

Directions: *The following is set of instructions about how to use washing machines. After reading it, you are required to complete the answers that follow the questions (No. 56 to No. 60). You should write your answers **in not more than 3 words** on the Answer Sheet correspondingly.*

To effectively use this washing machine, you must complete four steps carefully: loading (装载) the clothes, pouring in the detergent (洗涤剂), adjusting the water temperature, and putting in the coins. First, throw clothes of similar color into the machine; for example, whites, colored clothes, and towels should be washed separately. While completing this step, you must be careful not to overload the machine. Second, you should read the directions on your detergent box to find out the correct amount for your particular load. Next, select one of three possible water temperatures: hot, warm, or cold. Generally, hot temperature is used for white clothes, warm temperature for light colored clothes, and cold temperature for dark or brightly colored clothes.

Finally, after closing the door of the washing machine, put in the proper amount of money.

In summary, by following these simple directions, the washer will give you a clean load of wet clothes.

56. Why should you follow the directions carefully when using the machine?
    To use the washing machine _____.

57. What is the first step for using the machine to wash your clothes?
    To throw the clothes of _____ into the machine.

58. Where can you find the correct amount of the detergent to be used?
    On _____.

59. What temperature is recommended for washing light colored clothes?
    _____.

60. When should you put in the money?
    After _____ of the washing machine.

Part IV Translation — English into Chinese (25 minutes)

Directions: *This part, numbered 61 through 65, is to test your ability to translate English into Chinese. Each of the four sentences (No. 61 to No. 64) is followed by four choices of suggested translation marked A, B, C and D. Make the best choice and write the corresponding letter on the Answer Sheet. Write your translation of the paragraph (No. 65) in the corresponding space on the Translation/ Composition Sheet.*

61. Two assistants will be required to check reporters' names when they arrive at the press conference.
    A. 两位助手要求记者在到达新闻发布会时通报他们的姓名。
    B. 两位助手到达新闻发布会时被记者要求通报他们的姓名。
    C. 有两位助手检查记者的姓名并通告他们新闻发布会的时间。
    D. 要有两位助手在记者到达新闻发布会时核对他们的姓名。

62. A guest paying full fare can invite another guest to join the tour at half price.
    A. 支付全额费用的客人，每位可以再带一位客人参加旅游，按半价付费。
    B. 支付全额费用的客人，每位需要再邀请一位客人参加旅游，按半价付费。
    C. 每位按半价付费参加旅游的客人，必须再找到一位全额付费的客人参加。
    D. 支付全额费用的客人，如邀请另外一位客人参加旅游，可退还一半费用。

63. Congratulations on purchasing from our company the C800 Coffee Maker, which is suitable for home use.
    A. 我公司隆重推出 C800 型家用咖啡壶，欢迎各界人士惠顾。
    B. 您从我公司购买了最新款的 C800 型家用咖啡壶，值得祝贺。
    C. 恭喜您购买本公司 C800 型咖啡壶，此款咖啡壶适合居家使用。
    D. 您购买的咖啡壶是我公司最新产品——C800 家用型，特此致谢。

64. Last month I booked a double room in the name of Mr. Brown for a week from the 14th, January.

    A. 上个月我以布朗先生名义预定了一间双人房，为期一周，从 1 月 14 日起算。

    B. 上个月 14 日我为布朗先生预定了一间房间，到现在已有一周时间了。

    C. 上个月我为布朗先生预定了一个双人间，到 1 月 14 日止刚好为期一周。

    D. 上个月，布朗先生为我预定了两个房间，到 1 月 14 日为止，共一周时间。

65. Thank you for choosing our restaurant during your visit to London. Services to guests of the restaurant are a large part of our tasks, and we are grateful for the opportunity to serve you. We would like to invite your comments on our performance and to learn from your experiences. Please take a few moments to complete our customer response form so that we may serve you better in the future.

Part V Writing (25 minutes)

Directions: *This part is to test your ability to do practical writing. You are required to write a note asking for sick leave based on the following information given in Chinese. Remember to do your writing on the Translation/Composition Sheet.*

说明：假设你是公司职员刘斌，给经理 Mr. Johnson 写一张请假条。

时间：2008 年 6 月 19 日，星期四

    1）咳嗽特别厉害，想去医院看病；

    2）因本周大部分工作已经完成，故星期五请假一天；

    3）看完病后，会给经理打电话；

    4）对由此造成的不便表示歉意；

    5）希望能得到经理的批准。

To: _____

From: _____

Date: _____

Subject: <u>Leave of Absence</u>

_____

_____

_____

_____

2007年12月高等学校英语应用能力考试（B级）真题

Part I Listening Comprehension (15 minutes)

Directions: *This part is to test your listening ability. It consists of 3 sections.*

Section A

Directions: *This section is to test your ability to give proper responses. There are 5 recorded questions in it. After each question, there is a pause. The questions will be spoken two times. When you hear a question, you should decide on the correct answer from the 4 choices marked A, B, C and D given in your test paper. Then you should mark the corresponding letter on the Answer Sheet with a single line through the center.*

Example: *You will hear:* Mr. Smith is not in. Would you like to leave him a message?

You will read: A. I'm not sure.   B. You're right.

C. Yes, certainly.   D. That's interesting.

From the question we learn that the speaker is asking the listener to leave a message. Therefore, "C. Yes, certainly." is the correct answer. You should mark C on the Answer Sheet. Now the test will begin.

1. A. Yes, it is.   B. No, thanks.   C. Never mind.   D. Certainly.

2. A. Thank you.   B. Sorry, he's not here.   C. I'm sorry.   D. My name is Jack.

3. A. After December 24.   B. It's too hot in June.

   C. My pleasure.   D. No problem.

4. A. Yes, please.   B. For two months.   C. Every day.   D. Yes, I will.

5. A. Nice to meet you.   B. Thanks anyway.   C. Very interesting.   D. Not bad.

Section B

Directions: *This section is to test your ability to understand short dialogues. There are 5 recorded dialogues in it. After each dialogue, there is a recorded question. Both the dialogues and questions will be spoken two times. When you hear a question, you should decide on the correct answer from the 4 choices marked A, B, C and D given in your test paper. Then you should mark the corresponding letter on the Answer Sheet with a single line through the center.*

6. A. Snowy.   B. Cloudy.

   C. Windy.   D. Rainy.

7. A. By car.   B. By train.
   C. By plane.   D. By ship.
8. A. Calling the police.   B. Booking a ticket.
   C. Giving information.   D. Asking the way.
9. A. Patient and doctor.   B. Husband and wife.
   C. Teacher and student.   D. Manager and secretary.
10. A. Buy a new phone.   B. Use her phone.
    C. Have the phone repaired.   D. Try the phone again.

Section C

Directions: *In this section you will hear a recorded short passage. The passage is printed in the test paper, but with some words and phrases missing. The passage will be read three times. During the second reading, you are required to put the missing words or phrases on the Answer Sheet in order of the numbered blanks according to what you hear. The third reading is for you to check your writing. Now the passage will begin.*

Welcome to the Public Bus System. Its bus network operates 365 days of the year and has _____11_____ that can take you to your destination (目的地) quickly and easily.

You can travel round the city for just $ _____12_____ a day with Type-A bus tickets. Type-B bus tickets are even _____13_____. You can get on and off as many times _____14_____, so you can tour the city at your own pace.

You can buy tickets at most newspaper stands.

If you want to get _____15_____, call the office of the Public Bus System.

Part II Vocabulary & Structure (15 minutes)

Directions: *This part is to test your ability to use words and phrases correctly to construct meaningful and grammatically correct sentences. It consists of 2 sections.*

Section A

Directions: *There are 10 incomplete statements here. You are required to complete each statement by choosing the appropriate answer from the 4 choices marked A, B, C and D. You should mark the corresponding letter on the Answer Sheet with a single line through the center.*

16. It suddenly occurred to me that we could _____ the police for help.
    A. ask   B. look   C. tell   D. meet
17. Many companies provide their employees _____ free lunch during the weekdays.
    A. by   B. with   C. to   D. for

18. Life is more enjoyable to people _____ are open to new ideas.

    A. whose   B. whom   C. who   D. which

19. I _____ my former manager when I was on a flight to Beijing.

    A. ran into   B. took away   C. put on   D. shut down

20. It has been quite a long time _____ the two companies established a business relationship.

    A. although   B. because   C. if   D. since

21. The house was sold for $60,000, which was far more than its real _____.

    A. money   B. payment   C. value   D. profit

22. Customers consider location as the first factor when _____ a decision about buying a house.

    A. make   B. made   C. to make   D. making

23. The work seemed easy at first but it _____ to be quite difficult.

    A. broke out   B. turned out   C. worked out   D. set out

24. The small company is _____ to handle this large order.

    A. able   B. probable   C. reasonable   D. possible

25. If I _____ that your business was growing so rapidly, I wouldn't have been worried about it.

    A. know   B. knew   C. had known   D. have known

Section B

Directions: *There are 10 incomplete statements here. You should fill in each blank with the proper form of the word given in brackets. Write the word or words in the corresponding space on the Answer Sheet.*

26. David will go on holiday as soon as he (finish) _____ the project.

27. Although the small town has been changing slowly, it looks quite (difference) _____ from what it was.

28. My father is a sports fan and he enjoys (swim) _____ very much.

29. The small village has become (wide) _____ known in recent years for its silk exports.

30. The fast (develop) _____ of the local economy has caused serious water pollution in this region.

31. Thank you for your letter of April 15, (tell) _____ us about Mr. John Brown's visit to our company on May 10.

32. The (late) _____ model of the racing car will be on display at the exhibition this week.

33. Miss Li was (luck) _____ enough to get the opportunity to work in that world-famous company.

34. Last year, customers (buy) _____ a total of 90 million iPods and 2 billion songs from the iTunes store.

35. Yesterday, the secretary (give) _____ the task to make arrangements for the annual meeting.

Part III Reading Comprehension (40 minutes)

Directions: *This part is to test your reading ability. There are 5 tasks for you to fulfill. You should read the reading materials carefully and do the tasks as you are instructed.*

Task 1

Directions: *After reading the following passage, you will find 5 questions or unfinished statements, numbered 36 to 40. For each question or statement there are 4 choices marked A, B, C and D. You should make the correct choice and mark the corresponding letter on the Answer Sheet with a single line through the center.*

Cars are lots of fun, but they could also be dangerous. We have to be careful when we drive them or ride in them.

It's always a good idea to put on your seat belt when you're in a car. Why? Think about this example: You put an egg on a skateboard (滑板) and give it a push. If the skateboard hits a stone, it will stop, but the egg won't. It will fly through the air, hit the ground and break.

Now, think what would happen if you tied the egg to the skateboard. When the skateboard hits a stone, the egg won't go flying. It will stay safely on the skateboard.

Volvo, a famous Swedish carmaker, was the first to use seat belts in 1949. Air bags are also very important for car safety, because sometimes a seat belt isn't enough. If the car is going really fast and runs into something, seat belts could even hurt the people who wear them.

Most newer cars have air bags in front of and next to the seats. When a car hits something, its airbags will come out quickly—in less than one second—to keep the people inside safe.

36. We have to be careful in driving a car mainly because it could be _____.

    A. little fun   B. a pleasure   C. a lot of trouble   D. a great danger

37. The example of an egg on a skateboard is used to show that _____.

    A. eggs break easily on a moving skateboard

    B. cars should not be stopped suddenly

    C. seat belts are important to safety

    D. driving is a dangerous act

38. Which of the following statements is TRUE?

    A. People with seat belts tied will always be safe in cars.

    B. Volvo was the first carmaker to use seat belts in cars.

    C. Air bags will come out before the cars hit something.

    D. All cars have air bags in front of the seats.

39. According to the passage, air bags are another device that _____.

    A. adds safety to car driving   B. is going to replace seat belts

    C. comes out slowly to function   D. prevents cars from running too fast

40. The best title for this passage is _____.

    A. Buy a Volvo with Airbags   B. Make a Car Safe Inside

    C. Fasten Your Seat Belts   D. Add Air Bags to Cars

Task 2

Directions: *This task is the same as Task 1. The 5 questions or unfinished statements are numbered 41 to 45.*

    The Museum of Contemporary (当代的) Art (MOCA) has started a new series of programs, known as "*Art Makes Good Business.*" It is designed to educate company managers about why art makes good business and how to take full advantage of it.

    The event is open to new and current corporate (企业法人的) members of MOCA. An understanding and appreciation of art is becoming a must in today's business world. Art can be a valuable tool for seeking new ways to communicate with customers and raising public awareness of your company's role in the community.

    During the coming months the series will look into the relationship between art, business and community. The series will cover how to understand modern art and how art can help improve a company's image. *Art Makes Good Business* speakers will include leaders from the business and art worlds. Bookings are required. Space is limited. For more information call 305-893-6211 or visit www.momanomi.org.

41. The purpose of the museum's new programs is to show _____.

    A. the management of business by artists   B. the role of art in improving business

    C. the education of modern artists   D. the way to design art programs

42. The Art Makes Good Business program is intended for _____.

    A. the general public   B. modern art lovers

    C. corporate members of MOCA   D. people involved in art business

43. MOCA members who take part in the programs can learn _____.

    A. to become leaders in business and art worlds

    B. to cooperate with other members of MOCA

    C. the new ways of communication between people

    D. about the relationship between art, business and community

44. Those who want to attend lectures by Art Makes Good Business speakers must _____.

    A. make a booking   B. pay additional fees

    C. understand modern art   D. be successful managers

45. This advertisement aims to _____.

    A. improve the relationship between companies

    B. stress the important role of art in education

    C. attract MOCA members to the programs

    D. raise funds for museums of modern art

Task 3

Directions: *The following is an advertisement. After reading it, you should complete the information by filling in the blanks marked 46 through 50 **in not more than 3 words** in the table below.*

Make our Tourist Information Centre your first call when planning your visit to Cheltenham. Our friendly team can provide a wide range of services to make your stay enjoyable and unforgettable. We can book your accommodation (住宿), from a homely bed and breakfast to a four-star hotel. We can provide tickets for local events and we are booking agents (代理商) for National Express and other local coach companies.

In summer we organize our own various programs of Coach Tours of the Cotswolds, plus regular walking tours around Cheltenham, all guided by qualified guides. We also stock a wide range of maps and guidebooks plus quality gifts and souvenirs (纪念品). We can help you with advice on what to see, where to go and how to get there.

We look forward to seeing you in Cheltenham.

Tours of Cheltenham

Tour Services Provider: ____46____

Services Offered:

    1) booking accommodation

    2) providing tickets for ____47____

    3) booking tickets from National Express and other ____48____

    4) organizing Coach Tours and regular ____49____ in summer

    5) providing various maps, ____50____, gifts and souvenirs

---

Task 4

Directions: *The following is a menu of a mobile (移动的) phone. After reading it, you are required to find the items equivalent to (与……等同) those given in Chinese in the table below. Then you should put the corresponding letters in the brackets on the Answer Sheet, numbered 51 through 55.*

A — phone book   B — tools

C — calculator   D — message saving

E — phone setting   F — backlight setting
G — key lock   H — automatic redial
I — sound volume   J — ring type
K — voice mail   L — additional functions
M — own number   N — alarm
O — new message   P — network
Q — delete all

Examples: （C）计算器   （K）语音信箱

51. （ ）自动重拨	（ ）本机号码
52. （ ）闹钟	（ ）音量
53. （ ）网络	（ ）信息储存
54. （ ）工具箱	（ ）背景光设置
55. （ ）电话簿	（ ）话机设置

Task 5

Directions: *The following is a letter. After reading it, you are required to complete the answers that follow the questions (No. 56 to No. 60). You should write your answers **in not more than 3 words** on the Answer Sheet correspondingly.*

Dear Guests,

In order to serve you better, we are carrying out a reconstruction program at the hotel, which will improve our fitness (健身) facilities.

We are currently working on our program on the 6th floor. We regret that the tennis court is not in operation.

However, you are still welcome to use the swimming pool. Please change into your swimsuit in your room.

While this program is in progress, drilling (钻孔) work may create some noise during the following time schedule:

9:00 am to 11:00 am

4:00 pm to 6:00 pm

We apologize for the inconvenience (不便). Should you require any help during your stay with us, please call our Assistant Manager. He will be at your service any time of the day and night at 6120.

Once again, thank you for your kind understanding and have a pleasant stay!

Yours faithfully,

Arthur White

General Manager

56. What's the purpose of the hotel's reconstruction program?

  To improve its _____.

57. Where is the reconstruction work going on at the moment?

  On the _____.

58. Where should guests change into their swimsuits before going swimming?

  In their _____.

59. Why does the hotel apologize to the guests?

  Because of _____ caused by the reconstruction

  program.

60. Who should the guests turn to if they have any problem?

  They should call the _____.

Part IV Translation — English into Chinese (25 minutes)

Directions: *This part, numbered 61 through 65, is to test your ability to translate English into Chinese. Each of the four sentences (No. 61 to No. 64) is followed by four choices of suggested translation marked A, B, C and D. Make the best choice and write the corresponding letter on the Answer Sheet. Write your translation of the paragraph (No. 65) in the corresponding space on the Translation/Composition Sheet.*

61. I will give you a clear idea of the market conditions in the region as soon as possible.

  A. 我会尽快让你们清楚地了解该地区的市场情况。

  B. 我将尽可能设法弄清楚该地区的市场销售情况。

  C. 我会尽早向你们清楚地说明该地区的市场状况。

  D. 我将尽可能对该地区市场状况提出明确的想法。

62. One more assistant will be required to check reporters' names when they arrive at the press conference.

  A. 还需要一位助手在记者到达新闻发布会时核查他们的姓名。

  B. 还需要一位助手在记者到达新闻发布会时登记他们的姓名。

  C. 还有一位助手在到达新闻发布会时请记者通报他们的姓名。

  D. 还有一位助手要记者在到达新闻发布会时通报他们的姓名。

63. Mr. Smith has cancelled his trip because an urgent matter has come up which requires his immediate attention.

  A. 史密斯先生推迟了旅行，因为发生了一件大家都十分关注的突发事件。

  B. 史密斯先生取消了旅行，因为发生了一件紧急的事情需要他立即处理。

  C. 史密斯先生取消了旅行，因为有一件棘手的事情需要他予以密切关注。

  D. 史密斯先生推迟了旅行，因为要处理一桩已引起公众关注的突发事件。

64. The library is trying in every possible way to raise more money to meet its increasing running costs.

   A. 这个图书馆正尽一切努力增加更多收入以满足不断增长的日常开支。

   B. 这个图书馆正想尽一切办法提高收费标准并不断降低经营管理成本。

   C. 这个图书馆正尝试用各种办法提高收费标准以便尽早收回投资成本。

   D. 这个图书馆正想尽一切办法筹集更多资金满足越来越多的日常开支。

65. Worktrain is a website for jobs and learning. It puts the most popular services for job seekers online. This makes it easy for you to get the information you need. At this site, you'll find over 300,000 jobs, plus thousands of training opportunities and information on job markets. And because Worktrain uses the power of the Internet, it gives you what you need faster and more easily than ever before.

Part V Writing (25 minutes)

Directions: *This part is to test your ability to do practical writing. You are required to write a Notice according to the information given below in Chinese. Remember to write the notice on the Translation/Composition Sheet.*

说明：写一份英语通告，涵盖以下内容，不要求逐词翻译。

东方电子有限公司为一家中外合资企业，主要生产制造电子产品。该公司将于2007年12月26日（星期三）在我校学生俱乐部举行招聘会。招聘的职位有：办公室秘书、市场营销人员和实验室技术员。我们希望有兴趣的同学于当天下午1：30到2号会议室参加招聘会，并请携带身份证、个人简历、英语应用能力考试合格证书以及计算机等级证书。

Words for reference:

招聘：recruitment

身份证：ID card

实验室技术员：laboratory technician

B级证书：the certificate of PET (Level B)

Notice

Dong Fang Electronics Ltd. is a joint venture, which _____

_____

_____

2007 年 6 月高等学校英语应用能力考试（B级）真题

Part I Listening Comprehension (15 minutes)

Directions: *This part is to test your listening ability. It consists of 3 sections.*

Section A

Directions: *This section is to test your ability to give proper responses. There are 5 recorded questions in it. After each question, there is a pause. The questions will be spoken two times. When you hear a question, you should decide on the correct answer from the 4 choices marked A, B, C and D given in your test paper. Then you should mark the corresponding letter on the Answer Sheet with a single line through the center.*

Example: *You will hear: Mr. Smith is not in. Would you like to leave him a message?*

You will read: A. I'm not sure.　　　　B. You're right.

C. Yes, certainly.　　　　D. That's interesting.

From the question we learn that the speaker is asking the listener to leave a message. Therefore, "C. Yes, certainly." is the correct answer. You should mark C on the Answer Sheet. Now the test will begin.

1. A. I'm sorry. B. It's my pleasure. C. Yes, I am. D. Yes, I do.

2. A. Not yet. B. Most of the time. C. Yes, I know. D. Please do.

3. A. Yes, I'd love to. B. At half past eight. C. Eight hours. D. It's early.

4. A. It's terrible. B. No, thank you. C. Nothing serious. D. Yes, I have.

5. A. No, not yet. B. No, thanks. C. Yes, I do. D. Yes, I often go.

Section B

Directions: *This section is to test your ability to understand short dialogues. There are 5 recorded dialogues in it. After each dialogue, there is a recorded question. Both the dialogues and questions will be spoken two times. When you hear a question, you should decide on the correct answer from the 4 choices marked A, B, C and D given in your test paper. Then you should mark the corresponding letter on the Answer Sheet with a single line through the center.*

6. A. Cold. B. Warm. C. Wet. D. Hot.

7. A. Buy a book. B. Meet him tomorrow.

C. Go to Beijing. D. Book a ticket.

8. A. He's kind.　　　　　　　　　　　　B. He's careless.

   C. He's serious.　　　　　　　　　　　D. He's polite.

9. A. They won't go to the party.　　　　B. They won't be late.

   C. They will be late.　　　　　　　　D. They will stay at home.

10. A. She wants to ask for help.　　　　　B. She wants to work for the man.

    C. She doesn't like the man.　　　　　D. She doesn't need his help.

Section C

Directions: *In this section you will hear a recorded short passage. The passage is printed in the test paper, but with some words and phrases missing. The passage will be read three times. During the second reading, you are required to put the missing words or phrases on the Answer Sheet in order of the numbered blanks according to what you hear. The third reading is for you to check your writing. Now the passage will begin.*

The world population today is about 6 billion. But only about 11 percent of the world's land is suitable for farming. However, the area of farmland is becoming smaller and smaller ____11____. So it will be difficult to feed so many mouths. There are several reasons why farmland is being ____12____. First, a lot of the land is being used for the ____13____ of houses. Secondly, some of the land has become wasteland because wind and ____14____ have removed the top soil. Thirdly, some of the land has become too salty to ____15____. Therefore, a big problem that we face today is hunger.

Part II Vocabulary & Structure (15 minutes)

Directions: *This part is to test your ability to use words and phrases correctly to construct meaningful and grammatically correct sentences. It consists of 2 sections.*

Section A

Directions: *There are 10 incomplete statements here. You are required to complete each statement by choosing the appropriate answer from the 4 choices marked A, B, C and D. You should mark the corresponding letter on the Answer Sheet with a single line through the center.*

16. This new style of sports shoes is very popular and it is _____ in all sizes.

    A. important　　　　B. active　　　　　C. available　　　　D. famous

17. _____ a wonderful trip he had when he traveled in China!

    A. Where　　　　　B. How　　　　　　C. What　　　　　　D. That

18. She gave up her _____ as a reporter at the age of 25.

    A. career　　　　　B. interest　　　　　C. life　　　　　　　D. habit

19. She didn't receive the application form; it _____ to the wrong address.

    A. sent   B. be sent   C. was sent   D. being sent

20. Time _____ very fast and a new year will begin soon.

    A. takes off   B. goes by   C. pulls up   D. gets along

21. I didn't answer the phone _____ I didn't hear it ring.

    A. if   B. unless   C. although   D. because

22. We're going to _____ the task that we haven't finished.

    A. take away   B. carry on   C. get onto   D. keep off

23. The general manager sat there, _____ to the report from each department.

    A. to listen   B. listen   C. being listened   D. listening

24. In this report of the accident he _____ some important details.

    A. missed   B. wasted   C. escaped   D. failed

25. It is necessary to find an engineer _____ has skills that meet your needs.

    A. whom   B. which   C. whose   D. who

Section B

Directions: *There are 10 incomplete statements here. You should fill in each blank with the proper form of the word given in brackets. Write the word or words in the corresponding space on the Answer Sheet.*

26. She managed to settle the argument in a (friend) _____ way.

27. I would rather you (go) _____ with me tomorrow morning.

28. If I (be) _____ you, I wouldn't ask such a silly question.

29. You should send me the report on the program (immediate) _____.

30. As soon as the result (come) _____ out, I'll let you know.

31. If you smoke in this non-smoking area, you will (fine) _____ $50.

32. It is quite difficult for me (decide) _____ who should be given the job.

33. The new flexible working time system will enable the (employ) _____ to work more efficiently.

34. The more careful you are, the (well) _____ you will be able to complete the work.

35. I'll put forward my (suggest) _____ now so that he can have time to consider it before the meeting.

Part III Reading Comprehension (40 minutes)

Directions: *This part is to test your reading ability. There are 5 tasks for you to fulfill. You should read the reading materials carefully and do the tasks as you are instructed.*

Task 1

Directions: *After reading the following passage, you will find 5 questions or unfinished statements, numbered 36 to 40. For each question or statement there are 4 choices marked A, B, C and D. You should make the correct choice and mark the corresponding letter on the Answer Sheet with a single line through the center.*

We've found that eating habits vary (变化) so much that it does not make sense to include meals in the price of our tours. We want to give you the freedom of choosing restaurants and ordering food that suits your taste and budget (预算).

As our hotels offer anything from coffee and toast to a full American breakfast at very reasonable prices, it will never be a problem for you to start the day in the way you like best. At lunch stops, your tour guide will show you where you can find salads, soups, and sandwiches.

Dinner time is your chance to try some local food. Sometimes the tour guide will let you have dinner at a restaurant of your own choice. At other times he or she will recommend a restaurant at your hotel. Years of research have taught us which restaurants reliably serve a good choice of delightful dishes at down-to-earth prices.

In Mexico, Alaska, and the Yukon, where your restaurant choice may be limited, we include some meals. The meals provided are clearly stated on the tour pages.

36. According to the passage, most meals are not included in the price of tours mainly because _____.

  A. meals make up a large part of the tour budget

  B. meals prices vary a lot from place to place

  C. people dislike menus offered by tour guide

  D. people have different eating habits

37. We can learn from the passage that _____.

  A. the hotels where you stay will offer you free breakfast

  B. dining information can be obtained from your tour guide

  C. you can have a complete choice of local dishes at the hotel

  D. a full list of local restaurants can be found on the tour pages

38. Which of the following statements is TRUE?

    A. Tour guides are supposed to arrange dinner outside the hotel.

    B. Tour guides' recommendations on food are unreliable.

    C. Tourists must have lunch in the hotels they stay in.

    D. Tourists may taste local dishes during dinner time.

39. The word "down-to-earth" (Line 4, Para. 3) most probably means _____.

    A. changeable   B. expensive   C. reasonable   D. fixed

40. Meals are included in the tour price in some places where _____.

    A. restaurant choice may be limited

    B. there are many nearby restaurants

    C. delightful dishes are not served

    D. food may be too expensive

Task 2

Directions: *This task is the same as Task 1. The 5 questions or unfinished statements are numbered 41 to 45.*

Some cities have planned their transportation systems for car owners. That is what Los Angeles did. Los Angeles decided to build highways for cars rather than spending money on public transportation.

This decision was suitable for Los Angeles. The city grew outward instead of upward. Los Angeles never built many tall apartment buildings. Instead, people live in houses with gardens.

In Los Angeles, most people drive cars to work. And every car has to have a parking space. So many buildings where people work also have building lots.

Los Angeles also became a city without a Central Business District (CBD). If a city has a CBD, crowds of people rush into it every day to work. If people drive to work, they need lots of road space.

So Los Angeles developed several business districts and built homes and other buildings in between the districts. This required more roads and parking spaces.

Some people defend this growth pattern. They say Los Angeles is the city of the future.

41. According to the passage, Los Angeles is a city where _____.

    A. there is no public transportation system

    B. more money is spent on highways for cars

    C. more money is spent on public transportation systems

    D. public transportation is more developed than in other cities

42. "The city grew outward instead of upward" (Line 1, Para. 2) means _____.

    A. the city became more spread out instead of growing taller

    B. there were fewer small houses than tall buildings

    C. rapid development took place in the city center

    D. many tall buildings could be found in the city

43. According to the passage, if a city has several business districts, _____.

    A. people won't have to drive to work every day

    B. there have to be more roads and parking spaces

    C. companies would be located in between the districts

    D. there would be no need to build parking spaces within the districts

44. According to the growth pattern of Los Angeles, homes were mainly built _____.

    A. in the city center

    B. along the main roads

    C. around business districts

    D. within the business districts

45. The passage is mainly about _____.

    A. the construction of parking spaces in Los Angeles

    B. the new growth pattern of the city of Los Angeles

    C. the public transportation system in Los Angeles

    D. the problem of traffic jams in Los Angeles

Task 3

Directions: *The following is an instruction of writing a trip report. After reading it, you should complete the information by filling in the blanks marked 46 through 50 **in not more than 3 words** in the table below.*

Trip Reports

    Many companies require their employees to hand in reports of their business trips. A trip report not only provides a written record of a business trip and its activities, but also enables many employees to benefit from the information one employee has gained.

    Generally, a trip report should be in the form of a memorandum (内部通知), addressed to your immediate boss. The places and dates of the trip are given on the subject line. The body of the report will explain why you made the trip, whom you visited, and what you did. The report should give a brief account of each major event. You needn't give equal space to each event. Instead, you should focus on the more important events. Follow the body of the report with a conclusion.

A Trip Report

Reported by: an employee back from a business trip

Addressed to: his or her immediate ___46___

Used for:

    1) serving as a written record

    2) giving helpful ___47___ that can be shared by others

Written in the form of: a(n) ___48___

Information to be included in the report:

    1) the places and dates of the trip on ___49___

    2) major event(s) during the trip in the ___50___ of the report

    3) conclusion

Task 4

Directions: *The following is a list of terms used in railway services. After reading it, you are required to find the items equivalent to (与……等同) those given in Chinese in the table below. Then you should put the corresponding letters in the brackets on the Answer Sheet, numbered 51 through 55.*

A — information desk

B — ticket office

C — half-fare ticket

D — waiting room

E — excess baggage charge

F — baggage check-in counter

G — security check

H — platform underpass

I — ticket agent

J — departure board

K — railroad track

L — traffic light

M — railroad crossing

N — soft sleeping car

O — hard sleeping car

P — hard seat

Q — baggage-claim area

Examples: （Q）行李认领处   （E）超重行李费

51. （ ）硬座	（ ）软卧
52. （ ）开车时间显示牌	（ ）信号灯
53. （ ）站台地下通道	（ ）候车室
54. （ ）问询处	（ ）安全检查
55. （ ）半价票	（ ）售票处

Task 5

Directions: *The following is the Trouble-Shooting Guide to a microwave oven. After reading it, you are required to complete the answers that follow the questions (No. 56 through No. 60). You should write your answers **in not more than 3 words** on the Answer Sheet correspondingly.*

Problems	Probable causes	Suggested solutions
The display is showing the sign ":".	There has been a power interruption.	Reset (重新设置) the clock.
The fan seems to be running slower than usual.	The oven has been stored in a cold area.	The fan will run slower until the oven warms up to normal room temperature.
The display shows a time counting down but the oven is not cooking.	The oven door is not closed completely.	Close the door completely.
	You have set the controls as a kitchen timer (定时器).	Touch OFF/CANCEL to cancel the Minute Timer.
The turntable (转盘) will not turn.	The support is not operating correctly.	Check the turntable support is properly in place, and restart the oven.
The microwave oven will not run.	The door is not firmly closed.	Close the door firmly.
	You did not touch the button "START".	Touch the button "START".
	You did not follow the directions exactly.	Follow the directions exactly.

56. What should you do if the display is showing the sign ":"?
    Reset _____.

57. What is the probable cause if the fan seems to be running slower than usual?
    The oven has been put in _____.

58. What are you advised to do if you have set the controls as a kitchen timer?
    Touch OFF/CANCEL to cancel the _____.

59. What is the cause for the turntable to fail to turn?
    _____ is not operating correctly.

60. What will happen if you do not touch the button "START"?
    The microwave oven _____.

Part IV Translation — English into Chinese (25 minutes)

Directions: *This part, numbered 61 through 65, is to test your ability to translate English into Chinese. Each of the four sentences (No. 61 to No. 64) is followed by four choices of suggested translation marked A, B, C and D. Make the best choice and write the corresponding letter on the Answer Sheet. Write your translation of the paragraph (No. 65) in the corresponding space on the Translation/Composition Sheet.*

61. The manager tried to create a situation in which all the people present would feel comfortable.

    A. 经理在设法创造条件，让所有的人都得到令人满意的礼物。

    B. 经理试图营造一种氛围，让所有在场的人都感到轻松自在。

    C. 经理在设法创造一种条件，让所有人都能够显得心情舒畅。

    D. 经理努力营造一种气氛，让所有的人到场时都觉得畅快。

62. Mr. Smith demands that all the reports be carefully written and above all be based on the facts.

    A. 史密斯先生要求把所有的报告都写好，还要求全部都应该是事实。

    B. 史密斯先生需要的报告都应该写得详细，而且全部都只能是事实。

    C. 史密斯先生所需要的报告都写得很完整，而且包括了所有的事实。

    D. 史密斯先生要求认真写好所有报告，最重要的是应以事实为依据。

63. Obtaining enough food is the first concern for every nation; in some countries food shortages have become a serious problem.

    A. 生产足够的粮食是各国的首要国策；有些国家已面临粮食减产这一重大问题。

    B. 能否获得充足的粮食关系到每个国家的生存；有些国家粮食短缺的问题日趋严重。

    C. 获得足够的粮食是所有国家的头等大事；粮食短缺已成为一些国家的严重问题。

    D. 首先每个国家对生产足够的粮食都会关心；有些则已经解决了粮食短缺的重大问题。

64. Candidates should be given the company brochure to read while they are waiting for their interviews.

    A. 求职者应帮助公司散发有关的阅读手册，同时等候面试。

    B. 在阅读了公司所发给的手册之后，求职者才能等待面试。

    C. 在求职者等待面试时，应该发给他们一本公司手册阅读。

    D. 求职者在等待面试时，可要求得到一本公司手册来阅读。

65. The new Holiday Inn has everything you need for a weekend of family fun or business travel. Conveniently located, the Holiday Inn is within walking distance to the hot springs and the downtown shopping area. Each room has a refrigerator, coffee maker, and hair dryer. Guests will enjoy the Holiday Inn's swimming pool, as well as a free Western or Chinese breakfast every morning.

Part V Writing (25 minutes)

Directions: *This part is to test your ability to do practical writing. You are required to write an email according to the information given below in Chinese. Remember to write the email on the Translation/Composition Sheet.*

说明：假设你是王军。根据以下内容以第一人称发一封电子邮件。

内容：

1）发件人：王军

2）收件人：Anna

3）发件人电子邮件地址：wangjun11007@hotmail.com

4）收件人电子邮件地址：anna11008@hotmail.com

5）事由：

王军在网站 www.ebay.com.cn 上卖出了一本书；书名：《电子商务导论》。买家是美国客户 Anna Brown。

6）邮件涉及内容：

① 感谢对方购买《电子商务导论》；

② 书已寄出，预计一周内到达；

③ 希望收到书后在网站上留下反馈意见；

④ 如果满意，希望向其他客户推荐；

⑤ 最后还会推出一些新的书，欢迎选购；再次购买可以享受折扣。

Words for reference:

反馈意见：feedback

电子商务导论：Introduction to E-commerce

注意：email 的内容要写成一个段落，不得逐条罗列。

Email Message

From: _____

To: _____

Subject: Feedback of the transaction

Dear Miss Anna Brown,

_____

_____

_____

_____

Sincerely,

Wang Jun

2006 年 12 月高等学校英语应用能力考试（B 级）真题

Part I Listening Comprehension (15 minutes)

Directions: *This part is to test your listening ability. It consists of 3 sections.*

Section A

Directions: *This section is to test your ability to give proper responses. There are 5 recorded questions in it. After each question, there is a pause. The questions will be spoken two times. When you hear a question, you should decide on the correct answer from the 4 choices marked A, B, C and D given in your test paper. Then you should mark the corresponding letter on the Answer Sheet with a single line through the center.*

Example: *You will hear: Mr. Smith is not in. Would you like to leave him a message?*
You will read: A. I'm not sure.   B. You're right.
*   C. Yes, certainly.   D. That's interesting.*

From the question we learn that the speaker is asking the listener to leave a message. Therefore, "C. Yes, certainly." is the correct answer. You should mark C on the Answer Sheet. Now the test will begin.

1. A. Who's calling, please?   B. How are you?
   C. Where is she?   D. No, you can't.
2. A. It's possible.   B. That's all right.   C. No way.   D. My pleasure.
3. A. Yes, of course.   B. Is it true?   C. You're welcome.   D. No, thanks.
4. A. Yes. When?   B. Yes. What?   C. Well, how?   D. Well, who?
5. A. Never mind.   B. Not likely.   C. I'm afraid I can't.   D. Quite well.

Section B

Directions: *This section is to test your ability to understand short dialogues. There are 5 recorded dialogues in it. After each dialogue, there is a recorded question. Both the dialogues and questions will be spoken two times. When you hear a question, you should decide on the correct answer from the 4 choices marked A, B, C and D given in your test paper. Then you should mark the corresponding letter on the Answer Sheet with a single line through the center.*

6. A. Holiday food.   B. Children's food.   C. Chinese food.   D. Western food.

7. A. In a bookstore. B. In a theatre. C. At the Customs. D. At a bank.

8. A. There is a visitor at the door. B. The woman is calling Jack.

 C. The door is open. D. The telephone is ringing.

9. A. To finish her work. B. To attend a meeting.

 C. To get an important paper. D. To meet somebody.

10. A. To get some medicine. B. To have a check-up.

 C. To visit a patient. D. To look after the man.

Section C

Directions: *In this section you will hear a recorded short passage. The passage is printed in the test paper, but with some words and phrases missing. The passage will be read three times. During the second reading, you are required to put the missing words or phrases on the Answer Sheet in order of the numbered blanks according to what you hear. The third reading is for you to check your writing. Now the passage will begin.*

Scientists have discovered that tea is good for us. It tastes good and it is refreshing. In recent ____11____ studies, tea has been found to help prevent heart attacks and cancer.

One study suggests that both black tea and green tea help ____12____ the heart. In the study, tea drinkers had a 44 percent ____13____ death rate after heart attacks than non-drinkers. Other studies have shown that tea, like fruit and vegetables, helps fight against chemicals that may ____14____ the development of certain cancer.

Many people really like tea. Next to plain water, it's the world's most ____15____ drink.

Part II Vocabulary & Structure (15 minutes)

Directions: *This part is to test your ability to use words and phrases correctly to construct meaningful and grammatically correct sentences. It consists of 2 sections.*

Section A

Directions: *There are 10 incomplete statements here. You are required to complete each statement by choosing the appropriate answer from the 4 choices marked A, B, C and D. You should mark the corresponding letter on the Answer Sheet with a single line through the center.*

16. It is the general manager who makes the _____ decisions in business.

 A. beginning B. finishing C. first D. final

17. Never _____ such a good boss before I came to this company.

 A. do I meet B. had I met C. I met D. I had met

18. If the machine should _____, call this number immediately.

    A. break down   B. set out   C. put on   D. go up

19. The manager showed the new employee _____ to find the supplies.

    A. what   B. where   C. that   D. which

20. Look at the clock! It's time _____ work.

    A. we started   B. we'll start   C. we're starting   D. we have started

21. The sales department was required to _____ a plan in three weeks.

    A. turn up   B. get up   C. come up with   D. put up with

22. Price is not the only thing customers consider before _____ what to buy.

    A. deciding   B. decided   C. to decide   D. having decided

23. All the traveling _____ are paid by the company if you travel on business.

    A. charges   B money   C. prices   D. expenses

24. Sorry, we cannot _____ you the job because you don't have any work experience.

    A. make   B. send   C. offer   D. prepare

25. This article is well written because special attention _____ to the choice of words and style of writing.

    A. had been paid   B. has been paid   C. will be paid   D. will have been paid

Section B

Directions: *There are 10 incomplete statements here. You should fill in each blank with the proper form of the word given in brackets. Write the word or words in the corresponding space on the Answer Sheet.*

26. It is a fact that traditional meals are (healthy) _____ than fast foods.

27. Nurses should treat the sick and wounded with great (kind) _____.

28. All visitors to the lab (expect) _____ to take off their shoes before they enter.

29. (Personal) _____, I think he is a very nice partner, though you may not agree.

30. They talked to him for hours, (try) _____ to persuade him to change his mind.

31. His efforts to improve the sales of this product have been very (help) _____.

32. When we arrived, there was a smell of cooking (come) _____ from the kitchen.

33. We have to find new ways to (short) _____ the process of production.

34. By this time next year my family (live) _____ in this small town for 20 years.

35. Jane, as well as some of her classmates, (work) _____ in the Quality Control Department now.

Part III Reading Comprehension (40 minutes)

Directions: *This part is to test your reading ability. There are 5 tasks for you to fulfill. You should read the reading materials carefully and do the tasks as you are instructed.*

Task 1

Directions: *After reading the following passage, you will find 5 questions or unfinished statements, numbered 36 to 40. For each question or statement there are 4 choices marked A, B, C and D. You should make the correct choice and mark the corresponding letter on the Answer Sheet with a single line through the center.*

People who work night shifts are constantly fighting against an "internal clock" in their bodies. Quite often the clock tells them to sleep when their job requires them to remain fully awake. It's no wonder that more accidents happen during night shifts than at any other time. Light therapy (照光治疗法) with a bright light box can help night-shift workers adjust their internal clock. However, many doctors recommend careful planning to help improve sleep patterns. For example, night-shift workers often find it difficult to sleep in the morning when they get off work because the body's natural rhythm (节律) fights back, no matter how tired they are. Some experts recommend that night-shift workers schedule two smaller sleep periods—one in the morning after work, and another longer one in the afternoon, closer to when the body would naturally need to sleep. It's also helpful to ask friends and family to cooperate by avoiding visits and phone calls during the times when you are sleeping.

36. Night-shift workers are those who _____.

    A. have to rely on their internal clock   B. need to re-adjust their clock

    C. fall asleep late at night   D. have to work at night

37. In order to remain fully awake at work, people working night shifts should _____.

    A. have longer sleep periods after work   B. make the light darker than usual

    C. try to re-set their "internal clock"   D. pay more attention to their work

38. Many doctors think it is helpful for night-shift workers _____.

    A. to sleep with a bright light on   B. to plan sleep patterns carefully

    C. to avoid being disturbed at work   D. to sleep for a long time after work

39. Night-shift workers often find it difficult to sleep in the morning because _____.

    A. their internal clock will not allow them to

    B. they are often disturbed by morning visits

    C. they are not trying hard enough to do so

    D. they are too tired to go to sleep well

40. According to the passage, some doctors recommend that night-shift workers should _____.

  A. have frequent visits and phone calls   B. improve their family relationship

  C. have two smaller sleep periods   D. rely mainly on light therapy

Task 2

Directions: *This task is the same as Task 1. The 5 questions or unfinished statements are numbered 41 to 45.*

A few ways Greyhound can make your next trip even easier

Tickets by mail. Avoid lining up altogether, by purchasing your tickets in advance, and having them delivered right to your mailbox. Just call Greyhound at least ten days before your departure (1-800-231-2222).

Prepaid tickets. It's easy to purchase a ticket for a friend or family member no matter how far away they may be. Just call or go to your nearest Greyhound terminal (车站) and ask for details on how to buy a prepaid ticket.

Ticketing requirement. Greyhound now requires that all tickets have travel dates fixed at the time of purchase. Children under two years of age travel free with an adult who has a ticket.

If your destination (目的地) **is to Canada or Mexico.** Passengers traveling to Canada or Mexico must have the proper travel documents. US, Canadian or Mexican citizens should have a birth certificate, passport or naturalization (入籍) paper. If you are not a citizen of the US, Canada or Mexico, a passport is required. In certain cases a visa may be required as well. These documents will be necessary and may be checked at, or before, boarding a bus departing for Canada or Mexico.

41. From the passage, we can learn that "Greyhound" is probably the name of _____.

  A. an airline   B. a hotel   C. a website   D. a bus company

42. Why should people call Greyhound for tickets in advance?

  A. To avoid waiting in lines at the booking office.

  B. To hand in necessary traveling documents.

  C. To get tickets from the nearest terminal.

  D. To fix the traveling destination in time.

43. What can we learn about the Greyhound tickets?

  A. They are not available for traveling outside the US.

  B. Travelers should buy their tickets in person.

  C. Babies can not travel free with their parents.

  D. They have the exact travel date on them.

44. When people are traveling to Canada or Mexico, a passport is a must for _____.

   A. American citizens　　B. Japanese citizens　　C. Mexicans citizens　　D. Canadians citizens

45. This passage mainly offers information about _____.

   A. how to prepare documents for traveling with Greyhound

   B. how to purchase a Greyhound ticket and travel with it

   C. how to make your trip with Greyhound interesting

   D. how to travel from the US to Canada and Mexico

Task 3

Directions: *The following is a letter of complaint. After reading it, you should complete the information by filling in the blanks marked 46 through 50* **in not more than 3 words** *in the table below.*

December 10th, 2006

Dear Sirs,

I know that your company has a reputation (声誉) for quality products and fairness toward its customers. Therefore, I'm writing to ask for a replacement for a lawn mower (割草机).

I bought the mower about half a year ago at the Watchung Discount Center, Watchung, Nebraska. I'm enclosing a copy of a receipt for the mower.

A month after I bought the lawn mower, the engine failed, and it was repaired under warranty (保修期). So far, I have had the engine repaired four times.

Now the engine has broken down again.

I have already spent more than $300 on repairs, and I am beginning to seriously question the quality of your mowers.

I am requesting that you replace this mower with a new one.

I hope that you will live up to your reputation of the good customer service that has made your business successful.

Faithfully,

Rod Green

Letter of Complaint
Purpose of the letter: requesting a(n) ___46___ for a lawn mower
Time of purchase: about ___47___ ago
Trouble with the machine: ___48___
Times of repairs so far: ___49___
Money spent on repairs: more than ___50___

Task 4

Directions: *The following is a list of terms of modern business management. After reading it, you are required to find the items equivalent to (与……等同) those given in Chinese in the table below. Then you should put the corresponding letters in the brackets on the Answer Sheet, numbered 51 through 55.*

A — employee turnover
B — life-long employment
C — role conflict
D — profit sharing
E — scientific management
F — comparable worth
G — flexible working hours
H — social support
I — survey feedback
J — core competence
K — public relations
L — group culture
M — wage and salary surveys
N — honesty testing
O — human resource planning

Examples: (I) 调查反馈　　　　　　　　(A) 人员流动

51. (　) 测谎	(　) 工薪调查
52. (　) 社会支持	(　) 终身雇用制
53. (　) 团队文化	(　) 公共关系
54. (　) 利润分享	(　) 人力资源策划
55. (　) 科学管理	(　) 弹性工作时间

Task 5

Directions: *The following is a letter applying for a job. After reading it, you are required to complete the answers that follow the questions (No. 56 to No. 60). You should write your answers **in not more than 3 words** on the Answer Sheet correspondingly.*

Dear Sirs,

For the past 8 years I have been a statistician (统计员) in the Research Unit of Baron & Smallwood Ltd. I am now looking for a change of employment which would broaden my experience. A large and well-known organization such as yours might be able to use my services.

I am 31 years old and in excellent health. I majored in advertising at London University and I am particularly interested in work involving statistics (统计).

Although I have had no experience in market research, I am familiar with the methods used for recording buying habits and trends. I hope that you will invite me for an interview. I could then give you further information.

I am looking forward to hearing from you soon.

Yours faithfully,
Mike Smith

56. What's Mike Smith's present job?

He's working as a(n) _____.

57. What was Mike Smith's major at London University?

_____.

58. What kind of work does he like to do?

Work involving _____.

59. In what area does he lack experience?

He has no experience in _____.

60. What's the purpose of the writer in sending this letter?

To be invited for _____.

Part IV Translation — English into Chinese (25 minutes)

Directions: *This part, numbered 61 through 65, is to test your ability to translate English into Chinese. Each of the four sentences (No. 61 to No. 64) is followed by four choices of suggested translation marked A, B, C and D. Make the best choice and write the corresponding letter on the Answer Sheet. Write your translation of the paragraph (No. 65) in the corresponding space on the Translation/ Composition Sheet.*

61. For safety, all passengers are required to review this card and follow these instructions when needed.

A. 为了安全，请各位乘客反复阅读本卡片，务必按照各项规定执行。

B. 为了保险起见，请各位乘客务必阅读本卡片，并参照相关内容认真执行。

C. 为了保险起见，要求所有乘客在需要时都能看到这张卡片及以下这些内容。

D. 为了安全，要求所有乘客仔细阅读本卡片各项内容，必要时照其执行。

62. Peter misunderstood the instructions his boss gave him and mailed the wrong documents to the supplier.

A. 彼得按照老板给他的指示把单据误寄给了供货商。

B. 彼得误解了老板的指示，向供货商发错了单据。

C. 彼得对老板的指示还没理解就把错误的单据交给供货商。

D. 彼得没来得及听取老板的指示就给供货商寄去了有错误的单据。

63. People now have more leisure time, which is the reason why the demand for services has increased so rapidly.

A. 如今人们有更多的时间去娱乐，从而影响了劳务资源的快速上升。

B. 如今希望有时间娱乐的人越来越多，这是因为服务质量在迅速提高。

C. 如今人们有了更多的闲暇时间，因而对各种服务的需求增长得如此快。

D. 如今人们有了更多的空闲时间，这就是要求迅速提高服务质量的原因。

64. Passengers going to the airport by arranged buses must take the bus at the time and place as shown below.

A. 搭乘专车前往机场的旅客，务必在下列指定的时间和地点乘车。

B. 乘公共汽车去机场的旅客必须乘这路车，时间和地点安排如下。

C. 经安排搭乘汽车去机场的旅客，应按指定的时间和地点上车。

D. 机场即将为旅客安排汽车，请注意下列指定的上车时间和地点。

65. I'm writing to confirm our telephone conversation of Thursday, the 7th, about our visit to your company. Next Monday, December 11, will be fine for us and we hope that it will suit you, too. My secretary, Miss Mary Brown, and Sales Manager, Mr. Zhang Ming, will be coming in the morning. It's unfortunate that I will not be able to with them.

Thanks again for giving us this opportunity to visit with you.

Part V Writing (25 minutes)

Directions: *This part is to test your ability to do practical writing. You are required to complete a Visitor's Message according to the instructions given below in Chinese. Remember to do your writing on the Translation/Composition Sheet.*

假定你是假日酒店的前台工作人员 Linda。根据以下内容填写来访客人留言表。

内容：

1）来访客人：李华，男，PKK 公司总经理助理；联系电话：65734363

2）来访时间：12 月 20 日上午 10 点

3）被访客人：Mr. John Smith，住假日酒店 422 房间

4）事由：李华来酒店与 Mr. John Smith 商谈工作，Mr. John Smith 外出

5）留言：李华约 Mr. John Smith 明天去 PKK 公司洽谈业务。李华明天上午 9:00 驾车来酒店接他；下午安排 Mr. John Smith 参观公司一条新建成的生产线。

Words for reference:

驾车接人：pick sb. up

生产线：assembly line

总经理助理：Assistant to General Manager

Holiday Inn

Visitor's Message

Mr./Ms. (1) Mr. John Smith   Room No.: __(2)__

While you were out

Mr./Ms. ____(3)____ of ____(4)____   Telephone: (5) 65734363

☐ Telephoned   ✓ Came to see you

☐ Will call again   ☐ Will come again

☐ Asked you to call back

Message:

(6) _____

_____

_____

Clerk: __(7) Linda__   Date: __(8)__   Time: __(9)__

注意：请将要求填写在表格中的内容按顺序填入答题卡中的 Writing 部分并注明所填内容的顺序号！即：

(1) Mr. John Smith

(2) _____

(3) _____

(4) _____

(5) 65734363

(6) _____

_____

_____

(7) Linda

(8) _____

(9) _____

2006 年 6 月高等学校英语应用能力考试（B 级）真题

Part I Listening Comprehension (15 minutes)

Directions: *This part is to test your listening ability. It consists of 3 sections.*

Section A

Directions: *This section is to test your ability to give proper responses. There are 5 recorded questions in it. After each question, there is a pause. The questions will be spoken two times. When you hear a question, you should decide on the correct answer from the 4 choices marked A, B, C and D given in your test paper. Then you should mark the corresponding letter on the Answer Sheet with a single line through the center.*

Example: *You will hear: Mr. Smith is not in. Would you like to leave him a message?*
You will read: A. I'm not sure.   B. You're right.
*   C. Yes, certainly.   D. That's interesting.*
From the question we learn that the speaker is asking the listener to leave a message. Therefore, "C. Yes, certainly." is the correct answer. You should mark C on the Answer Sheet. Now the test will begin.

1. A. So do I.   B. Thank you.   C. Yes, I like it.   D. Yes, of course.
2. A. Yes, it is.   B. Yes, I have.   C. I like the city.   D. It's a famous city.
3. A. My pleasure.   B. Not at all.
   C. Nothing, thank you.   D. Sure.
4. A. I often drink tea at home.   B. No, thanks.
   C. Not likely.   D. No problem.
5. A. Thank you.   B. It's important.   C. Yes, I will.   D. No, it isn't.

Section B

Directions: *This section is to test your ability to understand short dialogues. There are 5 recorded dialogues in it. After each dialogue, there is a recorded question. Both the dialogues and questions will be spoken two times. When you hear a question, you should decide on the correct answer from the 4 choices marked A, B, C and D given in your test paper. Then you should mark the corresponding letter on the Answer Sheet with a single line through the center.*

6. A. A business plan.　　　　　　　　B. A working schedule.

　　C. A computer problem.　　　　　　D. A computer class.

7. A. She's a manager.　　　　　　　　B. She's a secretary.

　　C. She is an engineer.　　　　　　　D. She's a teacher.

8. A. A list.　　　B. A product.　　　C. A contract.　　　D. A book.

9. A. In a post office.　　　　　　　　B. In a restaurant.

　　C. At the airport.　　　　　　　　D. At a railway station.

10. A. Anytime today.　　　　　　　　B. This morning.

　　C. Next afternoon.　　　　　　　　D. Tomorrow morning.

Section C

Directions: *In this section you will hear a recorded short passage. The passage is printed in the test paper, but with some words or phrases missing. The passage will be read three times. During the second reading, you are required to put the missing words or phrases on the Answer Sheet in order of the numbered blanks according to what you hear. The third reading is for you to check your writing. Now the passage will begin.*

Modern technology has a big influence on our daily life. New devices are widely used today. For example, we have to ____11____ the Internet every day. It is becoming more and more ____12____ to nearly everybody. Now it's time to think about how the Internet influences us, what ____13____ it has on our social behavior and what the future world will look like. The Internet has ____14____ changed our life; there is no doubt about that. I think the Internet has changed our life in a(n) ____15____ way.

Part II Vocabulary & Structure (15 minutes)

Directions: *This part is to test your ability to use words and phrases correctly to construct meaningful and grammatically correct sentences. It consists of 2 sections.*

Section A

Directions: *There are 10 incomplete statements here. You are required to complete each statement by choosing the appropriate answer from the 4 choices marked A, B, C and D. You should mark the corresponding letter on the Answer Sheet with a single line through the center.*

16. My impression of the service in the hotel was that it had really _____.

　　A. improved　　　　B. implied　　　　C. imported　　　　D. imagined

17. The policeman stopped the driver and found that he _____ alcohol.

　　A. drinks　　　　B. has drunk　　　　C. is drinking　　　　D. had drunk

18. There are three colors in the British flag, _____ red, white and blue.

    A. rarely   B. namely   C. really   D. naturally

19. I can't find the key to my office. I _____ have lost it on my way home.

    A. would   B. should   C. must   D. ought to

20. David has _____ much work to do that he is staying late at his office.

    A. such   B. so   C. very   D. enough

21. I tried hard, but I couldn't find the _____ to the problem.

    A. solution   B. help   C. reply   D. demand

22. _____ writing a letter to the manager, he decided to talk to him in person.

    A. Due to   B. Because of   C. As for   D. Instead of

23. As far as I'm concerned, I don't like _____ in that way.

    A. to be treated   B. to treat   C. treated   D. treating

24. Lisa was busy taking notes _____ Mark was searching the Internet for the information.

    A. until   B. unless   C. while   D. if

25. There was a heavy fog this morning, so none of the planes could _____.

    A. get through   B. take off   C. pull out   D. break away

Section B

Directions: *There are 10 incomplete statements here. You should fill in each blank with the proper form of the word given in brackets. Write the word or words in the corresponding space on the Answer Sheet.*

26. Of all the hotels in the city, this one is the (good) _____.

27. Yesterday they received a written (invite) _____ to a dinner from Mr. Black.

28. That new film is worth (see) _____ for the second time.

29. Next week we (sign) _____ the sales contract with the new supplier.

30. (general) _____ speaking, he is a person that you can trust.

31. The new machine ought to (test) _____ before it is put to use.

32. If your credit (信誉) is good, you will be allowed (use) _____ the credit card.

33. It will be very (help) _____ if each member presents his or her own opinion at the meeting.

34. The number of sales people who have left the company (be) _____ very small.

35. It is well-known that sports will (strength) _____ the friendship between nations.

Part III Reading Comprehension (40 minutes)

Directions: *This part is to test your reading ability. There are 5 tasks for you to fulfill. You should read the reading materials carefully and do the tasks as you are instructed.*

Task 1

Directions: *After reading the following passage, you will find 5 questions or unfinished statements, numbered 36 to 40. For each question or statement there are 4 choices marked A, B, C and D. You should make the correct choice and mark the corresponding letter on the Answer Sheet with a single line through the center.*

Dear Sir or Madam,

The MDC Company was established in 2001 and in four short years has become one of the most successful companies in the market place. For this, we are pleased, proud and grateful.

We are pleased because our customers have confirmed our belief that if the products we offer are new, exciting, innovative (有创意的) and of excellent quality, they will be purchased.

We are proud because we know we are a company that keeps its word to its customers; that guarantees that any product can be returned within 30 days if it proves to be unsatisfactory in any way; and that always lets our customers know if there is to be a delay in delivery.

We are grateful to customers like you, because you confirm our beliefs that good service and quality result in satisfied customers. Without you, there would be no reason for us to be pleased or proud. We thank you for your orders and for giving us the opportunity to be of service to you.

Our special summer catalogue (商品目录) is at the printers and should be in your home soon. We hope that you will be pleased with the new selections.

Yours faithfully,
John Brown

36. From the passage we can learn that MDC Company always _____.

    A. keeps its promise   B. provides the same products

    C. sells its products at a low price   D. delivers its products without delay

37. MDC Company believes that its customers are satisfied because the company_____.

    A. gives them opportunities to order   B. provides good service and quality

    C. guarantees the quickest delivery   D. sends new catalogues to them

38. The customers will be informed if _____.

    A. the product can't be delivered on time

    B. the product is out-of-date and unsatisfactory

    C. the company doesn't accept the returned product

    D. the company can't send a new catalogue on time

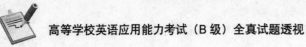

39. The purpose of this letter is to _____.

    A. tell the customers about the quality of their products

    B. express the company's thanks to the customers

    C. prove the excellent service of the company

    D. inform the customers of a new catalogue

40. What can we learn about the company?

    A. It has the largest number of customers.   B. It is grateful for its employees' efforts.

    C. It is successful in the market place.   D. It charges the least for its services.

Task 2

Directions: *This task is the same as Task 1. The 5 questions or unfinished statements are numbered 41 to 45.*

    Unlike Britain, the US does not have a national health care service. The government does help pay for some medical care for people who are on low incomes and for old people, but most people buy insurance (保险) to help pay for medical care. The problems of those who cannot afford insurance are an important political subject.

    In Britain, when people are ill, they usually go to a family doctor first. However, people in America sometimes go straight to an expert without seeing their family doctor first. Children are usually taken to a doctor who is an expert in the treatment (治疗) of children. In Britain, if a patient needs to see a specialist doctor, their family doctor will usually recommend a specialist.

    Doctors do not go to people's homes when they are ill. People always make appointments to see the doctor in the doctor's office. In a serious situation, people call for an ambulance (救护车). In America, hospitals must treat all seriously ill patients, even if they do not have medical insurance. The government will then help pay for some of the cost of the medical care.

41. Some medical care is paid by the US government for _____.

    A. people living in the country   B. non-government officials

    C. people with insurance   D. the poor and the old

42. Most people in the United States buy insurance _____.

    A. to pay for their own medical care

    B. to help to live on their low incomes

    C. to improve the national health care service

    D. to solve one of the important political problems

43. What do British people usually do when they are ill?

    A. They go to see their family doctor first.   B. They go to see a specialist doctor first.

    C. They call for a specialist doctor.   D. They call for a family doctor.

44. In America, seriously ill patients will _____.

    A. be treated if they have an insurance   B. make an appointment with a specialist only

    C. receive treatment even without insurance   D. normally go to see an expert for treatment

45. Which of the following would be the best title for this passage?

    A. Types of Doctors in the United States

    B. Health Care in the United States and Britain

    C. Treatment of Sick Children in the United States

    D. Medical Insurance in the United States and Britain

Task 3

Directions: *The following is a part of the guide for a transit system: Metro. After reading it, you should complete the information by filling in the blanks marked 46 through 50 **in not more than 3 words** in the table below.*

Thanks for using Metro (地铁)

    Clean. Modern. Safe. And easy to use. No wonder Metro is considered the nation's finest transit (公交) system. This guide tells how to use Metro, and the color-coded map on the inside will help you use Metro to get all around the Nation's Capital.

Metro-rail fares

    • Each passenger needs a fare-card. (Up to two children under 5 may travel free with a paying customer.)

    • Fares are based on when and how far you ride. Pay regular fares on weekdays 5:30-9:30 a.m. and 3:00-7:00 p.m. Pay reduced fares at all other times.

    • Large maps in each station show fares and travel times. Please ask the station manager if you have any questions.

    • Fare-card machines are in every station. Bring small banknotes because there are no change machines in the stations and fare-card machines only provide up to $5 in change (in coins). Some machines accept credit cards (信用卡).

A Transit System Metro

Features of the system: 1) ___46___,

                    2) modern,

                    3) safe, and

                    4) ___47___

Fares for weekends: ___48___ fares

Place showing fares and travel times: large maps in ___49___

Change provided by fare-card machines: up to $ ___50___

Task 4

Directions: *The following is a list of signs for public attention. After reading it, you are required to find the items equivalent to (与……等同) those given in Chinese in the table below. Then you should put the corresponding letters in the brackets on the Answer Sheet, numbered 51 through 55.*

A — Buses Only　　　　　　　　　B — No Parking

C — No Standing　　　　　　　　　D — Police Cars Only

E — No U-Turn　　　　　　　　　　F — No Admittance

G — No Entry by This Door　　　　　H — One Way Street

I — One Lane Bridge　　　　　　　　J — Admission by Ticket Only

K — Admission Free　　　　　　　　L — Keep Away

M — House to Let　　　　　　　　　N — Keep Order

O — Wet Paint　　　　　　　　　　P — Line Up for Tickets

Q — No Posting of Signs　　　　　　R — Seat by Number

S — Wheelchairs Only

Examples:　（Q）请勿张贴　　　　　　　（C）禁止停车候客

51. （　）禁止停车	（　）禁止掉头
52. （　）此门不通	（　）不得入内
53. （　）房屋出租	（　）单行道
54. （　）排队购票	（　）凭票入场
55. （　）公交专用道	（　）对号入场

Task 5

Directions: *There are two business letters here. After reading them, you are required to complete the answers that follow the questions (No. 56 to No. 60). You should write your answers in **not more than 3 words** on the Answer Sheet correspondingly.*

Letter 1

June 10, 2006

Dear Sir or Madam,

Last night the central heating system that you installed (安装) in our factory exploded. The explosion caused a great deal of damage and our stock of fashion clothes has been completely ruined.

We must insist that you replace the heating system immediately and pay for our damaged stock, valued at $400,000.

We look forward to your reply.

Yours faithfully,

Bill Black

Assistant Manager

Letter 2

June 15, 2006

Dear Mr. Black,

We are writing in connection with the recent explosion at your factory.

We would like to point out that we have been manufacturing heating system for over 25 years and we have never had a complaint before. We have asked a surveyor to find out the cause of the explosion.

We are hoping that we can provide you with a satisfactory answer soon.

Yours sincerely,

Mary Miller

Service Manager

56. What happened in the factory last night?

The central heating system _____.

57. What was the damage caused to the factory?

The stock of _____ was ruined.

58. How much was the stock valued at?

It was valued at _____.

59. What did Bill Black demand in his letter?

To replace _____ and pay for the damage.

60. What has been done by the heating system supplier?

_____ has been asked to find out the cause of the accident.

Part IV Translation — English into Chinese (25 minutes)

Directions: *This part, numbered 61 through 65, is to test your ability to translate English into Chinese. Each of the four sentences (No. 61 to No. 64) is followed by four choices of suggested translation marked A, B, C and D. Make the best choice and write the corresponding letter on the Answer Sheet. Write your translation of the paragraph (No. 65) in the corresponding space on the Translation/Composition Sheet.*

61. All in all, the ABC Company offered me the experience to advance my career in China.

   A. 总而言之，ABC 公司使我有了工作经历，我要在中国发展我的事业。

   B. 总而言之，ABC 公司的历程有助于我实现在中国发展事业的目标。

   C. 总而言之，ABC 公司使我有了在中国拓展我的职业生涯的经历。

   D. 总而言之，ABC 公司的历程使我认识到我应该在中国发展事业。

62. We are confident that we will get rid of those difficulties since the government has agreed to give us some help.

   A. 由于政府已经同意给予我们一些帮助，我们有信心克服那些困难。

   B. 自从政府同意给予我们帮助以来，我们才下了脱贫致富的决心。

   C. 政府同意给我们一些帮助，因此我们要下定决心直面困境。

   D. 我们有信心克服困难，争取政府同意给我们一些资助。

63. Both late sleepers and early risers find the fixed hours of a nine-to-five workday a problem.

   A. 早起和晚睡的人都发现了问题，应该把朝九晚五的工作时间定下来。

   B. 早起和晚睡的人都发现了朝九晚五这种固定工作时间带来的问题。

   C. 早起和晚睡的人都认为朝九晚五这种固定的上班时间有问题。

   D. 早起和晚睡的人都认为应该把工作时间定为朝九晚五。

64. Not surprisingly, many scientists predict that such changes in the climate will probably result in hotter days.

   A. 毫不奇怪，许多科学家都预计气候的这些变化可能会导致天气变暖。

   B. 毫不奇怪，许多科学家认为这样的变化可能会导致热天更多。

   C. 许多科学家对于气候变化和炎热天气所产生的后果毫不惊讶。

   D. 许多科学家都认为天气变暖会改变气候，这并不令人怀疑。

65. We are glad to welcome our Chinese friends to this special Business Training program. Here, you will have a variety of activities and a chance to exchange ideas with each other. We hope that all of you will benefit a lot from this program. During your stay, please do not hesitate to speak to us with questions or concerns. We believe this will be an educational and enjoyable program.

Part V Writing (25 minutes)

Directions: *This part is to test your ability to do practical writing. You are required to write a Memo (内部通知) according to the instructions given in Chinese below. Remember to write your memo on the Translation/Composition Sheet.*

说明：假定你是销售部经理 John Green，请以 John Green 的名义按照下面的格式和内容给本公司其他各部门经理写一个内部通知。

主题：讨论 2006 年第三季度（the 3rd quarter）销售计划

通知时间：2006 年 6 月 16 日

内容：本部门已制定 2006 年第三季度的销售计划，将于 2006 年 6 月 19 日下午 1:00 在本公司会议室开会讨论这一计划，希望各部门经理前来参加。如不能到会，请提前告知本部门秘书。

Words for reference:
告知：notify
提前：in advance

SALES DEPARTMENT
MEMO

DATE: _____

TO: _____

FROM: _____

SUBJECT: _____

_____

_____

_____

2005 年 12 月高等学校英语应用能力考试（B 级）真题

Part I Listening Comprehension (15 minutes)

Directions: *This part is to test your listening ability. It consists of 3 sections.*

Section A

Directions: *This section is to test your ability to give proper responses. There are 5 recorded questions in it. After each question, there is a pause. The questions will be spoken two times. When you hear a question, you should decide on the correct answer from the 4 choices marked A, B, C and D given in your test paper. Then you should mark the corresponding letter on the Answer Sheet with a single line through the center.*

Example: *You will hear: Mr. Smith is not in. Would you like to leave him a message?*

You will read: *A. I'm not sure.*　　　*B. You're right.*

　　　　　　　C. Yes, certainly.　　　*D. That's interesting.*

From the question we learn that the speaker is asking the listener to leave a message. Therefore, "C. Yes, certainly." is the correct answer. You should mark C on the Answer Sheet. Now the test will begin.

1. A. With pleasure.　　B. That's great.　　C. What a pity!　　D. Please don't.
2. A. About 10 dollars.　　　　　　　　B. By 12 o'clock.
   C. In the photo shop.　　　　　　　　D. A moment ago.
3. A. Why not?　　B. I see.　　C. I don't think so.　　D. Go ahead.
4. A. Yes, please.　　B. No problem.　　C. Don't worry.　　D. Thank you.
5. A. What's there?　　B. Can I help you?　　C. No trouble.　　D. Thank you very much.

Section B

Directions: *This section is to test your ability to understand short dialogues. There are 5 recorded dialogues in it. After each dialogue, there is a recorded question. Both the dialogues and questions will be spoken two times. When you hear a question, you should decide on the correct answer from the 4 choices marked A, B, C and D given in your test paper. Then you should mark the corresponding letter on the Answer Sheet with a single line through the center.*

6. A. The man will do everything.　　　　B. The man needs a rest.
   C. Alice offers to help.　　　　　　　　D. Alice is quite busy.

7. A. They are free.   B. They are charged.

   C. They are expensive.   D. They are cheap.

8. A. Many people died in a fire.   B. Two persons were injured.

   C. There was a traffic accident.   D. There was an air crash.

9. A. Buy a train ticket for her.   B. Enjoy a concert with her.

   C. Go to the meeting with her.   D. Drive her to the railway station.

10. A. Where to have the meeting.   B. When to have the meeting.

    C. Who to attend the meeting.   D. What to discuss at the meeting.

Section C

Directions: *In this section you will hear a recorded short passage. The passage is printed in the test paper, but with some words and phrases missing. The passage will be read three times. During the second reading, you are required to put the missing words or phrases on the Answer Sheet in order of the numbered blanks according to what you hear. The third reading is for you to check your writing. Now the passage will begin.*

Good evening, ladies and gentlemen!

First of all, let me thank you for inviting us to such a great Christmas party. We ____11____ enjoyed the delicious food and excellent wine. Also, the music was perfect, so if I were a better dancer, I would have enjoyed the party twice ____12____. I enjoyed meeting and ____13____ to you, and sharing the time together. I hope we'll be able to keep this good relationship and make ____14____ another great one together.

Thank you again for the ____15____ party. We have had a great time.

Part II Vocabulary & Structure (15 minutes)

Directions: *This part is to test your ability to use words and phrases correctly to construct meaningful and grammatically correct sentences. It consists of 2 sections.*

Section A

Directions: *There are 10 incomplete statements here. You are required to complete each statement by choosing the appropriate answer from the 4 choices marked A, B, C and D. You should mark the corresponding letter on the Answer Sheet with a single line through the center.*

16. I am looking forward to _____ from you as soon as possible.

    A. hear   B. be hearing   C. hearing   D. have heard

17. He _____ that the people he works with are all very interested in their jobs.

    A. feels   B. tries   C. looks   D. asks

18. _____, a friend of Mrs. Black found the watch she had lost two days before.

    A. Especially   B. Usually   C. Generally   D. Fortunately

19. Few people _____ applied for the position meet the requirements of the company.

    A. whom   B. who   C. what   D. whose

20. Why didn't you _____ that pencil which was on the floor?

    A. pick up   B. bring up   C. get up   D. put up

21. Mary found _____ extremely difficult to pass the examination.

    A. it   B. this   C. that   D. what

22. She tried hard, but she still couldn't make us _____ our mind.

    A. to change   B. changed   C. change   D. changing

23. I was late for the interview because the bus _____ on the way to London.

    A. got off   B. brought in   C. kept off   D. broke down

24. The manager required that all the employees _____ at the office before 9:00 in the morning.

    A. will arrive   B. arrive   C. arrived   D. have arrived

25. She was talking about her _____ as a nurse in a hospital, which we had never heard of.

    A. expenses   B. excuses   C. experiences   D. expressions

Section B

Directions: *There are 10 incomplete statements here. You should fill in each blank with the proper form of the word given in brackets. Write the word or words in the corresponding space on the Answer Sheet.*

26. The children looked (health) _____ with bright smiles on their faces.

27. (work) _____ as a team, the foreign and Chinese engineers cooperated closely and successfully.

28. We were surprised at the (achieve) _____ the young man had made in the last three years.

29. The survey shows that green food is becoming (popular) _____ than traditional food.

30. The price of oil in the world market has (great) _____ increased in recent months.

31. I (work) _____ in the Human Resources Department for five months since I joined the company.

32. The flexible working time system will enable the (employ) _____ to work more efficiently.

33. Jane (praise) _____ many times by the general manager when she was working as the office secretary.

34. The railway station was crowded with people (say) _____ goodbye to their friends and relatives.

35. The professor, as well as his assistants, (do) _____ the experiment in the lab forty hours a week.

Part III Reading Comprehension (40 minutes)

Directions: *This part is to test your reading ability. There are 5 tasks for you to fulfill. You should read the reading materials carefully and do the tasks as you are instructed.*

Task 1

Directions: *After reading the following passage, you will find 5 questions or unfinished statements, numbered 36 to 40. For each question or statement there are 4 choices marked A, B, C and D. You should make the correct choice and mark the corresponding letter on the Answer Sheet with a single line through the center.*

Most people buy a lot of gifts just before Christmas. But some people think they buy too much. They have started a special day called Buy Nothing Day. They don't want anyone to go shopping on that day.

Buy Nothing Day is November 29. It's 25 days before Christmas. The idea for Buy Nothing Day started in Vancouver, British Columbia. Now people all over the United States celebrate Buy Nothing Day. In California, parents and children get together to read stories, sing songs and paint pictures. The children talk about why they don't need a lot of toys.

This year in Albuquerque, New Mexico, high school students wanted to tell other students about Buy Nothing Day. They organized a simple dinner to give people information about Buy Nothing Day. They asked restaurants in the neighborhood to donate (赠送) the food. They made posters (海报) and talked to other students about it. The dinner was a big success, and many students agreed not to buy anything on November 29. The students at the high school liked the idea of this new tradition. Next year, they want to have another dinner to inform more people about Buy Nothing Day!

36. Some people start Buy Nothing Day because they think _____.

    A. people need more time to do other things

    B. people buy too many gifts for Christmas

    C. people can hardly afford to buy a lot of gifts

    D. people waste too much time going shopping

37. The idea for Buy Nothing Day first started in _____.

    A. California   B. Albuquerque

    C. British Columbia   D. New Mexico

38. To make Buy Nothing Day more popular, the students in Albuquerque plan to _____.

    A. provide free food to more people

    B. persuade more restaurants to donate food

    C. put up more advertising posters on that day

    D. have another dinner to inform more people of the Day

39. According to the passage, which of the following statements is TRUE?

   A. Buy Nothing Day has become popular in the United States.

   B. Restaurants have a tradition of donating food on holidays.

   C. Gift shops are expected to be closed on Buy Nothing Day.

   D. Children like the idea of Buy Nothing Day best.

40. The best title for the passage might be _____.

   A. Buy Nothing Day in the U.S.　　　　B. The Future of Buy Nothing Day

   C. Free Dinners on Buy Nothing Day　　D. Students' Activities on Buy Nothing Day

Task 2

Directions: *This task is the same as Task 1. The 5 questions or unfinished statements are numbered 41 to 45.*

December 13th, 2005

Dear Sirs,

   I am very happy to apply for the position of secretary, which you advertised in *China Daily* of December 10, 2005.

   I have been working as a secretary at a college office. Because I am the only secretary in the office, it is necessary for me to work quickly and efficiently and to be flexible in my daily work. Professors value my work and my ability to meet their needs.

   Although I am happy now, I feel that my promotion (晋升) is limited here, and I would like to have a more challenging job. Therefore, I enrolled (参加) in a program to expand my knowledge of international business affairs. Now, both my English and Chinese have been improved and I am ready to begin working as a bilingual secretary in an international company like yours, and I believe I can be a great help to your firm.

   The enclosed resume gives further details of my qualifications, and I would appreciate it if you could give me an opportunity to have an interview. I am looking forward to receiving your call at 62428866 or please use the enclosed pre-paid postcard to send me your reply. Thank you very much for your consideration.

Faithfully yours,

Mary Lee

41. The writer wants to change her job because _____.

   A. she has difficulty handling her daily work efficiently

   B. she can hardly get a chance to be promoted

   C. she finds her present job too challenging

   D. she is tired of her duties at the college

42. In order to prepare herself for a more satisfactory fob, the writer _____.

    A. has taken part in a special business program

    B. tries to get the professors' high praises

    C. has worked much harder on her job

    D. has to prove herself to be efficient

43. A bilingual secretary (Line 4, Para. 3) differs from other secretaries in that he or she can _____.

    A. operate a computer

    B. do the job efficiently

    C. speak two languages

    D. write official documents

44. The writer of the letter enclosed a pre-paid postcard to _____.

    A. request a written reply

    B. make an appointment

    C. get more information

    D. express her thanks

45. By sending this letter, the writer expected to _____.

    A. draw the attention of the company

    B. get an opportunity for an interview

    C. apply for a suitable position in *China Daily*

    D. obtain more in formation about the company

Task 3

Directions: *The following is a report. After reading it, you should complete the information by filling in the blanks marked 46 through 50 **in not more than 3 words** in the table below.*

A Report on New Factory Location

The committee initially (最初) considered three possible locations for the proposed new factory. Of the three cities, Chicago presently seems to the committee to offer the greatest advantages. Here are our observations of the city.

Though not at the geographical center of the United States, Chicago is centrally located in an area that contains more than three-quarters of the US population. It is within easy reach of our head office in New York. And it is close to several of our most important suppliers of components (配件) and raw materials — those, for example, in Columbus, Detroit, and St. Louis.

The city is served by several major railroads. Except during the winter months when the Great Lakes are frozen, it is an international seaport. Chicago has two major airports and both home and international air cargo (货物) services are available.

A Report on New Factory Location

Location recommended: ___46___

Advantages of the location:

    1) in the ___47___ part of an area with a huge population;

    2) within easy reach of the ___48___ in New York;

    3) close to the important ___49___ of components and raw materials;

    4) convenient in rail, water and ___50___ cargo transport.

Task 4

Directions: *The following is a list of telephone operating instructions. After reading it, you are required to find the items equivalent to (与……等同) those given in Chinese in the table below. Then you should put the corresponding letters in the brackets on the Answer Sheet, numbered 51 through 55.*

A — Internet access

B — Open dial-up connection window

C — Enter card number in the "user name" box

D — Enter ID number in the "password" box

E — Enter 17200 in the "phone number" box

F — Connecting

G — Please input your account number

H — Please enter your ID number

I — Please enter the number you wish to call

J — Get current credit

K — Inquire abbreviated number

L — Transfer credit money from other cards to this card

M — Please enter your new ID number

N — Modify the ID number

O — Modify the abbreviated number

P — Account recharge

Examples: （E）电话号码输入栏键入 17200   （O）修改缩位号码

51. ( ) 键入呼叫号码		( ) 输入账号
52. ( ) 在密码栏中键入密码		( ) 互联网接入
53. ( ) 修改密码		( ) 打开拨号连接窗口
54. ( ) 在用户名栏中键入本卡卡号		( ) 将其他卡上的金额转移到本卡
55. ( ) 账户充值		( ) 连接中

Task 5

Directions: *There is an advertisement below. After reading it, you are required to complete the answers that follow the questions (No. 56 to No. 60). You should write your answers* **in not more than 3 words** *on the Answer Sheet correspondingly.*

Amway (China) Daily Necessities Company Limited

Amway is a leading international company engaged in daily necessities（必需品）with an annual sale of 16 billion US dollars worldwide. We are looking for qualified personnel to fill the following positions in our Beijing office.

1. Purchasing Manager
* College diploma（文凭）with technical background
* At least 3 years' experience in the field of chemicals and packaging materials
* Able to work independently and to set up purchasing procedures
* Good computer skills
* Excellent negotiation（谈判）techniques
* Fluent in English, but not essential

2. Personnel Manager
* College diploma in Human Resources Management
* At least 2 years' experience in Human Resources Management
* Good computer skills
* Fluent in English

3. Sales Manager
* College diploma
* Knowledge in product sales
* Fluent in English
* Active and hard-working

56. What line of products is Amway engaged in?

    _____.

57. What skills should a purchasing manager have?

    Good _____.

58. What foreign language should the personnel manager speak fluently?

    _____.

59. What qualities should a candidate have if he wants to be the sales manager?

    He must be active and _____.

60. How many positions does the company offer in the advertisement?

    _____.

Part IV Translation — English into Chinese (25 minutes)

Directions: *This part, numbered 61 through 65, is to test your ability to translate English into Chinese. Each of the four sentences (No. 61 to No. 64) is followed by four choices of suggested translation marked A, B, C and D. Make the best choice and write the corresponding letter on the Answer Sheet. Write your translation of the paragraph (No. 65) in the corresponding space on the Translation/Composition Sheet.*

61. It is reported that air pollution affects rivers and lakes indirectly because it causes acid rain.

A. 据报道，空气污染导致酸雨，因而对河流和湖泊造成间接影响。

B. 据报道，空气污染了河流和湖泊，间接的原因是因为有酸雨。

C. 据报道，空气污染间接来源于河流和湖泊的污染，因为后者会导致酸雨。

D. 据报道，空气污染对河流和湖泊的影响是间接的，因为它的成因是酸雨。

62. We are lucky to have the most up-to-date equipment in our laboratory, with which we can complete our research in time.

A. 我们很幸运能够拥有最先进的实验室，可以随时用来进行研究。

B. 很幸运，我们及时地找到了从事研究所需要的最完整的资料和设备。

C. 很幸运，我们实验室拥有最先进的设备，可以用来及时完成研究任务。

D. 非常幸运，我们实验室拥有的先进设备最多，能够完成所有的研究任务。

63. All of our four objectives of this trip have been fulfilled, which is more than I had expected.

A. 我们此行四个目标的完成情况比我预期的要好。

B. 我们此行的目标一共有四个，比我预期的还多。

C. 我们此行总共完成了四个目标，比我预期的要多。

D. 我们此行的四个目标均已达到，比我预期的要好。

64. You may use this computer, on condition that you are able to handle it properly so as not to damage it.

A. 这台计算机你可以使用，但如有损坏，你要有条件进行维修。

B. 只要你能正确地使用计算机，不损坏它，你就可以使用。

C. 你可以使用这台计算机，条件是如有损坏，你能维修。

D. 在有条件的情况下你可以使用计算机，千万别损坏它。

65. We are writing this letter to tell you that up to now no news has come from you about the goods we ordered on May 25th. As you have been informed in our letters, our customers are in urgent need of those machines. They are asking repeatedly for an early delivery (交货). We hope that you will try your best to arrange all this without further delay.

Part V Writing (25 minutes)

Directions: *This part is to test your ability to do practical writing. You are required to write an email according to the information given in Chinese. Remember to do the writing on the Translation/Composition Sheet.*

说明：根据下列内容写一封电子邮件。

发件人：John Smith（js456@vip.163.com）

收件人：假日酒店（电子邮箱 marketing@expedia.com）

发件时间：12 月 10 日

事由：

1）因行程改变，取消 12 月 5 日以 John Smith 的名义在贵酒店预订的 12 月 12 日到 15 日的两个单人房间；

2）表示歉意，并询问是否需支付违约金；

3）要求回信确认。

Words for reference:

违约金：cancellation penalty

假日酒店：Holiday Inn

以……的名义：in the name of

确认：confirm

Email Message

To:

From:

Date:

Subject: Cancellation of Hotel Booking

Dear Sir or Madam,

I am writing to inform you that _____

_____

_____

_____

Yours faithfully,

John Smith

2005 年 6 月高等学校英语应用能力考试（B 级）真题

Part I Listening Comprehension (15 minutes)

Directions: *This part is to test your listening ability. It consists of 3 sections.*

Section A

Directions: *This section is to test your ability to give proper responses. There are 5 recorded questions in it. After each question, there is a pause. The questions will be spoken two times. When you hear a question, you should decide on the correct answer from the 4 choices marked A, B, C and D given in your test paper. Then you should mark the corresponding letter on the Answer Sheet with a single line through the center.*

Example: *You will hear: Mr. Smith is not in. Would you like to leave him a message?*
            You will read: A. I'm not sure.   *B. You're right.*
                             C. Yes, certainly.   *D. That's interesting.*

   From the question we learn that the speaker is asking the listener to leave a message. Therefore, "C. Yes, certainly." is the correct answer. You should mark C on the Answer Sheet. Now the test will begin.

1. A. Yes, I know that.
   C. Yes, I'm all right.
   B. Yes, I'd like to.
   D. Yes, I'm sure.

2. A. Leave it to me.
   C. That's great.
   B. That's a good idea.
   D. Ten o'clock.

3. A. Chinese history.
   C. Too difficult.
   B. I'm twenty.
   D. I like football.

4. A. They are too big.
   C. They are thirty dollars.
   B. They are the same size.
   D. They are in fashion.

5. A. I'm sorry to hear that.
   C. My pleasure.
   B. No, thanks.
   D. Yes, I'd love to make it.

Section B

Directions: *This section is to test your ability to understand short dialogues. There are 5 recorded dialogues in it. After each dialogue, there is a recorded question. Both the dialogues and questions will be spoken two times. When you hear a question, you should decide on the correct answer from the 4 choices marked A, B, C and D given in your test paper. Then you should mark the corresponding letter on the Answer Sheet with a single line through the center.*

6. A. In a post office.   B. On board a ship.
   C. In a booking office.   D. On an airplane.

7. A. Look for Jack.   B. Buy some medicine.
   C. Call for a doctor.   D. Send Jack to school.

8. A. $ 5.   B. $10.
   C. $ 15.   D. $ 20.

9. A. He has no idea about it.   B. He's quite interested in it.
   C. He enjoys it.   D. He doesn't like it.

10. A. She is very nice.   B. She is impatient.
    C. She is careless.   D. She is very rich.

Section C

Directions: *In this section you will hear a recorded short passage. The passage is printed in the test paper, but with some words and phrases missing. The passage will be read three times. During the second reading, you are required to put the missing words or phrases on the Answer Sheet in order of the numbered blanks according to what you hear. The third reading is for you to check your writing. Now the passage will begin.*

Some managers have noticed recently that the employees in the company are taking advantage of the policy of having breaks. The workers have two 15-minute breaks per ____11____. However, the two breaks are lasting ____12____ as 25 to 30 minutes each. The workers complain that the factory work is so ____13____ that they need longer breaks. Also the dining hall is so ____14____ that it takes too long to walk there and back. But the company is losing hundreds of work hours each year. Should employees be paid for the time they are not working? The general manager has to call a meeting to ____15____ this matter.

Part II Vocabulary & Structure (15 minutes)

Directions: *This part is to test your ability to use words and phrases correctly to construct meaningful and grammatically correct sentences. It consists of 2 sections.*

Section A

Directions: *There are 10 incomplete statements here. You are required to complete each statement by choosing the appropriate answer from the 4 choices marked A, B, C and D. You should mark the corresponding letter on the Answer Sheet with a single line through the center.*

16. Judging from his accent, I can _____ that he is from the south.

    A. speak   B. look   C. tell   D. show

17. We won't be able to leave the office until the rain _____.

    A. will stop   B. stops   C. stopped   D. is stopping

18. The boss told his secretary to _____ the documents for later use.

    A. put away   B. turn on   C. make up   D. break out

19. Mary says this is the _____ decision she has ever made in her career life.

    A. bad   B. worst   C. worse   D. badly

20. We all think that John is the only candidate _____ will get the job.

    A. whom   B. whose   C. who   D. whoever

21. The fact _____ Mary was late for the meeting again made me angry.

    A. that   B. why   C. what   D. which

22. Most of the machines in the workshop _____ next month.

    A. are repaired   B. have been repaired   C. were repaired   D. will be repaired

23. _____ is quite difficult for Mary to pass the interview.

    A. What   B. This   C. That   D. It

24. If I work in a small factory, it is not _____ for me to gain much experience.

    A. weekly   B. friendly   C. likely   D. lively

25. The villagers have offered much help to us and we think we should do something for them _____.

    A. in return   B. in place   C. in fashion   D. in danger

Section B

Directions: *There are 10 incomplete statements here. You should fill in each blank with the proper form of the word given in brackets. Write the word or words in the corresponding space on the Answer Sheet.*

26. Some people do believe that smoking will (certain) _____ cause lung cancer.

27. If the team members hadn't helped me, I (fail) _____ in the last experiment.

28. I asked him not (say) _____ anything about our contract until the end of the month.

29. We usually (go) _____ abroad for our holiday, but this year we are staying at home.

30. With the (develop) _____ of foreign trade, more and more people are doing import and export business.

31. (See) _____ from the top of the hill, the village is very beautiful.

32. It was very (help) _____ of you to make all the necessary arrangements for us.

33. On hearing the good news that our new products sold well in the market, we all got (excite) _____.

34. Mark was a little upset, for the manager didn't allow him (take) _____ his holiday the following week.

35. Some American businessmen in China are spending a lot of time in (learn) _____ Chinese.

Part III Reading Comprehension (40 minutes)

Directions: *This part is to test your reading ability. There are 5 tasks for you to fulfill. You should read the reading materials carefully and do the tasks as you are instructed.*

Task 1

Directions: *After reading the following passage, you will find 5 questions or unfinished statements, numbered 36 to 40. For each question or statement there are 4 choices marked A, B, C and D. You should make the correct choice and mark the corresponding letter on the Answer Sheet with a single line through the center.*

It is often difficult for a man to be quite sure what tax (税) he ought to pay to the government because it depends on so many different things: whether the man is married; how many children he has; whether he supports any relations; how much he earns; how much interest he receives; how much he has spent on his house during the year, and so on and so forth. All this makes it difficult to decide exactly how much the tax is.

There was a certain artist who was always very careful to pay the proper amount.

One year, after posting his check as usual, he began to wonder if he had paid enough, and after a lot of work, with a pencil and paper, decided that he had not. He believed that he owed the government something.

He was just writing another check to send to the tax-collector when the postman dropped a letter into the box at the front door. Opening it, the artist was surprised to find inside it a check for five pounds from the tax-collector. The official explained that too much had been paid, and therefore the difference was now returned to the taxpayer.

36. According to the passage, to decide the exact amount of tax to be paid is _____.

　　A. simple　　　　　　B. easy　　　　　　C. difficult　　　　　D. interesting

37. It is mentioned in the passage that one has to pay tax according to _____.

　　A. how much education one has received　　　B. whether one is single or married

　　C. how old one's children are　　　　　　　D. where one lives

38. The word "proper" in the first line of the second paragraph means _____.

　　A. small　　　　　　B. big　　　　　　　C. right　　　　　　D. wrong

39. After a lot of work, the artist thought that he had paid the government _____.

　　A. less tax than he should have　　　　　　B. more tax than he should have

　　C. as much tax as usual　　　　　　　　　D. just enough tax

40. Why did the tax-collector send a letter to the artist?

　　A. To send him a new tax form.　　　　　　B. To return the money over-paid.

　　C. To remind him of paying the tax.　　　　D. To explain the rules of tax-paying.

Task 2

Directions: *This task is the same as Task 1. The 5 questions or unfinished statements are numbered 41 to 45.*

Pressure Cooker (压力锅) Safety

When you are cooking with a pressure cooker, you should learn a few common sense (常识) rules:

1) Never leave the cooker unwatched when it is in use.

2) Add sufficient liquid but never past the recommended fill point. Overfilling the cooker may block the vent pipe (排气孔) and cause the cooker to explode.

3) Set the cooking time. Too much time may overcook the food or too much pressure may build up in the cooker. Too little time will lead to undercooked food.

4) If you are new to pressure-cooking, follow the cooking instructions carefully. Heat and time can either result in a great meal or a ruined one.

5) Never try to force a pressure cooker cover open. Allow the cooker to cool or run it under cool water before trying to open the cover.

6) Clean the cooker thoroughly after each use. Mild detergent (洗涤剂) and hot water work the best. Do not use stove ash or sand for they may damage the cooker. The gasket (密封圈) is best cleaned in warm soapy water and then dried. Store the gasket in the bottom of the pot.

41. According to the first rule, the user should _____.

　　A. keep the cooker under close watch　　　　B. always keep the cooker half full

　　C. never leave the cooker empty　　　　　　D. never turn off the stove

42. According to the second rule, too much liquid in the cooker may result in _____.
    A. a ruined meal
    B. undercooked food
    C. too little pressure
    D. a blocked vent pipe

43. According to the fifth rule, a pressure cooker cover should be opened _____.
    A. as soon as the cooking is finished
    B. while it is still on the stove
    C. with force when it is hot
    D. after it is cooled down

44. According to the instructions, which of the following is TRUE?
    A. The gasket should be cleaned thoroughly with cold water.
    B. Mild detergent and hot water can best clean the cooker.
    C. Soapy water will often damage the cooker.
    D. Sand can be used to clean the cooker.

45. Which of the following operations may be dangerous?
    A. Overfilling the cooker with food and water.
    B. Cleaning the cooker with detergent.
    C. Cooling the cooker with cold water.
    D. Setting too little cooking time.

Task 3

Directions: *The following is an advertisement. After reading it, you should complete the information by filling in the blanks marked 46 through 50 **in not more than 3 words** in the table below.*

When someone is sick at home, the mother usually makes the first diagnosis (诊断). So we do everything we can to give her all the information she needs.

Take *Columbia One Source*. It's our monthly magazine which outlines practical ways to live a healthier life.

Then there's our website on the Internet that provides doctors' advice and other healthcare information.

Of course, if you ever need more than just information, *Columbia One Source* offers our patients the special knowledge of the nation's largest network of homecare services, hospitals and outpatient surgery (门诊手术) centers.

Our goal is to provide a series of services possible.

For more information, see our site on the Web or call 1-800-*Columbia* for a doctor's treatment or to get your free copy of *Columbia One Source*.

Columbia One Source

Services offered by *Columbia One Source*:

1) Information on ___46___ to live a healthier life

2) Doctors' advice and other ___47___

3) Special knowledge of the nation's ___48___ of homecare services

Ways to get more information from *Columbia One Source*:

1) See the site on ___49___

2) Call 1-800-*Columbia* for a doctor's treatment

3) Get a ___50___ of *Columbia One Source*

Task 4

Directions: *The following is a list of terms frequently used in medical services. After reading it, you are required to find the items equivalent to (与……等同) those given in Chinese in the table below. Then you should put the corresponding letters in the brackets on the Answer Sheet, numbered 51 through 55.*

A — severe pain   B — surgeon

C — skin test   D — blood test

E — eyesight test   F — sick-leave certificate

G — operation   H — blood pressure

I — toothache   J — stomachache

K — heart disease   L — infection

M — mental disease   N — nervous disease

O — lung disease   P — high fever

Q — dentist

Examples: （N）神经疾病   （L）感染

51. （　　）牙科医生	（　　）肺病
52. （　　）验血	（　　）精神疾病
53. （　　）病假证明	（　　）高热
54. （　　）血压	（　　）视力检查
55. （　　）胃痛	（　　）手术

Task 5

Directions: *There is an advertisement below. After reading it, you are required to complete the answers that follow the questions (No. 56 to No. 60). You should write your answers **in not more than 3 words** on the Answer Sheet correspondingly.*

Fly with Singapore Airlines to Australia and you could win free tickets.
There is a winner every day from January 1st to April 30th 2005.

Lucky Promotion (促销)

Fly between January 1st and April 30th 2005, and you could win free tickets daily, plus a chance to win one of the 2 Great Prizes:

First Prize: One pair of First Class return tickets on Singapore Airlines to any of our destinations (目的地) in Australia, 5 nights' accommodation (住宿) in a 5-star hotel and US $5,000 cash.

Second prize: One pair of Business Class return tickets on Singapore Airlines to any of our destinations in Australia, 5 nights' accommodation in a 5-star hotel and US $3,000 cash.

Plan your holiday to Australia on Singapore Airlines now and try your luck for the good chance!

For more information, contact the Singapore Airlines office at your place or visit our websites at *www.singaporeair.com* or *www.australia.com.*

56. How long does the Lucky Promotion last?

From January 1st to _____, 2005.

57. What could you win if you fly with Singapore Airlines within the period mentioned?

You could win _____ every day, plus a chance to win great prizes.

58. How many First Class return tickets can you get if you win the first prize?

_____ return tickets.

59. What kind of hotel can you stay in free of charge if you win a second prize?

A(n) _____.

60. Where can you get more information about the promotion?

Contact the _____ or visit its websites.

Part IV Translation — English into Chinese (25 minutes)

Directions: *This part, numbered 61 through 65, is to test your ability to translate English into Chinese. Each of the four sentences (No. 61 to No. 64) is followed by four choices of suggested translation marked A, B, C and D. Make the best choice and write the corresponding letter on the Answer Sheet. Write your translation of the paragraph (No. 65) in the corresponding space on the Translation/ Composition Sheet.*

61. What our company values most in employing people is their basic quality and practical skills.

　　A. 我们公司的最大价值在于它所雇用的员工具备了基本素质和实用技能。

　　B. 在培训员工时，我们公司大多会重视人的基本素质和实际技能。

　　C. 在招聘员工时，我们公司最看重的是人的基本素质和实际技能。

　　D. 我们公司最值得称道的是它培训员工的基本素质和实用技能。

62. It is obvious that Jack can hardly understand the instructions of the mobile phone he is reading.

　　A. 杰克显然看不懂他正在阅读的手机说明书。

　　B. 杰克费了很大劲才看懂本来很明显的手机指令。

　　C. 显然，杰克努力去理解他正在阅读的手机指令。

　　D. 显然，杰克再费劲也看不懂他正在阅读的手机说明书。

63. Candidates who are not contacted within four weeks after the interview may consider their application unsuccessful.

　　A. 面试后四周内仍未接到通知的求职者可以考虑再申请。

　　B. 未在面试后四周内来联系的求职者则可考虑申请是否已失败。

　　C. 求职者在面试后四周内不来签订合同则被认为是放弃申请。

　　D. 求职者如果在面试后四周内尚未得到通知，则可以认为未被录用。

64. Making a speech is an art which is constantly used, and it has to be learned and practiced.

　　A. 演讲是一门难得一用的艺术，所以有机会就要学习和锻炼。

　　B. 演讲是一门普遍运用的艺术，需要学习和训练才能掌握。

　　C. 演讲是一门常用的艺术，而且需要学习和实践。

　　D. 演讲这门艺术经常使用才能学会并用于实践。

65. Card-holders of Holiday Sunshine Hotel automatically become registered members of its Reservation (预定) Network. They are able to enjoy the services offered by its member hotels. We encourage card-holders to use the card as often as possible, and they will be awarded with prizes when their marks (积分) reach a certain amount. Before checking into a hotel, please always reserve your room first. When you check out, you will only have to pay the member price.

Part V Writing (25 minutes)

Directions: *This part is to test your ability to do practical writing. You are required to complete the English Questionnaire (问卷调查) Form based on the information given in Chinese.*

说明：假定你是王明（中国籍），去海口旅游度假，于 2005 年 6 月 10 日入住白云宾馆 3002 房间，6 月 20 日离店。临走时填写了一份问卷调查表。

内容如下：

1）对酒店的总体管理感到满意；

2）对酒店提供的各种服务感到满意；

3）建议：

a．因酒店位于海边，交通并不方便，周围的商业设施比较少，建议酒店每天能提供免费班车，方便来海边度假的住店客人去市区购买所需商品；

b．建议酒店与相关公司联系，为住店客人提供租车服务。

Words for reference:

总体（的）：overall

商业（的）：commercial

班车：shuttle bus

相关公司：related company

QUESTIONAIRE

To improve the quality of our service, we would be grateful if you'd complete the following questionnaire.

Name: _____　　　Nationality: _____　　　Room Number: _____

Check-in Date: _____　　　Check-out Date: _____

Did you receive polite and efficient service when you arrived? _____Yes_____

Are you satisfied with the room service of our hotel? _____

What's your opinion of our health facilities? _____Good_____

Please give your impression of our restaurant service. _____

Have you any other comments to help us make your stay more enjoyable?

_____

_____

_____

_____

Baiyun Hotel

General Manager

117

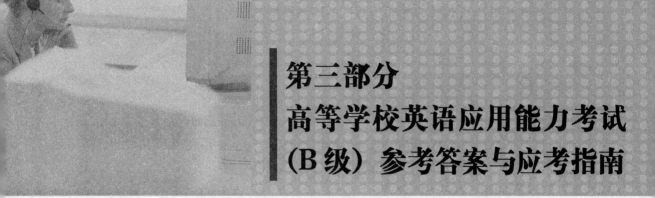

2009 年 12 月高等学校英语应用能力考试（B 级）参考答案与应考指南

Part I Listening Comprehension

1. B   2. A   3. D   4. D   5. C   6. C   7. A   8. D   9. B   10. D

11. show   12. factory   13. built   14. do our best   15. have a good time

Part II Structure

Section A

16.【答案】A

【考点】词义辨析

【译文】参加在线培训课程需要花多少钱？

【分析】本句中的 it 为形式主语，逻辑主语为后面的不定式 to take the online training course。give 意为"给予"；pay 意为"付款"，主语应该是人；spend 意为"花费"，主语也应该是人，可以表示花费时间、金钱、精力等。只有 A 选项 cost（花费）的主语是事物，且表示花费了金钱、时间、精力等。故 A 选项为正确答案。

【参考例句】The book cost me a lot of time.（这本书花了我很多时间。）

I spent a lot of time on this book.（我花了很多时间在这本书上。）

17.【答案】B

【考点】介词用法

【译文】如果您需要更多信息，请通过电话或电子邮件联系我们。

【分析】介词 by 在此处表示方式。选项 A，C，D 皆无此用法。

【用法拓展】短语 on the phone 在口语里表示"在打电话"。

18.【答案】C

【考点】词义辨析

【译文】史密斯先生曾经抽烟抽得很厉害，但他最近戒了。

【分析】此处需要一个副词来修饰动词 smoke。immediately 意为"立刻，马上"，roughly 意为"粗鲁地，粗略地，粗糙地"，heavily 意为"猛烈地，厉害地，严重地"，completely 意为"完全地"。只有 C 选项符合题意。

【参考例句】

Please return immediately.（请速归。）

Roughly speaking, about 100 people attended the meeting.（粗略说来，有 100 个人参加了会议。）

You are completely wrong.（你完全错了。）

19.【答案】D

【考点】固定结构

【译文】他说得如此快以至于我们很难听懂。

【分析】so...that... 引出结果状语从句，意为"如此……，以至于……"；so 后通常接形容词或副词。

【用法拓展】that 与 such 连用也可以引出结果状语从句，但 such 后通常接名词短语。

【参考例句】

His left in such a hurry that he forgot his key.（他走得如此匆忙，以至于忘了拿钥匙。）

20.【答案】D

【考点】词组辨析

【译文】请你一看到这则信息就立即给我打电话。

【分析】此题需要辨析四个含有 as...as... 的词组。as well as 意为"也，和"，as early as 意为"和……一样早"，as far as 意为"就……而言，在……范围内"，as soon as 意为"一……就……"。只有 D 选项符合题意。

【参考例句】

He has experience as well as knowledge.（他既有知识又有经验。）

Please come as early as possible.（请尽可能早来。）

As far as I know, he is honest.（就我所知，他是诚实的。）

21.【答案】A

【考点】词义辨析

【译文】我们无法为每个人都提供房间，所以你们中的一些人不得不合住。

【分析】share 意为"分享"，stay 意为"停留，保持"，spare 意为"节约，抽出（时间）"，live 意为"居住，生活"。只有 share 符合原句的意思。

【参考例句】

She <u>stayed</u> at school until five o'clock.（她一直到五点才离开学校。）

Could you <u>spare</u> a minute?（能耽搁您一会吗？）

I <u>live</u> in Wuhan.（我在武汉居住。）

22.**【答案】** B

　　【考点】 动名词

　　【译文】 在申请这个工作之前，你必须参加一项语言测试。

　　【分析】 根据空格前的介词 before，可知此处应填 apply 的动名词形式 applying。

23.**【答案】** C

　　【考点】 词组辨析

　　【译文】 如果你想要加入俱乐部，必须先填写这份表格。

　　【分析】 put up 意为"举起，建立，张贴"，try out 意为"试用，试验，选拔"，fill in 意为"填写"，set up 意为"建立，树立"。根据后面的宾语 this form，可以确定 C 选项为正确答案。

【参考例句】

We will <u>put up</u> a notice here.（我们将在这里贴一张通知。）

The idea seems good, but it needs to be <u>tried out</u>.（这个主意似乎不错，但必须经过检验。）

Many foreign firms have <u>set up</u> factories here.（很多外国公司在这里建立了工厂。）

24.**【答案】** D

　　【考点】 连词用法

　　【译文】 如果雨在 12 点之前停不了的话，我们将会取消比赛。

　　【分析】 此处需要一个引导状语从句的连词。分析逗号前面的"雨在 12 点之前停"和后面的"我们将取消比赛"，可知前者的对立面是后者的条件。故此处选择引导条件状语从句的连词 unless（除非）。

25.**【答案】** B

　　【考点】 动名词

　　【译文】 随着油价持续攀升，人们开车的花销更大了。

　　【分析】 keep（保持、继续）后接动名词作宾语。故 B 选项 going up 为正确答案。

Section B

26.**【答案】** wonderful

　　【考点】 词形转换

　　【译文】 那是多么棒的一个派对啊！在那里的每分钟我都很快乐。

　　【分析】 根据空格前的不定冠词 a 和后面的名词 party，可知此处应该填一个形容词修饰名词。故应使用动词 wonder 的形容词形式 wonderful。

27. 【答案】more successful

【考点】比较级

【译文】事实证明，电影比我们预料的还要成功。

【分析】根据横线后面的 than 可知此处应该填写形容词 successful 的比较级形式。由于 successful 是多音节单词，故它的比较级为 more 加上形容词原形，即 more successful。

28. 【答案】to bring

【考点】不定式

【译文】禁止读者在任何时候携带饮食进入图书馆。

【分析】allow 的宾语后接动词不定式短语作补语，即 allow sb. to do sth.。此句中的 allow 使用了被动语态，但后面依然要接不定式，即 to bring。

【用法拓展】其他常见的接不定式作宾语补足语的动词还有：advise, ask, enable, intend, force, lead, remind, tell, teach, want 等。

29. 【答案】immediately

【考点】词形转换

【译文】经理承诺马上处理这个问题。

【分析】此处需要一个词来修饰动词短语 deal with，故应填写形容词 immediate 的副词形式 immediately。

30. 【答案】working

【考点】动名词

【译文】我们期待着将来与您的合作。

【分析】在动词短语 look forward to（期待，盼望）中，to 是介词，其后应该接名词、名词短语或者动名词。故此处应填写 work 的动名词形式 working。

31. 【答案】communication

【考点】词形转换

【译文】如今，电子邮件已经成为了日常生活中的重要交流工具。

【分析】根据空格前的 an important means of 可知此处需要填一个名词。故应填写动词 communicate 的名词形式 communication。

32. 【答案】disappointed

【考点】词形转换

【译文】当游客们赶到博物馆的时候，很失望地发现它已经关门了。

【分析】根据空格前的 were 可知此处应填一个形容词。动词 disappoint 的形容词形式有 disappointed（感到失望的）和 disappointing（令人失望的）。此处这个形容词要表达的是游客们发现博物馆关门时的心情，故应选用 disappointed。

【参考例句】The result was rather disappointing.（结果相当令人失望。）

33. 【答案】improvement

【考点】词形转换

【译文】由于路况的改善，最近这里的事故减少了。

【分析】根据空格前的定冠词 the 可知此处应填动词 improve 的名词形式 improvement。

34.【答案】will meet

【考点】时态

【译文】您明天到的时候，我的秘书会去机场接您。

【分析】根据 tomorrow 可知 meet 这一动作发生在将来，应用一般将来时。arrive 这一动作也发生在将来，但在状语从句中，用一般现在时表示将来的动作。

35.【答案】joined

【考点】时态

【译文】自从 2002 年进入这家公司以来，约翰就一直担任销售经理一职。

【分析】本题考查 since 从句中的动词时态。since 表示某种情况在过去某个特定时刻开始并持续到现在，其后可接表示过去的时间或使用一般过去时的时间状语从句，而主句通常用现在完成时或现在完成进行时，故应使用 join 的过去式 joined。

Part III Reading Comprehension

▶（Task 1）大意

本文是 Calibre 盒式录音带图书馆给读者的一封信，介绍了图书馆的受众、规模及使用方法。

【核心词汇】

application	n.	申请	aim to		旨在，目的在于
sight	n.	视力	currently	adv.	现在
available	adj.	可用的，可得到的	in that case		如果那样的话
website	n.	网站			

36.【答案】D

【考点】细节题

【分析】本题询问根据第一段，图书馆将申请表寄给读者的原因是什么。根据本文第一段第三句 With it we are sending you an application form, so that you can join if you would like to try it 可知，图书馆寄申请表给读者的目的是为了读者能够加入，即能够使用图书馆的服务。故 D 选项为正确答案。连词 so that 是一个非常明显的表示原因的信号。

37.【答案】C

【考点】细节题

【分析】本题询问 Calibre 图书馆主要给什么样的人提供服务。根据第二段第一句 Calibre library aims to provide the pleasure of reading to anyone who cannot read ordinary print books because of sight problems 可知，图书馆的目标人群是有视力问题的人。故 C 选项为正确答案。

38.【答案】C

【考点】细节题

【分析】本题询问通过邮递来借书和还书的服务是怎样的。从第二段最后一句 They are sent and returned by post, free of charge 可知，邮递借书和还书的服务是免费的。故 C 选项为正确答案。

39.【答案】B

【考点】细节题

【分析】本题询问有一种使用图书馆服务的简单方法是什么。根据本文第三段第三句 The easy way to use Calibre library is to tell us what sorts of books you like, ... 可知，这种方法是告诉图书馆你喜欢什么种类的图书。故 B 选项是正确答案。

40.【答案】A

【考点】主旨题

【分析】本题询问这封信的主要目的是什么。这封信在开头简要介绍了图书馆的目标人群和规模之后，主要着墨于怎样申请加入、怎样借书还书、怎样借到自己想要的书等等。我们可以得出结论，这封信的主要目的是向读者介绍图书馆的服务。故 A 选项为正确答案。

▶（Task 2）大意

　　本文介绍和讨论了新的互联网网址系统将会使用包括中文在内的 16 种语言作为网址的情况。人们将能使用字符作为网址，而不仅仅是以前的罗马字母。而且网址的后缀将可以使用包括繁体中文和简体中文在内的其他 16 种语言。但由于一些语言，特别是中文，存在一词多义现象，也会导致一些问题产生。专家还预测公司之间会出现为了争夺流行语作为网址名的竞争。

【核心词汇】

native	adj.	本国的，本土的	governing	adj.	管理的，治理的
approve	v.	批准，赞同	up to		多达
other than		除了	traditional	adj.	传统的
simplified	adj.	简化了的	work out		解决
competition	n.	竞争	obtain	v.	获得，得到
approval	n.	批准，赞同			

41.【答案】A

【考点】细节题

【分析】本题询问中文使用者现在只能使用什么作为网络地址。根据第一段第二句 Neither can Chinese speakers, who have to rely on pinyin 可知，中文使用者现在只能依靠拼音作为网址。故 A 选项为正确答案。

42.【答案】D

　　【考点】推断题

　　【分析】本题询问 ICANN（互联网名称与数字地址分配机构）对 16 种语言使用的批准能够让网民们怎么样。从第一段第一句 People in some countries cannot use their native language for Web addresses 可知，以前人们无法用自己的母语作为网址。从第一段第三句 But last Friday, ICANN, the Web's governing body, approved the use of up to 16 languages for the new system 可知，经过 ICANN 的批准，情况有所改变。故 D 选项为正确答案。第二段第二句 People will soon be able to use addresses in characters other than those of the Roman alphabet. 也可说明这一点。

43.【答案】C

　　【考点】细节题

　　【分析】本题询问新系统将会允许网址的后缀以什么来表示。根据第二段最后一句 The change will also allow the suffix to be expressed in 16 other alphabets, including traditional and simplified Chinese Characters 可知，新系统将允许网址的后缀由繁体和简体中文在内的其他 16 种语言来表示。故 C 选项为正确答案。

44.【答案】A

　　【考点】细节题

　　【分析】本题询问使用新系统会出现哪种问题。根据第三段第一句 But there are still some problems to work out 和第二句 Experts have discussed what to do with characters that have several different meanings 可知，使用新系统将出现的问题是有些字符有好几种不同的意思。故 A 选项为正确答案。

45.【答案】D

　　【考点】细节题

　　【分析】本题询问很多专家不相信什么。从最后一段第一句 Most experts doubt the change will have a major effect on how the Internet is used 可知，大部分专家都觉得这个改变不会给互联网的使用带来大的影响。故 D 选项为正确答案。这一题的关键是要知道动词 doubt（怀疑）有否定语义，表示不相信某事，即 don't believe。

▶（Task 3）大意

　　本文为一则国际 IT 公司的招聘广告。广告包括岗位描述、对应聘者的要求及联系方法。

【核心词汇】

expanding	*adj.*	扩展的，扩充的	employee	*n.*	雇员
major	*v.*	主修	flexible	*adj.*	灵活的
efficient	*adj.*	效率高的，能干的	certificate	*n.*	证书
keyboard	*n.*	键盘	detail	*n.*	细节

46. 【答案】Hangzhou

　　【考点】细节题

　　【分析】本题询问此工作岗位的地点在哪里。根据文章第一部分最后一句话 You to be working in <u>Hangzhou</u> 可知，工作地点为杭州。

47. 【答案】Computer Science

　　【考点】细节题

　　【分析】本题询问应聘者需是什么专业的大学毕业生。根据文中第四部分的 A college graduate, majoring in <u>Computer Science</u> 可知，应聘者应该是计算机科学专业的大学毕业生。

48. 【答案】efficient

　　【考点】细节题

　　【分析】本题询问应聘者应该具备怎样的个人素质。根据文中第四部分的 Flexible, <u>efficient</u>, active 可知应聘者应该灵活、能干、活跃。

49. 【答案】unusual hours

　　【考点】细节题

　　【分析】本题询问本岗位的工作时间是怎样的。根据第四部分的最后一句话 Able to work <u>unusual hours</u>, e.g. 7 p.m. to 3 a.m. 可知，本工作岗位的工作时间是与众不同的。

50. 【答案】www.aaaltd.cn

　　【考点】细节题

　　【分析】本题询问访问哪个网站可以知道该工作的详情。根据全文最后一句话 For more details about the job, please visit our website: <u>www.aaaltd.cn</u> 可知正确答案。

▶ (Task 4) 大意

　　【答案】51. I, M　52. L, Q　53. N, G　54. E, B　55. K, P

　　【汉译】

A—年度奖金	B—基本工资	C—津贴	D—佣金
E—猎头	F—健康保险	G—住房基金	H—职业介绍所
I—招聘会	J—工作机会	K—劳务市场	L—劳动合同
M—最低工资	N—养老保险	O—试用期	P—失业保险
Q—福利			

▶（**Task 5**）大意

这是两封信。第一封信是销售经理罗伯特·罗福特斯写给约翰·坎贝尔的询价信，在信中他询问了山地自行车的价格及销售条件。第二封信是约翰·坎贝尔回复的报价信，他随信寄上了产品目录和价目单，并表示期待对方的订单。

【核心词汇】

mountain bike		山地自行车	terms	*n.* 条件，条款
favorable	*adj.*	有利的	inquire	*v.* 询问，打听
reasonable	*adj.*	合理的	price list	价目单
enclose	*v.*	附上	order	*n.* 订单，订货

56.【答案】mountain bikes

【考点】细节题

【分析】本题询问第一封信询问的是什么产品。根据第一封信第一句话 We...about your latest model of <u>mountain bikes</u>, in which we are very much interested 可知，第一封信询问的是山地自行车。

57.【答案】terms of sales

【考点】细节题

【分析】本题询问罗伯特·罗福特斯想知道山地车的什么信息。根据第一封信第三句话 Please send us further details of your prices and <u>terms of sales</u> 可知，他想知道的是山地车的价格和对方的销售条件。

58.【答案】price list

【考点】细节题

【分析】本题询问第二封信随信寄上了什么。根据第二封信第二句话 We are pleased to send you the catalogue and <u>price list</u> you asked for 可知，随信附上了目录和价目表。

59.【答案】sales

【考点】细节题

【分析】本题询问第二封信是谁写的。根据第二封信最后的署名 Jonh Campbell 及名字下面的 <u>Sales Manager</u> 可知，写信者 John Campbell 的职位是销售经理。

60.【答案】reasonable

【考点】细节题

【分析】本题询问约翰·坎贝尔认为他们对产品的报价是怎么样的。根据第二封信的第三句话 You will find our quotation <u>reasonable</u> with attractive terms of sales 可知，他觉得自己公司的报价合理，而且销售条件也很吸引人。

Part IV Translation — English into Chinese

61. 【答案】C—B—A—D

【分析】此句是一个倒装句。由于含有否定词的短语 not until 放到了句首，be 动词 were 提到了主语 they 前面，进行部分倒装。此句型应翻译为"直到……，才……"。解答本题还需要理解短语 be aware of（意识到，知道）。选项 A 和 D 结构翻译有问题。而 B 选项加译了"该修理了"。故选项 C 为最佳答案。

62. 【答案】B—C—A—D

【分析】解答本题的一个关键是要认清句中几个动作的关系。主句的动作 sent an email（发邮件）发生在一星期前。asking about the goods（询问货物）与 sent 同时发生，作伴随状语。we had ordered 作为一个省略了关系代词的定语从句修饰先行词 goods，表明这些货物是之前我们预订的。因此选项 B 为最佳答案。

63. 【答案】A—C—D—B

【分析】正确翻译此句的关键除了理解 candidate（候选人），apply for（申请），be expected to（被指望，被要求做某事）be skilled at（擅长），spoken English（英语口语）这几处之外，还要能分析出 applying for this job 是现在分词作后置定语修饰 candidates，即申请这份工作的应聘者。故 A 选项为最佳答案。B 选项将 expect 误译为了主动语态。C 选项没有译出 be good at，"受聘人员"也翻译得不准确。D 选项没有译出 be skilled at 和 spoken，并加译了"有可能"。

64. 【答案】D—C—B—A

【分析】此句中的 it 是形式主语，逻辑主语为后面的 that 从句。正确翻译此句需要理解 it is widely accepted that（人们普遍认为），cultural industry（文化产业）和 key industries（支柱产业）。还要注意此句的时态是现在完成时，宜翻译成"已……"。因此选项 D 为最佳答案。

65. 【答案】《学生报》现招聘记者。申请人必须是在校大学生，并且有至少一年的新闻报道写作经验。受聘者将负责报道本市新闻和校园新闻。如有兴趣，请将申请表于 6 月底前寄至《学生报》办公室。欲知更多信息，请访问我们的网站。

【分析】这是一则招聘广告，故翻译时应尽量使用书面语言。翻译时应注意根据中文习惯和招聘广告文体的需要，适当进行意译，不宜死抠字眼。如 look for 不宜翻译成"寻找"、should be studying at the university now 不宜翻译成"应该正在大学学习"、successful applicant 不宜翻译成"成功的申请人"。be expected to 本意为"被期待做某事、被要求做某事"，但此处引出的是记者的岗位描述，所以译为"将负责做某事"比较好。happenings 本意为事件，但此处翻译成"新闻"较好。

Part V Writing

【考点】商务信函

【解题技巧分析】本文要求写一篇信函。具体格式请参见本书第一部分"写作题型透析"。

【范文】

Dec. 20, 2009

Dear Zhang Wei,

We are going to hold a dinner party to celebrate the 30th anniversary of our company in the Holiday Inn on Tuesday, Dec. 29.

We would be greatly honored if you can come to our party, for you have supported and cooperated with us for years.

We sincerely hope you can attend.

Faithfully yours,

Mike Kennedy

General Manager

UST Electronics Corporation

2009 年 6 月高等学校英语应用能力考试（B 级）
参考答案与应考指南

Part I Listening Comprehension

 1. C 2. A 3. D 4. B 5. C 6. C 7. B 8. A 9. D 10. C

11. Welcome 12. local time 13. rain 14. arrive 15. stay

Part II Structure

Section A

16.【答案】A

 【考点】介词用法

 【译文】买卖双方最基本的差别是什么?

 【分析】介词 between 意为"在……之间"，用于两者之间，difference between 表示"两者之间的差别"。介词 among 意为"在……之间"，用于三者或三者以上。

 【参考例句】She is among the rich.（她是个有钱人。）

17.【答案】C

 【考点】词义辨析和句意理解

 【译文】杰克给航空公司打电话，确认今天早上飞往北京的航班。

 【分析】confirm 意为"确认"；improve 意为"改善"；believe 意为"相信"；insure 意为"确保，保证"。根据句意选项 C 为正确答案。

 【参考例句】

 （1）He has improved his health.（他改善了他的健康状况。）

 （2）I believe he will win at last.（我相信他最后一定会胜利。）

 （3）Their support will insure me success.（他们的支持将成为我成功的保证。）

18.【答案】B

 【考点】强调句型

 【译文】在 2002 年他们在中国建立了分公司。

 【分析】it 引导的强调句是用来对句中某一成分加以强调，其结构为：It is/was + 被强调部分 + that/who...，若去掉 It is/was...that/who...，句式结构和句意依旧完整。

【参考例句】

我昨天在街上遇见了约翰。

(1) <u>It was I that/who</u> met John in the street yesterday.（强调主语）

(2) <u>It was John that</u> I met in the street yesterday.（强调宾语）

(3) <u>It was yesterday that</u> I met John in the street.（强调地点状语，不可用 where）

19. 【答案】D

【考点】词组辨析和句意理解

【译文】你最好在做项目计划之前咨询一下。

【分析】ask for 意为"请求，要求"；put down 意为"记下，镇压"；take in 意为"吸收，理解"；turn out 意为"结果是，证明是"。根据句意选项 D 为正确答案。

【参考例句】

(1) Please <u>put down</u> what I told you just now.（请记下我刚告诉你的事情。）

(2) I couldn't <u>take in</u> the meaning of the word.（我不能理解这个词的含义。）

(3) It <u>turned out</u> to be a fine day.（结果那天是个好天气。）

20. 【答案】A

【考点】定语从句

【译文】现在年轻人的生活方式是他们父辈们从来没有梦想过的。

【分析】关系代词 which 指代先行词 lifestyle，在定语从句中充当宾语。

【用法拓展】定语从句一般由关系代词或关系副词引导。当定语从句修饰人时，用关系代词 who, whom 或 that 引导；修饰物时，用关系代词 which 或 that 引导；修饰表示时间、地点或原因的名词时，则分别用关系副词 when, where 和 why 引导。

【参考例句】

(1) The person <u>who/that</u> talked to you just now came from Canada.（刚才和你讲话的那个人来自加拿大。）

(2) There are moments <u>when</u> I missed my mother very much.（有时候我很想念母亲。）

(3) This is the place <u>where</u> he works.（这是他工作的地方。）

(4) This is the reason <u>why</u> I have done it.（这就是我这样做的原因。）

21. 【答案】B

【考点】词组辨析和句意理解

【译文】在法国旅行的时候，他学会了些日常法语。

【分析】pick up 意为"捡起；获得；学会"；give up 意为"放弃，戒除"；draw up 意为"写出，草拟"；get up 意为"起床，起立"。根据句意选项 B 为正确答案。

【参考例句】

(1) We should never <u>give up</u> our dreams.（我们永远都不能放弃梦想。）

(2) We <u>drew up</u> the contract yesterday.（我们昨天拟订了合同。）

(3) I <u>get up</u> early every morning.（我每天早上起得很早。）

22.【答案】D

　　【考点】倒装结构和时态

　　【译文】我刚到办公室电话就响了。

　　【分析】hardly 放在句首时句子要倒装。动作 arrive 在动词 ring 之前发生，ring 使用了过去时，故 arrive 要使用过去完成时，故选项 D 为正确答案。

　　【用法拓展】否定词开头的句子要用倒装结构，这类词有 not only...but also..., never, not until, hardly, seldom, by no means 等。

　　【参考例句】

　　（1）Never shall I forget the day.（我绝不会忘记这一天。）

　　（2）Not only does he like English, but also he learns it well.（他不仅喜欢英语，而且学得很好。）

23.【答案】C

　　【考点】词义辨析和句意理解

　　【译文】为了有效使用机器，你必须仔细阅读说明。

　　【分析】efficiently 意为"有效率地"；firstly 意为"首要地"；naturally 意为"自然地"；generally 意为"通常地"。根据句意选项 C 为正确答案。

　　【参考例句】

　　（1）There are three reasons why I support this idea. Firstly, we may get lots of benefits from it.（我支持这个观点有三点原因。首先，我们能从中受益。）

　　（2）Her hair is naturally wavy.（她的头发天生卷曲。）

　　（3）The child generally has little to say.（这个小孩总是没什么话要说。）

24.【答案】A

　　【考点】连词用法

　　【译文】如果今天我们不能做最后决定，明天还得继续讨论。

　　【分析】unless 意为"如果不，除非"，相当于 if...not...，引导条件状语从句；because 意为"因为"，引导原因状语从句；when 意为"当……时候"，引导时间状语从句。

25.【答案】A

　　【考点】词义辨析和句意理解

　　【译文】如果你有三年的工作经验，你将是这个工作最合适的人选。

　　【分析】person 意为"人"，泛指；passenger 意为"乘客"；tourist 意为"游客"；customer 意为"顾客"。根据句意选项 A 为正确答案。

Section B

26.【答案】successfully

　　【考点】词形转换

　　【译文】据报道，运动会组织得非常成功。

　　【分析】修饰动词 organize 需要用 successful 的副词形式。

　　【用法拓展】大部分副词由 "adj. + ly" 构成，如：kind (adj.) → kindly (adv.), brave (adj.) → bravely (adv.) 等。

27. 【答案】more

　　【考点】比较级

　　【译文】有些人想得更多的是他们的权利而非他们的义务。

　　【分析】由比较级标志性词语 than 得知，此处要用 much 的比较级 more。

28. 【答案】rose

　　【考点】过去时

　　【译文】据报道，去年该国进口车的销售增长了 8%。

　　【分析】由 last year 得知，该句应使用过去时态。

29. 【答案】(should) start

　　【考点】虚拟语气

　　【译文】顾问建议玛丽应尽快开始训练课程。

　　【分析】recommend 后接的 that 引导的宾语从句要使用虚拟语气，动词形式为 (should) do。

　　【用法拓展】suggest（建议），order（命令），demand（要求）等后接由 that 引导的从句时也要使用虚拟语气，动词形式为 (should) do。

　　【参考例句】

　　（1）He <u>suggested</u> that we (should) start now.（他建议我们现在就开始。）

　　（2）Workers <u>demanded</u> that they (should) get more money.（工人们要求获得更多的钱。）

　　（3）He <u>orders</u> that we (should) leave now.（他命令我们现在就离开。）

30. 【答案】attractive

　　【考点】词形转换

　　【译文】这个工作薪水很高，而且每年还有 20 天的假期，所以当然很吸引人。

　　【分析】修饰名词 offer 应该用 attract 的形容词形式 attractive。

　　【用法拓展】很多形容词以 -tive 结尾，如：active（积极的），creative（有创造力的），competitive（竞争的）等。

31. 【答案】was announced

　　【考点】被动语态和过去时

　　【译文】昨天宣布该比赛将在一周后开始。

　　【分析】事情是被宣布，故用动词 announce 的被动语态，从句中使用了将来时的过去时态 was to，故主句也要使用过去时。

32. 【答案】additional

　　【考点】词形转换

　　【译文】因为有很多人会参加该会议，所以我们需要更多的椅子。

　　【分析】修饰名词 chairs 需要用 addition 的形容词形式 additional。

　　【用法拓展】很多形容词以 -al 结尾，如：national（全国的），emotional（激动的）等。

33. 【答案】to take

    【考点】动词不定式

    【译文】不允许读者把参考书带出阅览室。

    【分析】allow 的用法为 allow sb. to do sth.，意为"允许某人做某事"。

    【用法拓展】有些动词后只能接动名词形式，如：finish, avoid, enjoy, mind, consider 等。

    【参考例句】

    （1）I am considering going abroad.（我正在考虑出国。）

    （2）He has finished doing his work.（他已经干完了他的工作。）

34. 【答案】to practice

    【考点】动词不定式的并列结构

    【译文】设计该课程是为了概要地介绍计算机知识和开展实际技术培训。

    【分析】to provide 和 to practice 是并列结构。

35. 【答案】make

    【考点】had better 的用法

    【译文】我们在巴黎只呆一天，所以我们最好充分利用时间。

    【分析】had better 后接动词原形，表示"最好做某事"。

Part III Reading Comprehension

▶ （Task 1）大意

本文为说明文。文章围绕美国地铁、公交车和出租车的基本情况介绍了美国的交通状况。

【核心词汇】

subway	n.	地铁	purchase	v.	购买
suburb	n.	郊区	available	adj.	可获得的
schedule	n.	时间表；预定计划	fare	n.	车票

【难句分析】第一段第一句话：Subways are underground trains, which usually operate 24 hours a day. 该句是含有 which 引导的定语从句的复合句。operate 意为"运行，起作用"，故该句意思是"地铁是地下火车，通常一天24小时运营"。

36. 【答案】D

    【考点】细节题

    【分析】根据题干关键词 subways 可将答案定位在第一段，由第一段第二句话中 …run between the suburbs and the downtown area 得知，选项 D 为正确答案。

37. 【答案】D

    【考点】细节题

    【分析】根据题干关键词 subways 可将答案定位在第一段，由该段第三句话 Maps and schedules are available from the ticket office 得知，选项 D 为正确答案。

38.【答案】C

【考点】细节题

【分析】根据四个选项的关键词 bus 可将答案定位在第二段，由该段最后一句话 Fare is paid by exact change in coins... 得知，选项 C 为正确答案。

39.【答案】B

【考点】细节题

【分析】根据题干关键词 taxi 可将答案定位在第三段，由该段第二句话 If you use a taxi, be sure you ask the amount of the fare before you agree or ride 得知，选项 B 为正确答案。

40.【答案】C

【考点】主旨题

【分析】本题询问全篇大意，选项 A，B 和 D 都只涉及到一个方面，选项 C 最为全面，能概括大意，故选项 C 为正确答案。

▶（Task 2）大意

本文由两封信组成。第一封信中玛丽向安询问成功举办晚宴的秘诀，第二封信中安告诉玛丽成功举办晚宴的基本原则。

【核心词汇】

comfortable	adj.	舒适的	treat	v.	款待，请客
offer	v.	提供	naturally	adv.	自然地
provide	v.	提供	atmosphere	n.	气氛，氛围

【难句分析】第二封信最后一段第二句话：Treat your guests as you want them to treat you when you're in their home—that is, act naturally toward them, and don't try too hard to be polite. 该句较长，正确的理解为"招待你的客人就像当你在他们家时你希望他们对待你那样——那就是自然地对待他们，不要因为出于礼貌而过于热情"。

41.【答案】A

【考点】推断题

【分析】根据第一封信的最后一句话 What's the secret of giving a successful party? 得知，玛丽向安询问成功举办晚宴的秘诀，与该句意思相符的只有选项 A。

42.【答案】D

【考点】细节题

【分析】根据题干关键词 first piece of advice 可将答案定位在第二封信的第一段，由该段第二句话 If a guest offers to help you in the kitchen, accept the offer 得知，选项 D 为正确答案。

43.【答案】A

　　【考点】细节题

　　【分析】根据题干关键词 drinks 可将答案定位在第二封信的第二段，由该段第一句话
　　　　　　...while your guests make small talks...offer them drinks 得知，选项 A 为正确答案。

44.【答案】D

　　【考点】细节题

　　【分析】本题询问就餐时该如何招待客人。根据第二封信的第三段第一句话 At the
　　　　　　dinner table, let your guests serve themselves 得知，选项 D 为正确答案。

45.【答案】B

　　【考点】细节题

　　【分析】根据题干关键词 the most important rule 可将答案定位在第二封信的第四段，由
　　　　　　该段第一句话 Perhaps the most important rule of all is to be natural 得知，选项 B
　　　　　　为正确答案。

▶（Task 3）大意

　　本文是一则公告，告知人们看见犯罪活动时该如何举报，可以拨打举报热线，拨打工
作人员电话或拨打警长电话。

【核心词汇】

crime	*n.*	犯罪	contact	*v.*	联系
officer	*n.*	政府官员	chief	*n.*	长官
staff	*n.*	工作人员	reply	*n.*	回答

46.【答案】information

　　【考点】细节题

　　【分析】本题询问举报犯罪时可以匿名提供什么。根据第二段第二句话 You can leave
　　　　　　information anonymously... 得知，可以匿名给出信息 information。

47.【答案】call you back

　　【考点】细节题

　　【分析】本题询问在留下名字和电话号码后，需等工作人员怎么样。根据第二段第二
　　　　　　句话中 ...an officer will call you back 得知，需等工作人员给你回电话。

48.【答案】8:00—16:00

　　【考点】细节题

　　【分析】本题询问警察在工作日的工作时间。根据第三段第一句话 ...who receives the
　　　　　　call weekdays, 8:00—16:00. 得知，警察的工作时间为工作日的上午 8 点到下午
　　　　　　4 点。

49.【答案】612-349-7200

　　【考点】细节题

　　【分析】本题询问警察局的电话号码。根据第三段第二句话 Call <u>612-349-7200.</u> 可知答案。

50.【答案】half a day

　　【考点】细节题

　　【分析】本题询问当多久没有收到举报热线的回复时需要给警长打电话。根据最后一段第一句话 If you haven't received any reply to your Tip Line information for <u>half a day</u>, directly call 612-349-7100... 得知时间 half a day。

▶（Task 4）

　　【答案】 51. C, F　　52. M, I　　53. K, H　　54. E, G　　55. D, L

　　【汉译】

A—微风	B—平静海面	C—天气放晴
D—天气干燥	E—有雾	F—大雪
G—海面大浪	H—小雨	I—局部多云
J—阵雨	K—东南风	L—暴风雨
M—最高温度	N—最低温度	O—台风
P—潮湿	Q—有风	

▶（Task 5）大意

　　本文由两则广告组成。第一则广告提出了招聘销售部经理个人助理的要求，第二则广告提出了招聘兼职司机的要求。

【核心词汇】

personal	*adj.*	个人的	hire	*v.*	雇佣
assistant	*n.*	助理	license	*n.*	许可证，执照
previous	*adj.*	先前的	acceptable	*adj.*	可以接受的

56.【答案】the sales department

　　【考点】细节题

　　【分析】本题询问广告一中公司的哪个部门招聘经理助理。根据广告一的第二句话 We are looking for someone to assist the manager of <u>the sales department</u>... 可知是销售部门。

57.【答案】from abroad

【考点】细节题

【分析】本题询问经理助理的主要职责是什么。根据广告一的第二句话 ...in dealing with foreign customers and orders <u>from abroad</u> 可知其主要职责是处理国外客户和海外定单。

58.【答案】Spanish and Italian

【考点】细节题

【分析】本题询问在广告一中经理助理申请者的优势是什么。根据广告一第一段的最后一句话 Some knowledge of <u>Spanish and Italian</u> would be an advantage 可知优势是会西班牙语和意大利语。

59.【答案】21

【考点】细节题

【分析】本题询问广告二中招聘兼职司机职位的年龄限制。根据广告二中 Must be <u>21</u> years or older 可知年龄限制是 21 岁或以上。

60.【答案】Washington State

【考点】细节题

【分析】本题询问申请者申请兼职司机必须有哪里的驾照。根据广告二 have a <u>Washington State</u> driver's license 可知必须要有华盛顿州的驾照。

Part IV Translation — English into Chinese

61.【答案】B—D—A—C

【分析】此句含有由 so...that... 引导的结果状语从句。此句中 so...that... 意为"如此……以至于……"，inexperienced lawyer 意为"缺乏经验的律师"。选项 D"不敢接手处理"不够准确，选项 A"不敢接手"语意不正确，选项 C"不应让有经验的律师来处理"语意完全背离本意，故最佳答案选 B。

62.【答案】D—B—C—A

【分析】此句含有由 no matter how 引导的让步状语从句。此句中 no matter how 意为"不管……"，operate the machine 意为"操作这台机器"，at a loss 意为"困惑"。选项 B"机器的用法"不够精确，选项 C"他们不相信我的话"语意不正确，选项 A"把机器开动了"，"觉得非常失望"语意完全背离本意，故最佳答案选 D。

63.【答案】A—D—C—B

【分析】此句中 returns or exchanges 意为"退或换"，within 30 days 意为"30 天内"，purchase 意为"购买"。选项 D"30 天之内购买的手机"不够准确，选项 C"30 天内可以购买手机"表意不正确，选项 B"试用"完全背离此句的意思，故最佳答案选 A。

64.【答案】C—B—D—A

【分析】此句含有由 which 引导的定语从句，which 指代先行词 environment。value 意为"重视"。选项 B"应该"一词翻译不够精确，选项 D"为了共同的目标"是"创造良好的工作氛围"的目的，应该放在此句之后，选项 A"要做好经理"语意完全背离本意，故最佳答案选 C。

65.【答案】如果你想要获得驾照，你必须向驾照办公室提出申请。你需要参加该地区考驾照的笔试。还需要通过视力测验。如果你需要戴眼镜，请务必携带。此外，你还必须通过实际（道路）驾驶测试。如果你没有通过笔试或者实际驾驶测试，你可以择日再考。

【分析】段落翻译时需要注意翻译技巧，在对英语结构和句意理解的基础上还要注意符合汉语的表达习惯。apply 意为"申请"，require 意为"要求"，in addition 意为"此外"。

Part V Writing

【考点】信函写作

【解题技巧分析】信函写作应注意格式（具体格式参见第一部分"写作题型透视"）。写作过程中若能把握好格式、表达和语言三方面就能拿高分。

【范文】

Dear Mr. Baker,

　　Welcome to Fuzhou.

　　Considering your journey here, our company has already booked a room for you in Orient Hotel, which is about 20 kilometers away from the International Airport. You can get there by taxi or shuttle bus. I will appreciate it if we can have a negotiation about our business the following day after you arrive.

　　Call us if you need help, and I hope you will have a nice trip.

Yours sincerely,

Wang Dong

Hongxia Trading Company

2008 年 12 月高等学校英语应用能力考试（B 级）
参考答案与应考指南

Part I Listening Comprehension

1. A   2. B   3. C   4. B   5. D   6. B   7. D   8. A   9. D   10. C

11. on business   12. safe   13. For example   14. helpful   15. always

Part II Vocabulary & Structure

Section A

16.【答案】C

【考点】动宾搭配

【译文】有关这个新系统的信息很容易在互联网上找到。

【分析】该句中的主语 information 是空格处动词的逻辑宾语。根据题意与 information 搭配的动词只能是 find, 故选项 C 为正确答案。

17.【答案】B

【考点】动名词

【译文】我们交谈了三个多小时连一杯茶都没有喝。

【分析】介词 without 后的宾语需要由名词、代词或动名词来充当, 选项 B 是 have 的动名词形式, 故为正确答案。

18.【答案】A

【考点】词组辨析

【译文】这家大型的信息技术公司将会在这座城市建立一个新的研究中心。

【分析】空格处需填入的动词词组与后面的 a new research center 构成动宾关系, 符合题意的只有 set up, 意为"建立, 设立"。break up 意为"破裂, 分解", get up 意为"起床", turn up 意为"出现, 调高"。

19.【答案】D

【考点】名词辨析

【译文】昨天晚上我们和他一起讨论了这个问题。

【分析】explanation 意为"解释, 说明", impression 意为"印象", exhibition 意为"展览", discussion 意为"讨论", 根据题意, 选项 D 为正确答案。

【用法拓展】have a discussion with sb. about sth. 意为"与某人讨论某事"。

20.【答案】D

【考点】固定搭配

【译文】她简要地跟我们说了他们是怎样成功开发新产品的。

【分析】固定搭配 succeed in doing sth. 意为"成功做某事"，故选项 D 为正确答案。

21.【答案】A

【考点】连词用法

【译文】虽然她进公司才一年，但已经得到两次晋升了。

【分析】although 意为"虽然，尽管"，引导让步状语从句；because 意为"因为"，引导原因状语从句；if 意为"如果"，引导条件状语从句；when 意为"当……时候"，引导时间状语从句。从句中的 joined the company only a year ago 与主句中的 been promoted twice 存在一种让步关系，故选项 A 为正确答案。

22.【答案】C

【考点】词组辨析

【译文】因为已经用完了所有的资金，所以他们不得不放弃那个计划。

【分析】run out of 意为"用完，耗尽"，come up to 意为"达到，符合"，get along with 意为"与……相处"，take charge of 意为"负责，掌管"。根据题意选项 C 为正确答案。

【参考例句】

（1）He didn't come up to my need.（他不能达到我的需求。）

（2）Do you get along with your boss?（你跟老板合得来吗?）

（3）I'll take charge of this project.（我将负责这项工程。）

23.【答案】D

【考点】过去进行时

【译文】当警察拦住我时，我正以每小时 130 公里的速度驾驶。

【分析】该句的从句中 stopped 为过去时态，主句强调过去某个时间点正在进行的动作，用过去进行时，故选项 D 为正确答案。

【用法拓展】when 引导时间状语从句可引出一个过去进行时态的句子，表示在某事发生的过程中另一件事正在发生。

【参考例句】

When they arrived, we were having dinner.（他们到时，我们正在吃饭。）

24.【答案】A

【考点】词义辨析

【译文】据报纸报道，两个人在此次事故中丧生。

【分析】该句的从句内容是一则新闻报道，动词 say 意为"报道，宣布，公布"，常用于报纸、广播和社论等，故选项 A 为正确答案。

25.【答案】B

【考点】固定搭配

【译文】我想把你介绍给我们部门的新经理——詹姆斯·斯图尔特。

【分析】固定搭配 introduce sb./sth. to sb. 意为"向某人介绍某人 / 某物"，故选项 B 为正确答案。

Section B

26.【答案】national

　　【考点】词形转换

　　【译文】新的国家博物馆将于下周向公众开放。

　　【分析】修饰名词 museum 应使用形容词形式。

　　【用法拓展】名词加后缀 -al 可构成形容词，表示"……的，具有……特性的"，如：
traditional（传统的），formal（正式的），original（最初的）等。

27.【答案】more difficult

　　【考点】形容词比较级

　　【译文】这个问题比我刚才回答的问题更难。

　　【分析】than 是比较级的标志性词语，故使用 difficult 的比较级 more difficult。

28.【答案】manager

　　【考点】词形转换

　　【译文】这个秘书已经为同一个经理工作了五年多。

　　【分析】the same 后接表示人的名词，work for sb. 意为"为某人工作"，故空格处应填名词 manager。

　　【用法拓展】manage 的名词形式有两种：manager（经理），management（管理）。

29.【答案】built

　　【考点】非谓语动词

　　【译文】这座建于 100 年前的宾馆看上去仍然很新。

　　【分析】该句有谓语动词，空格处只能填非谓语动词形式。动词 build 的逻辑主语与主句主语 the hotel 相同，并与 the hotel 存在被动关系，故用 build 的过去分词形式作定语修饰 the hotel。

　　【用法拓展】非谓语动词有三种形式：动词不定式、过去分词和现在分词。作定语时，动词不定式表示将来要发生的动作，过去分词表示动作已经发生并与逻辑主语构成被动关系，现在分词表示动作正在进行与逻辑主语构成主动关系。

　　【参考例句】

　　（1）The meeting to be held tomorrow is put off now.（明天要举行的会议现在推迟了。）

　　（2）Most people invited to the party were old friends.（被邀请参加聚会的多是些老朋友。）

　　（3）Who is the man talking to your sister?（正在跟你妹妹谈话的那个人是谁？）

30.【答案】was solved

　　【考点】一般过去时和被动语态

　　【译文】我们很高兴地了解到那个问题在昨天的会议上已经解决了。

　　【分析】从句的主语 the problem 与动词 solve 之间存在逻辑上的被动关系，并且从句中 yesterday 表示过去发生的事情，故空格处应填一般过去时的被动语态。

31.【答案】to point out

　　【考点】动词不定式

　　【译文】我想指出的是必须马上对那件事情做出决定。

【分析】动词 want 后常接动词不定式，want to do sth. 意为"想做某事"。

【用法拓展】want doing 意为"需要"，表示被动含义，主语通常指物。英语中用这种
　　　　　　形式表达被动关系的还有 need, require。

【参考例句】

Your coat <u>wants washing</u>. （你的衣服该洗了。）

32.【答案】experienced

　　【考点】词形转换

　　【译文】虽然她对这份工作来说还很年轻，但是她很有经验。

　　【分析】系动词 be 后一般接形容词或名词作表语，副词 very 通常用来修饰形容词，故
　　　　　　使用 experience 的形容词形式 experienced。

33.【答案】widely

　　【考点】词形转换

　　【译文】环境保护的新规则已经被公众广泛接受。

　　【分析】修饰动词 accept 应使用副词形式。

　　【用法拓展】副词可以修饰动词、形容词和副词。形容词后加 -ly，或以 y 结尾的形容
　　　　　　词改 y 为 i 再加 ly 可以构成副词，如：bravely（勇敢地），sadly（伤心地），
　　　　　　happily（高兴地）等。

34.【答案】(should) tell

　　【考点】虚拟语气

　　【译文】我们要求导游立即告诉我们有关日程安排的任何变化。

　　【分析】demand 意为"要求"，属于表示命令、愿望、请求、建议等意义的动词，故其
　　　　　　后的宾语从句中谓语动词使用"should + 动词原形"的虚拟式，should 可以省略。

　　【用法拓展】具有相似用法的动词还有：advise, command, insist, order, recommend, request,
　　　　　　require, suggest 等。

35.【答案】inviting

　　【考点】非谓语动词

　　【译文】感谢您 11 月 15 日来信邀请我方参加 12 月 10 日的交易会。

　　【分析】动词 invite 与其逻辑主语 letter 之间构成主动关系，故使用现在分词形式，在
　　　　　　句中作定语。

Part III Reading Comprehension

▶（Task 1）大意

　　本文是一则豪尔集市（Hall Markets）招聘志愿者的启事。文章首先介绍了豪尔集市
的基本情况，然后说明了豪尔集市的开放时间以及开放目的，最后指出志愿者对豪尔集市
的重要作用并热烈欢迎广大志愿者的踊跃报名。

【核心词汇】

stay away		远离	income	*n.*	收入
grateful	*adj.*	感谢的			

【难句分析】第三段最后一句：Hartley Lifecare is always grateful to have you serve as volunteers with the Hall Markets. 该句中含有一个动词不定式作目的状语。整句话的意思为：哈特利公司将会非常感激您能来豪尔集市当志愿者。

36.【答案】A

【考点】细节题

【分析】本题根据文中第一段第二句 Come out to our Hall Markets in the beautiful countryside... 可知选项 A 为正确答案。

37.【答案】C

【考点】细节题

【分析】根据题干关键词 350 stalls 可以将答案定位在文中第一段最后一句：With over 350 stalls selling wonderful home-made and home-grown goods, this will surely be a great day out. 故选项 C 为正确答案。

38.【答案】B

【考点】细节题

【分析】根据题干关键词 income 可以将答案定位在文中第二段最后一句：All the income will go to help and support service for people with disabilities. disabilities 是 disabled 的同义派生词，故选项 B 为正确答案。

39.【答案】A

【考点】细节题

【分析】根据题干关键词 when...open 可以将答案定位在文中第二段第一句：The Hall Markets are held on the first Sunday of each month... 故选项 A 为正确答案。

40.【答案】D

【考点】主旨题

【分析】本题考察的是考生对文章主旨的把握。根据题干关键词 purpose of inviting 可以将答案定位在文中的最后一段，可知本文的目的在于招聘志愿者，故选项 D 为正确答案。

▶（Task 2）大意

本文主要是介绍一本新出版的英语词典。文章先后介绍了出版该词典的目的，该词典的特点，最后希望新词典能够给学习英语的学生和老师带来帮助。

【核心词汇】

produce	v.	生产	look up		查找，查阅
as a result of		作为……的结果	edit	v.	编辑
focus	v.	集中注意力于……	remove	v.	移除

【难句分析】第二段第一句：Examples help students to remember the word they have looked up in the dictionary because it is easier both to remember and to understand a word within a context. 该句是一个含有由 because 引导原因状语从句的复合句。主句中的定语从句 they have looked up in the dictionary 修饰先行词 the word。故该句意思是"例句有助于学生记住他们在词典中所查阅的单词，因为在上下文中理解并记忆单词更容易"。

41.【答案】B

　【考点】细节题

　【分析】根据题干关键词 aim of producing new dictionary 可将答案定位在第一段第一句：...our aim is always the same: what can we do to make the dictionary more helpful for students of English? 选项 B 与此句同，故为正确选项。

42.【答案】D

　【考点】细节题

　【分析】根据题干关键词 easier to remember and understand 可将答案定位在第二段第一句：...it is easier both to remember and to understand a word within a context. 由此可知，单词在上下文中更容易理解和记住。故选项 D 为正确答案。

43.【答案】C

　【考点】细节题

　【分析】根据第二段最后一句：...we have included 40 percent more examples in this new book. 可知选项 C 为正确答案。其他几项均不能说明这本新词典的特别之处。

44.【答案】A

　【考点】细节题

　【分析】根据题干关键词 removing difficult words in the examples 可将答案定位在第三段，故选项 A 为正确答案。

45.【答案】C

　【考点】主旨题

　【分析】本题考查的是考生对文章整体的把握。文章一开始就表明了出版这本新英语词典的目的，然后介绍了这本新词典的特点，最后表达了编者的良好愿望。由此不难判断出本文源自一本词典的介绍。故选项 C 为正确答案。

▶（Task 3）大意

本文是一封邀请函。信中开门见山地提到亚洲经济研究协会荣幸地邀请 Dr. Yamata 在当年举办的年度国际研讨会上做嘉宾发言人，随后介绍了研讨会举办的时间、主题、参会人员等，最后希望 Dr. Yamata 能在 12 月 1 日前告知是否能参会。

【核心词汇】

annual	*adj.*	每年的	expense	*n.*	花销，花费
topic	*n.*	主题	announce	*v.*	宣布，通告
attend	*v.*	参加	look forward to		盼望，期待
cover	*v.*	覆盖，够支付			

46. 【答案】John Smith
   【考点】细节题
   【分析】本题询问写信人，根据书信的一般格式，写信人的签名位于信函的最后。由此可知写信人是 John Smith。

47. 【答案】Asian Economic Studies
   【考点】细节题
   【分析】本题询问研讨会的组织者。根据第一段的第一句话 The Association of Asian Economic Studies is pleased to invite you to... 可知研讨会的组织者是亚洲经济研究协会。

48. 【答案】December 22nd
   【考点】细节题
   【分析】本题询问研讨会开始的日期。根据第一段的第二句话：The symposium will be held for 3 days from December 22nd to 24th, 2008. 可知研讨会的开始日期是 12 月 22 日。

49. 【答案】100 people
   【考点】细节题
   【分析】本题询问被邀请参会的人数。根据第一段的第四句话：About 100 people from various countries will be attending the symposium. 可知将有大约 100 个来自不同国家的参会人员。

50. 【答案】Economic Development
   【考点】细节题
   【分析】本题询问研讨会的主题。根据第一段的第三句话：This year's topic will be Economic Development in Asia. 可知今年的主题为"亚洲的经济发展"。

▶（Task 4）

【答案】51. H, E　　52. K, C　　53. P, L　　54. G, A　　55. M, F

【汉译】

A—售后服务	B—营业执照	C—商业风险
D—滞销品	E—百货商店	F—进口许可证
G—有限公司	H—净重	I—包装费
J—价格标签	K—购买力	L—卖方市场
M—装船日期	N—购物高峰期	O—展示窗
P—超级市场	Q—贸易协定	

▶（Task 5）大意

这是一则 Yanton 运动场委员会招聘场地管理员的招聘广告。文章首先说明了招聘原因，然后指出场地管理员的工作性质、工作职责以及能力要求，最后提供了应聘的联系方式。

【核心词汇】

fortunate	*adj.*	幸运的	equipment	*n.*	设备，装备
retire	*v.*	退休	register	*v.*	注册

56.【答案】Yanton Playingfield Committee

【考点】细节题

【分析】本题询问什么机构招聘场地管理员。根据文章的标题 Yanton Playingfield Committee Grounds-person Wanted 可知答案。

57.【答案】retire in July

【考点】细节题

【分析】本题询问招聘新的场地管理员的原因。根据第一段第二句话：...Eddie has decided it's time to retire in July. 可知招聘的原因是前任场地管理员将在七月份退休。

58.【答案】rolling and trimming

【考点】细节题

【分析】本题询问场地管理员的职责。根据第二段第三句话：The duties involve the mowing, rolling, and trimming of the field edges. 可知答案。

59.【答案】drive and use

【考点】细节题

【分析】本题询问求职人的能力要求。根据第二段最后一句话 Applicants need to drive and use the equipment needed for the above-mentioned duties 可知，求职人需要操作和使用上面提到的各项职责所需要的设备。

60.【答案】Hugh Morris

【考点】细节题

【分析】本题询问招聘机构的联系人。根据第三段第一句话 Applicants can either contact <u>Hugh Morris</u>... 可知答案。

Part IV Translation — English into Chinese

61.【答案】B—C—D—A

【分析】此句关键是对 energy-efficient（高效节能的），save（节省），so...that...（如此……以至于……）的理解。选项 A 将 energy-efficient 译为"功率很高的"不够准确，选项 C 增加了原文没有的内容"电费"欠妥，选项 D 将 save 译成"仅需支付"有明显错误，故最佳答案为 B。

62.【答案】A—D—B—C

【分析】此句关键是对 cancel（取消），could do nothing except（除了……没有办法，只得）的理解以及 because of 和 so 引导的短语和句子之间的因果关系的把握。选项 B 将 could do nothing except 译成"无法"有误，选项 C 将 could do nothing except 译成"坚持"不妥，选项 D 漏译了 cancel 不够精确，故最佳答案为 A。

63.【答案】C—D—B—A

【分析】此句的翻译关键在于理解 more than（不仅仅是）的意思。选项 A 将 more than 译为"如"翻译有误，选项 B 和选项 D 将 more than 误译为"更多"，故最佳答案为 C。

64.【答案】B—C—A—D

【分析】此句是一个由 seldom 引导的倒装句。翻译此句关键在于对 seldom（很少）和 front page（报纸的头版）的理解。选项 A 将 seldom 译为"不会"，将 front page 译为"前几页"都存在明显错误，选项 C 将 front page 译为"第一页"欠妥，选项 D 将 seldom 译为"从不查看"不够准确，故最佳答案为 B。

65.【答案】ABC 铁路公司已经大幅度改善了公司的公众热线服务。您只需拨打 3929-3499 就可以获得关于该公司的所有服务信息。电话信息系统全年为您提供 24 小时服务。客服人员也随时准备提供您所需要的信息。客服人员的工作时间是周一至周日早上七点至晚上九点。

【分析】段落翻译时需注意使用翻译技巧，在对英语结构和句意理解的基础上还要注意符合汉语的表达习惯。本段的第二句和第四句，在翻译时要按照汉语的表达习惯将后置定语提到中心词的前面。第三句在翻译时也要按照汉语的表达习惯将状语 all the year round 提到动词短语前。此段落是对某公司电话服务系统的介绍，翻译时措辞要礼貌得体，语言力求简洁。

Part V Writing

【考点】信函写作

【解题技巧分析】本题要求写一篇感谢信，应注意信函写作格式（具体格式参见第一部分"写作题型透视"）。此外，感谢信语气要诚恳，处处流露出对所受帮助或款待的感激之情。表示感谢的常用表达法有：(1) Thank you for...；(2) I'm grateful/thankful to you for...；(3) I'd like to express my appreciation for your kind...；(4) It's so nice/kind of you to...；(5) My gratitude to you is beyond words. (6) Thank you very much from the bottom of my heart.

【范文】

December 21, 2008

Dear Miss Jane Costa,

I would like to take this opportunity to express my heartful thanks to you for your hospitality in Paris.

Paris has left a good impression on me and the visit will surely become an unforgettable memory in my life. I like the French perfume very much. I learned a lot after visiting the factories and schools.

Again, I'd like to express my warm gratitude to you. I have no doubt that my visit would not have been the success without your hospitable reception. I am looking forward to meeting you again.

Yours sincerely,
Thomas Black

2008 年 6 月高等学校英语应用能力考试（B 级）参考答案与应考指南

Part I Listening Comprehension

1. A　　2. D　　3. B　　4. B　　5. C　　6. C　　7. A　　8. B　　9. A　　10. D

11. degree　　12. other kinds　　13. training class　　14. work　　15. better

Part II Structure

Section A

16.【答案】D

　　【考点】固定搭配

　　【译文】请将你已完成的工作做一份详细记录。

　　【分析】固定搭配 keep a record，意为"做记录"，所以选项 D 为正确答案。

　　【参考例句】Keep a record of how much you spend.（你花了多少钱要记账。）

17.【答案】C

　　【考点】固定搭配

　　【译文】让我们感到惊讶的是，这位新来的秘书会说四门外语。

　　【分析】固定搭配 to one's surprise，意为"让某人吃惊的是"，所以选项 C 正确。

　　【用法拓展】to one's 后的名词可以换成其他词，例如 astonishment, disappointment 等。

　　【参考例句】To our astonishment, Mary cried.（让我们惊讶的是，玛丽哭了。）

18.【答案】B

　　【考点】词组辨析

　　【译文】会议中部门经理提出了促销的新计划。

　　【分析】put forward 意为"提出"，take away 意为"拿走"，look after 意为"照顾"，get on 意为"相处"。

19.【答案】D

　　【考点】表语从句

　　【译文】他告诉我面试前我该做足准备。

　　【分析】本句是主系表结构。What he told me 是句子的主语，was 是句子的谓语动词，其后接的是表语从句。that 是表语从句的引导词，在从句中不充当任何成分。

　　【用法拓展】表语从句的连接词有：that, what, who, when, where, which, why, whether, how 等。

　　【参考例句】The problem is when we can get a pay raise.（问题是我们何时能加薪。）

20.【答案】A

　　【考点】词义辨析

　　【译文】当处理比较难的任务时，艾丽丝总是向周围的人求助。

　　【分析】主句意为"艾丽丝总是向周围的人求助"，可得知是遇到麻烦的事情。difficult
　　　　　意为"困难的"，wonderful 意为"精彩的"，funny 意为"搞笑的"，simple 意
　　　　　为"简单的"，所以选项 A 正确。

21.【答案】A

　　【考点】非谓语动词

　　【译文】计划买房的时候，买房人首先考虑（房子的）地段。

　　【分析】when 后接动词的现在分词，plan 和该句逻辑主语 customer 存在主动关系，故
　　　　　填 planning。

　　【用法拓展】连词后也可以接非谓语的形式。

　　【参考例句】Before writing an application letter, you should be aware what kind of people
　　　　　the employer needs. （在写求职信之前你必须知道雇主需要什么样的人。）

22.【答案】C

　　【考点】词义辨析

　　【译文】与去年相比，这个市的软饮料销售量增加了 8%。

　　【分析】pick 意为"捡起，挑选"，move 意为"移动"，push 意为"推"。只有 increase
　　　　　符合题意，意为"增加"。介词 by 表示幅度，后接具体数字。

23.【答案】B

　　【考点】虚拟语气

　　【译文】如果我昨天没参加一个重要会议，我就会来见你了。

　　【分析】从句和主句都表示所讲述内容与过去某个时间的事实相反，因此从句中使用
　　　　　了 if + 主语 + had done，而主句中用主语 + would have done。

　　【用法拓展】从句若表示与现在事实相反用 if + 主语 + 动词过去式，从句表示与将来事实
　　　　　相反用 if + 主语 + should/were to。主句若表示与现在事实相反用主语 + would + 动
　　　　　词原形；表示与将来事实相反用主语 + should/will/would + 动词原形。

　　【参考例句】

　　（1）If I were you, I would hurry up. （要是换了我，我就会加紧。）

　　（2）If I were to do it, I will do it in a different way. （如果我来做，我会用另一种方式。）

24.【答案】B

　　【考点】词义辨析

　　【译文】第一次若要拿到那个国家的入境签证，你必须亲自申请。

　　【分析】in part 意为"部分地"，in person 意为"亲自"，in turn 意为"依次，轮流，反过
　　　　　来"，in place 意为"在适当的位置，已准备好投产或使用"，所以选项 B 正确。

25. 【答案】D

　　【考点】非限定性定语从句

　　【译文】那辆车的新款于 2007 年投产了，这有助于再提供 1,400 个工作岗位。

　　【分析】which 指代逗号前的部分，并作为非限定性定语从句的主语。

　　【用法拓展】非限定性定语从句中，关系代词 which 可以指代前面的名词，也可以指代句子。

　　【参考例句】

　　(1) I gave him a large glass of whisky, <u>which</u> he drank immediately.（我给了他一大杯威士忌，他马上喝了。）

　　(2) The meeting was put off, <u>which</u> was exactly what he wanted.（会议延期了，这正是他求之不得的。）

Section B

26. 【答案】greatly

　　【考点】词形转换

　　【译文】我的印象是这家公司今年的销售量大幅提高。

　　【分析】用副词修饰谓语 have increased，所以将 great 转换成副词。

　　【用法拓展】大部分副词是在形容词形式后加 -ly 构成。

27. 【答案】was taken

　　【考点】被动语态

　　【译文】这张照片是一位年轻的记者上月在北京拍的。

　　【分析】picture 是主语，动词 take 的意思为"拍摄"，因此主语与谓语是被动关系，故用被动语态。时间是上个月，因此要用一般过去时。

28. 【答案】decision

　　【考点】词形转换

　　【译文】汤姆决定在这个公司申请一份工作。

　　【分析】the 后面应接名词形式。

　　【用法拓展】动词加 -ion 变为名词，例如：election（选举），communication（交流），reflection（反射，反映）等。

29. 【答案】to take

　　【考点】固定搭配

　　【译文】读者不能将任何参考书带出阅览室。

　　【分析】allow sb. to do sth. 是固定搭配，意为"允许某人做某事"，no reader 是句子主语，意为"没有哪位读者"，谓语动词是 allow，意为"允许"，主语与谓语是被动关系，因此用了被动语态。

30.【答案】succeed

　　【考点】词形转换

　　【译文】即使刚开始你可能不会成功，你也应该不断努力。

　　【分析】情态助动词 may 后需要用动词原形，故将 success 转换为动词形式。

　　【用法拓展】succeed in doing sth.（成功做某事）

31.【答案】faster

　　【考点】比较级

　　【译文】因为光速比声速快，所以在听见雷声之前就能看到闪电。

　　【分析】根据句意和语法结构，以及关键词 than 得知句子需要填入比较级。

　　【用法拓展】三音节或多于三音节词的比较级应在词的前面加上 more。例如：more sophisticated, more experienced 等。

32.【答案】(should) start

　　【考点】虚拟语气

　　【译文】医生建议玛丽尽快开始健身计划。

　　【分析】当表示建议、命令、请求、决定、必要性等语义的名词、形容词、动词出现时，句子的从句应使用虚拟语气的 be 型，即用 should + 动词原形，或者省略 should，直接用动词原形。

　　【用法拓展】表示请求：He asked that they (should) be allowed to leave.（他请求准许他们离开。）表示建议：My proposal is that the meeting (should) be postponed.（我的建议是把会议推迟。）表示必要性：It is imperative that he (should) make a quick decision.（他必须尽快做出决定。）

33.【答案】driving

　　【考点】固定搭配

　　【译文】我花了好几个星期才适应在伦敦的道路上靠左行驶。

　　【分析】get used to doing sth. 意为"习惯做某事"，get used to sth. 意为"对某事物习惯"，故句子中应填入 drive 的动名词形式。

　　【用法拓展】used to do sth. 意为"过去常常做某事"；be used to do sth. 意为"被用来做某事"。

34.【答案】effective

　　【考点】词形转换

　　【译文】如果用药的时间足够早，这种药对于治疗皮肤癌是十分有效的。

　　【分析】由句子结构得知需要填入一个词作句子的表语，而副词 highly 可修饰形容词，不能修饰名词，所以应填入形容词形式。

　　【用法拓展】effect 既可以作名词，也可以作动词，转换为形容词是 effective，副词是 effectively。

35.【答案】is

【考点】主谓一致

【译文】现在通过互联网在家工作的人数量还是很少。

【分析】主语是 the number，句中 of people who are working at home on the Internet 是主语的修饰限定成分，所以谓语应该使用与主语一致的单数形式。

Part III Reading Comprehension

▶（Task 1）大意

本文为说明文，主要说明导致老年人在家中死亡的原因中跌倒占据首位。其实只要做一些非常简单的改变，有一半的室内事故都可以避免发生。文章就此提出几条建议：用亮色的带子给容易发生事故的地方做标记；在浴室装上把手；携带私人报警器。

【核心词汇】

fall	n.	跌倒	spot	n.	地点
cause	n.	原因	tape	n.	带子
common	adj.	常见的	bathroom	n.	浴室
up to		达到	hang on to		扶住
prevent	v.	阻止	alarm	n.	警报

【难句分析】第二段第三句：Applying bright tapes and using bright light in these areas would make these spots easier to see. 该句主语为 Applying bright tapes and using bright light in these areas 意为"用上了亮色的带子和明亮的灯"。谓语是 would make 意为"会使得"。补语是 these spots easier to see，意为"这些地方更容易看清"。

36.【答案】D

【考点】细节题

【分析】第一段第四句提到 simple changes，句意为"只要做一些非常简单的改变，有一半的室内事故都可以避免发生"。结合第二句出现的 live safely at home if they make a few changes（如果他们能做一些改变，就可以安全在家生活），故选项 A 为正确答案。

37.【答案】B

【考点】推断题

【分析】整个第二段讲了用亮色的带子和明亮的灯给容易发生事故的地方做标记，就可以使人在这些地方看得更清楚，反过来可以推断出如果不用亮色的带子做标记，台阶的最后一节会很危险。故选项 B 为正确答案。

38.【答案】A

　　【考点】细节题

　　【分析】问题中 bathroom, unfortunate 这两个词可以在第三段第二句和第三句找到原句，意为"在浴室跌倒很不幸，因为要让这些地方变得安全而减少事故发生是很容易的。"故选项 A 为正确答案。

39.【答案】C

　　【考点】细节题

　　【分析】本题问到的 personal alarm 在文章第四段谈到，报警器的功能在第四段第二句，句意为"只要按下按钮，报警器就会自动发出信号，这会叫来其他人，来看看此人是否需要帮助"。故选项 C 为正确答案。

40.【答案】C

　　【考点】主旨题

　　【分析】本题为综合理解题，本文谈到老人在家跌倒是可以避免的，并提出几种措施。选项 A 偏离主旨，只提到了现象；选项 B 只提到半数事故可以避免却没有说前提——做一些简单的改变，因此意义涵盖不全；选项 D 在文中没有提到。故选项 C 为正确答案。

▶（Task 2）大意

　　本文为一则汽车租赁公司的广告。文章提到这个公司推出 99 美元驾驶 7 天不用额外付费的特惠价格，用其遍及全国各地的办事处、驾车和旅游向导以吸引各地租车的顾客。

【核心词汇】

create	v.	创造，制定	as long as		只要
rate	n.	率，价格	include	v.	包括
actually	adv.	事实上	state	n.	州
rent	v.	租用	guide	n.	向导
quality	n.	质量	no matter		不管，不论

【难句分析】第三段第一句：You can drive as far as you like without paying us a penny over the $99 as long as you return the car to the city from which you rented it. 该句有一个条件状语从句 as long as you return the car to the city from which you rented it，意为"只要您把车还到您租车的那个城市"。这个条件状语从句中有一个介词前置的定语从句 from which you rented it 修饰 city。整个句子的意思是"只要您把车还到您租车的那个城市，您想把车开多远都行，我公司只收取 99 美元租车费，多的分文不取。"

41.【答案】B

【考点】细节题

【分析】本题问 99 美元租金汽车的使用限制。文章第二段提到 we'll rent you cars of high quality for seven days for $99，限期是 7 天。故选项 B 为正确答案。

42.【答案】D

【考点】细节题

【分析】本题问到哪种费用是包括在租金里的，文章第三段讲到 Insurance is included，意为"保险费用包含在内"。由这句话得知选项 D 为正确答案。

43.【答案】A

【考点】推断题

【分析】本题问在什么条件下租金维持 99 美元不变。文章里并没有 remain 这个词，所以要从寻找条件着手，第二段有表示条件的词句 as long as，难句分析里已讲到本句的结构和句意，故选项 A 为正确答案。

44.【答案】C

【考点】推断题

【分析】本题问文章最后一句话"您租到的是一个公司"的说法是什么意思。文章第五段提到租车还可以享受遍及全国各地的驾车及旅游向导的服务，可以得知该公司服务可谓"全方位"。故推断出选项 C 为正确选项。

45.【答案】D

【考点】主旨题

【分析】本题为综合理解题，这则广告谈到汽车租金以及该公司提供的租车相关服务，故选项 D 为正确答案。

▶（**Task 3**）大意

这是一封由 Richard Smith 写给 Ms. Rennick 的求职信。Richard Smith 应聘一个管理职位。信中提到了他的资历和相关经验，最后也希望对方能给他面试的机会。

【核心词汇】

communication	v.	得到	resume	n.	简历
leadership	n.	领导才能	in addition		另外，此外
management	n.	管理	candidate	n.	候选人
enclose	v.	附上	opportunity	n.	机会

【难句分析】第一段第一句中 an adviser to your firm 是一个插入语，说明了 Professor Saul Wilder 的身份是对方公司的顾问。with excellent communication skills, organizational experience, and leadership background for a management position 是句子的状语，表示公司要招聘的人"应具有优秀的沟通能力、组织经验以及领导背景"。

46.【答案】management

　　【考点】细节题

　　【分析】本题关键词是 position，由第一段第一句最后三个词 a management position 可知本题答案。

47.【答案】communication skills

　　【考点】细节题

　　【分析】本题询问 excellent 这个词修饰的中心词，根据第一段第一句 with excellent communication skills 可知本题答案。

48.【答案】leadership

　　【考点】细节题

　　【分析】本题询问 background，根据文章第一段第一句话中 and leadership background 可知本题答案。

49.【答案】a sales manager

　　【考点】细节题

　　【分析】本题关键词是 last summer，根据第一段第三句中 as a sales manager last summer 可知本题答案。

50.【答案】(317) 555-0118

　　【考点】细节题

　　【分析】本题关键词是 contact，根据文章第二段第二句 contact me at (317) 555-0118 可知本题答案。

▶（Task 4）

【答案】51. O, B　　52. H, M　　53. G, P　　54. J, F　　55. C, E

【汉译】

A — 收寄局	B — 收寄日期	C — 收寄日戳
D — 投递日戳	E — 单位名称	F — 发件人地址
G — 用户代码	H — 文件资料	I — 包裹邮件
J — 内件品名	K — 报价金额	L — 交寄人签名
M — 邮政编码	N — 保价费	O — 费用总计
P — 收件人签名	Q — 备注	

▶（Task 5）大意

　　本文为洗衣机使用说明。说明中提到了洗衣机的洗涤程序、需洗涤衣物的颜色归类、洗涤剂的用量、水温，以及何时投入硬币让洗衣机工作。

【核心词汇】

effectively	*adv.*	有效地	overload	*v.*	使超负荷
adjust	*v.*	调整	direction	*n.*	说明
temperature	*n.*	温度	detergent	*adj.*	使洁净的
similar	*adj.*	相近的	select	*v.*	选择
separately	*adv.*	分开地	amount	*n.*	量，数量

56. **【答案】** effectively

    【考点】 细节题

    【分析】 本题询问为何使用洗衣机时要认真遵守说明。根据第一段第一句话 To effectively use this washing machine... 可知本题答案。

57. **【答案】** similar color

    【考点】 细节题

    【分析】 本题询问洗衣服第一步要做什么事情。根据第一段第二句 First, throw clothes of similar color into the machine 可知本题答案。

58. **【答案】** your detergent box

    【考点】 细节题

    【分析】 本题询问在哪里可以找到洗涤剂的正确用量。根据第一段第四句 Second, you should read the directions on your detergent box 可知本题答案。

59. **【答案】** Warm temperature

    【考点】 细节题

    【分析】 本题询问用什么水温洗浅色衣服。根据第一段第六句 ...warm temperature for light colored clothes 可知本题答案。

60. **【答案】** closing the door

    【考点】 细节题

    【分析】 本题询问什么时候放入硬币（使洗衣机工作）。根据第一段最后一句 Finally, after closing the door of the washing machine, put in the proper amount of money 可知本题答案。

Part IV Translation — English into Chinese

61. **【答案】** D—A—C—B

    【分析】 此句为含有 when 引导的时间状语从句的复合句。be required to check 意为"被要求核对"，从句中 they 指代记者，因为根据逻辑，即使两位助手不到场，记者的身份还是需要核对的。选项 A 将核对译为"通报"不够精确；选项 B 将主语和宾语颠倒，变成"被记者要求"，明显错了；选项 C "新闻发布会的时间"是错误的翻译。故最佳答案选 D。

62.【答案】A—D—B—C

　　【分析】此句主语是 a guest，定语是 paying full fare，意为"支付全额的客人"。句子的谓语是 can invite，意为"能邀请"。句子的宾语是 another guest，宾语补足语是 to join the tour at half price，意为"以享受半价优惠参加旅游的另一名客人"。选项 B 把谓语译为"需要邀请"、选项 C 把谓语译为"必须再找"不合词义；选项 D 把宾语补足语译为"退还一半费用"不合短语意义，故最佳答案为 A。

63.【答案】C—B—D—A

　　【分析】此句关键是考察介词 on 之后的短语理解，短语中含有一个非限定性的定语从句 which is suitable for home use，意为"这种型号的咖啡壶适合家庭使用"。congratulations 意为"恭喜，祝贺"。因此选项 A 译为"我公司隆重推出"以及"欢迎各界人士惠顾"是完全偏离题意的；选项 B 译为"值得祝贺"有些牵强，并且"最新款"的说法在原文里没有，属于臆造；选项 D"最新产品"也是臆造，"特此致谢"也不能在原文找到，故最佳答案为 A，最贴近原文。

64.【答案】A—C—B—D

　　【分析】此句考察了对介词短语连用的理解。book 意为"预定"，double room 意为"双人间"，in the name of 意为"以（某人）的名义"，for a week 意为"为期一周"，from the 14th, January 意为"从 1 月 14 日开始"。选项 B"上个月 14 日"是随意将两个时间状语连在一起，导致语意混乱，14 日应是 1 月的，而不是上个月，"到现在已有"意义上是截止目前，与原句语意相反；选项 C"到 1 月 14 日止"与原句语意相反；选项 D"布朗先生为我预定"也与原句语意相反，故最佳答案为 A。

65.【答案】感谢您在游览伦敦期间光顾本餐厅。为顾客服务是我们的主要任务，非常感谢您给我们这样的机会。敬请对我们的表现提出宝贵意见，我们将从您对本餐厅的感受中受益。占用您一点时间，请您填写顾客意见表以便我们将来更好地为您服务。

　　【分析】这是餐厅写给顾客的一段话，并希望顾客能在顾客意见本上留言。翻译时应注意措辞，力求正式、礼貌、简洁。

Part V Writing

【考点】请假条写作（便条写作）

【解题技巧分析】请假条的正文可采用信函的格式（具体格式参见第一部分"写作题型透视"）。假条最重要的是写明请假的原因，说明请假日期和天数，最后希望上级批准请假要求。此类写作常用的表达法有：(1) I'm writing to...；(2) I shall be appreciated if...；(3) I want to apply for two day's leave of absence from...to...；(4) Please give me an extension of leave（续假）for two days.

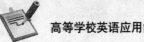

【范文】

To: <u>Mr. Johnson</u>

From: <u>Liu Bin</u>

Date: <u>June 19th, 2008</u>

Subject: <u>Leave of Absence</u>

Dear Mr. Johnson,

    I am afraid that I have to ask for a leave of absence because of my constant and serious cough for days. Having accomplished most of my work for this week, I would like to ask for a one-day leave on Friday. I'll call you after seeing a doctor. I am awfully sorry for the inconvenience caused by my absence.

    Your permission would be appreciated.

Yours truly,

Liu Bin

2007 年 12 月高等学校英语应用能力考试（B级）
参考答案与应考指南

Part I Listening Comprehension

1. D   2. B   3. A   4. C   5. D   6. A   7. B   8. D   9. A   10. C

11. services   12. 3   13. cheaper   14. as you like   15. more information

Part II Structure

Section A

16.【答案】A

　【考点】固定搭配

　【译文】我突然想到我们可以向警察求助。

　【分析】本题考查句意理解和动词短语搭配。It occurred to sb. that... 句型表示"某人突然想起……"。It 为形式主语，真正主语是由 that 引导的从句。题中所缺的动词应和后面的介词 for 搭配。ask sb. for help 表示"向某人求助"，符合题意。look 和 for 也可以搭配，但 look for sb./sth. 表示"寻找"，搭配形式和意义均不适合。而其他两个选项都不能和 for 搭配，故排除。因此选项 A 正确。

　【用法拓展】turn to sb. (for help) 也表示"向某人求助"。

17.【答案】B

　【考点】固定搭配

　【译文】许多公司工作日为员工提供免费午餐。

　【分析】动词 provide 一般有两种搭配形式，分别为 provide sth. for sb. 和 provide sb. with sth.，两者都表示"为……提供……"。本题应该选用 provide sb. with sth. 结构，因此正确答案为选项 B。

　【参考例句】

　（1）These books will provide us with all the information we need.（这本书将为我们提供所需要的全部信息。）

　（2）The hotel provides a reservation of tickets for its residents.（这家旅馆为旅客提供订票服务。）

18.【答案】C

　【考点】定语从句

　【译文】那些能够接受新思想的人会更享受生活。

　【分析】本题考查限定性定语从句中关系代词的使用。在限定性定语从句中，如果先

161

行词是人，关系代词用 who 或 whom（如果关系代词在定语从句中作主语，则选用 who；如果关系代词在定语从句中作宾语，则选用 whom）；如果先行词是物，关系代词则用 that 或 which。本题中先行词是 people，因此可以将答案锁定在 B、C 中，又因本句所缺的关系代词在其后的定语从句中作主语，故正确答案为选项 C。

【用法拓展】在限制性定语从句中，如果先行词是人，而关系代词在定语从句中作定语，则关系代词使用 whose。

【参考例句】

(1) This is the man who wanted to see you.（这就是要见你的那个人。）

(2) The doctor whom we all like very much is leaving.（我们非常喜欢的那个医生要走了。）

(3) There are still many people whose living conditions are miserable.（仍有许多人的生活条件是很艰苦的。）

19. 【答案】A

【考点】词组辨析

【译文】我在前往北京的航班上遇到了以前的经理。

【分析】本题需要结合四个选项的意思选择最佳答案。run into 意为"偶遇，撞上"；take away 意为"取走，拿走"；put on 意为"穿上，置……于……之上"；shut down 意为"关闭"。通读全句，选项 A 的意义最为符合。

20. 【答案】D

【考点】连词用法

【译文】两家公司建立业务关系已经很长时间了。

【分析】since 引导时间状语从句，表示"自从……以来"，其主句用完成时态，从句用一般过去时。although 用来引导让步状语从句，表示"尽管"；because 引导原因状语从句；if 引导条件状语从句。根据句意，选项 D 为正确答案。

【参考例句】

(1) We have been friends ever since we met at school.（自从我们在学校认识之后就一直是好朋友。）

(2) Although my uncle is old, he looks very strong and healthy.（我的叔叔虽然老了，但他看上去还是很健壮。）

(3) I bought the house simply because it was large.（我购买这房子，只是因为它面积大。）

(4) If weather permits, we will go to the park tomorrow.（如果明天天气好我们就去公园。）

21. 【答案】C

【考点】词义辨析

【译文】这栋房子售价达 6 万美元，远远超过了它的实际价值。

【分析】money 意为"金钱"；payment 意为"付款，支付"；value 意为"价值"；profit 意为"利益，好处"。根据题意，选项 C 最佳。

22.【答案】D

【考点】分词用法

【译文】在决定买房时，消费者将地段视为第一要素。

【分析】当从句的主语和主句的主语相同时，在从句中可以省略主语，动词采用分词形式。如果从句的动词和逻辑主语，即主句的主语，是主动关系，则使用现在分词；如果是被动关系，则使用过去分词。如果要强调分词短语与谓语动词所表示的时间关系，分词短语之前可用 when 或 while 等连词。本题中 when 引导一个分词结构在句中作状语。分词结构的谓语 make 和逻辑主语 customers 构成主动关系，所以使用 make 的现在分词形式。因此选项 D 为正确答案。

【用法拓展】分词短语作状语时，可以表示时间、原因、方式和伴随状况等。分词结构是常考考点，做题的关键是考察分词结构中的动词和逻辑主语的关系。

【参考例句】

（1）While <u>working</u> in the factory (= While I was working in the factory), I learnt a lot from the workers.（我在工厂工作期间，从工人那里学到了很多东西。）

（2）<u>Metals</u> expand when <u>heated</u> (= When they are heated).（金属受热后膨胀。）

23.【答案】B

【考点】词组辨析

【译文】这项工作起初看似简单，事实上却很难。

【分析】break out 意为"爆发"；turn out 意为"结果是，证明是"；work out 意为"解决，算出"；set out 意为"动身，出发"。根据题意，选项 B 为最佳答案。

24.【答案】A

【考点】词义辨析

【译文】这家小公司能够承担这个大订单。

【分析】able 表示"能够的"，be able to 是常见的搭配，意为"能够做……"；probable 和 possible 都表示"可能的"，这两个词一般用作定语或表语；possible 可以和不定式搭配构成 be possible to do sth. 表示"有可能做……"。根据本题中 small company 和 large order 的强烈对比，可以推测出题者想要表达的主要意思是"能不能够……"；reasonable 意为"合理的"，不符合本题的题意。因此选项 A 为最佳答案。

25.【答案】C

【考点】虚拟语气

【译文】如果知道你的事业发展得这么快，我就不会那么担心了。

【分析】根据主句 ...I wouldn't have been worried... 可以判断本题是与过去事实相反的虚拟语气，其结构为：从句的谓语动词用过去完成时，主句的谓语动词用 would/should/could/might + 现在完成时。因此选项 C 为正确答案。

【用法拓展】虚拟语气是常考的考点。详见附录 1。

Section B

26.【答案】finishes

【考点】时间状语从句

【译文】工程一结束，戴维就要去休假。

【分析】本题考查的是时间状语从句的时态。as soon as... 表示"一……就……"，引导时间状语从句时，主句用一般将来时，从句用一般现在时。

【参考例句】As soon as I get to Shanghai, I <u>will contact</u> you.（我一到上海就和你联系。）

27.【答案】different

【考点】词形转换

【译文】尽管小镇变化很慢，但是看上去还是和以前不大一样了。

【分析】本题考查的是形容词作表语的用法。本题中 look 是系动词，其后需要接形容词作表语。故需要填 difference 的形容词 different。

【用法拓展】有类似用法的可以作系动词的词还有：sound, smell, taste, feel, appear, seem 等。

28.【答案】swimming

【考点】动名词

【译文】我爸爸是个运动迷，非常喜欢游泳。

【分析】动词 enjoy 后面一般接动名词，不接动词不定式 to do，因此空格处需要填上 swimming。

【用法拓展】只能接动名词的动词还有 finish, keep, suggest, quit, mind 等。

29.【答案】widely

【考点】词形转换

【译文】近年来这个小村庄因出口丝绸而广为人知。

【分析】副词可以修饰动词、形容词和副词。此处空格后是 known，动词 know 的过去分词形式用作形容词。因而应填入副词修饰该形容词，填 widely。

30.【答案】development

【考点】词形转换

【译文】当地经济的快速发展造成了这一地区严重的水污染。

【分析】根据形容词 fast 和表示所属关系的介词 of 可知，空格处需要填一个名词。故动词 develop 的名词形式 development 为正确答案。

31.【答案】telling

【考点】分词作状语

【译文】感谢贵方4月15日的来信，告知我们约翰·布朗先生将于5月10日参观我公司。

【分析】分词短语作状语可以表示时间、原因、条件、让步和伴随等。当主句主语和分词之间是主动关系时，要用现在分词作状语；当主句主语和分词之间是被动关系时，要用过去分词作状语。本题中，letter 和 tell 之间构成主动关系，因此应使用 tell 的现在分词形式，表示伴随状况。

32.【答案】latest
　　【考点】最高级
　　【译文】这种赛车的最新款式将在本周的展览上展出。
　　【分析】形容词的最高级常和定冠词 the 连用，空格后为名词 model，因此空格处需要填形容词的最高级形式，即 late 的最高级 latest。

33.【答案】lucky
　　【考点】词形转换
　　【译文】李小姐很幸运，有机会在那个世界闻名的公司工作。
　　【分析】空格前面为系动词 was，空格处缺少一个形容词作表语。因此填 luck 的形容词形式 lucky。

34.【答案】bought
　　【考点】一般过去时
　　【译文】去年，顾客从 iTunes 商店共购买了 9,000 万部 iPod 机，并从网上 iTunes 商店买了 20 亿首歌曲。
　　【分析】本题解题的关键是表示过去的时间状语 last year，它明显表示对过去事实的阐述，句子的谓语动词需要使用一般过去时。因此空缺处需要填上 buy 的过去式 bought。

35.【答案】was given
　　【考点】被动语态
　　【译文】昨天秘书接到任务安排年会。
　　【分析】通过表示过去的时间状语 yesterday 可知，本题的谓语动词需要使用一般过去式，而通过解读题意可知，the secretary 是 give 的动作承受者，而不是动作的发出者，需要使用被动语态。故此处需要填上 give 的被动式的过去时态 was given。

Part III Reading Comprehension

▶（Task 1）大意

　　本文的主题是汽车内部的安全问题。文章以形象的例子说明了安全带对于保证车内人员安全所起的重要作用。文章进而又指出仅有安全带是不够的，汽车需要配备气囊才能在第一时间保证车内人员的安全。

【核心词汇】

fun	n.	乐趣	tie	v.	栓，系
belt	n.	带状物	safety	n.	安全
break	v.	打破	hurt	v.	受伤

36.【答案】D

【考点】细节题

【分析】本题询问开车需谨慎的原因。根据本文第一段第一句：Cars are lots of fun, but they could also be dangerous. We have to be careful when we drive them or ride in them.（汽车可以带来很多快乐，但也可能很危险。我们驾车或乘车时必须要小心。）可知开车小心的原因是其危险性。故选项 D 为正确答案。

37.【答案】C

【考点】推断题

【分析】本题询问举有关鸡蛋一例的意图。通过第二段的第一句：It's always a good idea to put on your seat belt when you're in a car. Why? Think about this example...（在车内，系上安全带不失为明智之举。为什么？看下面的例子……），在以鸡蛋为例之前，文章已经说明了用意，即为了证明系上安全带的重要性。故选项 C 为正确答案。

38.【答案】B

【考点】细节题

【分析】文章第四段第一句话：Volvo, a famous Swedish carmaker, was the first to use seat belt in 1949.（1949 年瑞典著名汽车制造商沃尔沃率先使用安全带）与选项 B 相符合。故选项 B 为正确答案。选项 A "系上安全带总能保证车内人员的安全"与文章的第四段第二句中 ...sometimes a seat belt isn't enough.（有时仅有安全带是不够的）有悖；选项 C "在汽车发生撞击前，气囊就会弹出"与本文最后一句话的意义相反，气囊在汽车撞击后第一时间弹出；选项 D "所有汽车的气囊都安装在座位的前方"，根据本文最后一段的第一句话"大多数的新车在座位前方或侧面装有气囊"可知选项 D 与原文不符。

39.【答案】A

【考点】推断题

【分析】本题询问气囊的作用。根据本文第四段的第二句话 Air bags are also very important for car safety（气囊对于汽车安全而言也是十分重要的）可知选项 A 为正确答案。

40.【答案】B

【考点】主旨题

【分析】本题询问文章的最佳标题。全文一直围绕着一个主旨展开，即汽车的安全问题，本文通过介绍两个构件来讲解如何维护车内人员的安全。故选项 B 为正确答案。

▶（Task 2）大意

　　本文意在介绍当代艺术博物馆（MOCA）所发起的一系列名为"艺术促进商务"的新活动。本文说明了该活动的主旨是教育公司经理如何利用艺术促进商务，活动的对象是 MOCA 的新老会员，活动的主题是探讨艺术、商务和社会三者的关系。本文还介绍了活动的参与方式。

【核心词汇】

design	v.	设计	communicate	v.	交流
educate	v.	教育	awareness	n.	意识
advantage	n.	优点	community	n.	委员会
current	adj.	目前的	improve	v.	提高
appreciation	n.	欣赏	image	n.	形象
valuable	adj.	贵重的	require	v.	要求
seek	v.	寻找	limit	v.	限制

【难句分析】第二段第三句：Art can be a valuable tool for seeking new ways to communicate with customers and raising public awareness of your company's role in the community. 该句大意是"艺术可以成为有效的工具，用来寻求与顾客交流的新方法，让公众更加了解公司的社会角色"。seeking new ways... 和 raising public awareness... 是并列结构，说明"艺术这一有效手段"的意义。

41.【答案】B

　　【考点】细节题

　　【分析】本题询问博物馆新开展活动的意义。根据本文第一段第二句：It is designed to educate company managers about why art makes good business and how to take full advantage of it.（该活动旨在教导公司经理为什么艺术能促进商务以及如何充分利用艺术促进商务。）故选项 B（艺术在促进商务中的作用）为正确答案。

42.【答案】C

　　【考点】细节题

　　【分析】本题询问该活动的参与对象。根据文章第二段第一句"活动面向 MOCA 现有和新进的企业法人会员"，可知选项 C（MOCA 企业法人会员）为正确答案。

43.【答案】D

　　【考点】推断题

　　【分析】本题询问参与该活动的 MOCA 会员将有什么收益。根据文章第三段第一句话"该系列活动将探讨艺术、商务和社会之间的关系"可推知选项 D 为正确答案。

44.【答案】A

【考点】细节题

【分析】本题询问参加该活动的人员需要做什么准备。根据最后一段的第四句 Bookings are required（请提前预约）可知参加该活动的人需要提前预约。故选项 A 为正确答案。

45.【答案】C

【考点】主旨题

【分析】本题询问该广告的目的。根据本文的主题以及广告本身的说服性本质，本广告的目的是说服 MOCA 会员参加此次活动。故选项 C 为正确答案。

▶（Task 3）大意

本文是一则旅游广告，向有意去切尔滕纳姆旅游的顾客介绍其游客服务中心，以及相关服务项目。同时该广告还介绍了该中心在夏季举行的各种项目，如科茨沃尔德长途汽车游等。

【核心词汇】

enjoyable	*adj.*	愉快的	regular	*adj.*	惯常的
unforgettable	*adj.*	难忘的	qualify	*v.*	使……有资格
local	*adj.*	当地的			

46.【答案】Tourist Information Centre

【考点】细节题

【分析】本题询问该旅游服务的提供者是谁。根据第一段第一句话"计划去切尔滕纳姆旅游，请首选致电我们的'游客服务中心'"，得知 Tourist Information Centre（客服中心）就是旅游服务的提供者。

47.【答案】local events

【考点】细节题

【分析】根据第一段最后一句话中 We can provide tickets for local events...，可知他们可以提供本地活动的入场券。

48.【答案】local coach companies

【考点】细节题

【分析】根据第一段最后一句话：...we are booking agents for National Express and other local coach companies. 可知他们是 National Express 和其他 local coach companies 的订票代理商。

49.【答案】walking tours

【考点】细节题

【分析】根据第二段第一句话：In summer we organize our own various programs of Coach Tours of the Cotswolds, plus regular walking tours around Cheltenham...，可知本题的答案是 walking tours。

50.【答案】guidebooks

【考点】细节题

【分析】根据第二段第二句话：We also stock a wide range of maps and guidebooks plus quality gifts and souvenirs. 可知答案为 guidebooks。

▶（Task 4）

【答案】51. H, M   52. N, I   53. P, D   54. B, F   55. A, E

【汉译】

A — 电话簿	B — 工具箱	C — 计算器
D — 信息储存	E — 话机设置	F — 背景光设置
G — 键盘锁	H — 自动重拨	I — 音量
J — 铃声类型	K — 语音信箱	L — 附加功能
M — 本机号码	N — 闹钟	O — 新信息
P — 网络	Q — 全部删除	

▶（Task 5）大意

本文是一封由某宾馆总经理所写的致歉信。由于该宾馆需要改善健身器材设施，宾馆六楼正在施工，网球场现不能开放。顾客仍然可以使用游泳池，不过须在客房内更换游泳衣。信上说明了施工时间，并对施工带来的噪音和施工期间给客人带来的不便表示歉意。

【核心词汇】

serve	v.	服务	in progress		正在进行
facility	n.	设施	apologize	v.	道歉
regret	v.	抱歉	at your service		随时效劳
operation	n.	运营			

【难句分析】第五段第二句：Should you require any help during your stay with us, please call our Assistant Manager.（如果您在入住期间需要任何帮助，请致电经理助理。）此句是 if 引导的虚拟条件句的倒装结构，未经倒装和省略之前，该句为：If you should require any help during your stay with us, please call our Assistant Manager. 若虚拟条件句中含有 were 或 had，should 等助动词或情态动词时，连词 if 可以省略，但应将 were, had, should 提到前面进行倒装。例如：Had I left a little earlier, I would have caught the train.（我如果早一点出发，就赶上火车了。）

56. 【答案】fitness facilities

　　【考点】细节题

　　【分析】本题询问该宾馆重建项目的目的。根据第一段第一句话：In order to serve you better... which will improve our fitness facilities. 可知该宾馆重建的目的是改善宾馆的健身设施。

57. 【答案】6th floor

　　【考点】细节题

　　【分析】本题询问目前重建工作正在哪里进行。根据第二段第一句话：We are currently working on our program on the 6th floor. 可知重建项目正在宾馆的六楼展开。

58. 【答案】(own) room

　　【考点】细节题

　　【分析】本题询问顾客游泳前在何处更换游泳衣。根据第三段第二句话：Please change into your swimsuit in your room. 可知顾客应该在自己的房间内更换游泳衣。

59. 【答案】the inconvenience

　　【考点】细节题

　　【分析】本题询问宾馆为何向客人致歉。根据倒数第二段第一句：We apologize for the inconvenience. 可知宾馆是因给客人带来不便而道歉。

60. 【答案】Assistant Manager

　　【考点】细节题

　　【分析】本题询问如果遇到困难，客人该向谁求助。根据倒数第二段第二句话：Should you require any help during your stay with us, please call our Assistant Manager. 可知客人可求助于经理助理。

Part IV Translation — English into Chinese

61. 【答案】C—A—D—B

　　【分析】解答此题的关键在于：as soon as possible 表示"尽早，尽快"；give sb. a clear idea of 表示"向……清楚说明……"；market condition 表示"市场状况，市场情况"。A 项"让你们清楚了解……"不如"向你们清楚说明……"贴切；D 项将 as soon as possible 译为"尽可能"不准确，而且该选项误解了 give sb. a clear idea of，将其译为"提出明确想法"也不合理；B 项不仅误译了 as soon as possible 和 give sb. a clear idea of，而且还把宾语 you 漏译了，造成译文与原文意义差别很大。故最佳答案为 C。

62. 【答案】A—B—D—C

　　【分析】解答此题的关键在于：one more assistant will be required 表示"还需要另一位助手"；check 表示"核查"。B 选项误将 check 译为"登记"；选项 D 将 one more assistant will be required 误译为"还有一位助手要求……"，而且将 check 误译为"通报"；选项 C 不仅误译了 one more 和 check 的意义，而且还擅自增加了"请记者通报他们的姓名"之意。故最佳答案为 A。

63. 【答案】B—C—A—D

【分析】解答此题的关键点在于：cancel 表示"取消"；an urgent matter 表示"一件紧急的事情"；requires his immediate attention 表示"需要他立即予以关注，需要他即刻处理"。选项 C 将 cancel 译为"推迟"有失偏颇，而且该项还把 urgent 误译为"棘手的"，把 immediate 误译为"密切的"；选项 A 中"大家都十分关注的"在原句中无对应，属于擅自添加句意；D 选项不仅擅自添加句意而且误译了 cancel。故最佳答案为 B。

64. 【答案】D—A—B—C

【分析】解答此题的关键在于：raise more money 表示"筹集更多的资金"；increasing 表示"越来越多的，日益增长的"；running costs 表示"日常开支"。A 选项将 raise more money 译为"增加更多收入"，与原句意义不符。B 选项中误将 raise more money 译为"提高收费标准"，而且该选项中的"降低经营管理成本"与原句无法对应；C 选项误译了 raise more money，而且原句中根本没有"尽早收回投资成本"之意。故最佳答案为 D。

65. 【答案】*Worktrain* 是一个提供工作和学习机会的网站。它给寻找工作的人提供最受欢迎的在线服务，让您轻松找到所需要的信息。在该网站，您可以找到 30 多万个职位，外加几千个培训机会和求职市场信息。由于 *Worktrain* 借用了互联网的力量，因此，它会比以往更便捷地提供您所要了解的信息。

【分析】*Worktrain* 是网站名称，在原文中用斜体表示，因此可以不用翻译。*Worktrain is a website for jobs and learning* 此句若直译，意义表达不清，需要根据汉语习惯增加动词使表达流畅，故译成"……是提供工作和学习机会的网站"。the most popular service 若直译为"最为流行的服务"让人不知所云，需要根据语境将其本义引申为"最受欢迎的服务"。uses the power of the Internet 可以直译成"借用因特网的力量"。than ever before 可以在汉语中找到相对应的成语进行翻译，即"前所未有"。

Part V Writing

【考点】通告写作

【解题技巧分析】本题需要考生书写一份通知。通知是上级对下级、组织对成员或者平行单位之间部署工作、传达事情等所使用的文体。一般而言，一则通知需要说明事件、时间、地点、参与人员、发出通知的时间和单位。通知中的语言要求简明扼要、一目了然，此外时间概念也很重要，必须写得十分明确，不容丝毫含糊。通知作为一种书面文体，有其独特的格式要求：

1）在通知的上方正中间写上 Notice（或者 NOTICE）；

2）另起一行在右边写上发出通知的时间；

3）再另起一行空四个字符开始写通知的正文内容，书面通知中不写称呼，也没有结束语；

4) 正文内容写完后需要处理落款，即发出通知的单位。一般要求在写好通知的正文内容后另起一行右侧写上发出通知的单位或部门名称，部门名称尾部与正文右侧大致保持右对齐即可。

【范文】

Notice

Dec. 21st, 2007

Dong Fang Electronics Ltd. is a joint venture, which mainly manufactures electronic products. The comptany will recruit new members in our school at Students' Club on Dec. 26th, Wednesday. The vacancies include office secretary, marketing personnel and laboratory technician. Students who are interested are expected to take part in this recruitment in Meeting Room No.2 at 1:30 p.m. on Dec. 26th. Please bring your ID cards, resumes, the certificates of PET (level B) and your certificates of Computer Rank Examination.

Students' Club

2007 年 6 月高等学校英语应用能力考试（B级）参考答案与应考指南

Part I　Listening Comprehension

　1. C　　2. A　　3. B　　4. D　　5. C　　6. A　　7. D　　8. C　　9. B　　10. D

11. every year　　12. lost　　13. building　　14. rain　　15. grow crops

Part II　Structure

Section A

16. 【答案】C

　【考点】词义辨析

　【译文】这种新款的运动鞋非常受欢迎，并且各种尺寸都有。

　【分析】available 意为"可用的，可获得的"，故选项 C 为正确答案。

　【参考例句】Several cars are <u>available</u> within this price range.（在这个价格范围内，有好几种汽车可供选购。）

17. 【答案】C

　【考点】感叹句

　【译文】他在中国的旅行多棒啊！

　【分析】what 用来修饰名词表示感叹。故选项 C 为正确答案。

　【用法拓展】感叹句表示喜怒哀乐等多种情绪，其中 what 用来修饰名词，how 用来修饰形容词或副词。

　【参考例句】

　（1）<u>What a</u> beautiful day it is!（多么美好的一天啊！）

　（2）<u>How beautiful</u> today is!（今天多么美好啊！）

18. 【答案】A

　【考点】词义辨析

　【译文】她 25 岁的时候放弃了记者的职业。

　【分析】career 意为"职业，事业"，interest 意为"兴趣，利益"，habit 意为"习惯"。故选项 A 为正确答案。

　【用法拓展】career woman 职业女性；career card 履历卡

19.【答案】C

　　【考点】被动语态

　　【译文】她没有收到申请表；申请表被送错地方了。

　　【分析】此句考查的是动词的时态和语态。前一个分句 she didn't... 为过去时，后一个
　　　　　　分句 it 代指 application letter, 与 send 是被动关系。故选项 C 为正确答案。

　　【参考例句】<u>Tom was sent to the hospital</u> because of his high fever. （汤姆因为发高烧被送
　　　　　　往了医院。）

20.【答案】B

　　【考点】词组辨析

　　【译文】时光飞逝，新的一年即将开始。

　　【分析】本题考查词组辨析。take off 意为"起飞", go by 意为"消逝", pull up 意为"向
　　　　　　上拉，停车", get along 意为"过活，前进，和睦相处"。故选项 B 为正确答案。

　　【参考例句】Time <u>goes by</u> like tears. （时光如泪水般流逝。）

21.【答案】D

　　【考点】原因状语从句

　　【译文】因为没有听到电话铃声，所以我没有接电话。

　　【分析】根据句意，我没有接电话的原因是没有听到铃声，从句和主句是因果关系。
　　　　　　unless 意为"除非", if 意为"如果"，都是引导条件状语从句, although 意为
　　　　　　"虽然"，引导让步状语从句。故选项 D 为正确答案。

　　【参考例句】I don't like him <u>because he is too rude</u>. （我不喜欢他，因为他太粗鲁了。）

22.【答案】B

　　【考点】词组辨析

　　【译文】我们将继续执行尚未完成的任务。

　　【分析】本题考查的是词组的辨析, take away 意为"带走，离开，消除", get onto 意
　　　　　　为"穿越，到达", keep off 意为"避开，远离", carry on 意为"坚持下去，
　　　　　　继续开展"。故选项 B 为正确答案。

　　【参考例句】They managed to <u>carry on</u> their experiments in spite of the difficulties. （虽然
　　　　　　有困难，他们还是设法使实验继续下去。）

23.【答案】D

　　【考点】分词用法

　　【译文】总经理坐在那里，听着各部门的报告。

　　【分析】本题考查分词作伴随状语，分词作状语时，句子主语和分词之间如果为主动
　　　　　　关系，则用现在分词。本句中 listening 和 general manager 之间是主动关系。
　　　　　　故选项 D 为正确答案。

　　【参考例句】<u>Sitting in the first row</u>, we heard the lecture clearly. （由于我们坐在第一排，
　　　　　　可以很清楚地听讲座。）

24.【答案】A

　　【考点】词义辨析

　　【译文】他在事故报告中遗漏掉了一些重要内容。

　　【分析】本题考查词义辨析，waste 意为"浪费"，escape 意为"逃跑，逃避"，fail 意为"失败"，miss 意为"错过，遗漏"。故选项 A 为正确答案。

　　【参考例句】He missed out something important when talking to his father. (他在和父亲的交谈中漏掉了一些重要内容。)

25.【答案】D

　　【考点】定语从句

　　【译文】找到一个能满足你需要的工程师是很有必要的。

　　【分析】本题考查定语从句用法，who 在本句中引导定语从句，在从句中作主语，而 whom 在引导的定语从句中应作宾语，which 在定语从句中指物，whose 在引导的从句中应作定语。故选项 D 为正确答案。

　　【参考例句】Is he the man who wants to see you? (他就是想见你的那个人吗？)

Section B

26.【答案】friendly

　　【考点】词形转换

　　【译文】她用一种友好的方式成功地解决了争论。

　　【分析】本题考查词性转换，名词 way 前面要用形容词作定语。所以 friend 的形容词形式 friendly 为正确答案。

　　【用法拓展】除了 friendly 之外，以 -ly 结尾的形容词还有：lonely（孤独的），lively（生动的），lovely（可爱的），ugly（丑陋的），silly（傻的）。

27.【答案】went

　　【考点】虚拟语气

　　【译文】我希望你明天早上能和我一起去。

　　【分析】本题考查虚拟语气，用在 would rather 之后的从句，表示"宁愿，宁可"之意。在虚拟语气中，表示与将来的事实相反的虚拟时，从句中的谓语动词用过去时。本句中的时间状语为 tomorrow morning，表示将来。所以谓语动词应该为 go 的过去时 went。

　　【用法拓展】类似 would rather 的用法还有 would sooner 等。

　　【参考例句】I would sooner that I had not left my hometown. (我宁愿没有离开家乡。)

28.【答案】were

　　【考点】虚拟语气

　　【译文】如果我是你，我不会问这么愚蠢的问题。

　　【分析】本题考查的是虚拟语气中的 were 式虚拟，if 引导的虚拟语气表示与现在的事实相反时，从句用 if + 主语 + 动词过去时，主句用主语 + would/should/could/might + 动词原形，但是 be 的过去式要用 were 而不用 was。

　　【参考例句】If I were you, I would accept his advice. (如果我是你，我就会接受他的建议。)

29.【答案】immediately

　　【考点】词形转换

　　【译文】你应该把这个计划报告立刻发给我。

　　【分析】本题考查词形转换，应该用副词修饰本句中的动词 sent, 所以要将 immediate 改为副词形式 immediately。

　　【用法拓展】大部分副词由 "*adj.* + ly" 构 成， 如：slow (*adj.*) → slowly (*adv.*), quick (*adj.*) → quickly (*adv.*)。

30.【答案】comes

　　【考点】动词时态

　　【译文】结果一出来，我就会让你知道。

　　【分析】as soon as 引导时间状语从句，意为"一……就……"，说明主句动作在从句动作之后，因此主从句时态要保持一致。此题主句时态为将来时，从句要用一般现在时表示将来，同时主语 result 为单数名词，所以动词应用 comes。

　　【参考例句】He will tell you <u>as soon as</u> he sees you. （他一看见你就会告诉你的。）

31.【答案】be fined

　　【考点】被动语态

　　【译文】如果你在无烟区吸烟，会被处以 50 美元的罚款。

　　【分析】本题中，主语 you 和动作 fine 之间是被动关系，应使用被动语态。因此，应为 be fined。

　　【参考例句】You will <u>be arrested</u> if you rob a bank. （你如果抢劫银行，会被逮捕。）

32.【答案】to decide

　　【考点】固定搭配

　　【译文】我很难决定把这份工作给谁。

　　【分析】本句中 it is difficult for sb. to do sth. 为固定句型，意为"某人做某事有困难"，it 为形式主语，真正的主语为不定式复合结构，因此应该填 to decide。

　　【参考例句】It is really difficult for me to quit that job. （我真的很难辞掉那份工作。）

33.【答案】employees

　　【考点】词形转换

　　【译文】新的弹性工作制将会使员工们的工作更有效率。

　　【分析】本题中 employ 为动词，意为"雇佣，使用"。根据句意，应填其名词形式 employee, 意为"雇员，员工"。

34.【答案】better

　　【考点】形容词比较级

　　【译文】你越细心，就能越好地完成工作。

　　【分析】本题考查 the more...the more... 句型，表示"越……越……"，所以应填 well 的比较级 better。

　　【参考例句】<u>The more</u> you learn, <u>the more</u> you earn. （学得越多，收获越多。）

35.【答案】suggestion

　　【考点】词形转换

　　【译文】我现在要提出我的建议，以便他在会议开始之前有时间考虑。

　　【分析】本句空格处应填宾语，为名词。所以 suggest 应转换为名词形式 suggestion。

Part III Reading Comprehension

▶（Task 1）大意

　　本文是一篇旅店提供的用餐提示，介绍了一日三餐在该旅店所能享受到的美味。早餐包括咖啡、吐司或者美式餐点，中餐包括沙拉、三明治和汤。晚餐更会有一些当地特色美食。旅店会以精美的食物和优惠的价格为游客服务。

【核心词汇】

habit	*n.*	习惯	reliably	*adv.*	可靠地
sense	*n.*	意思，意义	limited	*adj.*	有限的
suit	*v.*	适合	state	*v.*	陈述，声明
toast	*n.*	烤面包片			

【难句分析】第一段第一句：We've found that eating habits vary so much that it does not make sense to include meals in the price of our tour. 本句中包含了 so...that... 句型以及 make sense 的用法。so...that... 表示"太……而……"，make sense 表示"言之有理，有意义"。整句话的意思为：我们已经发现，人们的饮食习惯非常的不同，所以我们的旅游价目表上不可能包含餐饮。

36.【答案】D

　　【考点】细节题

　　【分析】根据题干关键词组 most meals are not included in the price of tours 可以将答案定位在文中第一段第一句：We've found that eating habits vary so much that it does not make sense to include meals in the price of our tour. 由此可知"人们有不同的饮食习惯"是其原因。故选项 D 为正确答案。

37.【答案】B

　　【考点】推断题

　　【分析】根据第二段第二句：At lunch stops, your tour guide will show you where you can find salads, soups, and sandwiches. 以及第三段第三句：At other times he or she will recommend a restaurant at your hotel. 中可知餐饮的具体事宜游客可以向导游咨询。故选项 B 为正确答案。

38.【答案】D

　　【考点】细节题

　　【分析】根据第三段第一句：Dinner time is your chance to try some local food. 可知"晚餐可以享用一些当地的美食"，故选项 C 为正确答案。

39. 【答案】C

【考点】推断题

【分析】根据第三段最后一句 Years of research have taught us which restaurants reliably serve a good choice of delightful dishes at down-to-earth prices 中的 reliably（可靠的），delightful dishes（可口的食物）可以推断出 down-to-earth 的意思为"合理的，实际的"。故选项 C 为正确答案。

40. 【答案】细节题

【考点】A

【分析】根据最后一段第一句：In Mexico, Alaska, and the Yukon, where your restaurant choice may be limited, we include some meals. 可知在餐馆选择有限的地方，我们提供餐饮服务。故选项 A 为正确答案。

▶（Task 2）大意

　　本文是一篇对美国洛杉矶交通系统的介绍。由于该城市是向外扩展而不是向上扩展，因此洛杉矶没有花钱来修建公共交通系统，而是为有车者修建高速公路。另一个原因就是洛杉矶没有中心商业区（CBD），不需要很多的道路空间，洛杉矶修建了若干个商业区来代替 CBD。很多人支持这种道路模式，声称洛杉矶是一座未来之城。

【核心词汇】

transportation	n.	交通	lot	n.	停车场
highway	n.	公路	district	n.	区域
outward	a.	向外的	crowd	n.	一伙，一群
upward	a.	向上的	defend	v.	防卫，保护
park	v.	停车			

41. 【答案】B

【考点】细节题

【分析】根据第一段第三句：Los Angeles decided to build highways for cars rather than spending money on public transportation. 可知"洛杉矶决定为有车的人修建高速公路，而不是花钱来建设他们的公共交通系统。"加之常识判断每个城市都应该有公共交通系统。故选项 B 为正确答案。

42. 【答案】A

【考点】词汇题

【分析】根据第二段最后两句：Los Angeles never built many tall apartment buildings. Instead, people live in houses with gardens. 可知"洛杉矶从来不建高层住宅，相反人们住在带有花园的房子里。"所以选项 A 为正确答案。

43.【答案】B

【考点】细节题

【分析】根据题干和关键词 business districts 可以将答案定位在第五段最后一句 This required more roads and parking spaces.（这就需要更多的道路和停车位），故选项 B 为正确答案。

44.【答案】C

【考点】细节题

【分析】根据第五段第一句：So Los Angeles developed several business districts and built homes and other buildings in between the districts. 可知"洛杉矶发展了几个商业区，同时在这些商业区之间修建住宅和其他建筑"。故选项 C 为正确答案。

45.【答案】B

【考点】主旨题

【分析】本文揭示了洛杉矶城市发展的特点：向外扩展而非向上扩展。同时文章介绍了该市交通、居民住宅、商业区的发展特点。特别是文章最后一句：They say Los Angeles is the city of the future.（他们说洛杉矶是未来之城）点明了主旨。故选项 B 为正确答案。

▶（Task 3）大意

本文是一篇关于怎样写出差报告的说明。出差报告不仅是出差活动的书面记录，同时也可以让公司其他员工从报告的信息中获益。文章着重阐述了出差报告应遵循的模式和需要注意的问题。

【核心词汇】

activity	n.	活动	subject	n.	主题
benefit	v.	受益	account	n.	陈述，报告
gain	v.	获得	equal	adj.	平等的

46.【答案】boss

【考点】细节题

【分析】本题询问出差报告应该交给的对象。根据第二段第一句：Generally, ...addressed to your immediate boss. 可知出差报告应该交给你的顶头上司，故答案为 boss。

47.【答案】information

【考点】细节题

【分析】本题询问出差报告可以提供什么供其他员工受益、分享。根据第一段第二句：A trip report..., but also enables many employees to benefit from the information one employee has gained 可知答案。

48.【答案】memorandum

【考点】细节题

【分析】本题询问出差报告的书写形式。根据第二段第一句：Generally, a trip report should be in the form of a memorandum... 可知答案。

49.【答案】the subject line

　　【考点】细节题

　　【分析】本题询问出差的地点和日期应写在报告的什么位置。根据第二段第二句：The places and dates of the trip are given on <u>the subject line</u>. 可知答案。

50.【答案】body

　　【考点】细节题

　　【分析】本题询问出差中的主要事件应写在报告中的什么位置。根据第二段第三句和第四句：The <u>body</u> of the report will explain why you made the trip, whom you visited, and what you did. The report should give a brief account of each major event. 可知答案。

▶（Task 4）

【答案】51. P, N　　52. J, L　　53. H, D　　54. A, G　　55. C, B

【汉译】

A — 问询处	B — 售票处	C — 半价票
D — 候车室	E — 超重行李费	F — 行李登记处
G — 安全检查	H — 站台地下通道	I — 票务代理
J — 开车时间显示牌	K — 轨道	L — 信号灯
M — 铁路交叉口	N — 软卧	O — 硬卧
P — 硬座	Q — 行李认领处	

▶（Task 5）大意

　　本文是一篇微波炉的使用说明书。阐述了微波炉在使用过程中可能会出现的一些问题、故障。本文不仅提出了问题产生的原因，更提供了解决问题的方法。

【核心词汇】

display	n.	显示	cancel	v.	取消
interruption	n.	中断	properly	ad.	合适地
store	v.	存放	exactly	ad.	精确地

56.【答案】the clock

　　【考点】细节题

　　【分析】本题询问当显示"："的时候需要采取什么措施。根据第一个问题的解决方法 Reset <u>the clock</u> 可得知答案。

57.【答案】a cold area

　　【考点】细节题

　　【分析】本题询问微波炉的风扇比平时转得慢的主要原因。根据第二个问题的主要原因阐述 The oven has been stored in <u>a cold area</u> 可得知答案。

58. 【答案】Minute Timer
【考点】细节题
【分析】本题询问如把遥控器设置成为厨房定时器，应采取什么措施。根据对第三个问题的解决方法 Touch OFF/CANCEL to cancel the Minute Timer 可知答案。

59. 【答案】The support
【考点】细节题
【分析】本题询问微波炉内转盘不转的原因。根据第四个问题的原因阐述 The support is not operating correctly 可得知答案。

60. 【答案】will not run
【考点】细节题
【分析】本题询问如果不按"开始"键，微波炉会怎样。根据最后一个问题 The microwave oven will not run 可得知答案。

Part IV Translation — English into Chinese

61. 【答案】B—D—C—A
【分析】此句为含有 in which 引导的定语从句。try to do 意为"尝试或设法做某事"，并不一定成功。in which 引导的定语从句修饰句中 situation 一词，意为"情况，处境"。present，形容词，意为"到场的，出席的"。选项 A 错把其翻译成"礼物"，且把 comfortable 误译为"令人满意的"，选项 C 错把 situation 翻译为"条件"，选项 D 把 comfortable 翻译为"畅快的"，不够准确，故最佳答案为 B。

62. 【答案】D—A—B—C
【分析】此句关键是要辨别出由 demand 引导的从句以及对词组 above all 和 be based on 的理解。demand，动词，意为"要求"。above all 意为"首先，尤其是"。be based on 意为"根据（以……为基础）"。选项 A 错把 above all 译为"还要求"，选项 B 把 demand 译为"需要"，above all 译为"而且"，不够精确。选项 C 整个句子存在明显错误，故最佳答案为 D。

63. 【答案】C—B—A—D
【分析】此句关键是对 obtain, concern, shortage 等单词的理解。obtain，动词，意为"获得，得到"。concern，名词，意为"关心，忧虑"。在本句中词组 the first concern 意为"头等大事"。shortage，名词，意为"不足，缺少"。选项 A 错把 obtain 译为"生产"，shortage 译为"减产"，选项 B 错把 concern 译为"生存"，选项 D 整个句子存在明显错误，故最佳答案选 C。

64. 【答案】C—D—B—A
【分析】此句关键是对被动句 should be given 和词组 the company brochure 的理解。句中主语 candidates 和 give 之间是被动关系，是动作的承受者。选项 A 错把关系翻译为主动。选项 D 错把 should be given 译为"可要求得到……"。选项 B 错把 the company brochure 译为"公司所发给的手册"，故最佳答案选 C。

65.【答案】新建的假日旅馆拥有家庭周末娱乐或者商务旅行所需要的一切。旅店所处位置便利，距离温泉及市中心购物区仅几步之遥。每个房间均配有冰箱、咖啡机和吹风机。旅客可以在假日旅店的游泳池内畅游，还可以每天早上享用免费的中式或西式早餐。

【分析】段落翻译时需要注意使用翻译技巧，在对英语结构和句意理解的基础上还要注意符合汉语的表达方法。第一句使用了换序法，即将 has everything you need（满足你所有的需要）的翻译放到后面去了。第二句使用了省词法，within（在……之内）的翻译省掉了。最后一句使用了转译法，即将 enjoy the Holiday Inn's swimming pool 翻译为"在假日旅店的游泳池内畅游"。同时还使用了换序法，即将 every morning（每天早上）的翻译放到句首。

Part V Writing

【考点】电子信函写作

【解题技巧分析】本文要求写一封商务电子邮件，正文部分与书面信函相同，具体格式参见本书第一部分"写作题型透视"。注意填写寄信人和收信人的名称及电邮地址。

【范文】

Email Message

From: Wangjun (wangjun11007@hotmail.com)

To: Anna (anna11008@hotmail.com)

Subject: Feedback of the transaction

Dear Miss Anna Brown,

Thanks very much for your purchase of the book *Introduction to E-commerce* on www.ebay.com.cn. The book has been sent out on time and is expected to reach you within a week. You are welcome to give me some feedback on the website after receiving it. I'll be so grateful if you could recommend this book to your friends. Recently some new-published books will be on sale, you could enjoy a discount for your next purchase.

Sincerely,

Wang Jun

2006 年 12 月高等学校英语应用能力考试（B级）
参考答案与应考指南

Part I　Listening Comprehension

1. D　　2. B　　3. C　　4. A　　5. D　　6. B　　7. D　　8. A　　9. C　　10. B

11. medical　　12. protect　　13. lower　　14. lead to　　15. popular

Part II　Structure

Section A

16.【答案】D

　　【考点】词义辨析

　　【译文】总经理拥有业务上的最终决定权。

　　【分析】beginning 的意思是"开始"，finishing"完成"，first"第一，首先"，final"最后的，最终的"。make the final decisions 表示"做最终决定"，选项 D 正确。

17.【答案】B

　　【考点】倒装结构

　　【译文】来这个公司前我从未遇到过这么好的老板。

　　【分析】表示否定意义的副词 never 位于句首，句子必须进行局部倒装，即把助动词提到主语之前，主动词位置不变，构成助动词 + 主语 + 主动词的形式。此外，met 这一动作发生在 came 之前，过去的过去应该使用过去完成时。故选项 C 正确。

　　【用法拓展】倒装结构分为全部倒装和局部倒装，常考查的是局部倒装。引起局部倒装的条件很多，本题考查的是当句首状语为否定词或带有否定意义的词语时，句子要发生局部倒装。常见的引起局部倒装的否定词有：seldom, hardly, rarely, little, few, not, never, no, no more, no longer, not until 等。

18.【答案】A

　　【考点】词组辨析

　　【译文】如果机器出现故障，立刻拨打这个电话。

　　【分析】break down 的意思是"（机械等）出故障，坏掉"，符合题意。set out 表示"出发，动身"，put on"穿上"，go up"升起，上升"，均不符合题意。

19.【答案】B

　　【考点】不定式

　　【译文】经理告诉新员工到哪里去领补给品。

【分析】 本题考查的是由疑问词引导的不定式。经分析可知 _____ to the find supplies 是直接宾语。根据题意，选项 B where 表示地点"在哪里"为正确答案。句中已有了宾语 the supplies，故 what 和 which 不合适，that 不是疑问词。

【用法拓展】 英语中，在一些动词之后可以接由疑问词引导的不定式，即疑问词＋不定式，以提供与行为相关的信息。可以这样使用的动词有 ask, describe, discuss, explain, guess, know, learn, see, show, teach, wonder, tell 等。

20. 【答案】 A
   【考点】 虚拟语气
   【译文】 看看几点了！该开始工作了。
   【分析】 在 It's (high/about/getting) time 后面的 that 从句中应使用虚拟式语气，主句若是一般现在时，则 that 从句中的动词用一般过去式。因此，选项 A 正确。

21. 【答案】 C
   【考点】 词组辨析
   【译文】 销售部门被要求三周后拿出计划来。
   【分析】 turn up 意为"出现"，get up 意为"起床"，come up with 意为"想出，找出"，put up with 意为"忍受"。根据句义，选项 C 正确。

22. 【答案】 A
   【考点】 动名词
   【译文】 在决定购买什么之前，顾客考虑的不仅仅是价格。
   【分析】 在介词之后，动词应使用动名词形式，且动词 decide 与主语 customers 之间是主动关系，故应使用 deciding，选项 A 正确。

23. 【答案】 D
   【考点】 词义辨析
   【译文】 如果出差的话，一切旅行费用由公司承担。
   【分析】 charge 表示"费用，控告"，但一般指商品或服务所需的费用；money"钱"，prices"价格"。expenses"费用，花销"，既符合题意又能与 traveling 搭配。因此，选项 D 正确。

24. 【答案】 C
   【考点】 词义辨析
   【译文】 对不起，我们不能为你提供这个工作机会，因为你没有工作经验。
   【分析】 make"使"，send"送"，offer"提供"，prepare"准备"。能与宾语 the job 搭配且符合句子意思的只有选项 C。

25. 【答案】 B
   【考点】 完成时
   【译文】 这篇文章写得很好，因为在写作过程中作者特别注意措辞及文体。
   【分析】 根据句子大意可知，因为在写作过程中作者特别注意措辞及文体，所以文章写得很好，要强调过去的动作对现在造成的影响应使用现在完成时。选项 B 正确。

Section B

26. 【答案】more healthy/healthier

　　【考点】比较级

　　【译文】事实上传统的饭菜比快餐更健康。

　　【分析】healthy 是形容词，其后有 than 这一比较级的标志性词语。因此，healthy 前应加 more 构成比较级，或者改为 healthier。

27. 【答案】kindness

　　【考点】词形转换

　　【译文】护士对待伤病员要体贴入微。

　　【分析】great 和 kind 都是形容词，故形容词 kind 应加名词后缀 -ness 构成名词 kindness，被 great 修饰。

28. 【答案】are expected

　　【考点】被动语态

　　【译文】所有参观者进入实验室之前都要脱鞋。

　　【分析】根据对句子的理解可知，主语 all visitors 是谓语动词 expect 动作的承受者，故应使用被动语态。此外，该句是警示句，常用一般现在时。因此，应填入 are expected。

29. 【答案】Personally

　　【考点】词形转换

　　【译文】就个人而言，我认为他是一个不错的合作伙伴，尽管你们可能不这么认为。

　　【分析】空格位于句首，并用逗号与主句隔开，很显然考查副词作状语。因此，形容词 personal 应加上副词后缀 -ly 构成 personally。此外，句首的单词首字母应大写。

30. 【答案】trying

　　【考点】分词

　　【译文】他们和他谈了几个小时，试图劝他改变主意。

　　【分析】主句在前，(try) _____ to persuade him to change his mind 作状语，表示伴随状况，对谓语加以说明。动词 try 与逻辑主语 they 是主动关系，故使用现在分词。

　　【用法拓展】非谓语动词中，若动词与逻辑主语是被动关系，应使用过去分词。

31. 【答案】helpful

　　【考点】词形转换

　　【译文】他为提高这种产品的销售量所做出的努力非常有成效。

　　【分析】help 是名词。空格处的单词位于 be 动词之后作表语。因此，名词 help 应加形容词后缀 -ful 构成形容词 helpful。

32. 【答案】coming

　　【考点】分词

　　【译文】我们到达时厨房里飘出一股饭菜的香味。

　　【分析】(come) _____ from the kitchen 作后置定语修饰名词词组 a smell of cooking，动词 come 与逻辑主语 smell 是主动关系，因此应使用现在分词 coming。

33.【答案】shorten

　　【考点】词形转换

　　【译文】我们必须找出新方法缩短生产过程。

　　【分析】short 是形容词。空格位于不定式符号 to 后、名词词组 the process of production 前，该处需要一个动词。因此，形容词 short 应加动词后缀 -en 构成动词 shorten。

34.【答案】will have lived

　　【考点】完成时态

　　【译文】到明年的这时候我家在这个小镇上就住了 20 年了。

　　【分析】句中表示将来的时间状语 by this time next year 和表示动作延续的状语 for 20 years 提示应使用将来完成时。故正确答案是 will have lived。

　　【用法拓展】现在完成时、过去完成时、将来完成时常与状语 by + 过去某时间 / 现在某时间 / 将来某时间连用。如果 by 后面是表示过去的时间，谓语应该使用过去完成时；如果 by 后面是表示现在的时间，谓语应该使用现在完成时；如果 by 后面是表示将来的时间，谓语应该使用将来完成时。

35.【答案】works

　　【考点】主谓一致

　　【译文】简和她的一些同学现在都在质量监察部工作。

　　【分析】时间状语 now 提示使用一般现在时。此外，虽然主语 Jane 后有 as well as 引出的从属结构，但谓语动词的数应不受影响，与主语保持一致。因此，正确答案是 works。

　　【用法拓展】当主语后有由 as well as, except, together/along with, including, with, rather than, instead of, in addition to 等引起的介词短语或从属结构时，其谓语的数不受影响。

Part III　Reading Comprehension

▶（Task 1）大意

　　本文是说明文，围绕值夜班的人的睡眠问题展开。文章首先介绍了经常值夜班的人的工作需要和体内生物钟的冲突，然后详细介绍了一些应对的方法。

【核心词汇】

shift	*n.*	轮班	schedule	*v.*	安排
awake	*adj.*	醒着的	cooperate	*v.*	合作；配合
recommend	*v.*	推荐；建议			

【难句分析】第六句：For example, night-shift workers often find it difficult to sleep in the morning when they get off work because the body's natural rhythm fights back, no matter how tired they are. 短语 get off work 表示"下班"，no matter how tired they are 是一个表示让步的状语从句。全句意思是"例如，值夜班的人经常会觉得在早上下班后无论多么疲惫都难以入睡，这是因为人体的自然节律在抵抗睡眠"。

36.【答案】D

【考点】细节题

【分析】本题问值夜班的工人是什么人。根据原文的第一、二句：People who work night shifts are constantly fighting against an "internal clock" in their bodies. Quite often the clock tells them to sleep when their job requires them to remain fully awake. 可知 night-shift workers 指的是那些必须夜间工作的人，故选项 D 正确。选项 A 意为"依赖他们体内的生物钟"，选项 B 意为"需要重新调整他们的时钟"，选项 C 意为"夜间很晚才睡觉"均不合原文意思。

37.【答案】C

【考点】细节题

【分析】本题问为了在干活时保持清醒，值夜班的人该怎么做。根据原文第四句：Light therapy with a bright light box can help night-shift workers adjust their internal clock. 可知用个明亮的灯箱进行的照光治疗法可以帮助值夜班的人调节他们体内的生物钟，故正确答案是 C（努力调整他们体内的生物钟）。选项 A 和 C 未提及，选项 B 与原文内容冲突。

38.【答案】B

【考点】细节题

【分析】根据题干中的 many doctors 可以定位到原文第五句。从 However, many doctors recommend careful planning to help improve sleep patterns 可知，许多医生建议仔细安排以帮助改善睡眠模式，故选项 B 正确。

39.【答案】A

【考点】细节题

【分析】根据 find it difficult to sleep in the morning 定位到原文第六句：For example, night-shift workers often find it difficult to sleep in the morning when they get off work because the body's natural rhythm fights back, no matter how tired they are. 可知值夜班的人觉得在早上下班后无论多么疲惫都难以入睡，是因为人体的自然节律在抵抗睡眠，故选项 A 正确。选项 B 和 D 不符合文意，选项 C 未提及。

40.【答案】C

【考点】细节题

【分析】根据短文倒数第二句：Some experts recommend that night-shift workers schedule two smaller sleep periods — one in the morning after work, and another longer one in the afternoon, closer to when the body would naturally need to sleep. 可知一些专家建议值夜班的工人安排两小段睡眠时间，其一安排在早上下班后，其二安排在下午，这一段时间可睡长些，它离人体需要睡眠的时间较近，故正确答案为 C。选项 A 和 D 不符合文意，选项 B 未提及。

▶（Task 2）大意

  本文介绍了美国著名的 Greyhound 公司提供的购票服务及旅行注意事项。文章首先介绍了邮寄购票、预付费购票两种方式及购票要求，然后介绍了前往加拿大或墨西哥的乘客应注意的事项。

【核心词汇】

avoid	v.	避免	document	n.	文件
deliver	v.	运送；递送	certificate	n.	证明
departure	n.	离开；启程			

【难句分析】第 四 段 最 后 一 句：These documents will be necessary and may be checked at, or before, boarding a bus departing for Canada or Mexico. 该句的主语是 these documents，两个谓语由 and 连接，board 表示"上（车、船、飞机等）"，位于介词 at 和 before 后变为了动名词形式，departing for Canada or Mexico 这一分词结构作后置定语修饰 a bus。全句意思是"这些文件是必要的，可能在驶往加拿大或墨西哥的巴士上或上车前被检查"。

41.【答案】D

 【考点】推断题

 【分析】根据短文第二段第二句：Just call or go to your nearest Greyhound terminal and ask for details on how to buy a prepaid ticket. 可知它应该是 a bus company，且文章最后一句也提到：These documents will be necessary and may be checked at, or before, boarding a bus departing for Canada or Mexico. 故正确答案是 D。

42.【答案】A

 【考点】细节题

 【分析】根据 tickets in advance 定位到原文第一段第一句：Avoid lining up altogether, by purchasing your tickets in advance, and having them delivered right to your mailbox. 可知为了避免排队，可提前买票并邮寄到邮箱，故正确答案是 A。

43.【答案】D

 【考点】细节题

 【分析】根据 tickets 一词可定位到前三段，根据第三段第一句：Greyhound now requires that all tickets have travel dates fixed at the time of purchase. 可知在购买时所有车票上都必须有准确的旅行时间，故正确答案是 D。

44.【答案】B

 【考点】推断题

 【分析】根据 Canada or Mexico 定位到最后一段的第二句：If you are not a citizen of the US, Canada or Mexico, a passport is required. 可知如果你不是美国人、加拿大人或墨西哥人，就必须带上护照，故正确答案是 B。

45. 【答案】B
　　【考点】主旨题
　　【分析】纵观全文可知文章提及到了购票方式、购票要求、凭票旅游的注意事项等，故正确答案是 B（如何购买 Greyhound 公司的车票以及如何凭此票旅行）。选项 A 是片面的，选项 C 和 D 未提及。

▶（Task 3）大意
　　这是一封投诉信。在信中作者首先陈述了公司在产品质量和售后服务方面的声誉，然后叙述自己购买的割草机引擎屡次出现故障，连续维修四次后仍旧无济于事，写信要求公司更换。

【核心词汇】

quality	adj.	优质的	repair	v.	修理
replacement	n.	替换；替换物	successful	adj.	成功的
receipt	n.	收据			

46. 【答案】replacement
　　【考点】细节题
　　【分析】该题询问写信的目的。根据正文第一段第二句：Therefore, I'm writing to ask for a replacement for a lawn mower. 可知作者写信的目的是要求更换一台割草机，故答案是 replacement。

47. 【答案】half a year
　　【考点】细节题
　　【分析】该题询问割草机购买的时间。根据原文第二段第一句：I bought the mower about half a year ago... 可知，购买时间为半年前，故答案是 half a year。

48. 【答案】engine failure
　　【考点】细节题
　　【分析】该题询问割草机的故障。根据正文第三段第一句：A month after I bought the lawn mower, the engine failed... 可知割草机买回来一个月后发动机就坏了，将 the engine failed 变换为名词形式 engine failure 填入即可。

49. 【答案】four
　　【考点】细节题
　　【分析】该题询问到目前为止割草机共维修了几次。根据第三段最后一句：So far, I have had the engine repaired four times. 可知到目前为止发动机已维修了四次，故答案是 four。

50. 【答案】$300
　　【考点】细节题
　　【分析】该题询问维修的费用。根据正文第五段第一句：I have already spent more than $ 300 on repairs... 可知答案为 $ 300。

▶（Task 4）

【答案】51. N, M   52. H, B   53. L, K   54. D, O   55. E, G

【汉译】

A — 人员流动	B — 终身雇用制	C — 角色冲突
D — 利润分享	E — 科学管理	F — 相对价值
G — 弹性工作时间	H — 社会支持	I — 调查反馈
J — 核心能力	K — 公共关系	L — 团队文化
M — 工薪调查	N — 测谎	O — 人力资源策划

▶（Task 5）大意

本文是一封求职信，求职者主要介绍了自己的工作经历、换职原因、健康状况、学历等，并请求得到一个面试机会。

【核心词汇】

employment	*n.*	工作；受雇	trend	*n.*	趋势；动向
broaden	*v.*	拓宽；增长	interview	*n.*	面试；采访
major	*v.*	主修	information	*n.*	信息
familiar	*adj.*	熟悉的			

56. 【答案】statistician

【考点】细节题

【分析】该题询问 Mike Smith 目前的工作。根据原文第一句：For the past 8 years I have been a statistician in... 可知近 8 年来他都在担任统计员，故答案为 statistician。

57. 【答案】Advertising

【考点】细节题

【分析】该题询问 Mike Smith 在伦敦大学时主修的专业。根据原文第二段第二句：I majored in advertising at London University and... 可知他在伦敦大学主修广告学，故答案为 Advertising。

58. 【答案】statistics

【考点】细节题

【分析】该题询问 Mike Smith 喜欢从事什么工作。根据原文第二段第二句：...and I am particularly interested in work involving statistics. 可知他对统计方面的工作特别感兴趣，故答案为 statistics。

59.【答案】market research

　　【考点】细节题

　　【分析】该题询问 Mike Smith 哪方面没有工作经验。根据原文第三段第一句：Although I have had no experience in <u>market research</u>... 可知他在市场研究方面没有经验，故答案是 market research。

60.【答案】an interview

　　【考点】细节题

　　【分析】该题询问作者写信的目的。根据正文第三段第二句：I hope that you will invite me for <u>an interview</u>. 可知答案为 an interview。

Part IV Translation — English into Chinese

61.【答案】D—A—B—C

　　【分析】此句翻译的要点是 for safety "为了安全"；review 表示"复习，回顾"，在此与 this card 搭配应引申为"仔细阅读"；follow "按照"；when needed "在必要的时候"。选项 A 将 require 译为"请"，降低了语气，漏译了 when needed；选项 B 漏译了 when needed（在必要的时候），将 for safety 误译为"为了保险起见"，将 follow 误译为"参照"，并增加了原文没有出现的"认真"一词；选项 C 将 for safety 错译成了"为了保险起见"，将 review 误译为"看到"，漏译了 follow，此外还弄错了 when needed 的修饰关系，when needed 修饰 follow these instructions 而不是 review this card。故最佳答案为 D。

62.【答案】B—C—D—A

　　【分析】此句翻译的要点是 misunderstood "误解"；his boss gave him 是一个省略了关系代词的定语从句，修饰先行词 instructions，即"老板给他的指示"；mail the wrong documents 表示"发错了单据"。选项 C 将 misunderstood 译为"没有理解"不够准确，另将 mail "邮寄"误译为"交给"；选项 D 将 misunderstood 误译为"没来得及听取"，且把 mailed the wrong documents 理解为单据本身有错误；选项 A 将 misunderstood 误译为"按照"，还将 mailed the wrong documents 误译为"把单据误寄给了"，弄错了 wrong 的修饰关系。故最佳答案为 B。

63.【答案】C—D—A—B

　　【分析】此句翻译要点是 leisure time "空闲时间，闲暇时间"；which 引导的非限制性定语从句表示原因，其中的 the demand for services has increased so rapidly 表示"各种服务需求迅速增长"。选项 D 把 the demand for services has increased so rapidly 误译为"要求迅速提高服务质量"；选项 A 将 leisure time 误译为"更多的时间去娱乐"，并将 the demand for services has increased so rapidly 错误地译为"劳务资源快速上升"；选项 B 将 the demand for services 误译为了"服务质量"，将主句 People now have more leisure time 严重误译为"如今希望有时间娱乐的人越来越多"，此外还颠倒了句中的因果关系。故最佳答案为 C。

64.【答案】A—C—B—D

【分析】此句翻译的要点是分词结构 going to the airport by arranged buses，它作定语修饰 passengers，即"搭乘专车去机场的旅客"，take the bus at the time and place as shown below "在下列指定的时间和地点乘车"。选项 C 把 going to the airport by arranged buses 翻译为"经安排搭乘汽车去机场"，从文字上看不如选项 A 的翻译"搭乘专车前往机场"流畅，此外将 must 译为"应"不够准确；选项 B 将 going to the airport by arranged buses 翻译为"乘公共汽车去机场"漏译了其中的 arranged；选项 D 把 going to the airport by arranged buses 严重误译为"机场即将安排汽车"，且增加了原文没有的"注意"一词。故最佳答案为 A。

65.【答案】现来信确认我们于 7 号周四在电话里商谈的参观贵公司一事。下周一，即 12 月 11 号，对我们比较合适，希望这个时间对贵公司也合适。我的秘书玛丽·布朗女士和销售经理张明先生将于早上前往。很遗憾，我不能和他们同去。

再次感谢贵公司给我们提供参观的机会。

【分析】这是一封商务函件，翻译时应注意尽量使用正式的书面语言，如 you "贵方"或"贵公司"。此外，在对文意理解的基础上，要综合运用词汇和句子层面的翻译技巧，使表达符合汉语的习惯，尤其注意语序的调整。

Part V Writing

【考点】留言表格写作

【解题技巧分析】本题考查应用文的写作能力，要求填写酒店来访客人留言表。填写留言表的关键是正确填写留言人、收受留言人、留言内容、留言时间等。考生首先应将提示的内容整理清楚，明确人物关系、留言内容、留言时间等以后，再动笔分项填写。

【范文】

(1) Mr. John Smith   (2) 422

(3) Mr. Li Hua   (4) Assistant to General Manager   (5) 65734363

(6) Mr. Li Hua wants to make an appointment with you to discuss business in PKK Company tomorrow. He will come to pick you up in this hotel at 9 a.m. He will also invite you to visit their newly-built assembly line in the afternoon.

(7) Linda   (8) December 20   (9) 10 a.m.

2006 年 6 月高等学校英语应用能力考试（B级）参考答案与应考指南

Part I Listening Comprehension

1. D　　2. A　　3. C　　4. B　　5. C　　6. C　　7. B　　8. A　　9. B　　10. D

11. deal with　　12. useful　　13. effect　　14. totally　　15. wonderful

Part II Structure

Section A

16.【答案】A

　【考点】词义辨析

　【译文】我的印象是这家酒店的服务的确改进了。

　【分析】句中 it 代指前文中的 service（服务），可与之搭配的只有 A 选项中的 improved（改进），即服务改进了。imply 意为"暗示"，import 意为"进口"，imagine 意为"想象"，放在此处皆不通。

　【参考例句】

　(1) His silence implied agreement.（他的沉默暗示他同意了。）

　(2) Computers are imported into that country every year.（那个国家每年都进口电脑。）

　(3) You can imagine how shocked I was.（你可以想象出我有多震惊。）

17.【答案】D

　【考点】动词时态

　【译文】警察拦住了那个司机，发现他喝了酒。

　【分析】通过 stopped 和 found 可知此句主要动作发生在过去。而驾驶员应该是已经喝了酒，drink 此动作应发生在过去的过去，故应使用过去完成时。

18.【答案】B

　【考点】词义辨析

　【译文】英国国旗上有三种颜色，即红白蓝。

　【分析】四个选项都是副词。rarely 意思是"很少地，难得地"，namely 意思是"即，也就是"，really 意思是"真正地，事实上"，naturally 意为"自然地"。后半句的"红白蓝"是对前面"三种颜色"的具体阐述，故 B 为正确答案。

　【参考例句】

　(1) I rarely play basketball.（我很少打篮球。）

　(2) It's really hot today.（今天真的很热。）

　(3) He speaks and behaves naturally.（他言谈举止很自然。）

19. 【答案】C

【考点】情态动词

【译文】我找不到办公室的钥匙了。我一定是在回家的路上把它弄丢了。

【分析】现在找不到钥匙，说明弄丢钥匙是以前发生的事情。must have done 表示对过去发生的事情的肯定推测。故 C 选项为正确答案。would have done 表示可以做的事情由于某种原因没有做。should have done 和 ought to have done 均表示该做的事情没有做，其中 should have done 的语气较重一些。

【用法拓展】should not have done 或 ought not to have done 表示本不该做的事情却做了。needn't have done 表示本不需要做的事情却做了。

【参考例句】

(1) You should/ought to have finished your homework yesterday. (你本该昨天完成作业。)

(2) You should not/ought not to have come. (你本不该来的。)

(3) You needn't have done it on your own. (你本不需要自己做这件事的。)

20. 【答案】B

【考点】固定结构

【译文】David 有如此多的工作要做，以至于他得在办公室里呆到很晚。

【分析】that 可与 so 连用引出结果状语从句。在此结构中，so 后面一般不接名词，但在 so many, so much, so little 等短语后可以接名词。故正确答案为 B。that 与 such 连用时，such 后通常接名词短语。very 和 enough 皆不能和 that 构成固定结构。

【用法拓展】so that 还可引出目的状语从句

【参考例句】I got up very early so that I wouldn't be late for school. (为了上学不迟到，我起得很早。)

21. 【答案】A

【考点】词义辨析和介词用法

【译文】我很努力了，但仍找不到这个问题的解决方法。

【分析】solution 意为"解决办法"，help 意为"帮助"，reply 意为"回复"，demand 意为"需求"。只有 solution 和 reply 这两个名词能与介词 to 搭配，但 reply to sth. 意为"对……的回复"，与句意不符。故正确答案为 A。

【用法拓展】可以与介词 to 搭配的名词还有 answer to（……的答案），key to（……的关键）等。

22. 【答案】D

【考点】词组辨析

【译文】他决定亲自去找经理谈谈，而不是写信给他。

【分析】due to 和 because of 都意为"因为，由于"，as for 意为"至于"，instead of 意为"代替，而不是"。从句意可知，writing a letter 和 talk to him 是一组二选一的动作，故 D 选项 instead of 为正确答案。

【参考例句】

(1) Her absence is due to illness. (她因病缺席。)

(2) I came back <u>because of</u> the storm.（由于暴风雨，我返回了。）

(3) <u>As for</u> you, you'd better be quick.（至于你，你最好快点。）

23.【答案】A

　　【考点】非谓语动词和语态

　　【译文】就我而言，我不喜欢被人那么对待。

　　【分析】动词 like 之后可以接不定式或者动名词。此句中的 I 和 treat 之间是被动关系，因此应使用被动结构。故只有 A 正确。

24.【答案】C

　　【考点】连词

　　【译文】利萨忙着做笔记，而此时马克正在网上查找信息。

　　【分析】四个选项都是引导状语从句的连词。其中 until（直到……时）和 while（当……的时候）引导时间状语从句，unless（除非，如果不）和 if（如果）引导条件状语从句。由句意可知，"做笔记"和"查找信息"是两个同时进行的动作。只有 C 选项的 while 能连接两个同时进行的、延续时间较长的动作。

　　【参考例句】

(1) I sat up <u>until</u> he came back.（我一直坐着等到他回来。）

(2) You will fail <u>unless</u> you work hard.（如果你不努力工作，就会失败。）

(3) <u>If</u> you work hard, you will succeed.（如果你工作努力，你会成功的。）

25.【答案】B

　　【考点】词组辨析

　　【译文】今天早上有大雾，所以没有飞机能够起飞。

　　【分析】前半句指出早上有大雾，据此可以推测出飞机无法起飞。故正确答案为 B 选项 take off（起飞）。get through 意为"结束，做完，通过"，pull out 意为"（火车等）离开"，break away 意为"突然离开，突然挣脱"。

　　【参考例句】

(1) Did you <u>get through</u> your examination?（你通过考试了吗？）

(2) The train <u>pulled out</u> of the station.（火车开出了车站。）

(3) The prisoner <u>broke away</u> from his guards.（囚犯从看守者手中逃走了。）

Section B

26.【答案】best

　　【考点】形容词最高级

　　【译文】这家酒店是这个城市所有酒店当中最好的。

　　【分析】根据句中的 of all the hotels，可知此处为三者或者三者以上进行比较，因此应用形容词最高级。故应填 good 的最高级 best。

　　【用法拓展】一些形容词的比较级和最高级的变化是不规则的，应特别加以记忆。如 bad—worse—worst, many/much—more—most, little—less—least 等。

27.【答案】invitation

【考点】词形转换

【译文】昨天他们收到了布莱克先生邀请他们赴晚宴的书面邀请函。

【分析】根据空格前面的不定冠词 a 和定语 written，可知此处应填动词 invite 的名词形式 invitation。

【用法拓展】-ation 为名词后缀，例如 information（信息），consideration（考虑）等。

28.【答案】seeing

【考点】固定结构

【译文】那部新电影值得看第二遍。

【分析】本题考察的是固定结构 be worth doing（值得做某事）。此结构中可以用动名词形式表达被动的意味。因此此处 worth 后面接 see 的动名词形式 seeing，可表达"被看"的意味。

29.【答案】will/shall/are going to/are to sign

【考点】时态

【译文】下周我们将会和新的供货商签署销售合同。

【分析】根据时间状语 next week，可知签合同一事发生在将来，故此处使用一般将来时。其形式比较多样，表示将来的 will, shall, are going to, are to 加上动词原形皆可。

30.【答案】Generally

【考点】词形转换

【译文】总的来说，他是一个你能够信赖的人。

【分析】此处需要一个副词来修饰动词的分词形式 speaking，因此应填 general 的副词形式 generally。因为在句首，应使用大写字母 G。此外也可将 generally speaking 作为一个固定短语来记忆。

【用法拓展】类似短语还有 personally speaking（就个人而言），frankly speaking（坦白地说）等。

31.【答案】be tested

【考点】被动语态

【译文】新机器在投入使用之前应该经过检修。

【分析】逻辑主语 the new machine 与 test 是被动关系，因此应使用被动语态，即 be 动词 + 动词的过去分词形式。又根据空格前面的情态动词 ought to 可知此处的 be 动词应使用原形。故 be tested 为正确答案。

32.【答案】to use

【考点】不定式

【译文】如果你信誉良好，就允许使用信用卡。

【分析】allow 后面应接不定式作宾语补足语，其固定结构为 allow sb. to do sth.，被动形式为 be allowed to do sth.。

【用法拓展】其他常接不定式作宾语补足语的动词还有 advise, allow, ask, expect, invite, tell, want 等。

33. 【答案】helpful

　　【考点】词形转换

　　【译文】如果每个成员都在会议上各抒己见，那将非常有帮助。

　　【分析】由空格前的 be 动词和副词 very，可知此处应填 help 的形容词形式 helpful。

　　【用法拓展】有很多形容词是以名词加上后缀 -ful 的形式构成的，如 care—careful, peace—peaceful, wonder—wonderful 等。

34. 【答案】is

　　【考点】主谓一致

　　【译文】已经离开这家公司的销售人员的数量很少。

　　【分析】此题的主语是 the number of sales people（销售人员的数量），是一个单数概念。故谓语动词也应采用单数形式 is。

35. 【答案】strengthen

　　【考点】词形转换

　　【译文】总所周知，体育运动能够加强国家之间的友谊。

　　【分析】根据空格前的 will 可知此处应填动词原形，故正确答案为名词 strength 的动词形式 strengthen。

　　【用法拓展】有些动词是由名词加上后缀 -en 构成，如 length—lengthen, fright—frighten 等。还有些动词是由形容词加上后缀 -en 构成，如 wide—widen, short—shorten 等。

Part III Reading Comprehension

▶ （Task 1）大意

　　本文是 MDC 公司的 John Brown 写给公司客户的一封信。在信件的开头，John Brown 介绍了公司的的成绩，并说明了取得这些成绩的原因，然后对客户表示了感谢，最后说明不久将会把公司的夏季商品目录寄给顾客，以期获得新的订单。

【核心词汇】

establish	v.	建立	unsatisfactory	adj.	令人不满的
confirm	v.	证实，确认	satisfied	adj.	感到满意的
keep one's word		遵守承诺	selection	n.	可供选择的东西
guarantee	v.	担保，保证			

【难句分析】（1）第二段：We are pleased because our customers have confirmed our belief that if the products we offer are new, exciting, innovative and of excellent quality, they will be purchased. 此句中包含一个 that 引导的同位语从句（that...purchased），做 belief 的同位语。而同位语从句中又包含一个 if 引导的条件状语从句（if...quality）。这句话的意思是"我们很高兴，因为我们的客户们使我们坚定了一个信念，那就是，如果我们提供的产品新颖、令人激动、有创意并且质量好，那么顾客们就会购买。"

（2）第三段：We are proud because we know we are a company that keeps its word to its customers; that guarantees that any product can be returned within 30 days if it proves to be unsatisfactory in any way; and that always lets our customers know if there is to be a delay in delivery. 此句中有一个 because 引导的原因状语从句（because...delivery）。而在此状语从句中，还有3个并列的由 that 引导的定语从句，用来修饰 company，指出这是怎样的一个公司。在其中第二个 that 引导的定语从句中，有一个 that 引导的宾语从句（that any product...in any way）和 if 引导的条件状语从句（if it proves to be unsatisfactory in any way）。此句的意思是"我们感到骄傲是因为我们知道我们是这样的一个公司：我们对顾客遵守承诺；我们保证如果任何商品在任何方面被证明是令人不满意的，可在30天内退货；如果交货有任何延误，我们都会告知顾客。"

36. 【答案】A

   【考点】细节题

   【分析】由第三段第一行的 we know we are a company that keeps its word to its customers 可知MDC公司遵守他们对顾客的承诺。句中的 keep its word 与A选项中的 keep its promise 意思对等，故选项A为正确答案。B选项和C选项中的内容文中均未提及。而根据第三段最后的 always lets our customers know if there is to be a delay in delivery（如果交货有任何延误，我们会告知顾客），可知公司并非一直都能按时交货，D选项错误。

37. 【答案】B

   【考点】细节题

   【分析】根据题干中的 its customers are satisfied 可快速定位到倒数第二段第一句中的 because you confirm our beliefs that good service and quality result in satisfied customers。据此可知顾客满意的原因是好的服务和质量，故选项B为正确答案。A选项的意思是公司给顾客订货的机会，与倒数第二段中的 we thank you for your orders and for giving us the opportunity to be of service to you（我们谢谢你们的订货，谢谢你们给机会让我们为你们服务）不符。C选项文中并未提及。D选项中的给顾客寄新目录只是此信的一个目的，而非顾客满意的原因，故可以排除。

38. 【答案】A

   【考点】细节题

   【分析】此题问的是在何种情况下顾客会被告知。根据题干中的 the customers will be informed 可以快速定位到第三段的 always lets our customers know if there is to be a delay in delivery，即送货如有延误会告知顾客。故选项A为正确答案。B，C，D选项文中均未提及。

39. 【答案】D

　　【考点】推断题

　　【分析】本题询问这封信的目的。此信从一开始介绍公司情况，到接下来感谢顾客的支持，都是为最后告知顾客夏季商品目录即将出炉、希望顾客能喜欢新产品做铺垫。即此信的最终目的是告知顾客夏季商品目录即将寄出。故选项 D 为正确答案。

40. 【答案】C

　　【考点】推断题

　　【分析】这封信的第一段中，John Brown 就说 The MDC Company...has become one of the most successful companies in the market place，据此我们知道此公司在市场上非常成功。故选项 C 为正确答案。其他三个选项文中均未提及。

▶（Task 2）大意

　　本文介绍了美国和英国的医疗制度和两国人民的就医方式。英国有国家医疗服务体制。当人们生病时，他们会先去找家庭医生。如果必要，家庭医生会推荐他们去看专科医生。美国没有国家医疗服务体制，大部分人都要自己买保险来支付医疗费用，但政府也会为没有买保险的急重病人或是老人、穷人支付部分医疗费用。

【核心词汇】

national	*adj.*	国家的	specialist	*n.*	专科医生
medical care		医疗保健	make an appointment		预约；约会
straight	*adv.*	直接地			

【难句分析】第一段第二句：The government does help pay for some medical care for people who are on low incomes and for old people, but most people buy insurance to help pay for medical care. 此句中的 does 表示强调。文中有一个 who 引导的定语从句（who are on low incomes），修饰说明 people。整句意思是"政府的确会帮助一些低收入的人和老人支付一些医疗费，但大部分人购买保险来支付医疗费。"

41. 【答案】D

　　【考点】细节题

　　【分析】根据题干中的 is paid by the US government 可以快速定位到第一段第二句话中的 The government does help pay for some medical care for people who are on low incomes and for old people，据此可知政府会为低收入的人和老人支付一部分医疗费用。题干只是将这句话变成了被动语态。故选项 D 为正确答案。美国没有国家医疗服务体制，故政府不会为国人的医疗买单，选项 A 错误。B 选项文中并未提及。从第一段第二句的后半句 but most people buy insurance to help pay for medical care 可知买保险的人是通过保险来支付医疗费，而非让政府支付，故可排除 C 选项。

42.【答案】A

【考点】细节题

【分析】从第一段第二句的后半句 but most people buy insurance to help pay for medical care 可知大部分人是通过购买保险来支付医疗费，故选项 A 为正确答案。文中并未提到 B 选项。美国没有国家医疗服务体制，故可以排除 C 选项。第一段最后一句话的确谈到了无力购买保险的人成为了一个重要的政治课题，但这一问题应是政府采取措施来解决，普通民众购买保险并非为了解决此政治问题，D 选项不可选。

43.【答案】A

【考点】细节题

【分析】此题问当英国人生病时通常会怎么样。根据题干中的 Britain 和 ill 可快速定位到第二段第一句话 In Britain, when people are ill, they usually go to a family doctor first。故选项 A 为正确答案。选项 B，C，D 皆与文意不符。

44.【答案】C

【考点】细节题

【分析】根据题干中的 America 和 seriously ill 可快速定位到最后一段的倒数第二句话：In America, hospitals must treat all seriously ill patients, even if they do not have medical insurance（在美国，重病患者即使没有医疗保险，也必须在医院得到治疗），据此可排除 A，并可知选项 C 为正确答案。专科医生 specialist 是在第二段谈及英国的医疗时提到的，因此可以排除 B 选项。由第二段第二、三句可知，美国人有时直接找专家看病，小孩也通常去找儿科专家看病，但并未提到 seriously ill patients 会找专家看病。故可以排除 D 选项。

45.【答案】B

【考点】主旨题

【分析】从文章第一句 Unlike Britain, the US... 可知此文是在拿两国的医疗保健做比较。全文介绍了两国的医疗制度和两国人民的就医方式，故选项 B（美英两国的医疗保健）为正确答案。A，C，D 皆不足以涵盖全文的内容。

▶ （Task 3）大意

本文是地铁公司的地铁使用指南。文章介绍了地铁的优点、怎样乘坐地铁及地铁票价的相关问题。

【核心词汇】

no wonder		难怪；怪不得	reduced	adj.	减少的，降低的
guide	n.	指南	banknote	n.	钞票，纸币
color-coded	adj.	用色彩做标记的	change	n.	零钱
up to		（数量上）多达	feature	n.	特征

46.【答案】clean

　　【考点】细节题

　　【分析】本题询问地铁的第一个特征。由题干中的 features 和后面的 modern 可快速定位到第一段中的 <u>Clean</u>. Modern. Safe. And easy to use. 由此可知地铁的第一个特征是 clean。

47.【答案】easy to use

　　【考点】细节题

　　【分析】本题询问地铁的第四个特征。由题干中的 features 和前面的 modern, safe 可快速定位到第一段中的 Clean. Modern. Safe. And <u>easy to use</u>。由此可知地铁的第四个特征是 easy to use。

48.【答案】reduced

　　【考点】推断题

　　【分析】本题询问周末的地铁票是怎样收费的。根据文章第二部分第二段的第二、三句话 Pay regular fares on weekdays 5：30-9：30 a.m. and 3：00-7：00 p.m. Pay <u>reduced</u> fares at all other times. 可知在工作日上午 5：30-9：30 和下午 3：00-7：00，乘客需支付常规票价，此外的任何时间都可以享受相对较低的票价。因此可以推断出周末的地铁票也是较低的，即 reduced fares。

49.【答案】each/every station

　　【考点】细节题

　　【分析】本题询问在何处的大地图可以告诉乘客票价和行程时间。根据文章第二部分第三段的第一句话：Large maps in <u>each station</u> show fares and travel times. 可知正确答案为 each station。填与之同义的 every station 也可以。

50.【答案】5

　　【考点】细节题

　　【分析】本题询问的是售票机能够提供的零钱最多为多少。根据文章第二部分最后一段第二句中的 fare-card machines only provide up to $<u>5</u> in change，可知正确答案为 5。

▶ (Task 4)

【答案】51. B, E　　52. G, F　　53. M, H　　54. P, J　　55. A, R

【汉译】

A — 公交专用道	B — 禁止停车	C — 禁止停车候客
D — 警车专用道	E — 禁止掉头	F — 不得入内
G — 此门不通	H — 单行道	I — 单行桥
J — 凭票入场	K — 免费入场	L — 请勿靠近
M — 房屋出租	N — 保持秩序	O — 油漆未干
P — 排队购票	Q — 请勿张贴	R — 对号入座
S — 轮椅专用		

▶（Task 5）大意

本部分有两封信。第一封是投诉信。Bill Black 投诉其工厂使用的中央供暖系统发生爆炸并造成了重大损失，要求供应商更换此系统并赔偿损失。第二封信是供应商的回复。供货商表示他们已派出调查员，待其找出爆炸的原因之后才能给出解决方案。

【核心词汇】

heating	*n.*	暖气装置	in connection with		与……有关
explode	*v.*	爆炸	manufacture	*v.*	生产
stock	*n.*	存货	complaint	*n.*	投诉；抱怨
ruin	*v.*	破坏；毁掉	surveyor	*n.*	调查员
replace	*v.*	更换；代替	satisfactory	*adj.*	令人满意的

56.【答案】exploded

　　【考点】细节题

　　【分析】本题询问头天晚上工厂里发生了什么事情。根据地点 factory 和时间 last night 及空格前的 central heating system 可快速定位到第一封信的第一句话：Last night the central heating system that you installed in our factory exploded. 由此可知头天晚上中央供暖系统爆炸了，故此处应填 exploded。

57.【答案】fashion clothes

　　【考点】细节题

　　【分析】本题询问工厂受到的损失是什么。根据第一封信第二句话：The explosion caused a great deal of damage and our stock of fashion clothes has been completely ruined. 可知工厂的损失是库存的时装都被毁了。故此处应填 fashion clothes。

58.【答案】$400,000

　　【考点】细节题

　　【分析】本题询问被毁库存时装的估价为多少。根据第一封信倒数第二句话中的 pay for our damaged stock, valued at $underlined{400,000} 可知，此处应填 $400,000。

59.【答案】the heating system

　　【考点】细节题

　　【分析】本题询问的是 Bill Black 在信中提出了什么要求。根据第一封信倒数第二句话中的 we must insist that you replace the heating system immediately and pay for our damaged stock 可知，Bill Black 要求更换中央供暖系统并由供货商赔偿损失。故此处正确答案为 the heating system。注意不要漏掉了定冠词 the。

60.【答案】A surveyor

【考点】细节题

【分析】本题询问的是供暖设备的供货商采取了什么措施。根据第二封信第二段的最后一句话：We have asked <u>a surveyor</u> to find out the cause of the explosion. 可知，供货商已经要求一位调查员查出此次爆炸的原因。故此处正确答案为 A surveyor。注意首字母要大写。

Part IV　Translation — English into Chinese

61.【答案】C—A—D—B

【分析】此句主干为 the ABC Company offered me the experience。后面的不定式短语 to advance my career in China 表示 experience 可以起什么作用。experience 与不定式在逻辑上有主谓关系。A 选项中的"我要"翻译得不准确。B 选项中的"有助于"和"实现……的目标"属于画蛇添足。D 项中的"使我认识到"、"应该"翻译有误。故最佳答案为 C。

62.【答案】A—C—D—B

【分析】此句中包含一个 since 引导的原因状语从句，应译为"因为，由于"。短语 get rid of 意为"摆脱，除去"，和后面的宾语 difficulties 一起应译为"克服困难"。这比按字面意思译为"摆脱困难"更加准确。confident 意为"有信心的"。B 选项的"自从"、"脱贫致富"、"下了……的决心"皆翻译错误。C 选项中的"下定决心"、"直面困境"翻译得不对。D 选项未能正确翻译出 since 引导的状语从句。故最佳答案为 A。

63.【答案】C—B—A—D

【分析】find something a problem 应译为"发现或认为……有问题"。fixed hours of a nine-to-five workday 应译为"早 9 晚 5 的固定上班时间"。A 选项中的"应该把……定下来"误译了形容词 fixed。B 选项中的"带来的问题"为误译。D 选项中"应该把工作时间定为早 9 点到晚 5 点"完全与原文意思相反。故最佳答案为 C。

64.【答案】A—B—C—D

【分析】此句中有一个 that 引导的宾语从句。not surprisingly 应译为"并不令人惊讶地，毫不奇怪地"。predict 意为"预计，预言"。such changes 应译为"这些变化，这样的变化"。result in 意为"导致"，故 such changes 和 hotter days 是因果关系。B 选项将 predict 误译为"认为"，漏译了 in the climate，并将 hotter days 误译为"热天更多"。C 选项没有弄清楚气候变化和炎热天气的因果关系。D 选项误译 not surprisingly 为"并不令人怀疑"。故最佳选项为 A。

65.【答案】我们非常高兴地欢迎中国朋友来参加这个特别的商务培训项目。在这里，你们将会参加各种活动，并有机会彼此交流思想。我们希望这个项目能让大家都受益匪浅。在此期间，如果你们有任何问题或困难，尽可告诉我们。我们相信这会是一次既具有教育意义又轻松愉快的培训。

【分析】本文是一篇欢迎辞。翻译时应注意口语化的特征。第一句话表达了发言者的欢迎之情。注意可加译动词"参加"。第二句介绍培训的内容，其中的 a variety of 意为"各种"。第三句中的 benefit from 意为"从……当中获益"，benefit a lot 可译为"受益匪浅"。第四句中的 during your stay 可灵活译为"在此期间"。hesitate 意为"犹豫"，但此句不宜译为"请不要犹豫告诉我们"，可稍加变化，译为"尽可告诉我们"更通顺直白。最后一句中要注意的是两个形容词 educational（有教育意义的）和 enjoyable（轻松愉快的）的翻译。

Part V Writing

【考点】内部通知写作

【解题技巧分析】内部通知又称为备忘录，常用于公司内部传递信息。其格式较为固定，通常包括标题、日期、接收方、发出方、主题和正文，而不需像信件那样使用称呼和结束语。内容应力求简洁明了。一些常用的词汇需要考生平时积累，如 sales manager（销售部经理），meeting room（会议室）等。

【范文】

SALES DEPARTMENT

MEMO

DATE: June 16th, 2006

TO: Managers of all the departments

FROM: John Green, Sales Manager

SUBJECT: Discuss the sales plan of the 3rd quarter of 2006

Sales Department has made the sales plan of the 3rd quarter of 2006. A meeting will be held in the meeting room of our company at 1:00 p.m. on June 19th, 2006 to discuss the plan. It is expected that the managers of all the departments will be present. If you can't attend the meeting, please notify the secretary of the Sales Department in advance.

2005 年 12 月高等学校英语应用能力考试（B 级）参考答案与应考指南

Part I Listening Comprehension

1. A　　2. B　　3. C　　4. B　　5. D　　6. D　　7. A　　8. C　　9. D　　10. B
11. really　　12. as much　　13. talking　　14. next year　　15. wonderful

Part II Vocabulary & Structure

Section A

16.【答案】C
　　【考点】介词 to 的用法
　　【译文】我期待尽早收到你的来信。
　　【分析】短语 look forward to (doing) sth. 的意思是"期待，盼望"。短语中的 to 是介词，
　　　　　　其后接名词或动名词。故选项 C 为正确答案。
　　【用法拓展】带介词 to 的短语还有 be used to，表示"习惯于"，object to 表示"反对"。
　　【参考例句】
　　（1）Tom is used to drinking coffee after breakfast.（汤姆习惯于早餐后喝咖啡。）
　　（2）Mr. Jones objects to my plan.（琼斯先生反对我的计划。）

17.【答案】A
　　【考点】词义辨析
　　【译文】他认为和他共事的那些人都对自己的工作很感兴趣。
　　【分析】feel 作及物动词，意思是"觉得，认为"，符合句意；try 表示"试图，尝试"，
　　　　　　其常见用法是"try to do sth./try to doing sth./try sth."；look 表示"看起来"，不
　　　　　　符合句意；ask 表示"询问，请求"，其后常接 how, what, why, who 等疑问代词
　　　　　　或副词引导的宾语从句，或用 ask sb. sth.。故选项 A 为正确答案。
　　【参考例句】
　　（1）I try to finish my work before 9.（我试图在 9 点前做完我的工作。）
　　（2）He asks how the computer works.（他问电脑如何运行。）

18.【答案】D
　　【考点】词义辨析
　　【译文】幸运的是，布莱克夫人的一位朋友捡到了她两天前丢失的手表。
　　【分析】四个选项均为副词。especially 表示"特别，尤其"；usually 表示"通常地"；
　　　　　　generally 表示"一般来说"；fortunately 表示"很幸运地"，符合句意。故选项
　　　　　　D 为正确答案。

19.【答案】B

　　【考点】定语从句

　　【译文】申请该职位的人中几乎没有人符合公司的要求。

　　【分析】Few people <u>who applied for the position</u> meet the requirements of the company. 此句的划线部分是定语从句，引导词 who 在从句中充当主语。注意：定语从句引导词中只有 who，that 和 which 能充当从句主语。whom 只能充当从句的宾语；what 不能引导定语从句；whose 表示所属关系，不符合句子要求。故选项 B 为正确答案。

　　【参考例句】Jane, <u>whose father is a professor</u>, is very interested in science.（简，她的父亲是位教授，对科学有着浓厚的兴趣。）

20.【答案】A

　　【考点】词组辨析

　　【译文】你为什么不捡起地上那支铅笔?

　　【分析】pick up（拾起，捡起）符合句意；bring up 表示"培养"；get up 表示"起床，起身"；put up 表示"举起，穿上"。这三项均不符合句意。故选项 A 为正确答案。

　　【用法拓展】词组 pick up 还有"（车辆）中途搭载（人、物）"的意思。

　　【参考例句】The train stopped to <u>pick up</u> some passengers.（火车停下来搭载了一些乘客。）

21.【答案】A

　　【考点】it 作形式宾语

　　【译文】玛丽觉得要通过考试是非常困难的。

　　【分析】在此句中，Mary 作主语，found（原形 find）作谓语。单词 it 充当形式宾语，而真正的宾语是不定式结构 to pass the examination。extremely difficult 作宾语补足语。

　　【用法拓展】it 作形式主语或形式宾语时，真正的主语一般是后面的不定式结构、分词结构，或名词性从句等。

　　【参考例句】I think <u>it</u> impossible <u>that he died in the car accident</u>.（我认为他不可能死于那场车祸。）

22.【答案】C

　　【考点】使役动词的用法

　　【译文】她努力尝试过，但还是没能改变我们的想法。

　　【分析】make 作使役动词的用法是"make + 宾语 + 省略 to 的不定式"，表示"使人（物）怎么样"，故选项 C 为正确答案。

　　【用法拓展】动词 let 作使役动词的用法同 make，但它多用于祈使句中。

　　【参考例句】<u>Let</u> me <u>help</u> you.（让我来帮你。）

23.【答案】D

【考点】词组辨析

【译文】我面试迟到了，因为在去伦敦的路上公共汽车抛锚了。

【分析】get off 表示"下车"；bring in 表示"引进，介绍"；keep off 表示"远离，不接近"；break down 表示"出现故障，中止"，符合句意要求。故选项 D 为正确答案。

24.【答案】B

【考点】虚拟语气

【译文】经理要求所有员工上午 9 点前务必到办公室。

【分析】题干中 require 的意思是"要求"。在表达愿望、要求、请求、建议、命令、必要性等意义的动词后，如果接 that 引导的宾语从句，则从句的谓语动词用（should +）动词原形的形式，should 可以省略。故选项 B 为正确答案。

【用法拓展】与 require 用法相同的动词还有：advise, command, demand, desire, order, propose, request, recommend, suggest, urge 等。

【参考例句】I suggest that the plan be checked again.（我建议对这项计划再检查一遍。）

25.【答案】C

【考点】形近词辨析

【译文】她正在谈论她在一家医院当护士的经历，这些经历我们从未听说过。

【分析】四个选项均为复数形式名词。expense 表示"花费，花销"；excuse 表示"借口"；experience 表示"经历"；expression 表示"词组，措辞，表情，表达"。选项 C 为正确答案。

【用法拓展】experience 表示"经历"时是可数名词，表示"经验"时是不可数名词。

【参考例句】Wang Ling is an excellent teacher of much teaching experience.（王玲是位优秀的老师，教学经验丰富。）

Section B

26.【答案】healthy

【考点】词形转换

【译文】孩子们笑容灿烂，看上去很健康。

【分析】此句题干中 look 是系动词，后面应该接形容词作表语。

【用法拓展】与 look 用法类似的还有单词 taste, sound, touch, feel, smell 等感官动词。

【参考例句】The food smells terrible.（这食物真难闻。）

27.【答案】Working

【考点】分词作状语

【译文】作为一个团队，中外工程师们紧密合作，卓有成效。

【分析】动词的现在分词和过去分词可以用作状语，表示原因、结果、条件、时间等。如果该句的主语与分词是主动关系，则用现在分词；如果该句的主语与分词是被动关系，则用过去分词。此句 work 与主语 engineers 是主动关系，所以用 working。注意句首单词首字母大写。

【参考例句】

(1) <u>Standing on the stage</u>, he felt nervous. （站在舞台上，他感到紧张。）

(2) <u>Scolded by his parents</u>, Terry is frustrated. （被父母批评了，泰里很难过。）

28. 【答案】achievement(s)

【考点】词形转换

【译文】我们对这位年轻人在过去三年中取得的成就感到惊讶。

【分析】此题中有两个关键点都提示该空缺应填上名词：一是空缺在介词 at 后；二是空缺在定冠词 the 后。单词 achieve 是动词，改成名词形式的方式是在词尾加 -ment。

【用法拓展】在动词词尾加 -ment 变成名词的单词还有：require(ment), develop(ment), equip(ment), settle(ment) 等。

29. 【答案】more popular

【考点】形容词比较级

【译文】调查表明绿色食品比传统食品更受欢迎。

【分析】题干中提示词 than 表明此空应该用 popular 的比较级。单词 popular 有三个音节，所以比较级是 more + popular 的形式。

【用法拓展】单音节形容词的比较级是在词尾加 -er，如 greater, harder, easier。双音节的形容词的比较级分两类：以元音结尾的双音节形容词，其比较级一般是在词尾加 -er（以 y 结尾的将 y 变为 i 再加 -er），如 healthier, happier；以辅音结尾的双音节形容词，其比较级是 more + 形容词的形式。多音节（三个及以上）形容词的比较级是 more + 形容词的形式，如 more difficult, more beautiful 等。

30. 【答案】greatly

【考点】词形转换

【译文】最近几个月全球市场的油价大幅上涨。

【分析】题干中 increase 是动词，前面修饰词需用副词，表示上涨的程度。

31. 【答案】have worked/have been working

【考点】动词时态

【译文】进入这家公司后，我在人力资源部门工作了 5 个月。

【分析】从题干中 since 一词可知，本句谓语动词 work 的时态应是现在完成时 have worked。如果强调 work 现在仍在进行，则可以用现在完成进行时 have been working。两种答案均正确。

32. 【答案】employee(s)

【考点】词形转换

【译文】弹性工作制可以使员工的工作更有效率。

【分析】题干中动词 enable 表示"使……发生，成为可能"，常用 enable sb. to do，所以此处需填一个名词作它的宾语。动词 employ 意思是"雇佣"，employee 表示"雇员"。

【用法拓展】employer 表示"雇主，老板"。

33.【答案】was praised

　　【考点】被动语态

　　【译文】简做办公室秘书的时候多次被总经理夸奖。

　　【分析】动词 praise 意思是"赞扬，夸奖"。题干中 by 提示了 Jane 是被总经理多次表扬，所以用被动语态结构：be + 动词过去分词。而题干中"...she was working as..."表明时态是过去时，所以用 was praised。

34.【答案】saying

　　【考点】分词短语作后置定语

　　【译文】火车站挤满了与亲友道别的人们。

　　【分析】动词的分词形式可以用来作后置定语，修饰前面的名词，表示状态。如果名词与分词是主动关系，则用现在分词；如果名词与分词是被动关系，则用过去分词。此句中 people 和 say 是主动关系，所以用 saying。注意：此空不可用谓语形式，因为介词 with 后只能接名词或名词性短语和从句。

35.【答案】does/did

　　【考点】主谓一致

　　【译文】这位教授和他的助手们每周在实验室做 40 个小时的实验。

　　【分析】此句的主语是 professor，而 as well as his assistants 是插入语作补充说明，不是主语，所以谓语要用 do 的第三人称单数形式 does。语境没有限定时间，因此也可以用 do 的一般过去时 did。

　　【用法拓展】与 as well as 用法类似的单词和短语还有：as much as, besides, except, including, in addition to, like, more than, rather than, with, along with, together with 等。

　　【参考例句】Cindy, along with her roommates, goes to the cinema.（辛迪和她的室友一起去看电影。）

Part III Reading Comprehension

▶（Task 1）大意

　　本文介绍了零购物日。有些人认为大家在圣诞节前购物过多，于是将 11 月 29 日定为零购物日。零购物日起源于大不列颠哥伦比亚省的温哥华市，现在在美国广受欢迎。今年，美国新墨西哥州阿尔布奎克市的高中生举办餐会来让更多人知道这个零购物日。

【核心词汇】

celebrate	v.	庆祝	tradition	n.	传统
paint	v.	绘制，画	inform	v.	告知，通知
organize	v.	组织			

36. 【答案】B

　　【考点】细节题

　　【分析】本题询问人们创立零消费日的原因是什么。本文第一段的前两句话指出很
多人在圣诞节前买很多礼物，有人认为他们购买过多。在第三句就点出创
立零消费日。可见前两句话就是其创立的原因。选项 A，D 不符合原文，
选项 C 的意思是人们买不起那么多礼物，是曲解原文。故选项 B 为正确
答案。

37. 【答案】C

　　【考点】细节题

　　【分析】本题询问零购物日这一想法起源地是哪里。根据原文第二段第二句可知这一
想法始于不列颠哥伦比亚省的温哥华市，故选项 C 为正确答案。

38. 【答案】D

　　【考点】细节题

　　【分析】本题询问阿尔布奎克市的学生打算做什么来让零购物日更普及。问打算
做（plan to do）什么表示还未做而将来要做。根据原文第三段最后一句中
next year 可知他们会再办餐会让更多人了解零购物日。故选项 D 为正确
答案。

39. 【答案】A

　　【考点】推断题

　　【分析】本题要求根据原文选出陈述正确的一项。根据原文第二段第三句可知如今美
国各地的人们都会庆祝零购物日，选项 A 陈述正确。选项 B 故意曲解原文，
文章第三段第三句说明学生们请附近的餐厅在那天赠送食物，并未说赠送食
物是餐厅的传统。选项 C、D 在文中都未提及。故选项 A 为正确答案。

40. 【答案】A

　　【考点】主旨题

　　【分析】本题要求选出文章最恰当的标题。文章主要介绍了美国的零购物日。第一段
说明了零购物日的由来；第二段交代了其起源地和在美国的普及情况；第三
段则介绍了美国学生宣传零购物日的活动。选项 A 符合要求。选项 B 的意思
是"零购物日的未来"，不合题意。文章只说了明年高中生的宣传计划，并没
有谈及零购物日的未来。选项 C、D 都只是零购物日的细节部分，不是主题。
故选项 A 为正确答案。

▶（Task 2）大意

　　本文是一封求职信。求职人要申请某公司的秘书一职。她简要介绍了自己的工作经
验、更换工作的原因、进修情况和中英文交流能力，并且希望获得面试机会。随信还附寄
了简历和一张邮资已付的明信片以便公司回复。

【核心词汇】

apply for		申请	firm	*n.*	公司
position	*n.*	职位，方位	enclosed	*adj.*	被附上的
advertise	*v.*	做广告	qualification	*n.*	资格
efficiently	*adv.*	高效地	appreciate	*v.*	欣赏，感谢
flexible	*adj.*	灵活的	pre-paid	*adj.*	已付款的
challenging	*adj.*	有挑战性的	postcard	*n.*	明信片
expand	*v.*	扩展	consideration	*n.*	考虑
bilingual	*adj.*	双语的			

41.【答案】B

【考点】细节题

【分析】本题询问求职者更换工作的原因。根据原文第三段第一句可知，她在原单位的晋升机会有限，所以想换个更富挑战性的工作。选项 B 中的 hardly 对应文中的 limited，而动词 promote 意思是"提拔，提升"，对应文中的 promotion。故选项 B 为正确答案。

42.【答案】A

【考点】细节题

【分析】本题询问求职人为了找到更满意的工作做了什么准备。根据原文第三段第二句可知，她学习了一门能拓展国际商务知识的课程。选项 A 中动词短语 take part in 的意思是"参加"，正好对应原文的 enroll in。故选项 A 为正确答案。

43.【答案】C

【考点】推断题

【分析】本题询问双语秘书与其他秘书的不同之处。问题的核心词是 bilingual，该词并非常见词汇，解题需要找到上下文的提示。根据第三段第三句 Now, both my English and Chinese have been improved and I am ready to begin working as a bilingual secretary... 可知，求职人现在的英语和汉语水平都提高了并准备成为一名双语秘书处理国际商务事宜。A，B，D 三项都和此句没有联系。故选项 C 为正确答案。

44.【答案】A

【考点】细节题

【分析】本题询问求职者随信附寄一张邮资已付的明信片的原因。根据最后一段第二句 ...please use the enclosed pre-paid postcard to send me your reply 可知，求职者希望公司能寄出其答复。故选项 A（请求获得书面回复）为正确答案。

45.【答案】B

【考点】细节题

【分析】本题询问求职者写信的目的。选项 A"吸引公司注意"，表达不清晰；选项

B "得到面试机会" 符合原文第三段第一句话 ...give me an opportunity to have an interview；选项 C "在《中国日报》求得一个合适的工作" 是曲解原文，原文第一段指出求职者看到登在《中国日报》上的招聘广告，而不是求职者去该报社求职；选项 D "得到更多公司信息" 原文没有提及。故选项 B 为正确答案。

▶（Task 3）大意

　　本文是一篇新工厂选址报告。在三个备选城市中，委员会认为芝加哥最具优势。芝加哥位于美国的人口密集区，距纽约的工厂总部不远，邻近配件和原材料供应商，且海陆空交通运输都很便捷。

【核心词汇】

location	n.	位置	quarter	n.	四分之一
committee	n.	委员会	supplier	n.	供应商
proposed	adj.	推荐的	raw material		原材料
observation	n.	观察	recommended	adj.	推荐的
geographical	adj.	地理的	convenient	adj.	便捷的，方便的
contain	v.	容纳，包括			

【难句分析】文章第二段第一句：Though not at the geographical center of the United States, Chicago is centrally located in an area that contains more than three-quarters of the US population. 本句中：Though (it is) not at the geographical center of the United States 是一个以连词 though 引导的让步状语从句，从句省略了主谓 it (Chicago) is。该从句的意思是 "尽管芝加哥不处在美国地理中心位置"。Chicago is centrally located in an area 是主句，意思是 "芝加哥位于某个区域的中心"。...an area that contains more than three-quarters of the US population 划线部分是一个定语从句，修饰 area。该句的意思是 "此区域容纳了美国四分之三的人口"。

46.【答案】Chicago

　　【考点】细节题

　　【分析】本题询问报告推荐的新厂址位置名称。根据文章第一段第二句可知委员会认为芝加哥最合适，所以答案应该是 Chicago。

47.【答案】central

　　【考点】细节题

　　【分析】本题询问芝加哥位于人口密集区的什么地方。根据第二段第一句话 ...Chicago is centrally located in... 可知该市位于中心区域。本题需要填写形容词修饰名词 part，所以应该用副词 centrally 的形容词形式 central。

48.【答案】head office
　　【考点】细节题
　　【分析】本题询问芝加哥离纽约的什么地方不远。根据第二段第二句可知是离纽约的
　　　　　　总部 head office 不远。

49.【答案】suppliers
　　【考点】细节题
　　【分析】本题询问芝加哥离配件和原材料的什么很近。根据第二段第三句可知对应信
　　　　　　息点 suppliers（供应商）。

50.【答案】air
　　【考点】细节题
　　【分析】本题询问芝加哥除铁路、水路运输便捷外，还有什么货物运输便利。根据第
　　　　　　三段最后一句可知是 air cargo services（航空货运服务），所以答案是 air。

▶（Task 4）
【答案】51. I, G　　　52. D, A　　　53. N, B　　　54. C, L　　　55. P, F
【汉译】

A — 互联网接入	B — 打开拨号连接窗口
C — 在用户名栏中键入本卡卡号	D — 在密码栏中键入密码
E — 在电话号码栏键入 17200	F — 连接中
G — 输入账号	H — 输入密码
I — 键入呼叫号码	J — 查询当前余额
K — 查询缩位号码	L — 将其他卡上的金额转移至此卡
M — 请键入新密码	N — 修改密码
O — 修改缩位号码	P — 账户充值

▶（Task 5）大意
　　本文是一则招聘广告。安利日用品公司招聘采购经理、人事经理和销售经理，并注明
了三个职位的招聘要求。
【核心词汇】

leading	adj.	领先的	independently	adv.	独立地
engage	v.	使从事，忙于	fluent	adj.	流利的
qualified	adj.	合格的	essential	adj.	必要的

56.【答案】Daily necessities
　　【考点】细节题
　　【分析】本题询问安利公司主要的产品类型是什么。根据第一段第一句话 ...company
　　　　　　engaged in daily necessities... 可知该公司的产品是日用品。

57. 【答案】computer skills

　　【考点】细节题

　　【分析】本题询问采购经理需要具备的良好技能。根据采购经理招聘要求第四项可知是良好的计算机技能。

58. 【答案】English

　　【考点】细节题

　　【分析】本题询问人事经理要能流利表达哪种外语。根据人事经理招聘要求第四项可知是英语。

59. 【答案】hard-working

　　【考点】细节题

　　【分析】本题询问销售经理候选人需要具备的素质。根据销售经理招聘要求第四项可知是"积极主动，工作刻苦"，所以答案是 hard-working。

60. 【答案】Three/3

　　【考点】细节题

　　【分析】本题询问该公司招聘几个职位。根据文章数字标注可知是 3 个。

Part IV Translation — English into Chinese

61. 【答案】A—D—B—C

　　【分析】本句是含有主语从句和原因状语从句的复合句。句首 it 作形式主语，真正的主语是 air pollution affects rivers and lakes indirectly，意思是"空气污染间接影响了河流湖泊"。...because it causes acid rain 意思是"空气污染造成酸雨"，句中的 it 指代 air pollution。本题难点在分析空气污染、酸雨、河流污染的因果关系。选项 D 错译了 cause，应该译为"造成"。选项 B 误解了 indirectly。选项 C 完全颠倒了因果关系。故最佳答案为 A 选项。

62. 【答案】C—A—D—B

　　【分析】本句是含非限定性定语从句的复合句。句中 ...with which we can complete our research in time 是非限定性定语从句，which 指代前文的 equipment。选项 A 漏译了 equipment，我们拥有的是最先进的"设备"而非"实验室"，并且错译了 complete（完成）和 in time（及时）。选项 D 错译了 the most，不是"最多"而是修饰 up-to-date 表示"最先进的"，该选项还擅自增加了"所有的"之意。选项 B 将整句的修饰关系译错：错译 have，漏译 in our laboratory，多译了"资料"。故最佳答案为 C。

63. 【答案】D—A—C—B

　　【分析】本句是含有非限定性定语从句的复合句。句中 which is more than I had expected 是非限定性定语从句，意思是"这事比我预期的好"。引导词 which 指代前半句所陈述的内容，即"此行的四个目标都已完成"这件事。选项 A 把 which 指代的内容译错。选项 C 错译了 all of 和 more than，原文没有比较目标个数之意。选项 B 除有选项 C 的错误外，还漏译了 fulfill。故最佳答案为 D。

64.【答案】B—D—C—A

【分析】本句是含有条件状语从句的复合句。句中 on the condition that you are able to handle it properly so as not to damage it 是条件状语从句，表示"如果你能正确使用电脑，不损坏它"。句中 so as (not) to 表示目的。选项 D 没有准确翻译条件状语从句，并漏译了 handle it properly。选项 C 译错了"可以使用电脑"的条件，并多译了"维修"。选项 A 除有选项 C 的错误外，还错译了"有条件地"。故最佳答案为 B。

65.【答案】兹去函告知，本公司于 5 月 25 日在贵公司所订货物至今未收到任何消息。我方已在之前的去函中告知了本方客户急需该批机器并多次提出早日交货这一情况。望贵方尽力安排此事，勿再延迟。

【分析】段落翻译时要注意翻译技巧。本文是商业信函的一个段落，翻译时应注意语气和措辞的简洁、礼貌。比如文中的 we 可译为"我方"或"本公司"，而 you 可译为"贵方"或"贵公司"。第一句交代写信的目的是催货，翻译时调整了主语，把客观事物（news）换成人作主语，更符合汉语表达习惯。第二、三句说明催货的原因，把被动句（have been informed）翻译成主动句。最后一句表达愿望，翻译时应避免用命令的语气，表达时尽量委婉。

Part V Writing

【考点】电子信函写作

【解题技巧分析】本文要求写一封取消酒店预订的电子邮件，正文部分与书面信函相同，具体格式参见本书第一部分"写作题型透视"。注意填写寄信人和收信人的名称及电邮地址。

【范文】

Email Message

To: Holiday Inn (marketing@expedia.com)
From: John Smith (js456@vip.163.com)
Date: Dec. 10th
Subject: Cancellation of Hotel Booking
Dear Sir or Madam,　I am writing to inform you that since my schedule has been changed, I have to cancel my reservation of two single rooms from Dec. 12th to Dec. 15th in your hotel. The reservation was made on Dec. 5th under the name of John Smith.　I feel extremely sorry and hope it may not cause any inconvenience to you. Please inform me of the cancellation penalty, if it should be paid.　I am looking forward to your reply and confirmation. Thank you! 　　　　　　　　　　　　　　　　　　　　Yours faithfully, 　　　　　　　　　　　　　　　　　　　　John Smith

2005年6月高等学校英语应用能力考试（B级）
参考答案与应考指南

Part I Listening Comprehension

1. B   2. D   3. A   4. C   5. B   6. A   7. C   8. B   9. D   10. A

11. day   12. as long   13. boring   14. far away   15. discuss

Part II Structure

Section A

16. 【答案】C

【考点】词义辨析

【译文】从他的口音判断，我能断定他来自南方。

【分析】speak 用作及物动词时，意为"说某种语言"；look 为不及物动词，需要与介词搭配才可接宾语；tell 除了可以表示"告诉，吩咐"外，还含有"辨别出，断定"的意思；show 意为"表明，显示"。根据句意可见 tell 最合适。

17. 【答案】B

【考点】主从句时态一致

【译文】直到雨停了我们才能离开办公室。

【分析】not...until... 句型表示"直到……才……"，如果主句动词用一般将来时，从句动词应选用一般现在时来表示将来。

【用法拓展】not 和 until 连在一起使用时，置于句首，主句需部分倒装。本句可改为：Not until the rain stops, will we be able to leave the office.

18. 【答案】A

【考点】词组辨析

【译文】老板吩咐秘书把文件收起来，以备今后使用。

【分析】本题考察动词短语。put away 意思是"把……收起来，放到其原来的位置"；turn on 意为"打开电器，呈现"；make up 意为"编造，化妆"；break out 意为"（战争、火灾等）突然爆发"。故选项 A 最符合句意。

【参考例句】

(1) Please turn on the radio. （请打开收音机。）

(2) The writer made up the plot. （作家虚构了剧情。）

(3) The fire broke out in the downtown area yesterday. （昨天城区爆发了一场火灾。）

19. 【答案】B

　　　【考点】形容词最高级

　　　【译文】玛丽说这是她职业生涯中做出的最糟糕的决定。

　　　【分析】根据定语从句 she has <u>ever</u> made in her career 中的时间副词 ever，可知其修饰的先行词 decision 前要采用形容词最高级。bad 的最高级为 worst。

　　　【参考例句】She is the <u>most beautiful girl</u> that he has <u>ever</u> seen.（她是他见过的最美的女孩。）

20. 【答案】C

　　　【考点】定语从句

　　　【译文】我们都认为约翰是唯一一能够得到工作的应聘者。

　　　【分析】candidate 意思是"候选人"，其后的句子是它的定语从句。先行词 candidate 在从句中作主语，则要选择关系代词 who 或 that。而 whom 是 who 的宾格形式，不能引导主语；whoever 表示"无论谁"，引导名词性从句而不能引导定语从句。故选项 C 正确。

　　　【用法拓展】定语从句常用的与人相关的引导词包括：who, whom, whose 和 that。who 和 that 在定语从句中通常作主语，也可作宾语；whom 在定语从句中作谓语和介词的宾语；whose 在从句中与所修饰名词表示所属关系。

　　　【参考例句】

　　　（1）The old man <u>whom</u> Mary is talking with is my father.（正和玛丽交谈的那个老人是我的父亲。）

　　　（2）My father loved the little boy <u>whose</u> mother died last year.（我父亲很爱那个小男孩，他的母亲去年过世了。）

21. 【答案】A

　　　【考点】同位语从句

　　　【译文】玛丽开会又迟到的事实让我生气。

　　　【分析】句子的主干为 The fact made me angry，fact 在其后的从句中不能担当任何句子成分，可判定 fact 后面的从句为同位语从句而非定语从句。同位语从句通常由 that 引导，但 that 在从句中只起到连接作用而不担当任何成分。

　　　【参考例句】The <u>news that the president was killed</u> shocked the whole country.（总统被杀的消息震惊了整个国家。）

22. 【答案】D

　　　【考点】一般将来时

　　　【译文】下个月将维修车间里的大部分机器。

　　　【分析】根据时间状语 next month 可以判断该句时态为一般将来时。句中物作主语，主语和谓语之间为被动关系，因此应为一般将来时的被动语态。

23. 【答案】D

　　　【考点】固定句型

　　　【译文】对于玛丽来说，通过面试太困难了。

　　　【分析】It is + *adj*. + for sb. to do sth. 为固定句型，本题中 it 作为形式主语指代后面的不定式短语，句子的真正主语为 to pass the interview。

　　　【参考例句】It is very important for me to get the job.（获得这份工作对我来说很重要。）

24. **【答案】** C

　　【考点】 形容词词义辨析

　　【译文】 如果我在一家小工厂工作，就不太可能获得许多经验。

　　【分析】 本题中 it is likely for sb. to do sth. 为固定句型，it 指代不定式短语 go gain much experience，意为"获得许多经验是……的"。weekly 表示"每星期的"，作名词时指"周刊，周报"；friendly 意为"友好的"；lively 意思是"活泼的"；只有 C 项 likely 意为"可能的"，在逻辑上符合句意。

25. **【答案】** A

　　【考点】 词组辨析

　　【译文】 乡亲们给我们提供了很多帮助，我们觉得应该做些什么作为回报。

　　【分析】 与介词 in 搭配的词组：in return 意思是"作为回报"；in place 表示"在适当的位置，适当"；in fashion 意思是"时髦的"；in danger 意为"处于危险之中"。根据句意，选项 A 为正确答案。

　【参考例句】

　（1）The picture is securely fixed in place.（这幅画安全地固定在适当位置。）

　（2）The shoes of this type are in fashion today.（如今正流行这种类型的鞋子。）

　（3）Everyone finds himself in danger.（人人自危。）

Section B

26. **【答案】** certainly

　　【考点】 词形转换

　　【译文】 一些人确信吸烟必定会导致肺癌。

　　【分析】 宾语从句中主谓宾成分完整，空格位于助动词 will 和谓语动词 cause 之间，因此缺少的只能是副词，用作状语以修饰动词。故应采用形容词 certain 的副词形式 certainly，意为"肯定，一定"。

27. **【答案】** would have failed

　　【考点】 虚拟语气

　　【译文】 要是没有队员们帮助的话，我上一次的实验就会失败。

　　【分析】 采用虚拟语气时，当 if 引导的非真实条件从句提出与过去事实相反的假设，从句谓语动词为过去完成时，主句则用 would have done 的形式。

　　【用法拓展】 本题中 if 也可省略，从句可以改写成：Had not the team members helped me, I would have failed in the last experiment. 该句与原句表示的意思相同。

28. **【答案】** to say

　　【考点】 动词不定式

　　【译文】 我要求他在本月底之前别说任何关于我们合同的事。

　　【分析】 本题中 ask sb. to do sth. 为固定词组，意为"要求某人做某事"。动词不定式 to do 用作宾语 sb. 的补足语。

【用法拓展】此外，不定式的否定方法就是直接在 to 的前面加 not，即 ask sb. not to do sth.，意为"要求某人不做某事"。

29.【答案】go

　　【考点】词形转换

　　【译文】我们通常到国外度假，但今年我们要呆在家里。

　　【分析】本题中副词 usually 意为"通常，经常"，暗示句子时态为一般现在时或一般过去时。but 连接两个简单句，根据两个并列句时态一致的原则，后半句采用现在进行时表示将来，前半句也应采用现在时。故采用 go 的第一人称复数的一般现在时态。

　　【用法拓展】英语中用现在进行时表示将来时的现象很普遍，一般表示谓语动作马上就会发生，而不是在遥远的未来。

　　【参考例句】The party is over, and I am leaving now.（聚会结束了，我现在就要走了。）

30.【答案】development

　　【考点】词形转换

　　【译文】随着对外贸易的发展，越来越多的人在做进出口生意。

　　【分析】空格位于定冠词 the 之后，且 with 介词短语中缺少核心名词，则应采用 develop 的名词形式 development。

31.【答案】Seen

　　【考点】分词短语

　　【译文】从山顶看去，这个村庄非常漂亮。

　　【分析】分词短语在句子中作状语分句时，有现在分词或过去分词两种结构。此时，是选用现在分词还是过去分词要根据分词与逻辑主语构成的主动或被动关系来判断。如果分词与其逻辑主语构成主动关系，则用现在分词；而如果分词与其逻辑主语构成被动关系，则用过去分词。本题中 see 的逻辑主语是主句的主语 village，两者构成被动关系，故采用 see 的过去分词形式 seen。

　　【用法拓展】当分词短语自带逻辑主语时，分词的形式（现在分词和过去分词）则由其与自带的逻辑主语关系决定，而不由其与主句的主语关系确定。

　　【参考例句】He rushed into the room, his face covered with sweat.（他满脸是汗地冲进房间。）

32.【答案】helpful

　　【考点】词形转换

　　【译文】你为我们做了所有必要的安排，真是帮了我们很大的忙。

　　【分析】本题中 It is + adj. + of sb. to do sth. 为固定句型，意为"某人做某事是……的"，其中的形容词通常为表示人的品质的词，如：kind, good, friendly 等，因此采用 help 的形容词形式 helpful。

33.【答案】excited

　　【考点】词形转换

　　【译文】听到我们的新产品在市场上销售得很好这个好消息时，我们都感到兴奋。

【分析】本题中主句是主系表结构，got 是系动词，其后缺少形容词作表语。动词 excite 的形容词有两种：exciting 和 excited。前者意为"令人兴奋的"，形容人或事本身具有的品质和能力；后者意为"感到兴奋的"，形容人的感受。显然句意表达人的感觉，故采用 excited。

【用法拓展】类似 excite 的动词还有：interest, confuse, shock 等。这类动词的现在分词和过去分词形式都可作形容词，前者描述某种状态，后者则描述人的心情和感受。如 shocking 表示"某件事令人震惊"，而 shocked 表示"令人震惊的心态"。

34. 【答案】to take

【考点】动词不定式

【译文】马克有点沮丧，因为经理没有准许他下星期休假。

【分析】本题中固定词组 allow sb. to do sth. 意为"允许某人做某事"，此时不定式作宾语补足语。故采用 to take。

35. 【答案】learning

【考点】动名词

【译文】一些在中国的美国商人会花很多时间学中文。

【分析】本题中 spend time (in) doing sth. 为固定短语，意为"某人花费……时间做某事"，in 可省略，因此采用 learn 的动名词 learning。

【用法拓展】spend 也可与 on 结合形成固定短语，即 spend time on sth. 或 spend money on sth.，意为"某人花费……时间在某事上"或"某人花费……金钱在某事上"。

【参考例句】

(1) I spent two hours on the lunch.（我花了两小时吃午饭。）

(2) I spent two dollars on the lunch.（我花了两美元在午饭上。）

Part III Reading Comprehension

▶（Task 1）大意

本文阐述了确定缴纳税款金额是件很困难的事情，它取决于多个因素。文章举了一个艺术家缴纳税金的例子。某次，艺术家自己计算缴纳的税金量竟然比税务官计算的还要多。

【核心词汇】

government	n.	政府	spend	v.	花费
depend	v.	取决	proper	adj.	适当的
support	v.	支持	owe	v.	亏欠
earn	v.	赚钱	check	n.	支票

【难句分析】第一段第一句：It is often difficult for a man to be quite sure what tax he ought to pay to the government because it depends on so many different things. 该句主干由主句 it is adj. for sb. to do sth. 句型加 because 引导的原因状语从句构成。主句

句型意思为"对于某人而言，做某事是……的"，其中 be quite sure 对应主句句型中 do，而 what tax he ought to pay to the government 不是疑问句，而是名词性从句，其功能相当于名词，对应 sth.。故该句的意思是"通常对人们而言，要非常确定他应该向政府支付多少税金是困难的"。

36. 【答案】C

　　【考点】细节题

　　【分析】根据文章第一段第一句话 It is often difficult for a man to be quite sure what tax he ought to pay to the government because it depends on so many different things... 可知，通常对人们来说，确定需要缴纳的税款是困难的，因为这取决于很多事情。故选项 C 为正确答案。

37. 【答案】B

　　【考点】细节题

　　【分析】文章第一段 it depends on so many different things 后列举了许多决定纳税金额的情况，其中包括 whether the man is married，这与选项 B 的内容一致。其他三项很明显不是文中列举的情况。故选项 B 为正确答案。

38. 【答案】C

　　【考点】词汇题

　　【分析】proper 意为"正确的，适当的"；right 意为"正确的"。文中详细描述艺术家的缴税情况，我们也可推出他是想缴纳正确的数额。故选项 C 为正确答案。

39. 【答案】A

　　【考点】推理题

　　【分析】从文中第三段 ...wonder if he had paid enough 和 He believed that he owed the government something 可知，他觉得他付费不够，欠政府什么。故选项 A 为正确答案。

40. 【答案】B

　　【考点】细节题

　　【分析】从文中最一句 The official explained that too much had been paid, and therefore the difference was now returned to the taxpayer 可知，信的内容为税务官将他多缴纳的部分返还给他。故选项 B 为正确答案。

▶（Task 2）大意

　　本文为说明文，阐述了使用高压锅的六条常识，包括：使用时要人看着；加入适量的水；设定合适的烹调时间；遵守烹调操作指导；勿强力打开压力锅的盖子；使用后彻底清洗压力锅。

【核心词汇】

sufficient	adj.	充足的	stove	n.	炉子
overfill	v.	使溢出	soapy	adj.	涂有肥皂的
undercooked	adj.	煮得欠熟的			

【难句分析】最后一段第三句：Do not use stove ash or sand for they may damage the cooker. 该句由主句祈使句 do not use stove ash or sand 和原因状语从句 for they may damage the cooker 构成。该句中 for 不是介词，不用来表示目的和对象。在语义和语法功能上 for 相当于 because，用来表示原因，引导原因状语从句，但是语气比 because 要弱很多。故该句意思是"请勿用炉灰或沙子以免损坏压力锅"。

41.【答案】A

　　【考点】细节题

　　【分析】本题询问了根据第一条规则，用户应该怎样。从 Never leave the cooker unwatched when it is in use 可知，在使用过程中应随时看守压力锅。故选项 A 为正确答案。

42.【答案】D

　　【考点】细节题

　　【分析】本题问及第二条规则。从 Overfilling the cooker may block the vent pipe and cause the cooker to explode 可知，压力锅里水填得过满会堵塞排气孔，从而导致爆炸。故选项 D 为正确答案。

43.【答案】D

　　【考点】细节题

　　【分析】本题问及第五条规则。从 Allow the cooker to cool or run it under cool water before trying to open the cover 可知，在打开压力锅之前要让其冷却下来或者置于流动的冷水中。故选项 D 为正确答案。

44.【答案】B

　　【考点】判断题

　　【分析】本题问及第六条规则。从 Mild detergent and hot water work the best 可知最好用中性洗涤剂和热水清洗。故选项 B 为正确答案。

45.【答案】A

　　【考点】判断题

　　【分析】本题涉及第二条规则。从 Overfilling the cooker may block the vent pipe and cause the cooker to explode 可知，压力锅里水填得过满会堵塞排气孔，从而导致爆炸。选项 B 和 C 均是文章中正确使用压力锅的方式，而 D 项的做法只会导致锅里的食物难以煮熟，不会产生危险。故选项 A 为正确答案。

▶（Task 3）大意

　　本文为一篇推销保健杂志的广告。该杂志向妈妈们提供保健信息和知识，以及医疗服务信息。

【核心词汇】

outline	*v.*	描画轮廓	network	*n.*	网络
website	*n.*	网站	goal	*n.*	目标
healthcare	*n.*	保健护理	treatment	*n.*	治疗

【难句分析】 第四段：Of course, if you ever need more than just information, *Columbia One Source* offers our patients the special knowledge of the nation's largest network of homecare services, hospitals and outpatient surgery centers. 该句中谓语动词 offer 后接双宾语：our patients 和 the special knowledge。名词词组 the special knowledge 后接两个 of 介词短语，第一个介词短语 of the nation's largest network 修饰 the special knowledge，第二个介词短语 of homecare services, hospitals and outpatient surgery centers 修饰 the nation's largest network。故该句意思是"当然，如果您不只需要信息，*Columbia One Source* 向病人们提供有关全国最大的家庭护理机构、医院和门诊手术中心等医疗机构网的特殊信息"。

46. **【答案】** practical ways

　　【考点】 细节题

　　【分析】 本题询问如何更加健康生活的信息。根据第二段第二句话 It's our monthly magazine which outlines practical ways to live a healthier life 可知，这是一本提供实用方法（practical ways）的月刊，它会带你走向更健康的生活。

47. **【答案】** healthcare information

　　【考点】 细节题

　　【分析】 本题询问了有关医生建议（doctors' advice）和其他信息。根据第三段 Then there's our website on the Internet that provides doctors' advice and other healthcare information 可知，该杂志在互联网上设有网站，提供医生的建议和其他保健信息（healthcare information）。

48. **【答案】** largest network

　　【考点】 细节题

　　【分析】 本题询问了向病人们提供家庭护理机构的特殊信息。根据第四段 *Columbia One Source* offers our patients the special knowledge of the nation's largest network of homecare services, hospitals and outpatient surgery centers. 可知，该杂志向病人们提供有关全国最大的（largest network）家庭护理机构、医院和门诊手术中心等医疗机构网的特殊信息。

49. **【答案】** the Web

　　【考点】 细节题

　　【分析】 本题询问了有关网址的信息。根据第六段 For more information, see our site on the Web 可知欲获取更多信息，请浏览网站（the Web）。

50.【答案】free copy

【考点】细节题

【分析】本题询问了有关获得该杂志的信息。根据最后一段 to get your free copy of *Columbia One Source* 可知，可免费领取一份（free copy）*Columbia One Source* 杂志。

▶（Task 4）

【答案】51. Q, O 52. D, M 53. F, P 54. H, E 55. J, G

【汉译】

A—剧痛	B—外科医生	C—皮肤检查
D—验血	E—视力检查	F—病假证明
G—手术	H—血压	I—牙痛
J—胃痛	K—心脏病	L—传染
M—精神疾病	N—神经疾病	O—肺病
P—高热	Q—牙科医生	

▶（Task 5）大意

本文是一篇航空公司促销的广告。文中介绍了在选择乘坐该航空公司航班时如何获得免费机票、现金奖励和获得大奖的方式。

【核心词汇】

airline	*n.*	航空公司	cash	*n.*	现金
prize	*n.*	奖品			

56.【答案】April 30th

【考点】细节题

【分析】本题询问该促销的持续时间。根据广告语 There is a winner everyday from January 1st to April 30th 2005 可知，持续时间为从 2005 年 1 月 1 日到 4 月 30 日（April 30th）。

57.【答案】free tickets

【考点】细节题

【分析】本题询问在促销期间内乘坐该航空公司航班可获得什么。根据广告正文第一段 ...and you could win free tickets daily, plus... 得知，可以获得免费机票（free tickets）。

58.【答案】One pair of/Two

【考点】细节题

【分析】本题询问有关获得一等奖机票的情况。根据正文第二段 One pair of First Class

return tickets on Singapore Airlines to any of our destinations in Australia... 可知，可以获得两张（One pair of/Two）新加坡航空公司飞往澳大利亚任一目的地的头等舱往返机票等。

59. 【答案】5-star hotel

　　【考点】细节题

　　【分析】本题询问获得二等奖入住酒店的情况。根据正文第三段 ...5 nights' accommodation in a 5-star hotel... 可知，可入住五星级酒店（5-star hotel）。

60. 【答案】Singapore Airlines office

　　【考点】细节题

　　【分析】本题询问获得更多有关促销信息的情况。根据正文最后一段 For more information, contact the Singapore Airlines office at your place... 可知，在新加坡航空公司（Singapore Airlines）办公室可获得更多信息。

Part IV　Translation — English into Chinese

61. 【答案】C—B—A—D

　　【分析】此句主干为主系表结构，主语为主语从句 what our company values most in employing people。解题关键在于对主语从句的正确翻译和对动词 value 和 employ 的正确理解。value 意为"重视，看重"；employ 意为"招聘，雇用"。选项 A 对主语从句谓语动词理解错误；选项 B 对 employ 翻译错误；选项 D 对词汇和句子结构的翻译错误。故最佳答案选 C。

62. 【答案】A—D—C—B

　　【分析】此句结构为 it + *adj.* + that，it 是句子的形式主语，而句子的真正主语是 that 引导的从句。解题关键包括正确理解：hardly 是否定副词，意为"几乎不，决不，一点也不"；he is reading 是一个定语从句，用来修饰 the instructions（说明书）of the mobile phone（手机）。选项 D 错译了 hardly；选项 B 和 C 错译了 instructions，且选项 B 错译 hardly。故最佳答案选 A。

63. 【答案】D—B—A—C

　　【分析】此句主干结构为 Candidates may consider their application unsuccessful，主语 candidates 其后跟有定语从句 who are not contacted within four weeks after the interview，意为"面试后四周内尚未得到通知的求职者"，因此本题关键在于定语从句的正确翻译。选项 B 将 contact 的被动关系翻译成主动关系；选项 A 没有翻译出 unsuccessful，且错译 consider；选项 C 语义理解错误。故最佳答案选 D。

64. 【答案】C—B—D—A

　　【分析】此句是一个含有定语从句的主从复合句，本题关键在于定语从句的正确翻译。定语从句 which is constantly used 修饰先行词 art，意为"一门常用的艺术"。逗号后 and 表示递进关系。此外，还要正确理解 constantly，其意为"经常地"。选项 A 错译 constantly used，且将句子间的递进关系错译为因果关系；选项 B 错译 constantly，多译"才能掌握"；选项 D 对句子关系和结构理解错误。故最佳答案选 C。

65. 【答案】"假日阳光大酒店"的持卡人自动成为其预定网络的注册会员。他们可以享用各加盟酒店提供的服务。我们鼓励持卡人尽量多地使用本卡。当持卡人的积分达到一定数量时，他们将获得奖励。在您入住酒店之前，请务必事先预订房间，这样当您退房时只需按会员价格付款。

【分析】此句翻译中应注意对以下几个语言点的正确理解：registered members 意为"注册会员"；在名词短语 the services offered by its member hotels 中，核心名词是 services，offered by its member hotels 为后置定语修饰名词 services，意为"由加盟店提供的服务"；as often as possible 意为"尽可能多地"，表频率；check in 意为"在旅馆登记住宿"；check out 意为"在旅馆结账退房"。

Part V Writing

【考点】问卷调查写作

【解题技巧分析】本文的体裁是问卷调查，要求对酒店的服务做出评价，并给出建议。本题已经给出了该问卷调查的格式和问题，只要求考生根据中文题目要求和问卷调查中给出的问题进行回答。因此，答题重点在于：书写建议时要表述准确、清晰，符合英文习惯。写作时要注意以下几点：要理顺句子间的逻辑关系，正确使用因果关联词，如：because, so that, therefore 等，尽量避免写成流水账；尽量使用一些固定短语或表达，如：it is advisable..., it is suggested..., be located in/by 等。

【范文】

QUESTIONNAIRE

To improve the quality of our service, we would be grateful if you'd complete the following questionnaire.

Name: Wang Ming   Nationality: Chinese   Room Number: 3002

Check-in Date: June 10, 2005   Check-out Date: June 20, 2005

Did you receive polite and efficient service when you arrived? Yes

Are you satisfied with the room service of our hotel? Yes

What's your opinion of our health facilities? Good

Please give your impression of our restaurant service. Overall good

Have you any other comments to help us make your stay more enjoyable?

There are two suggestions for you. First, because the hotel is located by the sea, tle traffic is inconvenient, and there are limited commercial facilities, it is advisable that you should provide free shuttle buses. It is convenient for guests who come here on holiday to go shopping in the downtown area. Second, it is suggested that the hotel should contact the related companies to offer guests the car renting service.

Baiyun Hotel

General Manager

2009 年 12 月高等学校英语应用能力考试（B 级）
听力录音文本

Section A

1. Are you Mr. Baker from America?
2. How do you like your work?
3. Would you please give me the report, Tom?
4. What's your father's job?
5. Would you like a cup of coffee?

Section B

6. W: What can I do for you, sir?
   M: Well, I want to buy a T-shirt.
   Q: What does the man want to buy?

7. M: What's your plan for the summer holiday?
   W: I'm going to Australia.
   Q: What's the woman going to do for the summer holiday?

8. W: May I use this telephone?
   M: Sorry, it doesn't work.
   Q: What does the woman want to do?

9. M: Excuse me, where is the manager's office?
   W: It's on the second floor.
   Q: On which floor is the manager's office?

10. W: May I have a double room for tonight?
    M: Sorry, there are only single rooms available.
    Q: Where does the conversation take place?

Section C

Ladies and Gentlemen,

Welcome to you all. We are pleased to have you here to visit our company.

Today, we will first (11) show you around our company, and then you will go and see our (12) factory and research center. The research center was (13) built just a year ago. You may ask any questions you have during the visit. We will (14) do our best to make your visit comfortable and worthwhile.

Again, I would like to extend a warmest welcome to all of you on behalf of our company, and I hope that you will enjoy your stay here and (15) have a good time.

2009 年 6 月高等学校英语应用能力考试（B 级）
听力录音文本

Section A

1. Can I see him in the office?

2. Hello, may I speak to Mr. Thomas?

3. How long may I keep the book?

4. Excuse me, is this train for London?

5. What do you think of the film we saw yesterday?

Section B

6. M: When does the plane arrive from Beijing?

   W: At twelve o'clock. You have to wait for another ten minutes.

   Q: When does the plane arrive?

7. W: I have not received your email yet.

   M: That's too bad. I'll send it to you again.

   Q: What's the man probably going to do?

8. M: Susan, why don't you have some wine?

   W: No, thanks. I'm driving tonight.

   Q: What can we learn from the talk?

9. W: Excuse me, where can I find English-Chinese dictionaries?

   M: They're on the second floor.

   Q: Where does the conversation most probably take place?

10. M: What's the matter, Mary?

    W: My computer doesn't work. Can you help me?

    Q: What does the woman ask the man to do?

Section C

Hello, everyone. This is the captain speaking. (11) Welcome to Flight JK900 leaving for Chicago.

Our flight time today is 2 hours and 35 minutes, and we will be flying at an average altitude of 31,000 feet. The (12) local time in Chicago is a quarter past twelve, and the current weather is cloudy, but there is a chance of (13) rain later in the day. We will (14) arrive at Gate 7 at the Chicago Airport.

On behalf of our Airlines, I wish you an enjoyable (15) stay in Chicago. Sit back and enjoy the flight.

2008 年 12 月高等学校英语应用能力考试（B级）
听力录音文本

Section A

1. Excuse me, are you Mr. Smith from America?
2. Mr. Johnson, when is the library open?
3. It's rather hot today, would you please open the window?
4. What do you think of your new boss?
5. What's the weather like in your city?

Section B

6. W: Are you coming for the basketball game?
   M: Yes, I got a ticket from my brother.
   Q: Where did the man get the ticket?

7. M: Can you stay for dinner?
   W: I'd love to, but I have to go to meet a friend at the airport.
   Q: What's the woman going to do?

8. W: I'm here to see Miss Brown.
   M: Miss Brown? Er…, she is in her office.
   Q: Where is Miss Brown?

9. M: Do you like your new job?
   W: Yes, I like it very much.
   Q: How does the woman feel about her new job?

10. W: Did you work as a salesman in that company?
    M: No, I was an engineer.
    Q: What did the man do in that company?

Section C

People visit other countries for many reasons. Some travel (11) on business; others travel to visit interesting places. Whenever you go, for whatever reason, it is important to be (12) safe. A tourist can draw a lot of attention from local people. Although most of the people you meet are friendly and welcoming, sometimes there are dangers. (13) For example, your money or passport might be stolen. Just as in your home country, do not expect everyone you meet to be friendly and (14) helpful. It is important to prepare your trip in advance, and (15) always be careful while you are traveling.

2008 年 6 月高等学校英语应用能力考试（B级）
听力录音文本

Section A

1. It's a fine day. Why not go to the zoo?

2. When can I take my winter vacation?

3. Did you enjoy the performance last night?

4. Can we have dinner together this weekend?

5. Professor Smith, may I ask you a few questions?

Section B

6. M: I prefer coffee to tea. What about you, Jane?

   W: Just water.

   Q: What would the woman like to have?

7. W: Excuse me, can you call a taxi for me?

   M: Sorry. The telephone is out of order.

   Q: What does the man mean?

8. M: What's wrong with me, doctor?

   W: Just a cold. Nothing serious.

   Q: What's the probable relationship between the two speakers?

9. M: Don't you usually drive to work?

   W: No. I walk to work every day.

   Q: How does the woman usually go to work?

10. M: My computer doesn't work.

    W: Why don't you have it repaired?

    Q: What does the woman think the man should do?

Section C

Today more and more people begin to understand that study does not come to an end with school graduation. Education is not just a college (11) degree; it is life itself. Many people are not interested in studying at college, and they are interested in (12) other kinds of learning. They may go to a (13) training class in their own field; they may improve their (14) work skills by following television courses. They certainly know that if they know more or learn more, they can get (15) better jobs or earn more money.

2007 年 12 月高等学校英语应用能力考试（B 级）
听力录音文本

Section A

1. It's getting dark. Would you please turn on the light?
2. Hello, may I speak to Bill please?
3. When can I have my holidays?
4. How often do you go online?
5. Hi, Mark! How are you getting on these days?

Section B

6. M: The streets are covered with snow.
   W: That's true. It has been snowing for a whole day.
   Q: What's the weather like?
7. W: You know I don't like to travel by plane.
   M: Yes, I see. Then let's go there by train.
   Q: How will the two speakers probably travel?
8. M: Is this the right way to the police station?
   W: No. It's in the opposite direction.
   Q: What's the man doing?
9. M: What's wrong with me, doctor?
   W: Nothing serious. You've just got a cold.
   Q: What's the probable relationship between the two speakers?
10. M: My mobile phone doesn't work.
    W: Why don't you have it repaired?
    Q: What's the woman's suggestion?

Section C

Welcome to the Public Bus System. Its bus network operates 365 days of the year and has (11) services that can take you to your destination quickly and easily.

You can travel round the city for just $ (12) 3 day with Type-A bus tickets. Type-B bus tickets are even (13) cheaper. You can get on and off as many times (14) as you like. So you can tour the city at your own pace.

You can buy tickets at most newspaper stands.

If you want to get (15) more information, call the office of the Public Bus System.

2007 年 6 月高等学校英语应用能力考试（B级）
听力录音文本

Section A

1. Are you going to buy a house?
2. Have you read today's newspaper?
3. What time do you usually go to work?
4. Have you received my letter?
5. Do you often go shopping at weekends?

Section B

6. M: It's very cold this morning.
   W: You are right. It's much colder than yesterday.
   Q: What's the weather like this morning?

7. M: I'm going to Beijing tomorrow. Would you please book a ticket for me?
   W: Sure, with pleasure.
   Q: What will the woman probably do?

8. M: What do you think of your new boss?
   W: I don't like him. He's too serious.
   Q: What does the woman think of her new boss?

9. W: I'm afraid we will be late for the party.
   M: Don't worry. There is still twenty minutes to go.
   Q: What does the man mean?

10. M: Is there anything I can do for you?
    W: Thank you very much, but I can do it all by myself.
    Q: What does the woman mean?

Section C

The world population today is about 6 billion. But only about 11 percent of the world's land is suitable for farming. However, the area of farmland is becoming smaller and smaller (11) every year. So it will be difficult to feed so many mouths. There are several reasons why farmland is being (12) lost. First, a lot of the land is being used for the (13) building of houses. Secondly, some of the land has become wasteland because wind and (14) rain have removed the top soil. Thirdly, some of the land has become too salty to (15) grow crops. Therefore, a big problem that we face today is hunger.

2006 年 12 月高等学校英语应用能力考试（B 级）
听力录音文本

Section A

1. Can I speak to Susan?

2. I'm terribly sorry we're late.

3. Thank you very much for your help.

4. Shall we meet again to discuss it further?

5. How does the new product sell in the market?

Section B

6. M: I wonder if you have a special menu for children.

   W: I'm sorry, but we don't have one.

   Q: What kind of food does the man ask for?

7. M: What can I do for you?

   W: I'd like to open a savings account here.

   Q: Where does the conversation most likely take place?

8. M: Someone is knocking at the door.

   W: I think it's Jack again.

   Q: What can we learn from the conversation?

9. M: Why are you in such a hurry?

   W: I left an important paper in the office.

   Q: Why is the woman going back to the office?

10. M: What's wrong with you, Helen?

    W: Nothing wrong. I just come for a medical check-up.

    Q: What does the woman want to do in the hospital?

Section C

Scientists have discovered that tea is good for us. It tastes good and it is refreshing. In recent (11) medical studies, tea has been found to help prevent heart attacks and cancer.

One study suggests that both black tea and green tea help (12) protect the heart. In the study, tea drinkers had a 44 percent (13) lower death rate after heart attacks than non-drinkers. Other studies have shown that tea, like fruit and vegetables, helps fight against chemicals that may (14) lead to the development of certain cancers.

Many people really like tea. Next to plain water, it's the world's most (15) popular drink.

2006 年 6 月高等学校英语应用能力考试（B级）
听力录音文本

Section A

1. Excuse me. Can I see your boss?
2. Is this your first trip to Beijing?
3. Is there anything you want me to do?
4. Would you like another cup of tea?
5. Will you attend the meeting this afternoon?

Section B

6. W: I've tried everything, but my computer still doesn't work.
   M: Let me have a look at your computer.
   Q: What are they talking about?
7. M: Mrs. Smith, have you got any work experience?
   W: Yes. I've been a secretary for five years.
   Q: What do we know about the woman?
8. W: Mr. Young, have you brought a price list with you?
   M: Yes. Here you are.
   Q: What does the woman want?
9. M: Would you like to see the menu, Madam?
   W: Oh, yes. What is today's special food?
   Q: Where does this conversation most probably take place?
10. W: What time should I check out if I leave the hotel tomorrow?
    M: Anytime tomorrow morning, Madam.
    Q: When will the woman check out?

Section C

　　Modern technology has a big influence on our daily life. New devices are widely used today. For example, we have to (11) deal with the Internet every day. It is becoming more and more (12) useful to nearly everybody. Now it's time to think about how the Internet influences us, what (13) effect it has on our social behavior and what the future world will look like. The Internet has (14) totally changed our life; there is no doubt about that. I think the Internet has changed our life in a (15) wonderful way.

2005 年 12 月高等学校英语应用能力考试（B级）
听力录音文本

Section A

1. Could you please send this letter for me?

2. When can I come to have my photos?

3. Excuse me. Is that seat taken?

4. Would you please tell me something about the machine?

5. Mr. Wang, shall I take a message for you?

Section B

6. M: Hi, Alice, how is everything with you?

　　W: As busy as usual.

　　Q: What can we learn from the dialogue?

7. W: Mike, may I use the telephone here?

　　M: Sure, and local calls are free here.

　　Q: What does the man say about local calls?

8. M: Did you hear about the bus accident last night?

　　W: Yes, it was terrible. Five people were injured.

　　Q: What happened last night?

9. W: I am going to the railway station. Can you drive me there?

　　M: Yes, it's my pleasure.

　　Q: What does the woman ask the man to do?

10. M: Shall we have the meeting at ten o'clock on Wednesday morning?

　　W: Wednesday morning at ten? It's OK for me.

　　Q: What are they talking about?

Section C

Good evening, ladies and gentlemen!

First of all, let me thank you for inviting us to such a great Christmas party. We (11) really enjoyed the delicious food and excellent wine. Also, the music was perfect, so if I were a better dancer, I would have enjoyed the party twice (12) as much. I enjoyed meeting and (13) talking to you, and sharing the time together. I hope we'll be able to keep this good relationship and make (14) next year another great one together.

Thank you again for the (15) wonderful party. We have had a great time.

2005 年 6 月高等学校英语应用能力考试（B 级）听力录音文本

Section A

1. Would you like to go swimming with me this afternoon?

2. What's the best time for us to leave?

3. Janet, what do you study at college?

4. Excuse me, how much are these shoes?

5. I'm going to make some coffee. Would you like some?

Section B

6. M: I want to mail these books to New York.

   W: By ship or by air, sir?

   Q: Where is the man?

7. W: Jack is ill. You'd better call the doctor.

   M: Sure, I'll do it right away.

   Q: What will the man probably do?

8. M: These cups look nice. How much are they?

   W: They are $10 each.

   Q: How much will the man pay if he buys only one cup?

9. W: Well, Mr. Black, what do you think of fast food?

   M: Oh, I don't like it.

   Q: What does the man think of fast food?

10. M: What do you think of our new boss?

    W: She's kind and patient.

    Q: What does the woman think of the new boss?

Section C

Some managers have noticed recently that the employees in the company are taking advantage of the policy of having breaks. The workers have two 15-minute breaks per (11) day. However, the two breaks are lasting (12) as long as 25 to 30 minutes each. The workers complain that the factory work is so (13) boring that they need longer breaks. Also the dining hall is so (14) far away that it takes too long to walk there and back. But the company is losing hundreds of work hours each year. Should employees be paid for the time they are not working? The general manager has to call a meeting to (15) discuss this matter.

附录1
必考及常考语言点
讲解与练习

从历年真题来看，高等学校英语应用能力考试中语法结构部分的考查重点是时态、语态、从句、非谓语动词、虚拟语气、主谓一致、倒装句、比较级、固定结构和固定搭配、词形转换等。以下我们将分类进行讲解和练习：

（一）时态

1.1 一般时态

● 谈及某人或某物经常或习惯性做的事情、提及某人或某事长期固定的状态、一般性真理、说明或报道、讨论电影、故事等时应使用**一般现在时**。

● 表示在过去某个时候发生并已完成的动作时用**一般过去时**。

● 预测某事将来会发生或表示说话者的打算时用**一般将来时**，其构成形式为 will/shall + v.。除此以外，be going to + v., be about to + v. 和 be to + v. 也都可以表示将要做某事。

其中应特别注意和掌握的常考语言点如下：

（1）状语从句中，用一般现在时表示将来的动作。例如：We won't start until he <u>arrives</u>.

（2）arrive/leave, begin/end, come/go, open/close 等动词的一般现在时与表示将来时间的状语连用，表示将来行为发生的计划性和规定性。例如：He <u>leaves</u> for Wuhan tonight.

1.2 进行时态

● 表示说话时正在进行的动作或存在的情况时用**现在进行时**；其构成形式为 am/is/are + doing。

● 表示特定的过去时刻正在发生的事情或重复发生的动作时用**过去进行时**；其构成形式为 was/were + doing。

● 表示某事肯定会发生、在将来特定时刻正在进行用**将来进行时**；其构成形式为 will/shall + be + doing。

注意：come, go, arrive, leave, start, begin, return 等词的现在进行时可以表示将来，即计划安排好要做的事情。例如：<u>I'm leaving</u> at eight tomorrow morning.

1.3 完成时态

完成时态是"语法结构"部分考查的重点之一，主要考查的是过去完成时、现在完成时和将来完成时。（1）过去完成时（had done）表示在过去某一时间或动作之前已经发生或完成的动作；换言之，它表示句子中描述的动作发生在"过去的过去"。（2）现在完成时（have/has done）表示与现在有联系的过去；动作发生在过去，但对现在有影响或产生了结果。（3）将来完成时 (will/shall have done) 用来表示在将来某一时间以前已经完成或一直持续的动作。

考生必须重点掌握以下相关的语言点：

● 现在完成时常与表示到现在为止历经一段时间的状语连用，如 all day, for 20 hours, since 2000, so far, up to now 等。例如：

I <u>haven't seen</u> her since she left school.

● 现在完成时、过去完成时和将来完成时常与状语"by + 现在 / 过去 / 将来某时间"连用。如果 by 后面表示的是现在的时间，谓语应使用现在完成时；如果 by 后面表示的是过去的时间，谓语应使用过去完成时；如果 by 后面表示的是将来的时间，谓语则应使用将来完成时。例如：

By <u>now</u>, we have learned 1,500 English words.

（到目前为止，我们已经学了 1,500 个英语单词。）

I had completed the course **by the end of** <u>last year</u>.

（到去年年底为止，我已经修完了这门课程。）

I will have completed the course **by the end of** <u>next year</u>.

（到明年年底为止，我将修完这门课程。）

● 在 It is/was first/second time/day/year (that)... 结构中必须使用完成时。如果前面的 be 动词是 is, that 从句中的动词使用现在完成时；如果前面的 be 动词是 was, that 从句中的动词使用过去完成时。例如：

It is the first time I <u>have been</u> in Wuhan.

It was the first time I <u>had been</u> in Wuhan.

● 在固定句型 hardly/scarcely...when... 和 no sooner...than...（均表示"一……就……"）中，前面的主句通常用过去完成时，后面的从句通常用一般过去时。例如：

No sooner <u>had we left</u> the village **than** it <u>began</u> to rain.

练习题：

1. I hope they ＿＿＿＿＿＿ this road by the time I come back next year.

    A. have repaired   B. will repair

    C. are to repair   D. will have repaired

2. I could have called you yesterday, but I ＿＿＿＿＿＿ your telephone number.

    A. didn't have   B. won't have

    C. hadn't had   D. wouldn't have

3. Hardly had we gathered in the square when it (begin) _____ to rain.

4. As soon as I (get) _____ home, it started to rain heavily.

5. When I found Kerry, she (play) _____ table tennis with her friend.

6. Up till now I (spend) _____ a great deal of money on books, magazines and newspapers.

答案：1. D　　2. A　　3. began　　4. got　　5. was playing　　6. have spent

（二）语态

　　动词的语态分为主动语态和被动语态。主语是动作的发出者时使用主动语态，主语是动作的接受者时使用被动语态。被动语态也是英语应用能力考试（B 级）的常考点之一。被动语态由动词 be + 过去分词构成。根据时态的变化，被动语态也有变化：一般现在时的被动语态为 am/is/are + 过去分词，一般过去时的被动语态为 was/were + 过去分词，一般将来时的被动语态为 will/shall be + 过去分词，现在进行时的被动语态为 am/is/are + being+ 过去分词，过去进行时的被动语态为 was/were + being + 过去分词，现在完成时的被动语态为 have/has been + 过去分词，过去完成时的被动语态为 had been + 过去分词。被动语态经常和时态联合起来成为考点。

　　需要注意的是，有时候主动形式也可以表示被动意义：

　　1) wash, cook, sell, write, cut, read, look 等词与副词如 well, easily, perfectly 等连用，描述事物的特性，用主动形式表示被动意义。例如：

　　The book **sells** well. （这本书很畅销。）

　　The pen **writes** well. （这只笔很好写。）

　　2) need, want, deserve, require, be worth 等动词或短语后可以接动名词，用主动形式表示被动意义。例如：

　　It **is worth** remembering all my life. （这值得我牢记一生。）

　　Your car **wants** repairing. （你的车需要修理。）

练习题：

1. Thirty percent of Jane's income _____ on clothing every year.

　　A. is spent　　　　　　　　　　　　B. is being spent

　　C. had been spent　　　　　　　　　D. has been spent

2. Since the introduction of the new technique, the production cost _____ greatly.

　　A. reduces　　　　　　　　　　　　B. is reduced

　　C. is reducing　　　　　　　　　　D. has been reduced

3. Nothing can (do) _____ unless we are given more information about the situation.

4. This film _____ this weekend.

　　A. will show　　　　　　　　　　　B. shows

　　C. is to show　　　　　　　　　　　D. is to be shown

5. Only people working in this factory (allow) _____ to enter this room.

答案：1. A　　2 D　　3. be done　　4. D　　5. are allowed

（三）从句

在考试中，对从句的考查不仅仅直接出现在"语法结构"部分，更多的则是渗透在"阅读理解"和"翻译"中。考生要读懂文章或翻译句子必须能够识别从句，分析句子的基本成分，因此此部分的掌握十分重要。

3.1 定语从句（Attributive Clause）

定语从句在句中作定语，修饰名词或代词。被修饰的名词或代词称为先行词；定语从句通常出现在先行词之后，由关系词（关系代词或关系副词）引出。

● 定语从句引导词

1. 关系代词引导的定语从句

关系代词所代替的先行词是表示人或物的名词或代词，并在句中充当主语、宾语等成分。关系代词在定语从句中作主语时，从句谓语动词的人称和数要和先行词保持一致。关系代词在定语从句中作宾语时可以省略。

1) who, whom, that 指代人，在从句中所起作用如下：

Is he the man **who/that** wants to see you?（关系代词 who/that 在从句中作主语，修饰 man）

He is the man **whom/who/that/×** you want to see.（whom/who/that 在从句中作宾语）

2) which, that 指代事物，在从句中可作主语、宾语等，例如：

He is reading a book **which/that** is very interesting.（which/that 在句中作主语）

Where is the book **which/that/×** I bought this morning?（which/that 在句中作宾语）

3) 带介词的关系代词。正式用法中，介词可置于关系代词之前。如果指人，关系代词用 whom；如果指物，关系代词用 which。例如：

Who is the man **with whom** you just shook hands?

Is this the car **for which** you paid a high price?

2. 关系副词引导的定语从句

关系副词可代替的先行词是表示时间、地点或理由的名词，在从句中作状语。关系副词 when, where, why 的含义相当于"介词 + which"结构，因此常常和"介词 + which"结构交替使用，例如：

Do you remember the day **when/on which** you joined our club?

Beijing is the place **where/in which** I was born.

I don't know the reason **why/for which** he was late for school.

（注意：why 引导的定语从句的先行词通常都是 **reason**。）

3. 关系限定词 whose 用于修饰人或物。它只能用作定语；指物时，还可同 of which 互换。例如：

Once there was a wise king **whose** name was Alfred.（修饰 a wise king）

Please pass me the book **whose cover is green**. = Please pass me the book **the cover of which** is green.（注意词序的不同）

注意：关系词在定语从句中作主语时不可以省略。

● 限制性和非限制性定语从句

定语从句可分为限制性定语从句和非限制性定语从句。

1. 限制性定语从句和先行词关系紧密，去掉它主句意思往往不明确；非限制性定语从句的作用相当于一种插入语或者对先行词的解释，和先行词之间的关系比较松散，它与主句之间通常用逗号分开。例如：

This is the car **which/that/×** she bought last year. （限制性定语从句）

The car, **which** she bought last year, is very expensive. （非限制性定语从句）

2. 非限制性定语从句还可以将整句话作为先行词，对其进行修饰。例如：

She passed the exam, **which** made her parents very happy. （which 代指前面的整个句子）

非限制性定语从句中的先行词也可是主句中的一部分内容。例如：

He said he was poor, **which** was untrue. (which 指代前面的 he was poor)

注意：非限制性定语从句中不能省略关系代词，也不能用 that。指人时，如果关系代词在从句中作主语，用 who；如果作宾语，用 whom；指物时，无论在从句中作主语还是宾语，一律用 which。whose, when, where 也可以引导非限制性定语从句，而关系副词 why 不能。

● 关系代词 that 的用法

1. 不用 that 的情况

1）在引导非限定性定语从句时不能用 that。

2）介词后不能用 that。例如：

This is the school **in which** I studied ten years ago. （✓）

This is the school **in that** I studied ten years ago. （×）

2. 只能用 that 而不能用 which 作为定语从句的关系代词的情况

1）在不定代词（如 something, somebody, someone, anything, anybody, anyone, nothing, nobody, no one, all 等）作先行词或先行词受 all, much, few, any, little 等限定词修饰时。例如：

Is there **anything** (that) I can do for you? (that 在从句中作宾语时可以省略)

The President is satisfied with **all** (that) you have done.

2）先行词有 the only, the very 修饰时。例如：

The only thing (that) you can do is to wait.

3）先行词被序数词或形容词最高级修饰时。例如：

This is the third book (that) I read this week.

He is the cleverest man (that) I have ever met.

4）先行词既有人又有物时。例如：

They talked about **things and persons** (that) they could remember.

练习题：

1. Our school has a lot of books, _____ are in English.
   A. many of which   B. many of them
   C. many ones   D. their many

2. We were talking about the American tourist _____ we met during our trip to the Great Wall.
   A. what   B. which
   C. whose   D. whom

3. On April 1st they flew to Beijing, _____ they stayed several days.
   A. when   B. where
   C. which   D. there

4. He suddenly left for Paris yesterday, _____ was more than we had expected.
   A. that   B. what
   C. which   D. this

5. The old man has two daughters, _____ are doctors.
   A. both of them   B. both of whom
   C. both who   D. they both

答案：1. A   2. D   3. B   4. C   5. B

3.2 同位语从句（Appositive Clause）

在复合句中用作同位语的从句叫同位语从句。它一般跟在某些抽象名词后面，用以解释说明该名词表示的具体内容。

● 同位语从句说明的抽象名词通常有 advice, belief, doubt, evidence, fact, feeling, hope, idea, message, news, order, opinion, promise, question, suggestion, thought 等。例如：

   I have a feeling **that** you are wrong.

● 英语应用能力考试中考到的同位语从句的引导词通常为 that。个别名词后还可接 whether 从句或 wh- 从句。例如：

   I have no idea **when** he will be back.

   We'll discuss the problem **whether** the meeting will be held on time.

● 有时同位语从句可以不紧跟在其说明的名词后面，而被别的词隔开。例如：

   The **thought** came to her **that** someone was following her.

练习题：

1. The news _____ the Chinese football team had won the match excited all of us.
   A. that   B. which
   C. what   D. as

2. He got a message from Miss Zhang _____ Professor Wang couldn't see him the following day.
   A. which   B. whom
   C. that   D. what

3. He often asked me the question _____ the work was worth doing.

    A. whether   B. where

    C. that   D. when

答案：1. A   2. C   3. A

3.3　状语从句（Adverbial Clause）

按照在句中的功能状语从句可以分为地点状语从句、时间状语从句、条件状语从句、原因状语从句、方式状语从句、目的状语从句、结果状语从句和让步状语从句。

● 地点状语从句通常由 where, wherever 引导，表示事件的地点。例如：

    Where there is a will, there is a way.

    Wherever I am I will be thinking of my motherland.

● 时间状语从句通常由 while, when, as 引导，表示事件的发生时间。此外，常见的一些时间状语从句引导词还包括：whenever, before, after, (ever) since, by the time, until, till, every/each time（每当），表示"一……就……"的 hardly/scarcely...when, no sooner than, as soon as, the moment, the minute, the instant 等。例如：

    Come **whenever** you like.

    Not until I heard the alarm clock did I wake up. (not until 在句首时，主句需部分倒装)

    Every time I went to her house, she was watching TV.

    No sooner had I arrived home **than** it began to rain.

    Hardly/Scarcely had I arrived home **when** it began to rain.

    I will telephone you **as soon as** I get there.

    I found myself in an entirely new world **the moment/the minute/the instant** I arrived in Beijing.

● 条件状语从句的连接词主要有 if（如果），unless（除非），as/so long as（只要），given that（如果），only if（只有在……情况下），provided/providing that（假如），in case（如果）等。例如：

    We will start the project **if the manager agrees**.

    We won't start the project **unless the manager agrees**.

    You will succeed one day **as/so long as** you work hard.

    Given that she is really interested in children, teaching was a proper career for her.

    Only if the case is urgent can you press that button.

    You can arrive in Beijing earlier for the meeting **provided/providing that** you don't mind taking the night train.

    In case we fail, we won't lose heart.

● 原因状语从句通常由 because, as, since, for, now that（既然，由于），seeing that（鉴于，由于），considering that（因为，鉴于），in that（因为）等来引导。例如：

    Now that everyone is here, let's begin.

    Seeing that it's raining hard, we'd better stay at home.

Considering that he has been studying Chinese for only one year, he speaks it quite well.

He didn't attend the meeting **in that** he was ill.

● 方式状语从句通常由 as, as if, as though 引导。

1. as 引导的方式状语从句通常位于主句后，说明某人做事或行为的方式。例如：

You must do everything **as I do**.

2. as if, as though 引导的状语从句中，谓语多用虚拟语气，表示与事实相反。当所说情况是事实或实现的可能性较大时，也可用陈述语气。例如：

He looked at me **as if** I were mad. （与事实相反，谓语用虚拟语气。）

He was lying on the bed **as though** he was very tired. （是事实的可能性较大，谓语用陈述语气。）

● 目的状语从句的常用引导词有 so that（以便），in order that（为了，以便），lest（唯恐，以免），for fear that（唯恐，以免），in case（以免）等。

Speak louder **so that/in order that** everyone can hear you.

He got up early **lest/for fear that** he should miss the flight.

Write the telephone number down **in case** you forget.

● 结果状语从句的常用引导词有 so...that, such...that, so that 等。

1. so...that 和 such...that 意为"如此……以至于……"。such 是形容词，修饰名词或名词词组；so 是副词，只能修饰形容词或副词。为加强语气，可将 so 及其引导的形容词或副词、such 或含有 such 的短语移到句首，主句使用部分倒装。例如：

He got up **so** early **that** he caught the first train.

= **So** early did he get up **that** he caught the first train.

She is **such** a good teacher **that** every student likes her.

= **Such** a good teacher is she **that** every student likes her.

2. so that 也可以引导结果状语从句，意为"结果是，以至于"。例如：

She is ill, **so that** she cannot be here tonight.

● 让步状语从句的常用引导词有 though/although, as, even if/though, whether...or..., whatever (whoever, whichever, whenever, however, wherever...)/no matter what (who, which, when, how, where...) 等等。

1. although 比 though 更正式。由 though, although 引导让步状语从句时，主句不能有 but。例如：

Although David is old, he looks very strong and healthy.

The report is very important **though** it is short.

2. as 引导的让步状语从句表示强烈的对比，从句必须用倒装结构。构成结构为：

1）形容词 + as + 代词 + 系动词。例如：

Strong as you are, you cannot lift it.

2）名词 + as + 代词 + 系动词。例如：

Child as he is, he knows a lot. （注意：as 前的名词不带冠词。）

3）副词＋as＋代词＋行为动词。例如：

<u>Hard **as** I tried</u>, I couldn't finish the assignment on time.

（注意：以上三种用法中的 as 都可以用 **though** 来替换。）

4）实义动词＋as＋代词＋情态动词。例如：

<u>Search **as** I would</u>, I could not find my purse.

3. ever if/though 表示"即使"。例如：

Even if/though it was snowing, she walked to work.

4. whether...or 意为"不管……都"，表示把两方面情况一起考虑都不会影响事情的结果。例如：

Whether she is sick **or well**, she is always cheerful.

Whether 也可与 or not 连用，例如：

Whether you like it **or not**, I will go with him.

5. whatever (whoever, whichever, whenever, however, wherever...)/no matter what (who, which, when, how, where...) 这一类词表示"无论……都……"。例如：

1) **Whatever/No matter what** happened, I would not mind.

2) The police will find the murderer **wherever/no matter where** he is.

3) **Whenever/No matter when** you call on us, you are welcome.

练习题：

1. I'll lend you my computer _____ you promise to take care of it.

　　A. unless　　　　B. as　　　　　C. while　　　　　D. if

2. We moved to London _____ we could visit our friends more often.

　　A. even if　　　　B. so that　　　C. in case　　　　D. as if

3. _____ the population is too large, the government has to take measures to control the birth rate.

　　A. Although　　　B. Since　　　　C. If　　　　　　D. Until

4. The machine will continue to make much noise _____ we have it repaired.

　　A. when　　　　　B. because　　　C. if　　　　　　D. unless

5. He bought an expensive coat _____ he just lost his job.

　　A. unless　　　　B. since　　　　C. although　　　D. till

答案：1. D　　2. B　　3. B　　4. D　　5. C

3.4 宾语从句（Objective Clause）

在句子中起宾语作用的从句叫做宾语从句。考生应该重点掌握以下几点：

● 如果从句是陈述句，引导词用 that（从句中的 that 通常可以省略）。从句仍用陈述语序。

例如：The teacher said **that** he was a clever boy.

如果从句是一般疑问句，引导词用 if 或 whether；如果从句是特殊疑问句，引导词用 what, who, when, where, why, which, how 等。此时从句的语序要由一般疑问句或特殊疑问句的语序变为陈述句的语序。例如：

He asked **whether/if** I could speak English.

I didn't know **why** he was so late.

No one can be sure **what** will happen.

He didn't tell me **when** we should meet again.

● 宾语从句应同主句在谓语时态上保持一致。

1. 如果主句谓语是现在时，宾语从句的谓语根据实际情况而定。例如：

Tell me <u>whether you **love** me or not</u>.

I think that <u>our team **will win** the match</u>.

2. 如果主句谓语是过去时，宾语从句的谓语必须是过去的某种时态（一般过去时、过去进行时、过去完成时、过去将来时等）。例如：

They wondered <u>whether he **was** honest</u>.

The reporter said <u>that the UFO **was traveling** east to west at that time</u>.

He asked <u>what **had happened**</u>.

I asked <u>if he **would come** and **fix** my TV set</u>.

如果宾语从句是客观真理，从句时态则不受主句时态限制，总是用一般现在时。例如：

He didn't know <u>that light **travels** much faster than sound</u>.

● 宾语从句之后带有补足语成分时，一般须用 it 作形式宾语，把宾语从句置于句末，此时的 that 不能省。例如：

She thinks **it** wrong <u>that he didn't answer the phone</u>.

We find **it** necessary <u>that we practice every day</u>.

练习题：

1. Please tell me _____ last year.
   A. where does your sister work   B. where did your sister work
   C. where your sister works   D. where your sister worked

2. She wanted to know _____ child it was on the grass.
   A. that   B. whose   C. what   D. whom

3. A computer can only do _____ you have instructed it to do.
   A. how   B. after   C. what   D. when

4. Linda said the moon _____ round the earth.
   A. travelled   B. has travelled C. travels   D. had travelled

5. He asked me _____ told me the accident.
   A. whom   B. which   C. who   D. whose

答案：1. D   2. B   3. C   4. C   5. C

（四）非谓语动词

非谓语动词分为不定式、分词和动名词。

4.1 不定式

动词不定式是由"不定式符号 to + 动词原形"构成的一种非谓语动词结构。高等学校英语应用能力考试主要考查不定式的被动式（to be done）、完成式（to have done, 用来表示不定式的动作发生在谓语动词之前）和否定式（not to do/not to have done, 注意否定词应置于不定式符号 to 之前）。例如：

He decided **to work** hard.（不定式的一般形式）

He preferred **to be given** heavier work to do.（不定式的被动形式）

I'm sorry **to have given** you so much trouble.（不定式的完成式）

Tell him **not to shut** the window.（不定式的否定形式）

He pretended **not to have seen** me.（不定式完成式的否定形式）

● 注意不定式在句中作定语、表语、状语时的不同作用。

1. 不定式作定语通常放在被修饰的词后面，表示将要发生。例如：

I will give a speech at the meeting **to be held** tomorrow.

2. 不定式也可放在 be 动词后面，作表语。例如：

Her dream is **to be a singer**.

3. 不定式作状语常表示目的、结果或原因等。例如：

She came here **to say goodbye to you**.（表示目的）

She returned **only to find** that no one was at home.（表示结果）

We were disappointed **to hear the news**.（表示原因）

● 注意区分两个易混淆的含有不定式的结构：It is + *adj.* + for someone to do... 和 It is + *adj.* + of someone to do...。前者中的形容词主要说明动作的特性，后者中的形容词主要说明人的品质和特性。例如：

It's **hard** <u>for him to</u> study two languages.

It's **very kind** <u>of you to</u> help me.

● 不定式的省略。

let, make, have 等使役动词以及 see, watch, notice, hear, feel 等感官动词后可接不带 to 的不定式短语作宾补。但以上动词凡可变成被动结构的，变成被动结构后都必须用带 to 的动词不定式。试比较：

I **saw** the man **enter** the bank.

The man **was seen to enter** the bank.

● 一些动词后可以接由疑问词引导的不定式短语，包括 decide, know, forget, learn, remember, show, understand, see, wonder, find out, explain, tell 等。例如：

Please show us <u>how to do that</u>.

I don't know <u>what</u> to do next.

● 一些含有不定式的固定结构如 too...to..., only to..., so as to (so as not to), so...as to, such...as to, in order to 等也是常考考点。例如：

He searched the room **only to** find nothing.（他搜查了房间，结果什么也没找到。）

He ran fast **so as to** catch the last bus.（他跑得很快以便赶上最后一班车。）

He ran **so** fast **as to** chase the thief.（他跑得那么快是为了追那个小偷。）

I'm not **such** a fool **as to** believe that.（我还不至于笨到相信那个事情的地步。）

● 常考的后面接不定式短语作宾语的动词有 afford, agree, aim, ask, choose, decide, demand, expect, fail, hope, intend, long, manage, prepare, pretend, refuse, tend, want 等。需要大家平时积累并加以记忆。

练习题：

1. She gave up her job as a nurse because she found the children too difficult _____.

    A. look after   B. to look after

    C. looking after   D. be looked after

2. Paul doesn't have to be made _____. He always works hard.

    A. learn   B. to learn

    C. learned   D. learning

3. More and more trucks are seen _____ between these two towns these days.

    A. run   B. to run

    C. be running   D. being run

4. I prefer (live) _____ in the country rather than in a city.

5. Please remember (lock) _____ the door when you leave.

6. If you intend (visit) _____ the National Garden, please contact me soon.

答案：1. B   2. B   3. B   4. to live   5. to lock   6. to visit

4.2 分词

分词是高等学校英语应用能力考试语法结构部分的常考考点。每年都会有涉及分词的考题，考生需特别注意。分词分为现在分词（-ing 分词）和过去分词（-ed 分词），主要考查点是分词作状语和定语。下面我们将具体介绍：

● 分词作状语

现在分词短语和过去分词短语均可作状语表示句子主语所做的另一个动作。我们可以把它的作用理解为一个状语从句。现在分词的意义是主动的，过去分词的意义是被动的。也就是说，现在分词的动作是句子的逻辑主语主动发出的，过去分词的动作是句子的逻辑主语被动接受的。分词作状语可表示原因、结果、条件、让步等。例如：

Not knowing what to do (=Because he didn't know what to do), he called the doctor.

（分词作状语表示原因）

Given better condition (=If they had been given better condition), my roses could grow better.（分词作状语表示条件）

有时候，分词短语的作用像一个并列分句，位于句后表示伴随状况。例如：

He sat in the armchair, **reading a book**. = He sat in the armchair **and read a book**.

现在分词短语作状语时，动作发生的时间与句子谓语动词通常是同时的。如果要强调这个动作发生在主要谓语动词之前，我们需要使用现在分词的完成式。例如：

Not having received any letter from my family, I was worried.

有时我们可在分词短语前加上 when, while, since, before, after, although, unless, if, so 等词，表示时间、让步、条件、结果等。例如：

While sitting in class, I fell asleep.

Although born in France, he works and lives in China.

之前出现的分词状语都是以主句的主语作为自己的逻辑主语，从而依附于主句。若分词带有自己的主语，在结构上不与主句发生关系，则被我们称为"独立主格"（absolute structure）。虽然称作独立主格结构，但它并不是真正的独立，它还是一种从属分句，在句中表示原因、条件、方式、伴随、时间等，通常起状语作用。独立主格主要有三种：现在分词、过去分词或无动词。例如：

There being nothing else to do, they have gone away.（现在分词独立主格结构，表示原因）

His homework done, Jim decided to go and see the play.（过去分词独立主格结构，表示时间）

Miss Wang came into the classroom, **books in hand**.（无动词独立主格结构，表示伴随）

英语应用能力考试常考的是前两种独立主格形式，主要考查学生对现在分词和过去分词之间的区别的掌握。做题时我们需要判断动作与状语的主语之间的关系来确定是使用现在分词还是过去分词：当动作由状语的主语发出时使用现在分词，而当状语的主语是受动者时则使用过去分词。

有时，独立主格的前面可加介词 with。这种结构主要表示伴随状况，有时也可表示原因。例如：

She stood there, **with her child playing beside her**.（表示伴随状况）

With the problem solved, she felt very happy.（表示原因）

练习题：

1. If _____ in the fridge, the fruit can remain fresh for more than a week.

　　A. keeping　　　　B. be kept　　　　　C. kept　　　　　D. to keep

2. The May Day Holiday _____ over, we must now get down to work.

　　A. be　　　　　　B. being　　　　　　C. to have been　　D. to be

3. While _____ in London, the young engineer picked up some English.

　　A. staying　　　　B. stay　　　　　　C. stayed　　　　　D. to stay

4. (Judge) _____ from last year's experience, the coach knows he should not expect too much of his team.

5. (see) _____ from the space, the earth looks like a big blue ball.

答案：1. C　　2. B　　3. A　　4. Judging　　5. Seen

● 分词短语作定语

分词短语作定语的作用如同一个定语从句，主要是用于修饰分词前面的名词或代词。**现在分词**短语作定语主要用来叙述和句子的主要动词几乎同时发生的动作或经常性、习惯性的动作，而且这个动作是前面它所修饰的名词或代词**主动发出**的。它相当于一个主动语态的定语从句。例如：

Who's the man **talking to your daughter** (=that is talking to your daughter)?

The girl **crossing the river** (=who was crossing the river) carried a basket.

过去分词短语作定语通常表示其动作在句子的主要动作之前已完成，或没有时间性，而且这个动作是前面它所修饰的名词或代词**被动接受**的。因此过去分词短语作定语相当于一个被动语态的定语从句。例如：

Is there anything **planned for your birthday** (=that has been planned for your birthday)?

Please keep a secret of the problem **discussed** (=that was discussed) yesterday.

* 如果强调叙述的动作与主要动词同时发生，我们通常使用现在分词的被动形式。例如：

Please keep a secret of the problem **being discussed** (=that is being discussed).

* 如果指的是未来的动作，则用不定式的被动形式。例如：

Please keep a secret of the problem **to be discussed** (that is to be discussed) tomorrow.

有时我们可用逗号将分词短语与句子的其他成分分开，相当于一个非限制性的定语从句，对所叙述的人或事物作修饰说明。例如：

The building, **completed in 2006** (=which was completed in 2006), is the highest in the world.

练习题：

1. What's the language _____ in Spain?

   A. speaking   B. spoken   C. be spoken   D. to speak

2. The computer center, _____ last year, is very popular among the students in this school.

   A. open   B. opening   C. having opened   D. opened

3. People (live) _____ comfortably in the towns hardly feel the pleasure of living in the country.

4. We were shocked to find that the man (come) _____ towards us was carrying a gun.

5. The problem (discuss) _____ at the meeting yesterday has not been solved yet.

答案：1. B   2. D   3. living   4. coming   5. discussed

4.3 动名词

● 常考的后面接动名词的动词有 admit, appreciate, avoid, complete, consider, delay, deny, dislike, enjoy, escape, feel like, finish, imagine, mind, risk, quit, suggest 等。需要大家平时加以积累和记忆。

- 某些常使用动名词的句子结构有 spend time (in) doing sth., it is no use/good/point doing sth., it is hard doing sth., cannot help doing sth., be busy doing sth., have a good/hard time doing sth., have trouble/difficulty (in) doing sth. 等。
- need, require, want, deserve 与 be worth 后也可接动名词表示被动意义。
- 区别不定式符号 to 与介词 to。由于介词后都接名词或动名词作其宾语，所以分清不定式符号 to 和介词 to 是非常必要的。常见的包含**介词 to** 的词组有：add to（增加），agree to（同意，答应），come to（到达，涉及到），get down to（开始，着手），get/be used to（习惯于），look forward to（盼望），object to（反对），resort to（诉诸于），refer to（提及），stick to（坚持，继续）等。
- 有些动词后面可以接不定式，也可以接动名词，但表达的意思是不一样的。如 stop, forget, remember, regret, mean 等。做题时需要仔细分辨。

练习题：

1. Jane always enjoys _____ to popular music at home on Friday evenings.
   A. listening   B. being listening
   C. to be listening   D. to listen
2. The thief took away the woman's money without _____.
   A. being seeing   B. seen
   C. being seen   D. seeing him
3. What a lovely party! It's worth _____ all my life.
   A. remembering   B. to remember
   C. to be remembered   D. being remembered
4. We appreciate (work) _____ with him, because he has a good sense of humor.
5. The teacher didn't mind (help) _____ the students in her spare time.
6. I wondered why the boy often avoided (talk) _____ with his classmates.

答案：1. A   2. C   3. A   4. working   5. helping   6. talking

（五）虚拟语气

虚拟语气表示动作或状态不是客观存在的事实，而是说话人的主观愿望或假想等。虚拟语气可分为 were 型虚拟语气和 be 型虚拟语气这两种。were 型虚拟语气是指不管主语是什么人称，动词一律用过去形式；be 型虚拟语气是指不管主语是什么人称、不管什么时间发生的动作，动词一律用原形。

5.1 were 型虚拟

- were 型虚拟常用于 if 引导的非真实条件句中，表示假设的或实际可能性不大的情况。根据谈论的事情所发生的时间不同，可分为以下三种情况：

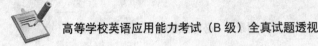

	条件从句	主句
与过去事实相反	过去完成时	would/could/might/should + have done
与现在事实相反	一般过去时（be 动词用 were）	would/could/might/should + 动词原形
与将来事实相反	should/were to + 动词原形	would/could/might/should + 动词原形

例如：If I **had worked** harder, I **would have succeeded**.（与过去事实相反）

If I **were** a bird, I **would fly** to you.（与现在事实相反）

If he **were to go** tomorrow, he **might tell** you.（与将来事实相反）

● 省略 if 的虚拟条件句

虚拟条件句的从句部分如果含有 **were**, **should** 或 **had**，可将 if 省略，再把 were, should 或 had 移至从句句首。例如：

If I **were** to have 3 days off, I would be very happy. = **Were** I to have 3 days off, I would be very happy.

If I **had** taken your advice, I wouldn't have made that mistake. = **Had** I taken your advice, I wouldn't have made that mistake.

If it **should** rain tomorrow, they wouldn't go for an outing. = **Should** it rain tomorrow, they wouldn't go for an outing.

● 有些虚拟条件句不使用 if 从句，而是借助一些介词短语来表达假设条件。常见的有 without（如果没有……），but for（要不是……），otherwise/or（要不然、否则）等。注意准确判断句子时间，决定谓语的形式。例如：

Without air, nothing could live.

But for the note you left, I would have forgotten to close the door.

We didn't know his telephone number; **otherwise/or** we would have telephoned him.

● 使用 were 型虚拟的一些特殊句型

1. **wish**

wish 后接宾语从句表达一种愿望。根据具体情况，从句中动词的时态会相应变化：

(1) 当表达对过去事情的愿望时，宾语从句的谓语动词使用过去完成时。例如：

I wish I hadn't said that.

(2) 表达对现在的事情的愿望时，宾语从句谓语动词使用一般过去时（be 动词用 were）。例如：I wish I had more free time.

(3) 表达对将来的事情的愿望时，宾语从句谓语动词使用 would/could/should/might + 动词原形。例如：I wish she would change her mind.

2. **would rather/would sooner**

would rather/would sooner 后可接一个从句，表示宁愿某事发生或没有发生。根据具体情况，从句中动词的时态也会相应变化：

(1) 当指的是现在或将来的事情时，从句的谓语动词使用一般过去时。例如：

I would rather <u>you paid me now</u>.

I would rather <u>they came tomorrow</u>.

（2）当指的是过去的事情时，从句的谓语动词使用过去完成时。例如：

I would rather <u>you hadn't told him the news that day</u>.

注意：如果 would rather/sooner 后直接接动词而不是从句，应使用动词原形。例如：

If you'd rather <u>be alone</u>, we'll all leave here.

3. if only

if only 引出感叹句，表达强烈愿望，意为"但愿……，要是……就好了"。谓语动词与 wish 引导的宾语从句中的虚拟形式相同。例如：

If only <u>I knew his name</u>!

If only <u>I hadn't been so careless in the exam</u>!

4. 在 **it is (about/high) time that**...之后的从句中，谓语动词常用一般过去时表示建议或忠告，意为"该做某事了"或"早该做某事了"。例如：

It's high time <u>that you went</u>.

It's time <u>that we went to bed</u>.

练习题：

1. I think it's high time we _____ strict measure to stop pollution.

    A. will take   B. take

    C. took   D. have taken

2. Mary feels tired, she wishes she _____ so late last night.

    A. didn't stayed up   B. wouldn't stayed up

    C. hadn't stayed up   D. wouldn't have stayed up

3. If I _____ harder at school, I would be sitting in a comfortable office now.

    A. worked   B. were to work

    C. had worked   D. were working

4. If we (know) _____ that the books were available, we would have bought them yesterday.

5. If I (leave) _____ a little earlier, I would have caught the rain.

答案：1. C   2. C   3. C   4. had known   5. had left

5.2　be 型虚拟

● 表示建议、命令、请求等

1. 在表示建议、命令、请求等动词后的宾语从句中谓语动词用 should + 动词原形。should 可以省去。这一类的动词有 advise, beg, command, demand, insist（坚持要求），order, propose, recommend, request, require, suggest（建议），urge 等。句型：sb. + v. + that... + (should) do。例如：

I **suggested** <u>that we (should) put off the meeting</u>.

His mother **advised** him <u>that he turn to his teacher</u>.

注意：当 insist 表示"坚持认为"、suggest 表示"表明，暗示"时，后面宾语从句的谓语动词不使用虚拟。例如：

He **insisted** that he hadn't been there before.

You pale face **suggests** that you are ill.

2. 在 advisable, desirable, essential, important, natural, necessary, urgent, vital 等形容词后的从句中谓语用 should + 动词原形。这些形容词主要表示必要性、重要性、强制性、合适性、义务性等。句型：It's *adj.* that... + (should) do。例如：

It is **necessary** that he (should) come to our meeting tomorrow.

It is **important** that the project be finished on time.

3. 在表示建议、命令、请求等名词后的同位语从句中谓语用 should +动词原形，should 可以省略。这样的名词有 advice, demand, desire, order, proposal, request, requirement, suggestion 等。句型：*n.* + that... (should) do。例如：

The manager accepted his **advice** that new technology be introduced.

I make a **proposal** that we (should) hold a meeting next week.

4. 在表示建议、命令、请求等动词被动式后的从句中谓语用 should + 动词原形。should 可以省去。句型：It + be 动词 + *v.*-ed + that... (should) do。例如：

It is politely **requested** by the hotel management that radios (should) not be played after 11 o'clock at night.

It is **required** that every employee should master a foreign language.

● lest/fearing that/for fear that 后使用 should/might + 动词原形，should/might 可以省去。意思是"避免，免于，免得……"。例如：

Hide it **lest** he (should) see it.

He told us to keep quiet **fearing that/for fear that** we might disturb others.

练习题：

1. He checked his car carefully lest it _____ on the way.

　　A. breaks down 　　　　　　　　　　C. would break down

　　B. broke down 　　　　　　　　　　D. should break down

2. Mike's uncle insists _____ in this hotel.

　　A. staying not 　　　　　　　　　　B. not to stay

　　C. that he would not stay 　　　　　　D. that he not stay

3. It is important that the committee _____ about the project at once.

　　A. will be informed 　　　　　　　　B. be informed

　　C. is informed 　　　　　　　　　　D. being informed

4. The suggestion that we _____ at once was accepted by everyone.

　　A. would go 　　　　B. ought to go 　　　　C. go 　　　　　　D. went

5. The chairman required that every speaker (limit) _____ himself to fifteen minutes.

答案：1. D　　2. D　　3. B　　4. C　　5. (should) limit

（六）主谓一致

英语应用能力考试中关于主谓一致的常考考点有：

- 由 and 连接不同事物的并列结构作主语时，动词用复数。例如：

  Lily and Lucy are planning their birthday party.

  但当由 and 连接的主语表示一个单一的概念，即指同一人、同一物或同一整体时，谓语动词用单数。例如：

  The iron and steel industry is developing rapidly.

  如果主语是由 and 连接的两个单数名词且前面由 every, each, no 等词修饰时，谓语动词用单数。例如：

  Every boy and girl in the village **is** taught to read and write.

- 当主语后有以 along with, as well as, in addition to, together with, with, except, instead of, rather than 等引起的介词短语或从属结构时，谓语动词的数不受影响。例如：

  Phelps, along with his coach, **has** just arrived.

- 由 or, either...or, neither...nor, not only...but also 连接两个主语时，谓语动词与其靠近的主语保持一致，即遵循"就近原则"。例如：

  Neither you nor **she is** wrong.

- 由 many a 或 more than one 所修饰的词作主语时，谓语动词多用单数形式。例如：

  Many a **student is** absent today.

- 有些复数名词没有以 -s 结尾，如 cattle, people, police 等；有些单数名词是以 -s 结尾的，如 news，一些以 -ics 结尾的学科名称（physics, politics, economics）和以 -s 结尾的国家名（United States）等。做题时需要仔细辨析。

练习题：

1. The owner and editor of the newspaper _____ the conference.

   A. were attending　　　　　　　　B. were to attend

   C. is to attend　　　　　　　　　　D. are to attend

2. Email, as well as telephones, _____ an important part in daily communication.

   A. is playing　　　　　　　　　　B. have played

   C. are playing　　　　　　　　　　D. play

3. Both of the twin brothers (be) _____ capable of doing technical work at present.

4. Not only I but also Jane and Mary _____ tired of having one examination after another.

   A. is　　　　　　　　　　　　　　B. are

   C. am　　　　　　　　　　　　　　D. be

5. Neither the clerks nor the manager (know) _____ anything about the new customer.

答案：1. C　　2. A　　3. are　　4. B　　5. knows

（七）倒装

倒装分为全部倒装和部分倒装。全部倒装是将句子中的谓语动词全部置于主语之前。部分倒装是指将谓语的一部分如 be 动词、助动词或情态动词倒装至主语之前。从历年真题来看，英语应用能力考试主要考查部分倒装。下面介绍几种常考的部分倒装的情况：

● 带否定意义的词或带否定词的短语位于句首时，句子要使用部分倒装，包括由 never, no, not, barely, hardly, rarely, scarcely, seldom, few, little 等词开始的句子或以含有 no 的介词短语开始的句子。例如：

Hardly <u>had she gone out</u> **when** a student came to visit her.

Never <u>will the boy do</u> **that** again.

● 在 so...that 和 so...as to 结构中，有时为加强语气，可将 so 及相关的形容词或副词移到句首，将 be 动词、助动词或情态动词移到主语前。例如：

So frightened <u>was he</u> **that** he did not dare to move an inch.

So loudly <u>did she shout</u> **as to** make everyone turn to her.

同样，在 such...that 结构中，为加强语气，也可将 such 或含有 such 的名词短语或介词短语移至句首，将 be 动词、助动词或情态动词移到主语前。例如：

Such a fool <u>was I</u> **that** I believed his words.

In such a hurry <u>was he</u> **that** he forgot to lock the door.

● 表示前面所述的情况适用于另一个人或事物时，使用部分倒装；其基本结构为"so/neither/nor + 助动词 / 情态动词 /be 动词 + 主语"，其中 so 针对前面的肯定性内容，neither 和 nor 针对前面的否定性内容。例如：

He can speak French and **so** <u>can I</u>.

I wasn't there and **nor** <u>were you</u>.

● 句首为表示限制意义的 only 或表示频度的 always, often, many a time 等副词时，应使用部分倒装。例如：

Only in this way <u>can we</u> solve the problem.

Many a time <u>did I</u> warn you.

练习题：

1. Seldom _____ to see his parents.

    A. he goes   B. goes he

    C. does he go   D. he does go

2. Not for a moment _____ the truth of your explanation about the event.

    A. we have doubted   B. did we doubt

    C. we had doubted   D. doubted we

3. Nancy works in a shop and _____.

    A. so does Alan   B. Alan too does

    C. does Alan too   D. so Alan does

4. By no means _____ look down upon the poor.

    A. we should   B. should we

    C. ought we   D. we shall

5. So loudly _____ that the audience in the back heard him clearly.

    A. does he speak   B. did he speak

    C. he speaks   D. he spoke

答案：1. C　　2. B　　3. A　　4. B　　5. B

（八）比较级和最高级

当表示"比较"和"最"的时候，形容词或副词要使用比较级和最高级。形容词或副词的原形称为"原级"。

8.1 形容词比较级和最高级

● 单音节及少数双音词形容词比较级的基本形式是单词后加 -er，最高级的基本形式是单词后加 -est。例如：strong—stronger—strongest；clever—cleverer—cleverest

    以 e 结尾的单词比较级后加 -r，最高级后加 -st。例如：wide—wider—widest

    以辅音字母加 y 结尾的单词，变 y 为 i 再加 -er 或者 -est。例如：busy—busier—busiest

    以一个辅音字母结尾的的重读闭音节单词双写结尾的辅音字母再加词尾 -er 或 -est 来构成比较级和最高级。例如：big—bigger—biggest

● 其他双音节词和多音节词的比较级和最高级的基本形式是在单词前加 more 和 most。例如：beautiful—more beautiful—most beautiful

8.2 副词的比较级和最高级

副词的比较级和最高级通常由 more 和 most 加副词构成。但有些常用的副词用 -er 和 -est 形式，如 fast, early, late, soon, far, long, near, hard, high 等。例如：quickly—more quickly—most quickly；fast—faster—fastest

8.3 有一些形容词和副词的比较级和最高级是不规则的，需要考生自己归纳掌握。例如：good/well—better—best；bad/badly—worse—worst；many/much—more—most；little—less—least；far（表示距离）—farther—farthest；far（表示比喻意义）—further—furthest

8.4 比较级形容词和副词可以用一个修饰语来说明程度。例如：

Your pronunciation is **far better** than mine.

This coat is **a bit more expensive** than that one.

I hope you'll do it **a bit more quickly** next time.

练习题：

1. One can jump (high) _____ on the moon than on the earth.

2. Nothing in the world can move (fast) _____ than light.

3. My father knows (much) _____ than I do.

答案：1. higher　　2. faster　　3. more

（九）固定结构和固定搭配

语法结构中也常常会涉及到一些固定结构和固定搭配，需要大家在平时积累记忆。如 the more...the more...（越……，越……），too...to...（太……而不能……），not until（直到…… 才……），be different from（与……不同），be interested in（对……感兴趣），be absent from（缺席），ask for（请求得到），pick up（无意中学会；拾起），turn to sb.（向某人求助），set up（建立），run out of（用完），to one's surprise（让某人惊讶的是），put forward（提出），in person（亲自），provide with（提供），run into（偶然遇到），turn out（结果是，原来是），carry on（继续进行），go by（时光流逝），break down（损坏，发生故障），come up with（提出，想出），take off（起飞），instead of（代替，而不是），put away（把……收好），in return（作为回报，作为报答），look into（调查），right away（立即，马上）等。

练习题：

1. The police are _____ the traffic accident that happened yesterday.

    A. looking down upon   B. looking forward to

    C. looking into   D. looking after

2. It will only take me a minute to get your watch fixed; it will be ready _____.

    A. by the way   B. right away

    C. at last   D. in that case

3. He _____ several jackets and finally picked out a blue one.

    A. tried on   B. went on

    C. took on   D. got on

4. I wish we had a color television; I'm _____ pictures in black and white.

    A. fond of   B. fed up

    C. tired of   D. interested in

答案：1. C   2. B   3. A   4. C

（十）词形转换

词形转换主要考查的是四大实词（名词、形容词、动词、副词）之间的转换。这里我们简单介绍一下这四类词常见的后缀。

● 常见的名词后缀有：-ment (government), -ship (friendship), -ness (kindness), -dom (kingdom), -th (length), -ar (liar), -or (actor), -ee (employee), -ian (musician), -ant (assistant), -al (refusal), -age (marriage), -hood (neighborhood), -ancy (expectancy), -ency (efficiency), -ance (performance), -ence (confidence), -ion (companion), -tion (pollution), -ation (modernization), -ty (safety), -ism (socialism), -ist (artist) 等。

● 常见的形容词后缀有：-ic (economic), -ical (historical), -ous (continuous), -ary (necessary), -ory (satisfactory), -ent (dependent), -able (imaginable), -ible (edible), -al (governmental), -like (childlike), -ish (foolish), -ive (attractive), -ful (colorful), -less (careless), -ly (friendly),

-an (American), -ed (married), -ing (encouraging) 等。

　　* 注意一些以 -ed 结尾的形容词和 -ing 结尾的形容词的意义区别。如 excited 与 exciting, interested 与 interesting, bored 与 boring 等。

● 常见的**动词**后缀有：-ize (modernize), -en (sharpen), -fy (beautify) 等。

● 常见的**副词**后缀有：-ly (possibly), -ward (downward), -wards (inwards), -wise (otherwise) 等。

练习题：

1. The local people are very (friend) _____ to the visiting tourists.

2. He is asked to (short) _____ his report to one page.

3. Going abroad to have a holiday will be an (excite) _____ experience for us.

4. Yao Ming, our favorite basketball (play) _____, is becoming a superstar in the world.

5. The manager has received only one (apply) _____ for this post.

答案：1. friendly　2. shorten　3. exciting　4. player　5. application

　　除上述几种常见的语法点之外，考试中也涉及强调句型、代词、情态动词、反意疑问句等语法点，需要大家自己多做题，多观察，多思考，做到举一反三。

附录 2
测试项目、内容、题型及时间分配表

序号	测试项目	题号	测试内容	题型	百分比	时间分配
I	听力理解	1 ~ 15	对话、会话、短文	多项选择、填空、简答	15%	15 分钟
II	词汇与语法结构	16 ~ 35	词汇用法、句法结构、词形变化等	多项选择、填空、改错	15%	15 分钟
III	阅读理解	36 ~ 60	语篇,包括简单的一般性和应用性文字	多项选择、填空、简答、匹配	35%	40 分钟
IV	英译汉	61 ~ 65	句子和段落	多项选择、段落翻译	20%	25 分钟
V	写作 / 汉译英		应用性文字(摘要、通告、简短信函、简历表、申请书等)	套写、书写、填写或翻译	15%	25 分钟
合计			65+1		100%	120 分钟

主要参考书目

1. 崔艳萍，冯新艳．高等学校英语应用能力考试（A级）全真试题透视．北京：外语教学与研究出版社．2009

2. 龚兵，马俊波．希望英语，第一册．北京：外语教学与研究出版社．2003

3. 顾伯清．高等学校英语应用能力考试应试必读．上海：复旦大学出版社．2007

4. 江沈英，房士荣．最新B级考试历年真题点评．大连：大连理工大学出版社．2009

5. 李防，王月会．高等学校英语应用能力考试考点分析与强化训练（B级）．北京：中国人民大学出版社．2007

6. 刘绍龙，王柳琪．B级考试：历年真题精解．北京：世图音像电子出版社．2009

7. 孟青，刘敏．高等学校英语应用能力考试A、B级过关必备——语法专项突破．郑州：河南教育出版社．2007

8. 牛慧霞．高等学校英语应用能力考试B级辅导大全．北京：外文出版社．2006

9. 谭海涛，邹渝刚．希望英语，第二册．北京：外语教学与研究出版社．2004

10. 王迈迈等．高等学校英语应用能力考试B级考试历年全真试卷与详解．北京：原子能出版社．2009

11. 于华，向俊．高等学校英语应用能力考试B级点评历年真题．北京：世图音像电子出版社．2009

12. 张成祎．大学英语语法手册．上海：上海外语教育出版社．2004

13. 章振邦．新编英语语法教程．上海：上海外语教育出版社．2000